THE
BROTHERHOOD
OF OLYMPUS
AND THE
TOWER OF
DREAMS

Written and Illustrated by

GUY T. SIMPSON, JR.

For more information please go to the author's website:

http://guysimpson.net

**MYTHIC
PUBLISHING**

ASGARD   GEHENNA   YELM

DEDICATION

To the many members of the Brotherhood of Olympus
over the years, your tales will continue to be told,

To my family for always believing in me,
even when I doubted,

To the people who love stories of myths, legends, basketball,
geeky kids, and dark adventure,

To the people who demonstrate agápe in their everyday lives,
you are truly heroic,

And especially to all of those that believed and trusted
—Dreams do come true.

Furfur and Tiamat

CONTENTS

ACKNOWLEDGMENTS

I would like to gratefully acknowledge the many people who have been touched by the tale told within these pages and the members of my family and friends whose echo can be seen in this story. I would also like to acknowledge my students, both current and past, for putting up with my stories throughout the years. The team of Sarah Mulkey, Mike Munro, Dan Helms, Ryan Healy, and Rebecca Latham who humored me by reading the incarnations of the first draft of this work and helped me shape it to what it has become.

The book clubs who read my work and discussed it with me, giving me insight to the supplemental materials included herein, and the team of dedicated English teachers who assembled those materials included in this edition, Rebecca Latham, Sarah Mulkey, Cami Krise, and Rebecca Bingham. My lovely editor, Becca Wolford. The fine folks at Mythic Publishing who gave my work an avenue to be read.

My children, Taylor, Kathryn, and Guy, III, for listening to me ramble on and on and on about the Brotherhood myths and legends and for being the most amazing children a dad could ever ask for—even as they now transition into their own adventures that may someday lead back to where they began. My best friend and wife, Rae—the distance has made our hearts grow fonder—and for truly learning how to let me create this world while supporting my dream.

And finally the author who inspired me all those years ago when I first read his work, the great J.R.R. Tolkien, without him the world would not be as rich and descriptive in my mind and whose shadow I hope to someday stand near.

And of course the Fans of the Brotherhood of Olympus without whom none of this would be possible, I salute you.

i

The PRUSSIAN FRONTIER, 1468

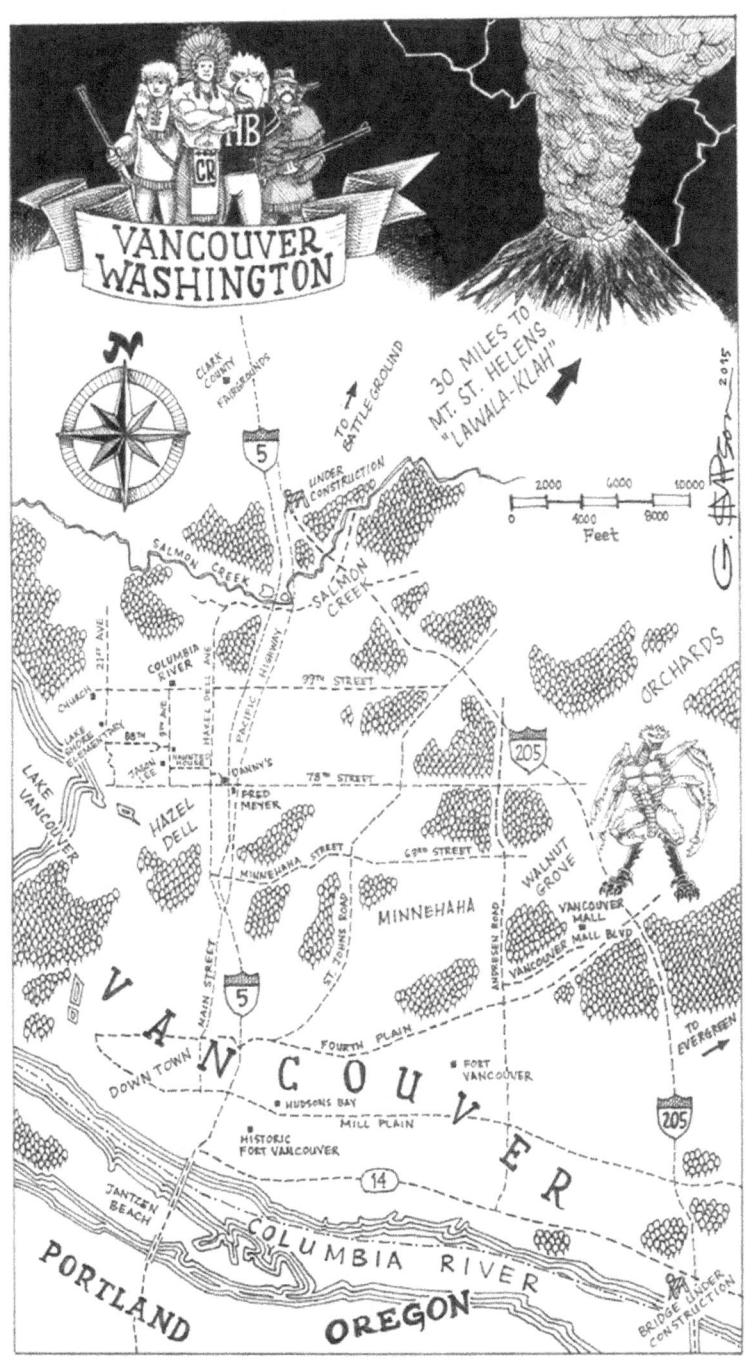

VANCOUVER WASHINGTON

BERCHTOLD
VON WENSING
EINSICHTMEISTER
MASTER OF
KNOWLEDGE

VALTEN
VON HOLDAU
ZAUBERMEISTER
MASTER OF
MAGIC

Prelude

BERCHTOLD AND VALTEN

THE BROTHERHOOD OF OLYMPUS AND THE TOWER OF DREAMS

WILHELM
VON ESSEN

UBERSINNLICHMEISTER

MASTER OF THE
SUPERNATURAL

LEOPOLD
VON SCHMIDT

TAKTIKMEISTER

MASTER OF
STRATEGY

Prelude

WILHELM AND LEOPOLD

THE BROTHERHOOD OF OLYMPUS
AND THE TOWER OF DREAMS

STEFFAN
VON DIENHEIM
WAFFENMEISTER
MASTER OF
WEAPONS

HEINRICH REUSS
VON PLAUEN
HOCHMEISTER
HIGH MASTER OF
THE TEUTONIC
KNIGHTS
THE LIVONIAN
BROTHERS OF
THE SWORD
AND THE
BROTHERHOOD
OF OLYMPUS

Prelude

STEFFAN AND THE HOCHMEISTER

THE BROTHERHOOD OF OLYMPUS
AND THE TOWER OF DREAMS

Last Stand of the Brotherhood of Olympus
Tower of Dreams Prelude
January 13, 1469
Mohrungen, Prussia

The snow-covered fields north of Mohrungen were muddied and cluttered with the carnage of battle, cloven shields, broken swords, spears, and hundreds of arrows rising up out of the slush — causing the field to look like a pincushion. Clusters of charred, dismembered, and broken bodies were scattered across the snow, illustrating exactly how the battle unfolded. Near each of these groupings of grisly remains were small steaming pools of blood that seeped into the vales and crannies of the plain. The cold winds blew ice particles off the drifting snow and over the battlefield, laying a thin, powdery white blanket over the death and destruction. The farmland was small, perhaps five acres ringed by gnarled forests, with a single rutted roadway cutting it in half from the north to south.

The fight that had been waged there was brutal and devastating for the three forces involved. None escaped without heavy casualties. But that was not what caught the eyes of Hochmeister Heinrich Reuss von Plauen, the Grandmaster of the Teutonic Knights, and his personal retinue of twenty knights and more than twice as many retainers, as they emerged from the dense forest on the south road.

"There it is, Hochmeister!" Gregor von Rautenberg exclaimed. He was a nobleman of Marienburg, whose blonde ringlets framed his pale face under the mail coif adorning his head. He was the Kanzler, or Chancellor of the Grandmaster, and it was his duty to care for the official keys and seals as well as being the recording clerk of the chapter. "The tower is real!"

"We can all see it, Gregor," the Hochmeister stated, in an attempt to calm the excitable Kanzler. The breath of the knights, men, and horses steamed into the chilled air.

Before the assembled knights of the order, in the middle of this small farmland, stood a massive black obelisk; it was a tower that stood out of place and time. It was nearly two hundred feet across at the base. There were no visible doors, windows, or any defensive arrow slits. But what awed the brethren was its height. It had no perceivable end. The top of the tower disappeared into the heavy gray clouds that rolled across the wintery sky, hundreds of feet above the Prussian wilderness. The stone surface of the tower was a shiny, nearly reflective black rock.

"It is constructed of obsidian," Berchtold von Wensing stated after eyeing the tower from top to bottom. He was a slender old man, disguised by the bulk of his decorative blackened plate armor, a large white Teutonic cross woven into a blue pentacle hung on a thick chain around his neck, and, like all Teutonic knights, he wore a thick white woolen cloak with a black Teutonic cross on the left shoulder. The Teutonic cross looked like four capital "T" letters joining together in a cross on their bases. Berchtold had seen too many winters, but his advanced age was pivotal in his position within the order. He was the Einsichtmeister, or knowledge master. It was his business to know everything about everything. His gear upon the flanks of his steed was the trappings of a scholar, not a fighter. Books, scroll cylinders, and archaic mechanical devices were packed tightly in his belongings. "Obsidian is an extremely rare volcanic rock. In Europe it can only be found in the Carpathians. To build a tower of this size out of such stones would be nigh impossible."

"Does obsidian have any properties, Valten?" the Hochmeister queried as his sinewy, white monk horse began to act skittishly. That was a highly unusual behavior for

Reuss von Plauen's large battle-trained steed.

"It would provide a measure of protection from magic, both spiritual and Eldritch, my Lord," Valten von Holdau, the Zaubermeister, or magic master explained. He was a tall man of dark complexion. He wore no helmet or mail coif like the other knights. Instead he wore a simple polished silver skullcap that fit tightly to his head. He had a dark, purplish-hued mail shirt under his white cape. He possessed the same medallion on a chain that von Wensing did, except his seemed to glow with a faint blue light in the woven pentacle. He carried no sword on his horse, but transported an equal number of books and scrolls, some rare herbs and other peculiar delicacies in darkened containers, and he favored a long, runic-carved wooden staff with polished silver metal caps on both ends. "And it may provide a focus point to use magic from within it. Do you concur, Wilhelm?"

"Aye," Wilhelm von Essen replied. He was a pale, almost sickly man, gaunt in features, thin straggly hair comprised his beard, and he was plagued by a chronic cough. He wore the medallion of his colleagues over a mail coat rumored to be magical silver. His head was hidden under a tall black helmet that had the face of a laughing demonic child adorning the crown. He was the most feared knight of the order. Von Essen was the Übersinnlichmeister, the master of the supernatural, and was known to commune with heathen gods, parley with daemons, was rumored to possess the skill of mind reading, and could move objects with a thought. He surely would have been excommunicated and executed long ago by order of the Pope himself if not for the service he had provided time and again, in defense against many dark forces. He looked intently upon the black obelisk. "It is indeed the Tower of Dreams, Hochmeister. It has haunted my dreams, and I sense the presence of Addraemyr the Keeper within. It is more than a mere coincidence that it appears now before us on the eve of what will be our end."

The steely eyes of the Hochmeister met the fanatical gaze of von Essen, and he knew the man spoke earnestly.

"So it is as it was told to us?" questioned Leopold von Schmidt as he moved his black gelding to the front near the Hochmeister. Von Schmidt was a fiery red-haired man with a full beard loosely braided in four roughly even tails below his chin. He wore a black helmet shaped to resemble a wolf, the medallion around his neck, a black coat of mail, the white cloak of the order, and had unsheathed his polished great sword in his right hand. He was the Taktikmeister, or master of strategy for the order. "The Brotherhood of Olympus dies today, unless we gain entry into that mythic tower?"

"It has been foretold as such, Leopold," von Essen turned to his brother. "The order to decommission the Brotherhood is following us even now from Rome. Ever since peace has come to the lands from the powers we have long fought, the Pope has no purpose for those of us who travel into the dark places to keep the world safe from what hides within that darkness."

"'Tis true," von Wensing stated, his gray beard frosting from his rapidly cooling breath. "There is no love lost between the Holiest of Holies and our little band here. We served a purpose prior to the Covenant of Reason being signed by the otherworldlies and the representative of his Holiness, Paul the Second. And in the months since, no otherworldlies have as much as stepped foot near, nor batted an eyelash, at mankind. His Holiness has obliged the will of the College of Cardinals and signed our death writ. The Teutonic order will continue, diminished of course, but the Brotherhood of Olympus, formed from the Livonian Brothers of the Sword long ago, shall perish."

"Is this true, Hochmeister?" questioned von Essen as he turned his brown monk horse toward Reuss von Plauen.

"Aye," the stern Hochmeister replied. "His Holiness has decreed our holdings forfeit. I would surmise that I may get a reprieve as the Hochmeister to the Teutonic order if I sought it, but you all, my brothers, shall not be spared the sword."

"Then I say we lay siege the Tower, and if God be

willing, live to see another day," announced Steffan von Dienheim as he positioned his gray-speckled, white gelding near the other masters of the order. He was a massive man, burly, and robust. His wild black hair waved in the breeze around his clearly dented great helm. He was the strongest of all the men in all of Eastern Europe, and went to great lengths to prove it before he joined the knighthood. He possessed nearly every weapon used by the Teutonic knights, either on his horse or on the mules carrying his weaponry. He often rode to battle with an overly large double-headed battle axe. Von Dienheim was the Waffenmeister, or master of weapons, of the order. He was a battle-hardened warrior with few peers and no equals.

"Hochmeister, there has to be another way?" the Kanzler queried from behind the other six knights. "Look at the carnage before us. The brethren of the order who preceded us here breathe no more. I fear we shall do no better in any such assault on this dread tower."

"Gregor," Heinrich Reuss von Plauen turned on his mount to face the Kanzler. The Hochmeister was a Thuringian nobleman and the nephew of the former Grandmaster who died in 1467. He assumed control of the order without having been elected Grandmaster, for that was a formality he took no comfort in. He was a war hero during the Thirteen Years' War against Poland, who commanded the destruction of the Polish army in the Battle of Konitz. Reuss von Plauen was a tall man, his long, brown, curly hair hung loose under the mail coif on his head. His mail coat was covered by a ruched royal blue jacket gathered in a series of silver buttons down the center of his torso. Like all of his master knights, he wore the cross and star medallion around his neck and sported the thick, white woolen cape. His beard was well manicured and his features were fair. He was a leader among leaders, and as such, it was up to him to make the difficult decisions. "Have care to my instructions, Kanzler, for the Teutonic order must survive this moment in time."

5

"Yes, Hochmeister," responded the Kanzler dutifully.

"Take all of the knights, less those who volunteer for the siege, and all of the men-at-arms," continued the Hochmeister as he turned his steed to face the brother knights assembled to the rear. "None must know of our folly here, and all of you are bound to utmost secrecy on this matter. Return forthwith to Mohrungen, Kanzler, and then you shall seek out my uncle's mute son Ludwig from the monastery in Konigsberg. He bears a likeness to me that neither the Poles nor the Pope will discern. Ludwig shall be but a puppet to allow you to complete my decree. Take care to dress him in my clothing and instruct him in the debt he owes me, his kin. You shall have to run the order in my absence, Kanzler. You have the keys and seals, make good on my plans to lead the order as I have decreed in my writ."

"Aye," the Kanzler replied taking mental note of the instructions and accepting a folded parchment from the Hochmeister.

"Hochmeister," von Schmidt began from his spot on the front line, "there are three forces gathering to assault the tower once more. A detachment of the Polish army to the forest on the right, a rabble of pagan heathens to the north, and an ungodly foe gathers on the left."

"I believe they have hellhounds in their midst," von Wensing added as he peered through a looking glass, "and what appear to be minor demons."

"Brother knights," the Hochmeister proclaimed as he rode his horse before the line of men, "I require five volunteers to ride forward with the Masters of the Brotherhood of Olympus to secure that tower yonder. Death is nearly certain. Glory shall not be shared of this day, save for in the company of our Heavenly Father, for none shall ever know that a few good knights rode to battle on this Friday, the thirteen of January, in the year 1469 of our Lord. I cannot command you to ride with me, nor can I condemn you if you choose otherwise. The path ahead for the Kanzler will be wrought with peril, and he will require all of you to be at his ready."

The Hochmeister turned his horse, drew his sword from its scabbard, and raised it above him as he rode in front of his men one final time.

"What say you, good brothers?" Reuss von Plauen shouted as he started his horse into a canter, "who shall ride with his Hochmeister? Death awaits us my lads, onward to battle, onward to glory!"

The brother knights erupted in a battle cry, raising their swords and lances. Five brave souls spurred their horses forward to join the masters, excitement and adrenaline coursing through their young bodies.

"Kanzler," von Schmidt stated as he neared the young nobleman, "do not record the deeds of the day. Should we be victorious, you will know upon our return. Look to the sky on the equinox to see any sign of our success. The tower rises in the west that night. No one must know of our duty here today."

"Aye, Einsichtmeister," the Kanzler replied. "It shall be done as the Hochmeister decreed."

"Good lad," von Schmidt continued as he turned his horse to join the others preparing to siege the tower. "And Gregor, tell our families that we lived honorably, and died likewise in the service of our Lord."

"Aye," the Kanzler responded with a tear forming in his eye.

The Hochmeister rode out before the brother knights and the masters of the order.

"Leopold!" Reuss von Plauen called out as his horse began to pick up speed. He was quickly followed by the five excited brother knights. "A plan might be good."

"We must make for the base of the tower, Hochmeister," von Schmidt answered quickly. "Surely there must be an entrance, and if not then we secure the base from the others."

"That's enough for me!" von Dienheim exclaimed as he spurred his horse to join the Hochmeister and raised his massive axe above him.

"Shall we?" von Essen asked with a forward motion of his hand. Von Holdau and von Wensing acknowledged the motion and together they spurred their horses to join the charge.

From his vantage point at the edge of the forest, Gregor von Rautenberg watched the horses charging toward the tower, the snow kicked up by their hooves fading into their steaming paths. He also took notice that the forces gathered on the three opposing sides began to surge toward the tower as well.

"God be with you my brothers," von Rautenberg said as he turned his horse back to the road south. "Brother knights, men-at-arms, we have our orders, back to Mohrungen."

The base of the monolithic tower was quickly gained by the charging knights. They pulled their horses to a halt before its massive black stone wall.

"Brothers, ride the perimeter of the tower, see if there are any doors or other possible ways of entrance," the Hochmeister commanded as he turned to look back to the south to see if the Kanzler had departed.

The knights circled the gigantic base of the tower, looking over the gleaming black stone of the structure, before returning back to the Hochmeister.

"I saw nothing, my Lord," stated the first brother knight to return to Reuss von Plauen.

"There was nothing that was any different than what is here before us, Hochmeister," the elderly von Wensing added as he pulled his horse to a stop. "I fear there is nothing physical about the tower that will let us gain entry."

"Valten, Wilhelm!" barked the Hochmeister as he dismounted from his steed. "I need you both to find us a way inside."

Both men quickly dismounted and pulled supplies from their horse's baggage, then sprinted to the base of the tower.

"What do you think, Wilhelm?" von Holdau queried as he held an oddly shaped device that had an internal gear mechanism that purred to life as he raised it near the obsidian of the tower.

"I think we better hurry, Valten," von Essen replied as he looked back over his shoulder, "our foes are nearly upon us."

"Brothers!" shouted von Schmidt as he turned his horse to the west and toward the onrushing demonic horde. "To arms, defend the perimeter in a tight formation!"

The mounted knights, along with the strategy master and the weapons master began to ride in a swift circle of sinewy horses and slashing blades. Von Schmidt had deployed this strategy successfully many times before. When done correctly it made a nearly unbreakable moving wall that defended a center point from an advancing foe. Von Schmidt also knew that to do it correctly required much more than seven riders.

The Polish army attacked from the east at nearly the same moment the demonic horde crashed into the circling riders on the west.

"Valten, Wilhelm!" the Hochmeister shouted as he positioned himself in front of the two other men. "I need you to hurry, we have no time to dawdle!"

"Hochmeister!" von Wensing called out as he dismounted his horse roughly. His aged body was not meant to be that agile, and he came up sorely limping. "I am better served being here trying to figure out our way in than on the field of battle."

The Hochmeister moved his sword into his left hand and clasped his right hand to the inside of von Wensing's right elbow, who returned the hand clasp.

"Aye, my friend," the Hochmeister agreed as he headed toward the circling knights.

At that moment, the tactic employed to delay the attacks on both sides failed, and the horses began to fall to the sharp fangs and claws of the monstrous hellhounds. The unhorsed knights struggled against their massing foes, their swords singing a song of bloody carnage honed by years of battle.

9

Two of the gallant knights failed to regain their footing and were rendered apart by the swarming demonic horde. The scaly reddish bodies of the demons spewed ichor from the savage cuts of the knight's swords. The black hellhounds stood half as tall as the knights, their bodies thick and rangy, nearly devoid of fur save the matted orange-brown wild tuft along the backs of their necks. Each had a ridge of skeletal spikes protruding from their spines, a barbed tail that could be fatal to a man if he were hit by it, and a most unnatural head. The hellhound heads appeared surprisingly human-like, except for the fact they were too big to be human and slightly canine in shape, their gaping mouths filled with long razor-sharp fangs, and gazing at their eyes was sure to cause madness. They cackled and howled as they moved about the knights. The demons were just as terrifying. Their bodies appeared to be insect-like in the way they bent and moved, had large heads, and sported equally large mouths filled with row upon row of shark-like teeth. Their fingers ended in long hooked claws and they took glee in ripping the flesh off the fallen horses. The three knights standing before the demons held their ground and turned them back twice.

On the opposite side, the Poles had dismounted von Schmidt, who stood alone. A moment before, the enraged von Dienheim rode out in a full charge into their ranks. His horse fell nearly forty yards out from were his brother now stood, the mighty weapons master was swallowed by the tide of the Polish militia. The solitary von Schmidt raised his sword and prepared for the end.

The Poles, armed with spears, advanced on von Schmidt. He hacked off their sharp spearheads as they pressed forward. In a flash of white cloak and burnished metal, the Hochmeister fell upon the Poles in a blaze of slashing steel, shattering spears, severing arms, gorging chests, and cleaving heads of the soldiers with little regard for his own safety. Von Schmidt took advantage of the attack and joined the Hochmeister in his frenzy. The lightly armored Poles fell back in their dismay, and broke into a run back toward the forest.

The demon horde slashed forward once again, a third knight falling to them, screaming in agony, as they tore him into shreds. Both von Schmidt and the Hochmeister turned and raced to aid their brothers in defending against the demons and hellhounds.

"I don't understand," von Wensing stated as he leaned against the cool obsidian of the tower. "These beasts should not be here, the Covenant of Reason forbids such incursions by otherworldlies."

"The tower itself is otherworldly, Berchtold," von Essen replied as he felt the side of the stone and appeared to be deep in thought. "If I can only contact Addraemyr, perhaps appeal to him, he might let us in."

The demonic horde took down another of the knights, as the Hochmeister and von Schmidt rallied to the surviving knight's aid. The three brothers pushed the horde back once again.

"Wilhelm, Berchtold, stand clear," Valten stated as he took his arcane staff and touched it against the obsidian. The hair on their bodies stood up as if electrified. A blinding flash leapt off the staff as thick coursing blue lightning arced off the tower from the dark clouds circling the top, and grounded itself into the metal cap of the staff.

"Valten, Wilhelm!" the Hochmeister hollered behind them. The last of the brother knights had fallen and the two masters were in dire need of support. "Some help over here!"

"Contact Addraemyr," Valten stated to Wilhelm as he turned and ran toward the fighting forms of von Schmidt and the Hochmeister. Once again a flash of lightning raged off the end of the staff, this time its target was the demonic horde. Charred demon flesh and hellhound hide smoldered around the three men. The demons fell back and regrouped as a dark robed figure stepped forward from within their ranks.

"They have a wizard," von Schmidt said as he turned and

looked at their own master of magic.

"I see that, Leopold," Valten replied coldly.

A pink gurgling aura radiated around the demonic wizard and it slowly expanded until a bolt of crimson energy shot out toward Valten, who quickly responded with the staff. Blue lightning sparked into the surging energy bolt and the two competing energy beams flashed and sparked against each other halfway between the two magic users. The demon horde rushed forward one more time. Von Schmidt and the Hochmeister braced themselves to defend Valten.

"I hate magic!" bellowed the slashed and bloodied, rambling form of von Dienheim from behind them, his massive axe raised, as he passed them by and crashed into the advancing demon horde. Parts of demons and hellhounds flew from the carnage that was the master of weapons.

"I thought he was dead!" exclaimed the Hochmeister.

"Should have known it would take more than a few hundred Poles to kill him," van Schmidt replied with a grin. Both men advanced to join von Dienheim in battle with the demons. Overhead, the clash of magic continued, but the blue lightning was pushing its way closer and closer to the black-robed wizard.

A second black-robed figure appeared from the demonic host and a gurgling purple mist began to form around it. At that moment the lightning struck the first demon wizard and blew it apart into fragments of cindered flesh. The demons and hellhounds retreated with the loss of their wizard, under the duress caused by the three knights slashing at them from the front. The second wizard continued casting its spell.

"I have contacted the Keeper!" shouted Wilhelm from beside the monolith. "He knows we are here and seeking entrance to the tower!"

The Hochmeister turned and looked toward the tower. He smiled broadly, as if he always had all the confidence in the world that they would succeed.

Forgotten during the battle at the base of the Tower of Dreams, the pagan heathen forces stood along the northern edge of the clearing. They had stayed clear as the larger forces clashed before them. They were poorly equipped, mostly farmers and a few huntsmen with bows. It was a particular huntsman from the Lithuanian lowlands who unleashed an arrow that found its mark, right below the medallion on the chest of the Hochmeister.

The thud of the arrow caused the five brothers to stand and stare at their leader. They had followed Heinrich Reuss von Plauen since the early 1440s when he took over the arcane order of the Brotherhood of Olympus. He was always right, and always willing to lead them wherever they needed to go, against whatever odds they faced, and they always prevailed.

Disbelief appeared in the Hochmeister's eyes as blood began to trickle from his mouth. How had his armor failed him? What fate would allow a simple arrow to pierce his armor that had repelled so many attacks through all those years?

Leopold von Schmidt rushed to his leader and grabbed him as he stumbled and nearly fell.

"Bring him back here!" von Wensing called out. "Put him against the tower."

Von Essen broke his connection with Addraemyr the Keeper inside and turned to assist the Hochmeister. The second demonic wizard had completed his spell. The purple mist blew rapidly toward the gathered Poles along the forest, circled the tower to flood across the heathen war party to the north, then frothed and boiled amongst the demons and hellhounds surrounding the wizard. On all three fronts the affected creatures began to howl and wail. Their eyes opened wide with madness, their mouths foaming with purple spittle.

Leopold sat the mortally wounded Hochmeister down with his back against the cool obsidian of the tower. He looked into the eyes of Wilhelm, who shook his head.

"It is a fatal wound," von Essen stated with tears in his eyes.

"Hochmeister," von Wensing stated as he knelt near

their leader, "it has been a pleasure and an honor to serve under your leadership."

"Berchtold," responded the Hochmeister as he placed his left hand upon his shoulder, "the Code, do you have a copy of it? Of course you do. May I have it?"

"Yes, my Lord," von Wensing replied as he fumbled for a parchment in a belt pouch that he quickly handed to the Hochmeister. The five knights gathered around the Hochmeister.

"My brothers," Reuss von Plauen began as he wiped the trickle of blood from his lips. "I know not where we go from here. I do not think this is the end of the Brotherhood, but a new beginning, a new chapter in our tale, told by minstrels who reveal not their sources. I know not if we have achieved victory this day. But I will forever know that I was honored to call each and every one of you my brother."

In turn each of the masters of the Brotherhood knelt and kissed the forehead of the Hochmeister.

"My brothers," the ever-observant von Schmidt announced as they turned away from the tower and the wounded Hochmeister, "the spell their wizard cast seems to be a rage spell and we are about to be set upon on all sides."

The five of them turned, each placing his right hand in the center of their impromptu circle. One by one they held their hands on top of each other's.

"This is truly the end then?" von Schmidt questioned as they broke their circle.

"As it would seem," von Essen replied as he looked down at the ground grimly. A dark shadow overcame him as electricity surged from his body.

"So be it," von Dienheim said as he ran his large hand along the blade of his massive axe, and turned to run toward the maddened demonic horde. "To the death!"

"Come on Berchtold," von Schmidt added as he grasped the elderly man's shoulder, "I will not let you fall as long as I draw breath."

In the distance the massive von Dienheim hacked apart

the enraged demons and hellhounds with machine-like precision. Valten channeled up the power of the mighty Staff of Orkan one last time and split the tide of the demons into a blackened pile of cooked flesh. Wilhelm moved into the Poles, his feet not touching the ground, as he hovered and advanced into them. Before him an unseen force crushed the maddened militia as he floated farther into their midst. Leopold held the line against the advancing heathen war party, hacking and parrying their attacks, and knocking arrows down with his sword. Berchtold stood beside him, his aged body resisting its breaking point and fighting beyond what he should have been capable of.

Two new demon wizards joined the other black-robed magic-user. Together, the three of them began to cast a new spell. Valten turned the staff upon them. Their magic clashed high above the battlefield as sparks of mana showered down upon the snow-covered fields.

Berchtold and Leopold heard a noise at the base of the tower. Both men turned to see that the Hochmeister was not there anymore. What appeared to be a passageway quickly closed in the wall of the tower. The distraction was enough to momentarily disrupt Leopold's martial skills. The heathen huntsmen had released a new volley of arrows. The dodging and diving Leopold could not reach them all with his sword, and one missile headed straight for Berchtold. Leopold threw himself in front of it. He felt the pain of the arrow deep in his chest, followed by an unusual numbness. He looked into Berchtold's eyes. The old man had begun to cry. Another arrow pierced Leopold's back with a sickening thud. Leopold looked at Berchtold again, and smiled. He gave him a wink and turned toward the heathens again with his sword arm swinging. Berchtold joined him in the battle once more. Two more arrows found their marks in Leopold's torso as he slumped to the ground. He looked up at Berchtold and saw that he, too, had been hit by arrows. Two bolts protruded from his body, one from his shoulder, another from his abdomen. The elderly man fell to his knees, his sword arm ruined by the arrow in his shoulder. Leopold moved before him.

"While I still draw breath, my brother," von Schmidt gasped as he rose up to defend the knowledge master.

The maddened heathens attacked with unnatural frenzy, cleaving into the armor of Leopold with scythes and axes. Overcome with blood loss, Leopold looked back and saw Berchtold on his knees, his lifeless eyes staring forward, ever forward, a third arrow sticking out from his heart. His brother was no more. One of the farmers advanced upon the slumped and severely bleeding Leopold, took his bloodied scythe, and with a mighty blow reaped the head of the knight from his body.

Valten von Holdau had long ago mastered the use of the Staff of Orkan, and he was without peer in the practice of magic in all of Europe. But his three foes before him were not from Europe, nor were they from anywhere good or natural. These unholy magi were spawned from the Abyss. In single numbers Valten would not fail, but out numbered three to one, Valten would have to be at his best to survive their magic. The three abyssal wizards formed into a triangle and brought their oozing essences together in a mixture of purple, green, and yellow energy. Valten struck first before their spell had time to mature. The lightning from the Staff of Orkan cracked through the sky causing a loud, banging thunderclap to roll over the plain. The lightning surged into the tri-colored triangle and did the impossible. It froze. Like a glowing twisted icicle stuck into the triangle all the way back to the staff, the lightning hung rigid in the air. Valten struggled but couldn't move the staff from the end of the sparkling ice. The three magi continued their demonic chanting, holding their triangle trap in place. A fourth black-robed figure emerged from the din of the battle, frothing orange energy rippling around it. A sudden shot of orange-hued light burst into Valten. He felt numbness below his waist and a sudden shift of weight upon his arms holding onto the frozen Staff of Orkan. He looked down to see that his body below his belt was gone. Valten was holding his torso up by the frozen staff. The three magi released their spell, and the Staff of Orkan fell to the ground. With a sickening thud, Valten's severed torso fell upon the staff. Valten looked at the snow mashed into his face. Snow was a curious thing. Slowly the tiny, pure-white crystals of frozen water turned red before him and he saw no more.

The massive form of Steffan von Dienheim cut a bloody swath of demonic ichor through the assembled frenzied horde of demons and hellhounds. By now they surely would have broken if they were not magically enraged. The weapons master was in his element—battle and bloodshed. He asked no quarter, and gave none to his enemies. The surging mass of the demonic horde had completely surrounded him, and he used his axe to its full extent, swinging it in long graceful circles above his head, around his body, to the front, the side, and behind him. Each swing cracked or sliced through another hapless demon or hellhound caught too close to him. The carnage piled up around him, and as it did it stopped his movement forward. Once stopped, his artistic skill with his axe diminished. He was getting pressed for room, and the pile of broken and cleaved bodies began to tumble into him. As his motion slowed, the horde pressed down. Claw and fang found flesh, tearing away his armor piece by bloody piece. Steffan was born of warfare, and in combat he was home, he always knew that someday battle would take him. He just never imagined it would be this day.

Suddenly, the horde pulled back, a pathway opening toward the forest beyond. From the darkness of the gnarled trees a huge, overly muscled creature emerged carrying a long curved black-bladed scimitar. His long, fiery red hair reminded Steffan of Leopold. The muscled form, vaguely human, moved closer, swinging his scimitar in such a way to loosen up his muscles and intimidate his foe. He wore armor crafted from bones wrought in black metal and thick iron-shod boots with a row of spikes along the toes.

17

"Steffan von Dienheim," he announced as he paced closer, the din of battle stopped around them, "long have I waited to meet you in combat."

Steffan spat blood from his mouth in defiance.

"I shall grant you no mercy, human," the barbaric daemon stated as he neared. "Before I kill you, I want you to know who I am."

"I know who you are, filth," von Dienheim retorted as he turned his slashed and bloodied body to face the new challenge. "Your cowardice and villainy precede you, Deshnak."

"That's Deshnak the Despoiler to you, human!" shouted the barbarian as he lunged forward with a slash of his scimitar. The blade was blocked by the sudden movement of von Dienheim, who countered with the haft of his axe.

Steffan climbed over the bodies of the fallen demons and hellhounds, turning to face the form of Deshnak as he spun back around from his first attack. The remaining demons formed a circular wall around the two large combatants. Deshnak advanced once again, his scimitar held tightly with both hands and raised into a ready position. With a growl, he swung as he passed von Dienheim. Steffan countered with a backward swing of his axe, spinning it upward into the boney armor of Deshnak's chest. The flat side of the ax shattered the layers of bone into ivory splinters.

The bigger daemonic barbarian turned and wildly swung his scimitar in a crude figure eight before crashing the blade into the thick armor still resting on von Dienheim's left shoulder. Pain radiated down Steffan's arm. He shifted his axe fully to his right hand and swung it with torrential rage, first downward, nearly striking Deshnak in his quickly retreating legs. Then back upward the axe rose, clipping across the shattered armor on his chest and gouging a jagged cut across the right side of his face from his jaw to his forehead. Bloody ichor spurted from the open wounds in his chest and upon his face.

With a wild scream Deshnak closed in on von Dienheim

before he could recover from his swing. He clasped him in a monstrous hug, grinding his broken armor into the open wounds of von Dienheim. The knight's arms were trapped beneath the arms of the daemonic barbarian, and they struggled for minutes in this way, both warriors flexing their muscles beyond human measure. The corded veins on their arms strained under the pressures applied. The hellhounds began to howl and bay as they circled closer and closer toward the two combatants. Their rabid jaws nipped ever so closely to the legs of the knight as he began to lose his struggle with the larger barbarian. With a sudden lunge the hellhounds tore into his legs. Von Dienheim screamed out in pain and loosened his struggle, giving Deshnak the opportunity he needed. In a quick move, Deshnak let the knight fall toward the ground and the ravening maws of the hellhounds, and just as quickly he caught him when his neck passed the barbarian's thick forearms.

"And now you die," Deshnak stated coldly. With a sudden flexing of his arms he twisted the neck of the struggling knight, snapping it with a loud crackle. He tossed the still form of von Dienheim to the ground. "Pathetic human."

The hellhounds tore into the fallen knight. Fortunately, the broken neck severed his nerves so he could not feel the hungry jaws of the slobbering hellhounds tearing him apart. He hoped he had bought his brothers the gift of time, as he slowly lost focus and saw no more.

Wilhelm von Essen hovered in the midst of the enraged Polish army. Those close enough lashed out at him with spears and swords only to be beaten back by a powerful unseen force. The dark energy surged through von Essen, crackling on the ground around him and melting the snow into muddied and blood-tainted slush. He had nearly crushed the entire force of the Poles who had gathered along the eastern edge of the clearing. None of these soldiers or poorly equipped men-at-arms could match the raw telekinetic fury of his mind fully unleashed. He violently ran down the last of the Poles and turned back in a graceful gliding motion toward the black tower standing in the middle of the fields of carnage.

The maddened heathens engaged him as he neared the tower. As he turned toward his new attackers, he vaguely saw the fallen forms of Berchtold and Leopold, and anger welled up inside him as he unleashed his fury on the wild men. The remaining heathen warriors crumpled before the raw power of von Essen. Those that resisted or retreated were simply crushed into the snowy field. Their lives ended by being broken by an unimaginable force, as if the weight of the moon settled upon their mortal forms. Once again, Wilhelm von Essen had cleaned a front of the battle and began to gracefully turn back toward the tower and the final massed foe, the horde of demonic forces that Steffan and Valten had launched themselves into. Of all his brothers, Steffan and Valten were the most capable in combat. He vaguely hoped that they might still be alive.

As Wilhelm glided forward into the gathered mass of the demon horde, he passed over the torso of Valten. Poor Valten, his closest friend did not deserve such a fate. Anger brewed deeper and darker in von Essen as he slowly moved into the gathering of demons, who seemed to be enthralled with something happening in a clearing in the middle of their masses, so much so that they did not realize their doom was upon them.

With renewed anger for his fallen friend Valten, Wilhelm crushed the life from his enemies with such vigor that many of them simply imploded into bloody pulp. In the opening before him Wilhelm saw the heavily muscled form of a man-like daemon holding his brother Steffan tightly by the neck. He saw the sudden snap, the toss to the ground, and the hungry attack of the hellhounds upon the broken body of his brother. Unbridled rage overtook him. Wilhelm had always guarded his use of anger or rage to fuel his psychic abilities. He knew that using anger in such a way was especially dangerous if he wanted to stay in control of his mind. Anger and hatred could cloud the focus of the mind, leading the unprepared psychic warrior to a very dark place, a place some never return from. That was a fear he lived with whenever he tapped into that dark power within him. Until this day, Wilhelm von Essen had always been able to control the power.

Seeing Steffan die before him, on top of the deaths of all of his brothers, tore his control away from him. Wilhelm ceased to exist at that moment. Darkness occupied his body, relegating his soul to the deepest recesses of his mind. He became a pure elemental force of destruction. The chitinous bodies of the demons snapped and crackled into nothingness before him. The hellhounds broke from their maddening rage and sprinted toward the forest. Wilhelm's power raced ahead of him, clipping most of the hellhounds as they ran, crushing them into fleshy pulp.

Only the massive Deshnak and the four dark, abyssal wizards stood their ground.

"Blind him with darkness," hissed the orange wizard. The other three wizards conjured up their energy and it shot out forming a thick black haze over the head of von Essen.

The hovering form of the knight stopped in the midst of the black haze. The elemental force had no direction to unleash itself without a visible target, so the usurped form of von Essen hovered in place. The orange wizard conjured up a mystic chain that he bound around the neck of the Wilhelm. The other magi turned and chanted as they walked toward the forest beyond. Deshnak picked up the axe of the fallen von Dienheim and looked at its edge. He shrugged and with a sudden swing he lopped off the head of its previous owner. With a wicked smile and a devilish chuckle he strode confidently toward the forest. The orange wizard tugged the mystic chain and moved the hooded form of the fallen knight behind him as they too disappeared into the gnarled woods.

With their passing into the forest, the fields around the Tower of Dreams fell silent save for the carrion call of crows that had been high in the air for much of the day.

It was recorded by the chroniclers of such events that the Brotherhood of Olympus ceased to exist on that grim Friday the thirteenth, in the year 1469, in the lands of Prussia. So, too, was the succession of knighthood ended, and the Code lost for antiquity.

1

FATE

THE BROTHERHOOD OF OLYMPUS
AND THE TOWER OF DREAMS

This tale is based upon actual events...

To Everything There is a Season
Chapter One
Autumn 1979
Hoquiam, Washington

Being sophomore class president was not really as bad as he thought it would be when he was elected into the position at the end of his freshman year. Nearly all August he dreaded coming back to school. By Labor Day those feeling had turned to anxiety. He knew he had to stand in front of the entire student body, almost six hundred kids, and say something into a microphone about his fellow tenth-graders. As a painfully shy, introverted bookworm, that was not his proverbial cup of tea. The odd thing about time was that it continued to pass at the same incremental rate whether you wanted it to go faster, slower, jump ahead, or just stop. It was like waiting for what seemed like forever for a desired holiday with presents, or how quickly the last days of summer dwindled away if you didn't want to go back to school. Time was a fickle concept at best.

Tuesday, September fourth, brought the inevitable welcome back-to-school assembly to Drake Fraser. He had prepared a speech that merged the message of Abraham Lincoln at Gettysburg, with the logical ramblings of Mr. Spock. It was a page and a half long. He practiced reading it, twice. He dressed in his hooded basketball sweatshirt from the year before, crisp new blue jeans, and his new Converse All-Star tennis shoes. Both the jeans and the shoes were his new school clothes for the year.

Drake had grown over the summer he stood an imposing six foot, four and one-half inches tall, but still lacked much girth. His straight black hair was now past his ears in length, in a rough bowl style. His Spanish, dark olive complexion had darkened over the summer as it always did from his time spent outside. He stood nervously next to the other class presidents, silently fidgeting, along the wall of the gym. He took the moment to review his speech one last time.

"My fellow sophomores, in the course of human events," Drake mumbled to himself as he began to read his handwritten monologue. The time slipped away, and the Associated Student Body advisor, Mr. Dawson, took over the microphone from the varsity cheerleaders.

"Thank you varsity cheerleaders," Mr. Dawson stated with his mouth a bit too close to the microphone. "And now, here are your three returning presidents to welcome each class back, sophomore Drake Fraser, junior Daphne Young, and senior Steve Hanson. Please give them a round of applause."

"Psst... Fraser," interrupted Steve. Drake had been reading his speech so intently that he didn't hear the introduction. "Let's go."

Drake and Steve followed Daphne to the center of the gym floor and they stood awaiting Mr. Dawson. Steve and Daphne waved to some of their friends and classmates to an increased amount of noise. Drake stood holding his speech. A noticeable tremor had started in his hands, and panic was welling up in him.

"First let's hear from your sophomore class president, Drake Fraser," Mr. Dawson's voice echoed through the gym. He turned and handed the microphone to Drake, who looked at it like it was an alien device. Time seemed to freeze. He noticed the gym full of students and staff, their eyes upon him. Even the kids who normally didn't pay attention, like his brother Mark, were looking at him, waiting.

"Drake," Daphne quietly encouraged him. "You have your speech, read it, they're waiting."

"Come on, man," Steve added with a slight nudge. "You

can do it."

Drake had to react. He looked at his paper, and it was blank. His heart beat so violently he was sure it would rip through his chest. He decided in that moment to improvise. He thought of something calming from the past year, raised the microphone, and opened his mouth.

"I'm very good at integral and differential calculus," he began in a low voice, barely audible through the sound system. The gym quieted and his voice grew stronger and louder. "I know the scientific names of beings animalculous."

The students in the gym were hanging on his words, trying to figure out the cryptic yet lyrical message he was delivering. The message was not lost on the choir, band, drama, and most of the art kids, and a particular blonde girl who caught Drake's eyes, who all started to sing with Drake as he finished his speech.

"In short, in matters vegetable, animal, and mineral," Drake stated as he held the microphone very close to his mouth, his voice now echoing through the large space. "I am the very model of a modern Major-General. May this year be awesome for you. Thank you"

The students singing along with his spoken words stood and clapped loudly, bringing his brother Mark to his feet, along with a quickly rising contingent of other students. Drake handed the microphone to Daphne, and he felt the heat of his body temperature radiate from him. He remembered very little of the rest of the assembly, or the first day of school, for that matter.

By the first Friday of school, many of the routines of the prior year had returned. Drake sat in the lunchroom at a table occupied by fringe kids, outsiders, invisibles, or socially awkward brains. He received more recognition from students passing by, but no invitation to join another table, though he never sought one out either.

He waited and hoped Rachel Finnegan would rejoin him

for lunches, like she did for most of last year. But through the first week he didn't see her at lunchtime. He'd thought a lot about her, how she infuriated him by nominating him for class president, how she always pestered him about his artwork, how she hung out with him at the Hoquiam Public Library for most of last year, and how she gave him the medallion which he still wore on her birthday two summers ago. She was in his mind, and despite the words of his deceased uncle Wally, 'girls have cooties,' still haunting him, he'd come to realize that he liked her. He liked her long blonde hair, her cheery attitude, her infectious smile, and her endearing support she'd demonstrated for him and his family.

He sat quietly and ate his somewhat warm 'hot' lunch.

"Hullo Drake," rang the familiar tone of Rachel as she appeared before him on the opposite side of the table. She stood there, her hair pulled back in a loose ponytail, wearing a green V-necked sweater and a knee-length black skirt. She looked down at him and he smiled, forcing his dimples to pop out. Rachel felt the temperature rise in the room. "Are you just gonna look at me, or are you gonna invite me to sit down?"

"Please," Drake said as he began to rise. He couldn't recall ever seeing her in a dress before, or wearing green, despite his insistence that she was Irish. "Join me."

"Thanks," she cooed as she tucked her skirt behind her, and sat down. "By the way, using the Major-General's song from the *Pirates of Penzance* was simply brilliant as your welcome back speech. The high school did that show last year. Very topical, Mister President, most of the kids still know that song. Didya like how we all sang the last part with you?"

"I didn't sing," Drake responded as he set down his fork. "I'm not a singer, you're the singer, remember?"

"Oh, that's right," she toyed with him as she opened her brown paper lunch bag. "You're an artist and all around genius, not a singer."

"I never said that," Drake interjected as he watched her.

28

"I know," Rachel said with a sly smile, "but that doesn't mean you aren't. Besides, that's my opinion."

Drake sat and forced himself to eat since he didn't like to eat while others watched him. Fortunately, Rachel was also occupied eating so it wasn't like she was staring at him like she did the first few times she sat with him last year. He thought of tangents and angles to try and broach the subject of liking her. Every one of them sounded completely lame in his head.

"Whatcha thinking?" Rachel queried as she studied his face doing what appeared to be mental gymnastics.

"Nothing," he quickly retorted.

"Oh, okay," she replied as she twirled a loose part of her hair with the index finger of her left hand. "How was your summer?"

"Well," Drake began as he pondered how to tell her all of the events of the summer, "you know Miss Furfur never came back to the library, right?"

"Yeah, good riddance," she responded with a wrinkled face. "I didn't like her Drake, she's a daemon and she threatened me. Didya know that?"

"Uh uh," he answered. "She isn't a daemon."

"Whatever," Rachel immediately rebutted. "What about your grandparents and the lawsuit? And that nasty *Spirit* Board game your brother had?"

"I don't remember you being that interested in all of that, Rachel," he replied as he ate, taking careful precaution to avoid talking with food in his mouth.

"Duh," she said with a giggle. "Don't you remember me hanging out in the library doing all that research with you? Of course I'm interested."

"Well," he began to explain, using his hands more to describe what he was saying, "the *Spirit* Board turned evil. It attacked us, or at least whatever was using it attacked us. It wrecked both of my brother's cars with a black tornado of death."

"Wow," she interrupted. "Really?"

29

"Yes," Drake continued intently, "and then we had to go into my grandparent's house to get the *Spirit* Board and burn it, but it was like haunted, and I had to fight mordgeists with my staff. My brother Dennis almost got pulled straight to Hell by a nasty purple tentacle and we all nearly died. But the board wouldn't burn because we'd forgotten some of it in the house."

"Wow," she responded again as she ate her orange, slice by slice. She struggled not to smile, that was like the most words Drake had ever said to her at one time. She was very happy, yet tried her best to remain serious. "That sounds incredible and really scary too."

"Well, we eventually got it to burn," Drake added as he moved his hands with an enthusiasm Rachel had never seen. "And when it did, I think it broke the cycle of evil. A few weeks later, in fact, the lawyers told my grandparents that the truck driver's family had dropped their lawsuit against them."

"Cool," she added as she watched him talk, carefully observing his body language. "Well, I'm glad you're okay, you and your whole family, right?"

"Yeah my family's okay now," Drake pondered about his family, his four brothers, his parents, his aunts and uncles, and his grandparents, as he replied to her question. "And you know what else is cool?"

"What's that Drake?" Rachel asked a question to his question.

"Well," he began with a spark in his eyes, "before we went into the haunted house I made us into a team, like heroes or something."

"Like the Superfriends?" she asked.

"No," he quickly answered. "Not like superheroes. Although that'd be really cool, too. We're like Knights of the Round Table, you know, we became the Brotherhood of Olympus."

"Oh, that is awesome Drake. I get the brotherhood thing, cause you're all brothers and all," she stated a bit confused by his gushing information to her. "But why

Olympus? Why not the Brotherhood of Fraser? Or the Brotherhood of Aberdeen? Or the Brotherhood of Grays Harbor? Or..."

"Hmmm..." Drake interrupted her before she took that tangent any further and then he responded thoughtfully. "I'm not sure, except that I recall being told that is what we should be called in a weird dream I had a couple years ago. Some god, I think he might've been Odin, you know, the chief god of the Norse pantheon. He told me all of that, and gave me a magical staff."

"Okay," she responded as she peered at him with doubtful eyes. She knew there were some very sinister forces at play last year around Drake and his family, Miss Furfur the daemon librarian was one, but getting magical weapons from ancient Norse gods was a bit of a stretch. "Drake Fraser, you're still a very weird boy."

Drake blushed. People around them began to clean up and get ready to go to fifth period.

"What do you think of my necklace?" she questioned, tactfully changing the subject as she raised it out from her pale skin above her cleavage. "It's a four leaf clover, and I put it under polished glass and made a charm out of it. I also made this bracelet the same way. Do you like 'em?"

Drake looked at both of the pieces of jewelry with admiration of her workmanship.

"Those are cool. You're very good at charm making," he said as he thought of his own medallion he wore that she had made. "But, Rachel, I do have another question for you. I noticed you're wearing a green shirt."

"Sweater," she interrupted.

"A green sweater," he continued, "and you have new jewelry made of four leaf clovers. Did your dad finally admit to being a leprechaun?"

"Drake Fraser, you take that back!" she snapped. He wasn't sure if she was being playful, or angry.

"I'm sorry," he said. "I didn't mean to offend you."

"It's time to go back to class," Rachel said as she rolled

up her lunch sack with a simple smile. "And Drake, you really need to get a clue about how girls work. Maybe you can look that up in the encyclopedia."

Drake wished there were such entries in the encyclopedia to help him better understand people, especially girls. Unfortunately, he never got to tell her that he liked her that day.

By late September, Drake had been having lunch with Rachel every day. He still couldn't muster the courage to talk to her about his feelings. He was getting comfortable talking with her during lunch though, and even began to forget about his inability to eat while someone watched him.

He also spent more time with some of the kids in his art class. He was by far the most accomplished at drawing in the entire school. Two of the guys in his class, who sat at his table of four, actually recruited him to come over after school and try playing bass guitar for their band. Bill Thompson and Pete Mason had both long admired Drake's artwork. They played guitar and drums and needed a bass player for their garage band, so they thought they would see if Drake could play.

Two or three times a week the guys would gather in Bill's garage. They had a trap set in one corner, and some amplifiers in another with a few twenty-five foot cables running out to guitar stands and microphones. Drake didn't like the look of the microphone, since it conjured up images of being made to talk in front of the whole school. But over time he learned a few bass progressions, could read a bass line on sheet music, and, most importantly, could keep a steady rhythm to blend the drums into the guitar.

They christened the name of their band FATE. Drake drew up a stylized logo, with each letter having an arrow-like end. They used their band name to work on a project in art. Each student had to make an album cover, paint it on tag board, and have it graded. The three boys made the self-titled first album, *FATE*, the second album, *The Rising Dead*, that featured a skull on the cover, and the third album, *Twisted Fate*, which had a giant screw going into a thick cluster of arrows all pointing away from each other. Drake drew the titles for each of the albums, along with some of the other more artistic details. He completed and turned in *The Rising Dead* album and earned an "A" grade on it.

By early October, Drake was writing some lyrical poetry that Bill and Pete were putting to music. Drake still didn't like to sing, but could be heard on a couple of their cassette tape recordings singing backing vocals. The three of them decided if they were going to be more than just a garage band in Aberdeen they would need a singer. There were many garage bands in the greater Grays Harbor area, and sometimes they would jam with other bands or musicians in the area. Two musicians they spent time with were Kirk Arrington, a classmate of Mark's, and Duke Erickson, a fellow sophomore, but unfortunately they also played drums and bass and neither of them wanted to be a lead vocalist. Drake enjoyed learning more complex bass riffs from Duke, who had been playing bass for a few years already, and whose nose he accidently broke in PE during eighth grade. Duke had always blamed the other kid next to Drake, and Drake had never felt up to taking the blame for it. He kind of just kept the status quo by remaining quiet about it.

Basketball would be starting up soon and Drake, as the tallest kid in school, would once again be the center. He knew he'd have to balance his time amongst all the things he was doing. He'd met a couple times with his oldest brother Martin when he was home from his duty assignment at Fairchild Air Force Base (AFB) to discuss the emotional high they felt with the whole founding of the Brotherhood of Olympus. They'd often sit and discuss possibilities until early in the morning and dream of a day when they could do something again to make a difference in the world.

Drake didn't realize it at the time, but he was beginning to blossom as an individual. The future, indeed, looked very bright for young Mr. Fraser.

125TH STS

2

PROJECT NORTH STAR

THE BROTHERHOOD OF OLYMPUS
AND THE TOWER OF DREAMS

Project North Star
Chapter Two
November 9, 1979
Portland, Oregon

The summertime at Fairchild AFB was hot, stuffy, and humid on days when the farmers watered their extensive croplands that bordered the lands near the military installation. Martin Fraser had demonstrated responsibility and leadership in his time as a Security Police Officer, and had quickly moved up to the rank of senior airman. Martin enjoyed being left in charge of his squad duties and thought his time in the Air Force was actually getting better. He had come a long way from the crying seventeen year-old that had to join the military or go to jail. He looked forward to his leave for two reasons, first he was re-connecting with his now bigger, little brother Drake, and he had continued to date Beth Scott, who he met in Aberdeen the previous spring. He had made plans to take his relationship with Beth to the next level when he bought a ring at a Spokane jewelry store in September.

When he came home in October, he spent part of a weekend talking to Drake about the formation, plans, and goals of the Brotherhood of Olympus. Martin felt that it needed a more military focus or regimentation, since that was his perspective from being in the Air Force. Drake agreed with many of the things Martin suggested.

"Do you think we need ranks?" Drake asked his older brother. Martin turned and looked at Drake. Martin was nearly as tall as his younger brother, standing almost six feet, four inches, and had the same dark hair, although his was dramatically shorter. The major differences between them were skin color. Martin was pale and Drake showed their Hispanic heritage, and of course, their eye color. Martin had blue eyes and Drake had deep brown eyes. "And if we have ranks, what should they be?"

"I'm not sure, little brother," Martin responded thoughtfully. "But I know we should have something like that."

"And who's the leader?" Drake queried, not sure he wanted that responsibility but equally not sure if he could fully trust Martin after the deep fracture that had happened between them because of the whole *Spirit* Board adventure. As time passed, Drake liked to think of it as an adventure instead of the nightmare made real that it was at the time.

"Well," Martin responded carefully, "I'm not sure. I mean, any of us could be. Except maybe Dennis and Albert obviously, since they are still so young and have a lot of growing up to do. But they were there, and should be considered. Mark could do it, but I don't think his heart is in it. So that leaves you and me. As the oldest I should probably do it, but the thing is, I don't have the time to devote to being the leader of a paramilitary ghost-fighting group. And besides, you are the smartest, and you are a leader at school now, too."

Drake was mystified that Martin was deferring leadership to him. This was so unlike Martin.

"What do you think, little brother?" Martin asked. "Do you think you want that responsibility, being a leader and all?"

"Maybe," Drake replied as he flipped open a notebook. "Any idea what our next adventure will be?"

"Hmmmm…" Martin thought about the question, pondering it for a few moments. "There're a couple things on the horizon that I cannot place. One of them seems really big, like a national security event. I tried to recall all the things on the list we burned in the envelope from Aunt Carmen. But most of those seemed vague."

"I never got to see what was in the envelope," Drake

responded as he began to doodle in his notebook. Martin was trying desperately to forget the references to the deaths of Drake and himself in 1984, which the *Spirit* Board foretold.

"There're some changes coming up too," Martin said as he looked away forlornly. "But not all of them are bad. Speaking of which, I've to go, cause I've to go meet Beth."

"You're spending a lot of time with her," Drake stated as he doodled a black obelisk on a desolate plain with dark rolling clouds crashing into it, making its top obscured.

"You need to mind your own business," Martin responded with a smile. "I may be spending a lot more time with her, if I get my way."

Drake nodded as he darkened in his doodle, losing focus on what Martin was talking about as he became absorbed by his drawing.

"I'll see you later Drake," Martin said as he headed for the door.

"Uh huh," Drake replied, completely immersed in his drawing.

Martin and Beth went to dinner that night at Danny's in downtown Aberdeen. As they finished their dessert, Martin fumbled and removed a small object from his pants pocket.

"What are you doing, Marty?" Beth questioned as she watched him. Beth was a slim, eighteen year-old, five foot, seven inch woman. Her oval-shaped face was framed by shoulder length red hair, her wide-set eyes were sparkly green with flecks of brown, and she had very full lips that she always seemed to have the brightest red lipstick on. She was the only person, other than Uncle Wally, to regularly call Martin by the Marty nickname. His brothers had tried it at various times during their lives and had always let it go. Martin was just Martin to them.

"Well, Beth," Martin stumbled on his words. "I've known you for almost seven months. I've grown a lot during that time. And, I think I'm maturing and becoming more of a man. I've always thought someday, when I got to a certain point in my life I would find someone. Someone I really liked and wanted to be around. Somebody who made me feel special and loved. Somebody who…"

"Marty," interrupted Beth as she was losing patience with his rambling and thought he should get to the point. "What're you trying to say to me? Are you asking me to marry you?"

"Beth," Martin continued, shocked at her perception. She had never fully believed his stories of psychic abilities, nor had he even tried to tell her the whole story about the *Spirit* Board. "Yes. I mean, Beth, will you marry me?"

Martin pulled a simple gold band with a single petite, diamond mounted upon it from his left hand and held it out to Beth.

"Oh Marty," Beth began to cry. "Yes. Yes, of course I will marry you."

The following week back at his duty assignment in Eastern Washington, Martin began to make arrangements to move out of the barracks and into base housing for him and his wife-to-be Beth. The commander had granted his move request, and he was able to begin moving right away since there were a number of base housing units sitting vacant.

Martin stood near the tall, open window of the second floor of the barracks that he had lived in since January. He was lost in thought about how his life was getting better and better every day. Unbeknownst to him, some of his friends had planned on surprising him on his last night in the barracks with them. Quietly John and Louis tiptoed up behind Martin, carrying a couple cold bottles of *Rainier* beer. Martin, usually perceptive of such things, did not hear them at all.

"Fraser!" shouted John as he touched him in the back of the neck with the cold beer bottle. Martin jumped from the startle and lost his footing as he banged his legs into the window casing below his knees. His arms flailed as he grasped for the sides of the window. In one singular motion he toppled out of the window head first and began a forward roll toward the ground.

"Oh my God!" Louis shouted at John as he quickly looked out the window to the dark ground below. The barracks were surrounded by large, jagged basalt rocks to keep weeds from growing around them. Those same rocks could prove to be fatal to someone falling from the second floor. "Oh my God, John, you killed him, oh my God!"

John panicked and fell to the floor in shock.

"John," Louis said with a sense of great urgency, "John, get up here and look out this window, now."

"I can't look at him down there," John said as he started to cry. His Air Force career would be over as he'd be prosecuted for the death of his superior.

"John," Louis commanded as he grabbed him by the shoulder and hauled him up to the open window. "Get up here airman, and look!"

John peered out the window and slowly looked down. The ground was about fifteen feet below the window, and he was not expecting what he saw. A couple feet above the sharp basalt rocks, Martin Fraser hung in the air, as if he were suspended by an invisible cushion that slowly jostled him as it deflated under him.

"What the hell!" John remarked with a shock. "How's he hovering there?"

Martin put his hands out and touched the ground and slowly got his knees to touch the ground before standing up and looking back up at his two friends.

"Are you a freaking witch?" John questioned with disbelief.

"I don't know what happened," Martin responded. "It must've been a freak air current or something."

Louis looked at Martin, unsure of what he had just witnessed. He'd seen Martin slow down almost immediately and float like a feather to the ground.

"That dude isn't right," John continued his tirade. "I'm going to report him to the C.O. as a freaking witch, or communist spy, or an alien, or something, cause what he just did wasn't natural."

"John," Louis reasoned with a sense of calculation, "you realize you'll get in more trouble if you report it, because you pushed him out the window."

"Damn it!" John realized Louis was right. He then leaned back out and pointed at Martin. "Damn it all to hell. You're not normal, you freak, and you better watch your back from here on out. You got that Fraser?"

"Yeah I got that," Martin responded as he walked toward the door at the front of the building. "I guess I don't have to worry about missing this place anymore."

Sitting in a car across from the barracks that night was an Air Force officer by the name of Captain Larry Spenser. Captain Spenser didn't intend to witness the event outside the barracks, but he did. That series of events changed many things for Martin Fraser.

On November first Martin received new orders. He was being transferred to the 125th Special Tactics Squadron in Portland, Oregon. It was largely an Air National Guard unit, which perplexed him as an active duty enlisted man. He packed up his belongings, which were never really unpacked from his move out of the barracks a week earlier and moved them in his car to Portland. He was to report to a building called The Greenhouse. During his drive to Portland he thought a greenhouse would be a weird duty assignment. He wasn't a botanist. He'd trained in security and warfare during his time in the Air Force.

He arrived on the base the afternoon of November ninth. It wasn't really a base like he had come to know, it was in fact more of an outpost on a small airfield outside downtown Portland. There was a single security police airman at the 'gate.'

"Welcome, and you are?" the SP questioned, as Martin rolled down his window. Martin noted that the SP was a single chevron airman.

"Senior Airman Fraser, reporting for duty," Martin snapped to the airman as he handed him his assignment papers. "Airman, where is The Greenhouse?"

"Senior Airman Fraser, sir, The Greenhouse is on the back side of the airstrip, behind the hangers, sir," the SP responded, almost like he was afraid of Martin. "You'll notice that it's painted green, sir."

"Thank you airman," Martin replied as he took his papers back and drove into the base with a wave.

Martin quickly found The Greenhouse beyond the hangers. It was an old World War Two era building, if it were a house it would only have room for maybe three bedrooms. It did look like it had an upstairs though, or at least an attic of some sort because there were small windows up under the roof. The green was a dark, Kelly green, which had seen better days, and was chipping off along the edges of the siding.

"Great," Martin thought, as he climbed out of his car and began to walk toward the front door of the building, "my new duty station is an old shack in Portland."

The door opened with a loud metallic squeak.

An Air Force officer came from one of the back rooms into the foyer of the building, which was very sparsely decorated with two simple folding chairs and a small end table holding some old magazines.

"You must be Martin Fraser," the officer said as he approached with his hand out for a handshake. He was a stout gray-haired man with steely blue eyes and a warm smile. He wore a light blue, Hawaiian print button-up shirt with two silver bars upon his collar, and blue jeans. He was definitely not in a standard uniform.

"Senior Airman Fraser reporting for duty sir," Martin retorted with a salute.

"Very well," the officer responded with a wry smile. "Captain Larry Spenser, I am your new C.O., and you are no longer Senior Airman Fraser anymore, son. With your new assignment comes a promotion. Fraser, you're now a Staff

Sergeant."

"Thank you sir," Martin responded, with a smile of his own. The extra money would help with his upcoming wedding. "Sir, about your uniform, sir?"

"Now Sergeant, the men in my unit have come to expect a certain amount of civilian privileges from being assigned here. I hope you aren't a stickler for those kind of rules, son?" Captain Spenser said as he began to walk back into the room he had previously emerged from. "Come with me, and let's talk about why you're here."

The entered a sparsely decorated room, military chic, Martin thought to himself. A single card table sat in the middle of the room with two folding metal chairs on opposite sides. On the table were two manila file folders, one absurdly overstuffed, and one that didn't appear to have much in it at all, if anything.

"Have a seat Martin," Captain Spenser offered as he sat on the far side of the table. Martin obliged and took a seat in the other chair. "First off, Martin, we don't really go for all that military stuff in this unit like I said about uniforms. We like to be familiar with each other and call each other by our first names. No ranks and no obstacles to our mission, so you can call me Larry. You okay with that, son?"

"Yes sir," Martin responded out of habit. "I mean yes, sir, Larry."

"Just Larry," Captain Spenser replied with a sly chuckle.

"Larry," Martin said to reassure Captain Spenser he had heard his direction.

"Okay," Captain Spenser began as he separated the two files and thumbed through the thicker one before opening the thinner one completely before him. Martin could make out the name Fraser on the tab of the file. "Let's start with why you've been assigned to this unit, Martin. Would you like to tell me about the report I have here regarding an incident at the barracks on Fairchild, on the evening of twenty-two October?"

"An incident?" Martin responded a bit shocked, he was

sure that neither Louis nor John reported his fall out the window. "I'm not sure what incident you're referring to, Larry?"

"Well," Captain Spenser continued with a doubtful look on his face. "I understand not wanting to draw attention to yourself, son, but what's in this report, this is exactly the kind of soldier we're looking for."

"I don't understand, Larry," Martin added tactfully.

"It states here that Senior Airman Martin Fraser, that's you right?" the Captain queried and Martin nodded, "at twenty-one hundred hours, fell from a second story window. But, here's the kicker—he never hit the ground. This is eyewitness testimony, mind you. It further states that Fraser appeared to be carried aloft by an invisible force, and something about unsubstantiated telekinetic powers."

"Eyewitness testimony, sir?" Martin responded as he tried to think if either of his two former SP squadron present that night would have actually talked, knowing what kind of trouble they could have gotten into.

"Call me Larry," the Captain continued as he closed the file. "Yes, Martin, eyewitness testimony. Now, don't get me wrong, I'm not trying to get you in trouble at all. As soon as I got this report I ran it right past General McCarty, and he pulled the trigger to get you transferred into my unit as quickly as humanly possible."

"I don't understand, Larry," Martin responded earnestly.

"What do you know of Project North Star, Martin?" the Captain asked as he opened the thick file again. Martin shook his head. "Very few have ever heard of it, it's a top secret project. Of course the Army is running their own version. They call it Project Star Gate, or something or other. They seem to change the name every year. We know the Russians are running at least two similar covert intelligence operations, and we think the Red Chinese may be attempting it as well."

Martin looked at Captain Spenser and couldn't get any read on him. He attempted to probe his mind, to see if he could read anything off him. The Captain was a blank wall.

"Those of us in this unit have learned from the very best, Martin," the Captain went on with his explanation, a wry smile on his face. "We're all trained in how to defend ourselves from psychic probing, like you just attempted with me."

Martin was shocked, a bit scared of his future within the Air Force and worried about what it all meant for his future wife and himself.

"Martin," the Captain continued, "Project North Star is a covert intelligence gathering unit of the United States Air Force. Our method of gathering information is through the use of trained psychics. We find them, we train them, and together we do our damndest to keep the country safe and strong."

"Psychics?" Martin queried, unsure of the intentions of the captain since he couldn't perceive anything off of him.

"Haven't you been paying attention, son?" Captain Spenser asked with a smile. "We have documented evidence that you're perhaps a grade five psychic, the Army has two grade four psychics, the highest grade we have are three's. None of our boys can do what you did, mastering telekinesis the way you did. You floated like a feather, for God's sake. There is only one other grade five psychic known to exist in the country right now, a gentleman known as Ingo Swann who resides in New York and helps train some of the best psychics used by the government."

Martin looked perplexed. He was unsure if he should open up to Captain Spenser, or if this was perhaps a test to see if he'd admit to having powers that could get him discharged from the Air Force.

"Yes, Martin," the Captain added trying to reassure the young Staff Sergeant, "I'm saying we know you're a psychic, and we want to use your powers to help the Air Force protect America. My God, son, I can't tell you how excited we were when we heard about you and your potential. You know how painfully slow the government moves in doing things, like promotions, or personnel transfers. Hell, when I was serving in Korea I waited two months before I got permission to take a dump."

Martin smiled and nodded in agreement over the perceived inefficiency of the government.

"I'm going to be frank with you Martin," Captain Spenser opened up to him, his facial expressions taking on a more serious tone. "Do you know what happened five days ago in Tehran? You know where Tehran is right? The capital of Iran? Well, Iranian 'student' revolutionaries stormed the U.S. Embassy and took over sixty American citizen's hostage. They have hunkered down and look like they have support of the Ayatollah Khomeini. Some of us believe it was Khomeini's plan all along to solidify his base amongst the revolutionaries. This has the potential to be a national crisis like we have never faced before. We've got no agents inside Khomeini's regime deep enough to get intelligence from the embassy. The CIA is crapping bricks, son. North Star and Star Gate are the go-to guys right now, and we need a star to lead us. I think you're that star, Martin."

Martin began to understand the need the government had for psychic spies, it made sense to attempt to utilize people possessing that gift for national security. And Martin certainly had the La Madrid gift that was further enhanced from training with the *Spirit* board. Including him in this was definitely doing more for his country than standing guard on an air base in Eastern Washington.

"Martin," Captain Spenser continued with his serious expression, "are you in? What are you thinking, son?"

"So how do you use psychics, Larry?" Martin questioned as he started to think the captain was being upfront with him.

"We do what's called CRV," Captain Spenser replied as he looked through the papers in his thick file. "Coordinate Remote Viewing. It's a way of looking at things in a controlled environment. It was first developed at the Stanford Research Institute by Dr. Harold Puthoff, a laser physicist who later trained Swann. The Army jumped in early, and the Air Force countered with our project here."

"How does it work?" Martin asked, becoming more open to the story Captain Spenser was sharing and intent on learning more about this use of psychic ability.

"Well," Captain Spenser responded as he pulled out a paper from the file, "let's say there was a military target we needed to know more about. In more conventional intelligence units they send operatives in undercover to observe or discover information. With technology being what it is today, we can utilize wireless eavesdropping, satellite reconnaissance, or electronic infiltration through what's called a Trojan horse virus inserted directly into a computer system. All of those intelligence-gathering techniques take risks of discovery, or are very costly. That's where we come in as a better alternative. What our unit does is this. We are given the target. We work as a team, the viewer and a monitor. The monitor knows some of the target information, sometimes, depending on the level of security, nothing more than basic information. The monitor provides coordinates and a description of the target, like a person or soft target, a place, a thing, a feeling, or a time."

"A time?" Martin asked with a raised eyebrow. "You can see into time?"

"Martin," the Captain responded, "the fabric of time and space are a roadmap for a skilled psychic. If you're trained well, you can go and see anything, anywhere, in time and space."

"Oh," Martin stated, as he thought about being able to travel and see his dead Uncle Wally, maybe before the accident that claimed his life and warn him to avoid that intersection on that fateful day last year. That also helped him understand his recurring dream where he first witnessed the mordgeists and their nefarious actions in causing all the struggles his family faced, and where he first heard the daemonic name that still haunted his dreams to this day—Succorbenoth.

"So the viewer," the Captain continued, holding up a

scribbled page with a random drawing on it that looked like one of the doodles Drake would often make as they talked abstractly, "is able to travel to the coordinates, not like an out of body experience, or astrally, but through their perception of the target in their minds-eye. They begin to report back what they see, hear, smell, taste, feel, or experience. Many times they will sketch a map or an image from their experience like this one here, what we like to call the Tower of Dreams."

"The Tower of Dreams?" Martin questioned. "What's that?"

"It's an outlier, it appears from time to time when we do some routine drills to sharpen our skills," Captain Spenser began to explain. "I think the first time we saw it was three or four years ago. This massive black tower on a desolate plain, we didn't even have a name for it. A couple years ago one of our viewers, who's no longer with us, actually went inside it. This sheet was one of her reports. She said she saw a gray alien, you know, like the Roswell aliens, which identified himself as the Keeper of the Tower of Dreams. Said his name was Addraemyr, and that his tower had existed since before many of humankind's old pagan gods did. Can you imagine that? Anyway, we use the Tower of Dreams as a test target to sharpen our skill, because it apparently moves around time and space."

The Captain chuckled as he put the tower doodle away and pulled out another sheet and held it up for Martin to see.

"This is more up our line of work, Martin," Captain Spenser continued. "Here we have the report of a Soviet agent who was undercover in our own research and development industry. We were given a soft target, coordinates to view, and our team found this spy who had been living in the country his whole life in New Mexico, but had arranged to sell secrets to the Soviets because he didn't like the prospect of nuclear war. As if selling our nuclear secrets to the Soviets would prevent that. Hell, he probably pushed the doomsday clock ahead a whole hour, the bastard.

Anyway, our viewers found him, visited his house, saw him doing his daily routine, and witnessed his traitorous actions. We forwarded enough information to the Defense Department that they were able to arrest him and help protect our national security."

"That's cool," Martin said. "So you think I can do this CRV?"

"Absolutely, son," Captain Spenser responded with a broad smile. "I plan on sending you to Manhattan to learn from Ingo Swann himself, if he'll teach you. He's a bit of an eccentric, but the man knows his stuff, an authentic expert on psychic phenomenon."

"I've never been to New York," Martin said with a smile.

"Son," Captain Spenser stated with his broad grin, "there are lots of places besides New York that you've never been to that you'll be visiting while you are working in this unit."

"Larry," Martin began as he thought of his fiancé, "where's the base housing? I'm getting married soon, and my new wife and I were going to be living on base at Fairchild."

"We'll pay for an apartment for you and your wife," Captain Spenser answered as he put away the papers into the thick file. "My recommendation, Martin is to find a place across the river in Vancouver. There're less curious people there, and the quality of life is pretty good, too. Once you find a place, submit the paperwork to our unit clerk. They will cut the check for deposits or whatnot."

"I appreciate that, Larry," Martin stated warmly.

"Well, Martin," Captain Spenser said as he reached out his hand to shake with Martin. Martin pushed his hand into the Captain's. "Welcome aboard Project North Star."

"Thank you, Captain," Martin said as they shook hands. "I mean, Larry. I cannot believe I am an official government psychic, this is so crazy and amazing at the same time."

"I can tell you," the Captain added as they separated their handshake, "that it was such a liberating thing for me to come into this unit and finally be able to embrace this dark part of myself that had been discouraged by everyone in my family, my church, and almost all of my friends. A little acceptance goes a long way to helping you mend the scars of the past, Martin."

"Thank you Larry," Martin said as they stood from the folding metal chairs.

"Let me show you around The Greenhouse and introduce you to your new unit," Captain Spenser stated as he began to walk to a door on the back wall. Martin began to follow his new commanding officer.

"So," Martin questioned as they walked through the doorway into the stark room beyond filled with cubicles, each with a table, two chairs, and a floor lamp. The walls were completely barren of decoration, no calendars, photographs, or paintings of any kind. "Maybe I'll get to view this Tower of Dreams sometime?"

"Oh," Captain Spenser replied as they paced into the room and into the gathered personnel who emerged from another conference room all dressed in varied civilian clothing with metal pins on their collars designating their rank. "Martin, my boy, you can count on it. And maybe you, as a class five psychic, will actually get us some real tangible information about it. It sounds like a pretty far out place, if it really exists at all."

Both Martin and Captain Spenser chuckled as they approached his new teammates.

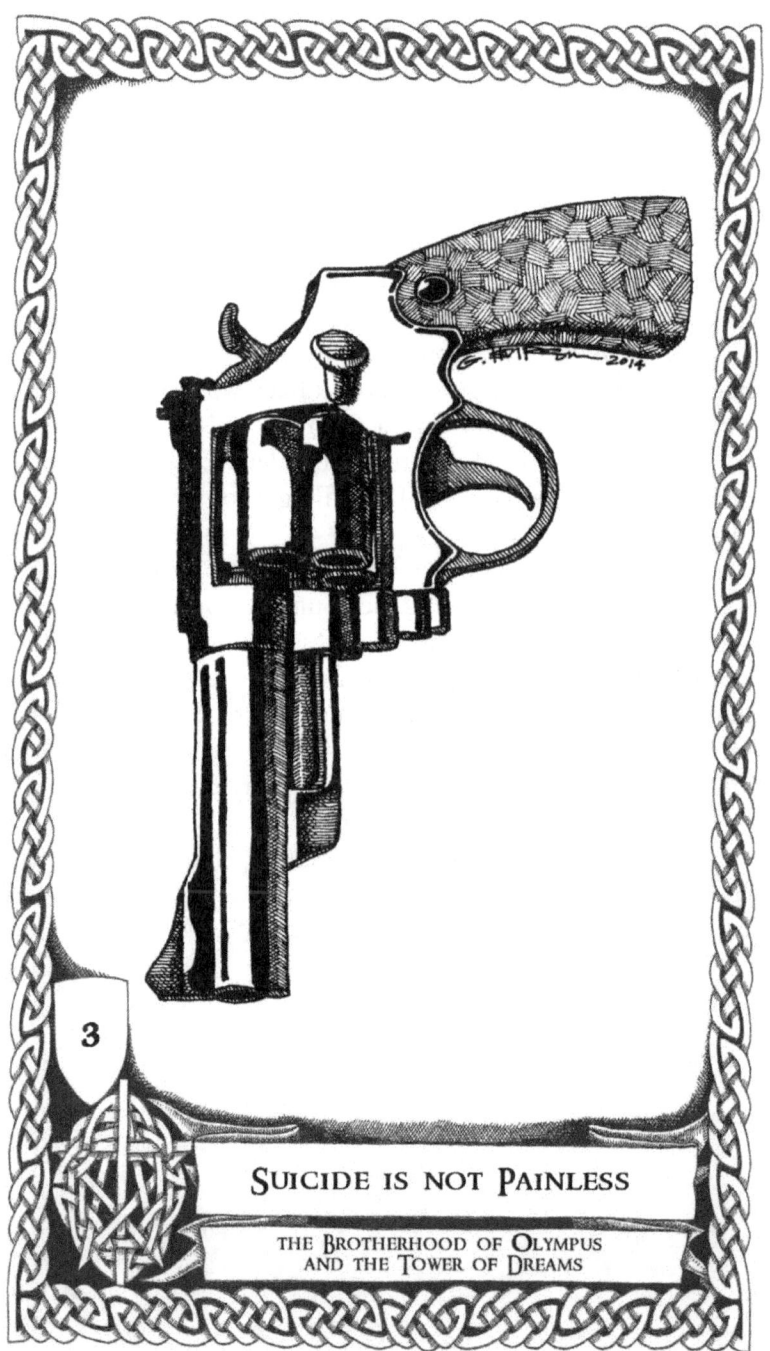

3

SUICIDE IS NOT PAINLESS

THE BROTHERHOOD OF OLYMPUS
AND THE TOWER OF DREAMS

It All Came Crashing Down
Chapter Three
November 21, 1979
Hoquiam, Washington

On a drizzly Saturday afternoon, the seventeenth of November, the Fraser family, parents Drake and Sophia, sons Mark, Drake, Dennis, and Albert played host to their extended family, friends of Martin and Beth, and her family for a modest little wedding at the Artic Community Center. Just down the road from the small cinder block building was the little bridge where Drake first observed the water-fearing behavior of the 'death tornado' that chased the five Fraser boys nearly half a year ago. The world had changed so much for the Fraser's as the darkness of the tragic loss of Uncle Wally was slowly being replaced by a new beginning. Dennis was healthy again, Albert had new friends at school and was playing youth league flag-football, Drake was in a band, playing basketball, and getting closer every day to telling Rachel Finnegan that he liked her. Mark was focused on his senior year of school. He wanted to be the first in the family to graduate from high school and he was actually thinking on going off to college or a technical school afterwards. Dad and Mom were both working full time and the family was doing better financially than it probably ever had. Martin was making something out of himself in the Air Force. He was newly promoted and working in a new unit closer to home, and was marrying a delightful young lady. From the perspective of many in attendance that day, the Fraser's were blooming like they never had before.

The bride wore a light blue above-the-knee, cocktail

dress and the groom wore his Air Force dress blues. After the short ceremony, presided over by a local pastor, food was served by some of the ladies in Martin's family.

"Where did he go?" mumbled Dennis. He had gained some weight over the summer. His brown hair was combed with a bit of *Brylcreem* to make it flip back from the part on the left. It was the same hairstyle favored by the father of the groom. His blue eyes scanned the big open room looking for his little brother. Although Albert was his younger brother by two years, he had recently grown taller than him.

"Who're you lookin' for?" Albert asked as he suddenly appeared behind Dennis, who reacted with a mild startle.

"For you, butthead," Dennis replied with a quick right hand jab to Albert's left shoulder.

"Ow," Albert stated with a chuckle. "That could've hurt."

Albert had the same brown hair color and same eye color as Dennis. However, he was more of a mix of his family heritage, having similar features of their oldest brother Martin and a bit darker complexion like Mark and Drake, blended though with the pasty complexions of Martin and Dennis. He was also the prototypical little brother who would go to great lengths to be involved with his older brothers, sought out negative attention because that was better than no attention, and seemed to get away with everything because he was the baby in their parents' eyes.

Drake and Mark had made their way to the covered porch area of the building where some of the older gentlemen were hanging out, drinking some canned beer and smoking. Mark was two years older than Drake, but only stood five feet, eleven inches in height. He was the tough and tumble brother. He had a similar Hispanic look as Drake did, so much so that they used to be confused by many as being twins when they were younger and the same height. Mark was the pragmatist, and the troublemaker. He had started smoking by the age of eleven, and quickly bummed a cigarette from one of their great-uncles.

"You guys want a beer?" Jacob Reuss asked as he pulled a cold *Rainier* can from a cooler. Jacob was a gray-haired, blue-eyed, six foot and one very proud inch, barrel-chested man. He was their grandfather Henry Reuss' older brother. He was quick to tell a story, usually involving his time spent in the Third Army under the command of General George Patton during the last two years of World War Two in Europe. He now worked as a car salesman at the dealership Mark had worked at as a lot boy two summers ago. "I was just saying it was a rainy day like this in France when Patton himself told me we were going to march across Europe and bring that bastard Hitler to his knees."

"Oh, don't believe that, fellas," John Reuss chuckled as he stood up and pulled another can of beer from the cooler and opened it with a sudsy pop. He tore the pull tab off the can and slurped some of the beverage. "Your Great-Uncle Jacob was in Patton's Third Army during the war, but he was the drummer in his band. He never actually saw any combat."

"Don't be so quick to think you know all the answers," Jacob responded to his youngest brother. They were separated by sixteen years, and John was plagued by the Reuss receding hairline like Henry, who was still inside trying to make sure the wedding reception was still going smoothly. John was the shortest of the three Reuss brothers. All of them bore a strong Germanic resemblance. John was the father of Ralph and Janet, who grew up in the valley with the other members of the Reuss extended family, including the Fraser boys' dearly departed Uncle Wally.

Drake would always remember the old photograph of the three oldest Fraser boys from 1965, sitting in DeWitt Park in Cosmopolis with Uncle Wally and Cousin Ralph. He had learned that those five boys were meant to become the Brotherhood of Olympus, but evil forces had acted against them causing the death of Wally, fracturing their relationship with Ralph, and left only the Fraser's to make the Brotherhood out of. That photograph had been the key to helping him remember what he was told in his dreams the summer before.

"Remember, Johnny," Jacob responded with a grin that made it difficult for Mark and Drake to determine if he was joking or mad, "you weren't even nine before the war ended, so I doubt you really know what happened. And you really don't have any idea what I saw, or had to do back then."

Both Jacob and John looked seriously at each other for a few moments before breaking into laughter. Mark turned and looked at Drake and raised one eyebrow.

"So, what are you guys up to?" John asked them, his words were delivered with the strong aroma of beer.

"Are you doing anything after high school, Mark?" Jacob asked. He had helped his nephew get the lot boy job at the car dealership and took a special interest in Mark.

"I think I am going to go to school, Uncle Jacob," Mark replied. "To be a mechanic."

"Mechanics can make some decent coin," John added with a pat on Mark's back. Jacob nodded in agreement.

"And what about you Drake, can you talk yet?" Jacob slurred. The effects of the alcohol were beginning to show. Both great uncles chuckled. Drake felt himself close off a bit in defense.

"Christ's sake, Drake," John announced as he changed the subject and loaded a large pinch of chewing tobacco into his cheek. "Are you done growing? You must be playing basketball for the high school, right?"

Drake nodded.

"Did you know that your uncle John used to play basketball, Drake?" Jacob declared.

"Oh, yeah," John added. "Though I was never as tall as you."

"But he was really good," Jacob continued as he moved over to pat Drake's shoulder. "Maybe he could show you how to play?"

"I'm sure he doesn't need any help from me," John replied.

Jacob finished his can of beer and quickly replaced it with another from the cooler.

"I'm sure any help is better than no help," Jacob stated with a loud slurp from his new beverage. "Right, Mark?"

Mark nodded slowly.

"His best moves on the court were these," Jacob declared as he placed his right heel on Drake's foot. "First, Johnny would stand on the other guy's foot like this. It'd make their height more equal since they couldn't jump. And his second move was to grab their shorts and pull them down. You'd be amazed how poorly a guy with his shorts around his knees plays in a game."

Jacob began to laugh a full hearty laugh. John joined his brother with a rolling chuckle. Drake looked back at Mark, raised an eyebrow and then walked back inside the community center.

The day, the wedding, and the reception were a success, and later the newlyweds moved into their new apartment in Vancouver, about three miles north of the Columbia River.

Wednesday, November twenty-first was the last day of school before the Thanksgiving break. Drake had thought a lot about Rachel after attending his brother's wedding. He had made up his mind. He was going to tell her he liked her before Thanksgiving. His time was running out, and he only had one more chance at lunch. Drake's mind raced at possible outcomes of his disclosure of emotion for the bubbly girl. She might say something rude and shut him down. But somehow, he knew that she really liked him and had been patiently waiting for him to admit he liked her too. Today was that day.

Rachel walked into the cafeteria carrying her brown paper lunch bag. She was a vision to Drake, her long, curly blonde hair cascading over her shoulders. She wore an orange V-neck sweater and a black skirt that came to her knees. On her feet she wore black Mary Jane shoes with a substantial heel over orange ankle socks with a lacy frill around them.

Drake's heart pounded in his chest. He realized his mouth was completely dry, and a scene from *Jaws* flashed in his mind. Richard Dreyfus' character, Hooper, was preparing to go into the water in his shark cage to face the mammoth great white shark. He attempted to spit into his mask to wet it unsuccessfully and looked up at Brody and Quint and stated, 'I got no spit.' Drake had no spit in his mouth. He was beyond parched and his tongue felt like it would break if he moved it.

"Hullo Drake," Rachel said as tucked her skirt and sat down across the table from the miraculously dehydrated boy. "Are you okay?"

Drake nodded and quickly took a drink from his milk carton. The cool milk didn't help him.

"I'm glad your brother got married," she rambled as she opened her lunch bag. "Weddings are so romantic. Someday when I get married, all my bridesmaids will wear a different color of the rainbow."

"I knew that already," Drake mumbled through his parched vocal cords. "But your dad's a leprechaun so I'd kind of expected you to want a rainbow at your wedding."

"Drake Fraser, he's not, and you know that," Rachel replied with a slight smile. Part of her had grown to appreciate his leprechaun taunting. Inside she was not happy, and she couldn't figure a way to explain why. She'd carried her unhappiness for the last month, always hoping she might be able to tell Drake, but afraid what it might do to the simple good times they shared at lunch. "I've something I need to tell you."

"Me too," Drake spurted out, seizing the opportunity to express his feelings for Rachel.

"Oh," she responded hoping his news was better than hers. "You first."

"That wouldn't be very gentlemanly of me," Drake insisted, hoping to buy himself more time.

"Okie Dokie Loki," she chirped as she tilted her head

slightly, hoping to find a tactful way to tell him her news. "Well, you know my father."

"The leprechaun," Drake said with a smile making his dimples pop out, and subsequently making Rachel smile and her eyes water.

"My dad," she began again as she struggled for the words, "my dad accepted a new job."

"Does it pay more money?" Drake asked in a very supportive way, still calculating how he might stretch out her news to delay his.

"Yeah, it does," Rachel said as she looked down at her lunch bag. "But, it's not in Hoquiam."

"Where, Aberdeen?" he responded and she shook her head. "Montesano?"

"No," Rachel replied as tears emerged from her eyes and slowly rolled down her beautiful cheeks. "Iowa. My dad got a job in Iowa, and we're moving."

"What?" Drake stated with a sudden croak of his voice. "When?"

"We're already packed up," she said somberly as her tears feely flowed down her cheeks. "We're leaving tomorrow morning."

Drake's head was pounding. He'd wanted to tell Rachel for nearly three months that he liked her, but could never find the strength or courage to do so. Now she was leaving. He'd likely never see her again. Part of him felt so empty and hollow inside. He couldn't explain it, nor could he understand the significance of the feeling. He felt sick, lightheaded, and the room began to spin before him forcing him to close his eyes tightly.

"What was your news?" Rachel said as she tried to compose herself and looked at the flustered boy across the table.

Drake shook his head.

"Okay," Rachel rolled up her lunch bag and stood up. "I have your address, I'll write to you after I get settled. Iowa should be fun right?"

Drake continued to look down. If he were capable of crying he'd have shed tears. He had not cried since the death of Uncle Wally on January thirteenth, 1978. He didn't know what to do or say.

"Well," Rachel said as she began to turn away, "I hope you find what you are looking for, Drake Fraser, and I'll never forget you."

Drake was crushed. He had dared to love this girl, and in his mind he had imagined what their future might be like. Maybe some day they would get married like Martin and Beth had. Maybe even with rainbow-colored bridesmaids. But he never told her. And now she was leaving. He couldn't imagine being able to care for another girl again for the rest of his life. He fought back the pain and looked up to call out to her. But she was already gone. Rachel Finnegan passed out of his life that day.

That evening, after Drake returned home from a rather bad day at basketball practice, he moped around the house and spent much of his time sitting quietly in his lilac painted room drawing an incredibly detailed picture. His mother worked night shift at the hospital as a licensed practical nurse, and she left for work at a little past ten o'clock. Martin and Beth had come back up from Vancouver to spend Thanksgiving with their families. Beth was spending the evening at her parents' house, and Martin had come over to hang out with his family for a while.

Mark and Martin sat in the living room talking to each other. Dennis had positioned himself in one of the five variously colored vinyl beanbag chairs to listen to their conversation. Albert stood in the kitchen, poking the thawing turkey in the sink that sat under cold running water. After a few minutes of this he tired of the turkey and walked through the living room.

"You can't hang out in here," Dennis scolded him as he walked past. "You're too young to be in here."

"Whatever," Albert chirped as he continued walking, his

left foot found the right calf of Dennis with a swift kick. He ran for the stairway, thumping up the stairs to avoid any chase from Dennis. The anticipated pursuit didn't come. Albert reached the top of the stairs and began to turn left to his small bedroom.

As he reached for the doorknob he paused. He heard an odd sound coming from his parent's closed bedroom door behind him. It was kind of a frantic sobbing and curiosity moved him to turn and silently approach the door. He stood there listening to the noise, and he was puzzled, because the only person in there was their dad. But Dad never cried. At least not like what he heard. Concerned, he slowly turned the doorknob and ever so quietly peered into the room from the widening crack in the doorway.

Dad sat on the edge of the bed, holding papers in his hand, crying. His deep sobs rasped through his chest, making him sound hoarse. Albert was shocked to his core. He had never seen this kind of raw emotion from his father.

Albert carefully turned and tiptoed away from the slightly ajar door, and quickly and quietly made his way down the stairs to alert his brothers.

"Dad's crying," Albert announced as he frantically entered the living room. "I think he's really hurt."

"What are you talking about, Albert?" Martin said distrustfully. They knew Albert wasn't above playing games to get them to chase after him. After all, attention was attention for their baby brother.

"Albert," Mark responded. "We're not gonna fall for it."

"No," Albert pleaded with a scared look on his face. Albert was quite convincing at times, but they had never seen him react this way. "I'm not kidding, Dad's hurt."

The boys got up and headed for the stairs. Mark led the way up the stairs, around the double landing and up the final flight of carpeted stairs. As they reached the top of the stairs they began to hear the irregular sobbing coming from their parent's room.

"Dad, are you okay?" Mark asked as he opened the door

into the spacious room. Martin, Albert, and Dennis followed him in. "Dad, what's wrong?"

He just sat there in his blue jeans and white t-shirt, barefoot, his eyes reddened, tears soaking his face and the front of his white shirt. He held a small stack of unfolded papers in his hands as he continued to cry.

"Dad," Martin asked as he and Mark turned in front of their father. "What's wrong?"

Dad sobbed heavily, he gasped for breath, and attempted to slow his tears so he could talk. The rasping of his crying had hurt his voice. Words didn't come. He looked at the papers in his hands and then up to his two oldest sons.

Martin and Mark tried to make sense of the scene. They looked into the pain-stricken eyes of their father and it hurt their souls.

"What is it, Dad?" Mark asked as he moved closer to him.

Dad looked into the faces of his boys. His heart was crushed and he couldn't bring himself to share why. With a pronounced and very loud sob he began to cry again. As his tears flowed, so too did the tears of Dennis and Albert. The two younger boys were terrified of what this meant and nearly immediately began to cry.

"What is it, Dad?" Mark asked again.

"What're the papers, Dad?" Martin questioned.

Dad didn't respond, he simply raised the stack of papers. Mark took the papers from Dad's hand and looked at them. They were letters. They were all addressed to 'My Darling Sophia.'

"Did you write these letters, Dad?" Mark asked as he handed them to Martin. Dad shook his head. He pointed to the bottom of the letters. They were signed in various ways, but the message most commonly on them was 'Your Lover, Paul.'

"Who's Paul?" Martin said, before the realization took over. "Oh my god, Dad, is Mom having an affair?"

Dad sobbed on the edge of the bed and nodded.

"What the hell!" Mark interjected angrily. "Who's this dude?"

"Some... some... one from the hospital," Dad responded with a heartbreaking cry. "I love your mother with all my heart. I can't live without her."

"Albert, Dennis," Martin said as he turned around to look at his crying little brothers. "Go get Drake. Hurry."

"This Paul dude, works with Mom?" Mark questioned as he looked at the letters again, taking the stack from Martin.

"Yes," Dad sniffed. "She's talked about him before. But I didn't know this was happening."

Mark was revolted as he read the graphic sexual content in the letters. He thought about going to the hospital right then and killing this Paul for what he had done to his parents, to his dad.

Drake quickly bolted into the room. Martin looked at Drake and made a motion with his eyes toward the rifles in the gun rack mounted on their parent's wall. Drake quickly went and removed the rifles and handed them to Albert and Dennis.

"Take these and go put them in the closet in your room, Dennis." Drake directed them quietly. "Take a pillow and blanket, and sit in there with the door locked. Keep these safe and out of reach, got it?"

Dennis and Albert nodded. They were visibly shaken. The only room with a lock on the inside was the old darkroom, the walk-in closet in Martin's old bedroom, now occupied by Dennis. Being on the inside and latching the lock behind them was the only way to secure the guns.

"I'll come get you later," Drake whispered. "Okay?"

Dennis and Albert nodded again and then turned and made their way down the stairs with the four rifles.

"This is messed up, man," Mark said as he continued to read the letters. "I can't believe Mom did this."

"I'm not leaving her at the hospital with Paul," Martin announced with a burst of visible anger. "I'm gonna go get her."

"I'm coming too," Mark said as they both turned and walked past Drake.

"Drake," Martin snapped as he headed for the stairs quickly. "Watch Dad."

Drake nodded and went to sit by his father.

He heard the front door slam as Martin and Mark left the house. Dad continued to sob, though his breathing had become more regular.

"Dad," Drake began, "would you like some water?"

Dad nodded. Drake got up and headed down to the kitchen. He did not see his father move toward the head of the bed and move his robe from the bedpost, revealing the fully loaded leather gun belt and twenty-two caliber pistol in the holster. The boys had always thought his gun belt looked like something a cowboy would wear in a western movie, or maybe something you would see on *Bonanza*.

Drake carefully ascended the stairs, not wanting to spill any of the water out of the glass he carried for his father. As he neared the bedroom doorway, he heard the sound of the chamber of the revolver spinning, the metallic click of the hammer pulling back. He realized too late what the source of the noise was as he raced into the room, dropping the glass in a loud shattering of jagged glass and water upon the carpeted floor. Dad had the gun to the right side of his head and he pulled the trigger.

A click was the result. The spin of the chamber had moved it to where the revolver was without a bullet. Dad cried loudly, having failed in his attempt. He pulled back the hammer again, holding the gun to his temple.

"Dad, no!" Drake shouted as he rushed to his father. Panic coursed through him. He could not lose his Dad, nor could he witness his dad's suicide. "Don't Dad! Please don't do it, Dad!"

Drake made it to his father. He was careful not to reach for the gun and accidently make his Dad pull the trigger. He fell to his knees putting his head on his dad's lap, hugging his blue jean covered legs.

"Dad, no!" Drake continued frantically. "Please don't do it! Please, Dad, no!"

Dad opened his eyes and looked down at his son. Drake was his namesake. He remembered the day he was born, the love he felt for his sons, his family, and his wife. He remembered the undying love for his wife, and the devotion he had always carried for her since that night they met at the Harborena Roller Rink all those years ago. He knew that he was gone a lot, because he worked over two hours away in Napavine, and they struggled financially after he was injured at work. But every family has hardships, every relationship, and every marriage has rough spots. He couldn't imagine why she did this to him. If she was unhappy, she should've told him. She should've given him a chance to fix things. Instead she found someone else, loved someone else, and threw his undying love and devotion away.

"I can't live without your mother," Dad cried as the gun twitched in his hand, cocked and ready to fire.

"I don't know why she did what she did, Dad," Drake reasoned with his father looking at his eyes and glancing at his index finger on the trigger of the revolver. "But, we can't live without you."

Dad looked at him through the tears in his eyes.

"We all need you," Drake continued. "Martin, Mark, Dennis, and Albert. I need you. Damn it Dad. I've already lost so much—Uncle Wally, my friend Rachel, and now Mom maybe. I can't lose you too, Dad. I love you, you're my father, and I can't survive without you."

"You're stronger than you think, Drake," Dad answered. His index finger was turning white from the pressure it applied on the trigger of the twenty-two. "Of all my boys, you'll survive this and be successful."

"You're stronger too, Dad," Drake answered. "You're the strongest man I know."

"Drake," Dad said as he shook his head. "I've never told you why I named you after me have I?"

"No," Drake replied as he reached up with his right

hand. "Dad, please give me the gun."

"I named Martin after my dad," Dad continued as he repositioned his hand on the gun. "Mark was a name your mother wanted for some reason. I hoped to name him after me, but only got her to agree on using my name as his middle name. Finally, when you were born, I had to name you after me. My dad told me when I was thirteen that he named me Drake because it was a family name in the land he came here from. He told me Drake was a name of kings, and he hoped I would grow up to be one some day. But, look at my life, I sell campground memberships for Christ's sake, I have a bad mortgage, an unfaithful wife, five sons, and most of my life has already happened. I'll never be a king, Drake. But, I named you, the name my father chose, so that you might grow up and be the man I couldn't be."

Drake looked into the eyes of his father. They were wet with moisture. What Dad had just said was profound, another reference to him growing up to be a king, just like the *Spirit* board and the psychic medium had last year. Tears ebbed in Drake's eyes, but didn't fall.

"Dad," Drake lobbied with his open hand still outstretched. "I need you in my life. You'll always be my dad, and I really need you. I love you so much. You're my captain, my king. Please, Dad, give me the gun."

Dad began to cry loudly again. Drake heard the hammer click on the revolver, and he held on to his father's legs. There was no noise, save for his father crying above him. Drake looked up, and saw that Dad had moved the gun from the side of his head and had let his finger off the trigger.

"Thank you, Dad," Drake responded, as he reached up for the gun. Dad gave it to him. "I'll always be there for you Dad."

They hugged as Drake moved the revolver away from his father, pointing it toward the far wall in case it accidently went off. Drake got up and grabbed the holster belt, putting the gun back inside it and snapping the leather strap over the end of it.

Drake sat and held his father for a long time as he sobbed silently in his son's arms. Nearly half an hour later the front door opened with a bang. Martin and Mark walked upstairs to the bedroom where Drake and Dad still sat. Mom followed them quietly.

"Boys," Mom said coolly as she walked past Martin and Mark. "Let your Dad and I talk."

Drake got up. He kissed his father upon the forehead, and turned to leave the room. He still carried the revolver in the holster, and he glared at his mother as he passed her. Martin and Mark turned to leave too.

"Guess what?" Drake said as he passed his brothers and over the wet broken glass on the floor. He held up the holster. "We forgot this one."

The three of them left the room. Mom came in and closed the door behind them. They stood in the hallway for some time, waiting for something to go wrong in the bedroom beyond the door, but eventually they made their way back downstairs for the comfort of the living room furniture. It wasn't until sometime after they had arrived downstairs that Drake remembered their younger brothers.

"Oh, crap," Drake stated as he walked into Dennis' room. He knocked on the closet door. Neither Dennis nor Albert answered. Drake knocked louder, and louder, before calling out to both of them. "Dennis, Albert, its Drake, open up the door. It's safe, come on, open the door."

He heard the metal hook of the lock move and the door swung open. Dennis stood there, with messed up hair and sleep in his eyes. Behind him, on the floor, lay Albert fast asleep under a blanket from his bed.

"You guys can come out and go to bed," Drake told them. "Mom's home and she's upstairs talking to Dad now. All we can do now is wait, and see what happens."

Albert stayed in the closet, sleeping. Dennis climbed in his bed and fell back to sleep. Martin and Mark sat in the living room and napped while Drake returned to his room to finish the drawing he was working on earlier before all of this erupted.

Drake dozed off after finishing his drawing. He woke up early on Thursday morning. He brushed his teeth, combed his hair, got dressed, put on his jacket and ran out the door with the picture he drew in his hand. It was almost half a mile to her oddly painted house. But Drake knew he needed to take his picture to her, to give her something to remember him by. He quickly ran toward her house. Soon he saw the garish blue and pink paint of the Finnegan home as he neared it. He turned onto the cement walkway and dashed up on the porch. He knocked on the door with an unknown passion. He waited, but nothing or no one stirred inside. He knocked again and waited some more. He repeated that numerous times before he stepped away and walked around the house toward the garage. There were no cars, and no truck loaded with personal belongings. He realized at that moment that he was too late, and the drawing he worked on so hard last night was a wasted effort. He couldn't give Rachel the unicorn she had always asked him to draw for her. He had lost her.

Sadly, he turned and walked silently home in the late November chill of a Grays Harbor morning.

Later, when he got home, Martin was up and getting ready to leave to go pick up Beth. Mark was still half asleep on the recliner.

Mom and Dad came down the stairs and entered the living room together. The boys knew the divorce announcement would be quickly coming.

"Boys," Mom began. "Your dad and I have been up all night talking. We've decided to… to stay together."

"But," Dad added, "we will not be staying here, so close to this other man. We are going to move to Vancouver as soon as your mother is able to get a job at a hospital down there."

Martin was shocked, but after the announcement he was suddenly okay with this change in family residence, since he currently lived in Vancouver as well. This meant his family would be living close by. Mark wasn't awake for the entire message but did hear the moving to Vancouver part. Since he was in the middle of his senior year in high school, this plan did not please him at all. In fact, he would've rather seen them divorce than move him.

Drake saw the bloom that was their family, blossoming as recently as the prior weekend at Martin and Beth's wedding, shriveling, turning brown, and withering on the vine. Personally he had lost Rachel, his mother betrayed his father, he nearly lost his father to suicide, and now he was going to lose all the benefits he'd worked for at school. His friends, his class presidency, his band, his place on the basketball team, and everything else he had slowly struggled to achieve. In his viewpoint, everything in his life had just come crashing down around him.

4

HIKARI

THE BROTHERHOOD OF OLYMPUS
AND THE TOWER OF DREAMS

Hikari
Chapter Four
December 6, 1979
Aberdeen, Washington

On a dry, deserted plain of low rolling hills stood a massive, shiny, black tower that rose upward into the brewing storm clouds that churned through the sky. A dull, primer-black car approached the base of the tower with its exhaust spewing a thick blue smoke from the rich burning of oil. Martin climbed out of the passenger side door, flipping the seat forward and letting a red-haired woman out of the back seat. It was Beth. She looked completely frazzled, like she was in a state of shock. Behind her a sinewy darker-skinned man emerged from the back seat of the car. He was a bit taller than Beth's height, but his proportions were beyond those of a typical man. He was built like a weight lifter, a profoundly gifted weight lifter. His rippling upper arms were bigger around than Martin's thighs. His neck was so thick it appeared to be just an extension of his shoulders. He carried two machetes, one in each hand.

The three of them turned and looked toward an unseen object, maybe it was another person who was with them. They appeared to be talking to each other and this other person. Off in the distance a wailing cackle was heard. It repeated from the other side. It began to get louder. Whatever was making the noises was getting closer. A sense of urgency came over the muscled man as he ran to the glistening exterior of the tower. Martin followed him and together they began to feel the smooth wall looking for something. The howls were getting ever so close now.

Martin yelled at the muscled man and the unseen person. The weight lifter found the crack Martin was pointing too and tried to get his fingers into it. He couldn't get a grip. He quickly stuck the end of one machete into the slim gap and pulled on it with a great flexing of his arms. The machete snapped in two near the tip of the black blade. He turned to the unseen person and stuck out his hand, demanding something. Suddenly a hand raised a shiny silver sword up before the weight lifter, and there was a side-to-side shaking like a camera moving.

The howling was now nearly upon them. Martin yelled something at them and they rushed back into the dust-covered car. They barely made it in and closed the doors before the windows were assaulted with loud thuds by large dog-like creatures with wild tufts of hair on the backs of their necks, a row of long bone-like spikes protruding from each of their spines, and overly large, human-like heads with rows of razor-sharp teeth in the slobbering maws.

With a sudden startle, Drake awoke from his nightmare, covered in a cold sweat. The images streaked across his psyche—the shiny black tower, Martin, Beth, and this dark weight lifter. The dreams were becoming more frequent. He remembered having the first one in early 1978, back when he did not know who the red-haired lady was with them. Now he knew who she was, his new sister-in-law, but he still didn't know the weight lifter and the older long-haired guy with thick black glasses who was inside the tower waiting for them in some versions of the dream. Drake slung himself out of bed, fumbled for the light switch on the wall, and walked over to his bookshelf and looked for the book. He had always used the same book to alter his thoughts when he had a bad dream, or struggled going to sleep at night because of the deep, dark questions his mind wrestled with—like how long was forever or what mystery awaited the human soul beyond this life. He quickly found the narrow book and pulled its worn green hardcover from the shelf. On the cover a cat, striped orange and black with a black eye-patch over its right eye played a violin tucked under its chin. Behind the cat was an odd assortment of dancing people, all dressed in what looked to be medieval clothing. *The Boy, the Cat and the Magic Fiddle* was a book Drake had gotten from his great-grandfather, Hector La Madrid, who had lived with his family in the last few years of his life. It was a whimsical tale of a boy who received three gifts to bring him luck upon his journey, an axe, a magic fiddle, and a talking cat. Drake knew that book with its illustrated pages would clear his mind and allow him to sleep soundly once again.

Drake turned off the room light, climbed back into his bed, pulled the thick covers back over him, and clicked on the reading light hanging from the headboard on his bed. As he usually did, he fell back to sleep before he finished the story, leaving the single light on above him.

After school on Friday, November thirtieth, Drake joined his parents and two younger brothers for their final visit to their grandparents' out in rural Brooklyn before they moved south to Vancouver. The ride over the Cosi hill had never been the same since that fateful day nearly two years ago, when Uncle Wally was killed in a horrible car accident at the junction of the roads at the base of the hill. Their hearts still sank as they passed the site of the accident on the left, and the location where they were attacked by the floating head in the clover field to the right, on the day they burned the *Spirit* Board last summer. The rest of the trip was long and uneventful. The family van finally turned into the sweeping driveway before the large, yellow two-story ranch style house.

The boys piled out the side door and were greeted by the massive Saint Bernard, Buddy. His thick tail wagged vigorously behind him as he covered them in long white hair and warm slobber.

"Thanks a lot, Buddy," Drake said as he wiped a thick strand of slobber off the back of his hand onto the hood of Dennis' jacket. According to Mark, that's what little brothers were for. Drake had taken his share of nasty things from his older brothers over the years.

"Stop it, Drake," Dennis snapped, unaware that the rubbing of his hood also involved dog slobber.

The five of them quickly walked to the front door. Albert pressed the white rectangular doorbell with a smile. Mom shook her head and opened the white metal storm door with its hinges on the right, and turned the knob opening the wooden door with its hinges on the left.

"Knock, knock!" Mom shouted as she stepped inside the entryway.

"Come on up!" was the reply from Grandma upstairs. Both Dennis and Albert avoided the knitted orange and black cat doorstop that had an eerie resemblance to *Garfield*. It sat in the hallway staring aimlessly toward the front door as both the boys turned up the stairway to the right, to follow Mom. Ever since the incident in the house last summer, Dennis was better going up the stairs. He still went slowly, taking them one step at a time, getting both feet on a step before moving up to the next. But that was way better than how he used to go up, scooting backwards on his butt.

Dad waited for Drake to come in so he could close the door. Drake paused to look at the storm door and wooden door hinges, he was always mystified by the fact that the two sets of hinges were on opposite sides. He never had the courage to ask his grandfather why he put the doors up that way.

"Come on Drake, its cold outside," Dad said as he motioned Drake inside the house and closed the door behind him.

The two of them, father and son, headed up the steep stairs, past the stained glass window on the wall at the landing, before turning up to the left for the rest of the climb to the upstairs beyond. When they reached the top of the stairs, Drake turned to the left and headed down the hallway toward the bathroom. Dad turned to the right and stepped into the wide living room, illuminated by the large windows that filled much of the two exterior walls. He walked across the carpeted floor and sat on the couch next to Albert. Dennis was slouching next to Albert, and Grandpa—Henry Reuss sat in his recliner where he could peer out the window that looked down the length of the road that led to their house. Grandpa was a large man of German descent, with sparkling blue eyes, gray receding hair, a heartwarming smile, a cleft chin, and a silent stoicism about him that always made people wonder what he was thinking.

As Drake walked the few steps to the bathroom, he passed some of the photographs that lined the walls. Hundreds of pictures were tacked on cork bulletin boards along both walls, interrupted by larger portraits of family members in frames. Just over five months ago Mark and Drake were assaulted by those same pictures. Even though the pictures were of his loved ones, the trauma of the event still haunted him, and the hallway would never feel the same for him after that. He quickly stepped into the bathroom and nearly slammed the door, because he had an odd, creepy feeling that he was being watched in the hallway. The hair on the back of his neck stood up, and his pulse raced. Drake took a few deep breaths to calm himself.

Mom was in the kitchen with Grandma and Aunt Carmen, who had stopped by to visit on her way home from work. The three women bore physical similarities. All three had prominent Spanish features, dark brown, nearly black hair, olive complexion, brown eyes, full lips, and warm friendly faces. Isabella had been born in Madrid in the spring of 1924 to the mysterious La Madrid family, rumored to be either mystical gypsies or Spanish royalty, or perhaps both. She had met Henry while attending high school in Aberdeen after her parents had moved to the United States in the summer of 1936, before the start of the Spanish Civil War. Had they not escaped Spain when they did, they undoubtedly would've been executed when the fascist Francisco Franco took power at the end of the war.

Both Sophia and Carmen were both taller than their

mother, by four or five inches. Sophia was nearly twelve when Carmen was born, and Carmen was six when Sophia had her first child, Martin. They had a slightly disconnected sister relationship due to the age difference. Where the three women excelled was in their choice of careers. Each had chosen to enter the medical field, and it allowed them to use their La Madrid gift as empathy in ways beyond what most humans could.

"So why are you really moving, Sis?" Carmen asked as she stirred some sugar into her coffee.

"Well," Sophia began after a long pause, "the nursing position at St. Joseph's Community Hospital is too good to pass up. And by moving into Hazel Dell, it'll make Drake's daily drive to work in Napavine shorter."

"A shorter drive is nice," Isabella remarked as she sipped some coffee.

"Is that all?" Carmen inquired with a raised eyebrow.

"Does there need to be more, Carmen?" Sophia replied in an almost motherly tone.

"What about the boys?" Carmen continued. "It's Mark's senior year, and Drake's doing so well in school."

"They'll adjust," Sophia answered. She was doing her best to conceal darker secrets in her mind. She had long been aware of the La Madrid gift of psychic abilities. She knew her sister was better with the power than she was, and she had to work hard to keep the secret of her affair and the real reason for the move from Carmen. "They're good kids and they will do fine in Vancouver. Their new school is amazing, it's a lot bigger, and we can get Mark in an automotive class for his last semester. Drake can join their basketball team and start playing right away. Of course, Dennis and Albert will do fine, too."

"You'll be closer to Martin and that delightful Beth of his, too," Isabella remarked. "They live in Vancouver."

"Are you sure you're not hiding something from me?" Carmen questioned.

"No!" Sophia snapped. "Of course not. The boys'll

love it there. Mark can transfer to the Danny's restaurant in Vancouver, and Drake…"

"What about me?" Drake said as he entered the kitchen on his way back from the bathroom.

"Who's Paul?" Isabella questioned her eldest daughter. Sophia's face turned red from shame and embarrassment. "Really, dear, you should've just shared with us. It would've made things so much easier for you."

"Oh my god," Carmen said as she found the truth in her sister's memories. Tears began to form in Sophia's eyes.

"Drake," Isabella called to her grandson. "Come here, my darling grandson."

Drake walked over to his grandmother, looked at his mother about to cry, and stared at the shocked face of his Aunt Carmen.

"Grandpa and I have something for you out in the shop," Grandma said as she patted the back of his hand. "Why don't you head down there and I'll send him right out to you."

"Okay Grandma," Drake responded as he turned and headed back toward the hallway and the steep stairs beyond. He was curious why his mother was nearly in tears, but thought it was better to leave well enough alone.

Drake quickly went down the stairs, rounding the landing before finishing the shorter stair section to the entryway below. Turning right, he headed to the door on the left at the corner of the hall, opened it, and walked into the darkened garage. He almost ran into grandma's car as he maneuvered through the darkness on instinct. This was a skill he was teaching himself after reading about it in one of the books Mark had taken from the secret Archive Room in the library in the spring. He easily found the doorknob on the opposite wall around the car. The cool damp air greeted him as he crossed the short breezeway to the door that led into the shop. Its bronze doorknob was chilled from the elements, and fortunately for Drake it was unlocked allowing him to quickly enter. Light streamed in from the row of large multi-paned windows along the long back wall to the right. Grandpa's large pickup truck was in the first stall before him. Drake curiously walked toward the workshop bench, past the welding equipment, and two large metal tool boxes on casters. He slowly ran his fingers over the wooden bench along the back wall below the windows. His grandfather was a skilled craftsman, capable of making nearly anything and this is where he did it.

"Drake," echoed the deep voice of his grandfather behind him. Drake jumped with a sudden startle. "There you are. Grandma said she sent you down here."

Drake quickly moved away from the bench and stood silently.

"Did Grandma tell you what we have for you?" Grandpa asked with a smile. Drake shook his head.

"Okay, come over here and sit down," Grandpa stated as he motioned to the two green webbed, aluminum framed, folding lawn chairs in the corner by the large assortment of cylindrical tanks holding the fuel needed for his welding. Drake sat in one of the chairs as Grandpa went and retrieved a cloth-wrapped item behind one of the large metal toolboxes.

"You like history?" Grandpa questioned as he sat opposite Drake and placed the long bundle across his legs. Drake nodded. "Well then, let me tell you a bit of a story."

"Okay," Drake said with a smile.

"Well," Grandpa began as he sat back in the lawn chair with a loud creak or the aluminum frame, "my grandfather moved into Aberdeen back in the late 1800s. My father was born here, and so was I. My father, and your great-grandfather, Pop, he used to own a lot of forest land around these parts before the Great Depression, and a few lots in town, too."

Drake nodded, he loved to learn about historical things. His impression of Pop had always been based on the kind of crotchety old man he knew. It had been on his lawn where he heard the 'crying only makes it hurt worse' statement from his Uncle Wally that now was so deeply bonded to him. Pop raised fighting chickens and Australian Blue Heelers, and had sicced them on the boys a couple of times in the past when they pestered him too much or were someplace they weren't supposed to be, like playing in one of his barns.

"Back then, Pop did a lot of horse logging on the property," Grandpa continued as he looked off into the distance. "And he'd sold a piece of land in South Aberdeen to a kind Japanese immigrant who had been a highly skilled metal smith in Japan. Pop thought the guy deserved a chance, and helped him set up a blacksmith shop. His name was Masao Norishige. Lots of people just called him Mark. He was close to our family, you know, and your mother named your older brother after him. Anyway, old Masao helped Pop shoe his horses and build rigs to help with logging. I even learned to weld from him, too."

"Cool," Drake interrupted involuntarily with wide open eyes.

"When the depression hit, Pop sold a lot of his land off to the Weyerhaeuser's and the Tacoma Paper Company for next to nothing," Grandpa began again with a more somber look on his face. "He only kept the land in this valley and up the hills a bit. I spent a lot of the 1930s scrounging firewood off the railroad tracks outside of town, doing odd jobs, or, if I was lucky, helping out Masao at his shop. Times were really tough for everyone back then."

"Was he able to stay in business?" Drake asked knowing that many businesses had failed during that bleak economic time.

"Barely," Grandpa replied. "Masao did a lot of his work in barter to keep his family going, and to help ours. Then in 1941 the Japanese bombed Pearl Harbor and all hell broke lose around these parts."

"What happened?" Drake questioned.

"After that attack," Grandpa added, "we had lots of civil defense drills here, being on the Pacific Coast and all. Up on the hillside behind and beyond your Uncle Jacob's house there are a couple of caves. We were so worried about a complete invasion that we moved a lot of provisions up in those caves, and we made them into defensible forts in case the Japanese Army ever did invade. Then in early 1942 something happened. The government began to look at the Japanese-Americans living out here, including our friend Masao Norishige and his family. The president signed Executive Order 9066, and anyone of Japanese descent was going to be relocated to internment camps in the interior of the country."

"That's horrible, Grandpa," Drake remarked with a frown.

"It was supposed to keep them safe," Grandpa replied thoughtfully. "And keep us safe as a country. I was eighteen and tried to enlist with Masao's seventeen-year-old son, Joji. He got in and went off to serve in Europe, and I got branded '4F' because I had flat feet. Like the bottom of my feet were going to stop me from fighting just as much as the guy next to me. Masao had his family relocated, and they were eventually taken to Minidoka, Idaho, and held there through the end of the war. Masao stayed to help fight the war here because his blacksmith skills were needed, but he wasn't able to be seen. He had a small room in the back of the woodshed. He worked out of Pop's old barn, and would hide out in the caves whenever anyone snooped around or we were on high alert for an invasion. He loved this country, his country, his son fought and died for this country, but we took his family and his property away from him."

Drake was amazed by the story. He had learned of the period in American History by reading the encyclopedia many years ago as well as a number of other historical books on the war, but he had never heard of the toll placed upon Masao and many other Japanese-Americans, or the internment camps.

"What happened to Joji, Grandpa?" Drake asked cautiously. "And Masao? Did I ever meet him?"

"Well, Drake," Grandpa answered, "Joji was part of the

442nd Regiment, and took part in the war in Europe. He was killed in action in Italy during 1945. Masao stayed out here on Pop's property during the whole war. He eventually was reunited with his family after the war and they moved down to California during the late 1950s. So no, you never got to meet Masao or his family. But that's only part of the story."

"Oh," Drake said surprised. "There's more?"

"Yeah, there's this," Grandpa replied with a pat on the wrapped object on his lap. "Masao was very grateful for what Pop and I did for him, so he made a few tokens of his appreciation to give to us. Pop has some very nicely crafted and very valuable, silver trinkets up in his attic. I got this."

"What is it Grandpa?" Drake inquired.

"Masao used to tell me stories about his ancestors while I worked in his smithy," Grandpa answered with another pat on the long wrapped item. "He was a descendent of a great metalworker in ancient Japan. His forefather was a student of Masamune, the master swordsmith of the golden age of the samurai. Legends say one of the students was known as Saeki Norishige from the Etchu Province, who was a great-great-great something-or-other of Masao. He crafted samurai swords with a distinctive pine tree bark pattern in the steel."

"That's cool," Drake said as he listened to the story, lost in the thoughts of swords. "I like swords."

"I hoped so," Grandpa said as he began to unwrap the object on his lap. "Masao made this for me, and I thought I would give it to my son Walter when he was ready."

Drake noticed Grandpa's sad expression when he mentioned Wally. Grandpa continued to remove the cloth from the item in his lap. He stood up from the chair, revealing what appeared to be a scabbard of a long sword.

"This is a samurai sword, a Tsurugi," Grandpa stated as he drew the blade from the crafted scabbard. It was a smooth silver blade, barely over three feet long and straight with sharp beveled edges on both sides. It had an odd pattern along the blade, an organic pattern that looked something like tree bark. "Not the curved katana swords you see in movies, mind you. Masao said it was an Ōdachi, a long sword, a rare double-edged, straight-bladed sword made in the samurai tradition, with the metals folded thousands of times onto each other, increasing their strength and driving out impurities. It's known as a Tsurugi."

"That's awesome, Grandpa," Drake said with great fascination. "I've never seen anything like it before, not even in books."

"It's extremely rare, no other sword was ever made this way," Grandpa said as he turned the blade before him allowing the light coming in from the windows to sparkle off the shiny metal. "Masao never finished the hilt, he left the tang unfinished when he gave it to me. He said he thought I possessed the skill to craft an honorable tsuka for the sword. I never got around to working on it, and after your uncle, well... it kind of just sat in the scabbard collecting dust."

"I'm sorry Grandpa," Drake said noticing a pooling of tears in his grandfathers eyes.

"Then Grandma said to me," Grandpa continued with a quick smile, "Henry, she said, we need to finish Mark's sword and give it to someone who needs it. And I said, what do you mean, Mother? And she said, our grandson needs that sword. Drake's going to need it. So I got busy, and made this hilt, the tsuka, with the family crest of Reuss and the Teutonic Cross upon it, carved from elk antler. Then as I was designing it, your Grandma and Aunt Carmen took the sword and added this to the end of the tsuka."

Drake stood up and looked at a silver crested medallion that had the name Walter Reuss engraved upon it in a circular motif surrounding a cross that resembled four capital "T" letters joined at the bases, Drake recalled this as the Teutonic Cross from his research of the order of knights last year. Grandpa turned it so Drake could see the medallion more clearly. Along its edge was a fine solder line. It was hollow like a locket.

"Your Grandma and Aunt said they made that especially for this sword," Grandpa said as he brought his left hand up and rubbed his index finger over the inscription. "They said they put some of Wally's ashes inside it before I sealed it. The sword has 'powers' so they say. I'm not real big on the whole La Madrid thing, Drake, but I know they can do things normal people can't, so I don't doubt that they did something. But, more than that, this is a special weapon made by a master swordsmith, in a style long since forgotten."

Drake stood silently before his grandfather.

"I'm giving it to you, Drake," Grandpa said sternly as he spun the sword around and handed to his grandson, the finely crafted hilt first, "if you'll promise to honor it and to keep it well because it holds the memories of a very special man in my life as well as the essence of my son. Can you do that?"

"Grandpa," Drake began as he thought about what his kindly grandfather had asked of him, "I'd be honored to accept this sword from you, and I promise to honor it and keep it well. Does it have a name? Almost every great sword in history had a name, like Excalibur."

Drake reached out and put his right hand on the tsuka of the sword, grasping it fully. Grandpa pointed to a symbol on the blade of the sword, a Japanese glyph that kind of resembled a little stick-figured man with a single beam of light coming off each shoulder.

"Masao said this was Hikari," Grandpa responded with a broad smile. "That means 'light' in English, and I assume it means the glowing kind rather than light in weight, because it isn't really, is it?"

"Oh," Drake responded as Grandpa released Hikari into his hand, the full weight of the sword pulled his arm downward before he adjusted his body position and raised it back up before him. Drake turned the sword in his hand as he raised the point up looking at the bark pattern on the blade. He smiled a wide toothy grin that made his dimples pop. "It's kind of heavy, isn't it, so why did he name it 'Light' then?"

Grandpa smiled, shrugged his shoulders then handed Drake the scabbard, and put the cloth over his shoulder before putting his hand up on his taller grandson's head and mussing up his hair with a hearty wiggle.

"You best wrap it all back up for the move to Vancouver," Grandpa remarked as he began to walk back toward the door outside. "You don't want your brothers playing with it, they might break it."

Drake nodded with a smile.

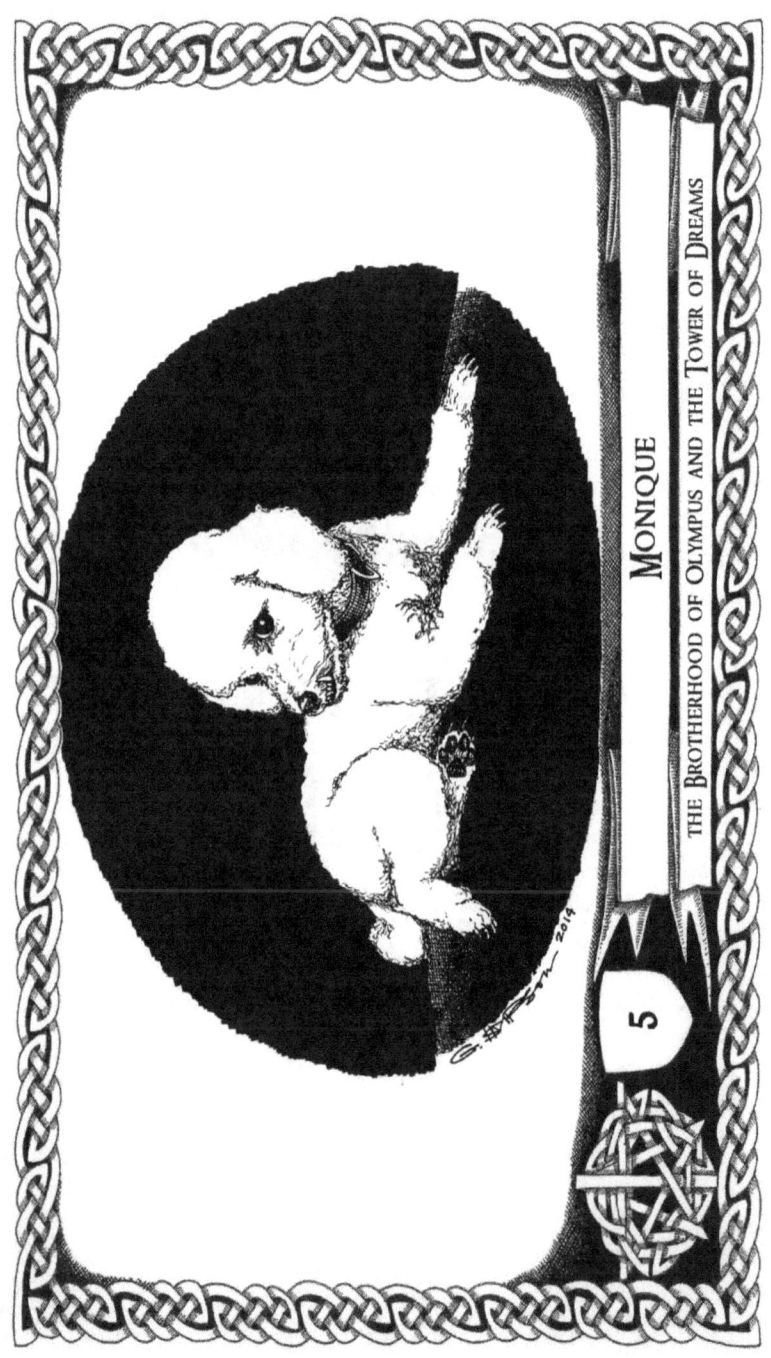

MONIQUE

THE BROTHERHOOD OF OLYMPUS AND THE TOWER OF DREAMS

5

The Journey South
Chapter Five
December 14, 1979
Aberdeen, Washington

On Thursday, December thirteenth, Drake spent his last day at the high school as sophomore class president. His last official duty in that office was signing a letter of resignation. He had spent the better part of two days crafting that letter which began:

> When in the course of human events it becomes necessary for one person to dissolve the political bands which have connected them to another people and relinquish the role of elected authority, it is prudent for that one person to do so in a proper and just way, guaranteeing the ongoing and continued success of the people in the absence of their duly elected official.

Drake had always been fascinated with American history and used classic references whenever he could, and this was a perfect opportunity for him. He delivered the resignation letter to Mr. Dawson's classroom during seventh period. The cluttered classroom was a testament to a long tenured history teacher, roll-down maps clustered along the top of the green chalkboard, student-made posters dominated the available wall space, and a colorful timeline of American presidential portraits—from Washington to Carter—lined the wall above the row of windows that looked down on the cold courtyard below.

Drake stood at the doorway and paused as he looked into the vacant room. The upbeat rhythm of the Neon Sign Symphony filled the space from a stereo behind the teacher's desk.

You're always braggin' bout your amazing life,
But it don't seem like you tell it right.
Your legend just grows more, more, more,
One more time and I'll be out the door,
Don't let me down.

Drake was sure he missed Mr. Dawson and began to walk to the teacher's desk in the front of the room to drop off the letter, the hardwood floor creaking underneath him as he approached the jumble of papers piled high upon the oaken desk. With a sudden turn, the high-backed red upholstered chair spun around revealing the startled Mr. Dawson.

Don't let me down.

"Holy crap, Drake!" Mr. Dawson shouted after he spit a mouthful of coffee across his desk. The rapid motion and reaction of the teacher made Drake flinch backwards.

Don't let me down.

"I'm sorry, Mr. Dawson," Drake began.

"You shouldn't sneak up on people," Mr. Dawson replied, as he attempted to clean wet coffee off of the stacks of paper with the sleeve of his brown sports jacket. The stains on his jacket sleeve indicated to Drake that he had used it before to clean coffee in such a manner.

Don't let me down.

"I didn't mean it," Drake continued, as he approached the cluttered desk. "I didn't know you were in here, I'm sorry Mr. Dawson."

Don't let me down.

"Stop saying you're sorry," Mr. Dawson interjected. "You didn't do it on purpose, and I asked you to come by and drop off your letter."

You only just started and now it's done,

Seeing you leave makes me wonder who won.

"Drake?" questioned Mr. Dawson. "You do have your resignation letter, right?"

"Oh... yes sir... Mr. Dawson," Drake stammered, as he held out the handwritten document. Mr. Dawson reached out and took the letter from him. "I'm sorry."

Your legend just grows more, more, more,

"You know, Drake," Mr. Dawson replied, as he shook his head, "the only thing I'm sorry about is that you're leaving. I've been impressed by how much you have blossomed this year. This school's going to miss you."

I should've never walked and left you on the floor,

"Are you playing in the game tonight?" asked Mr. Dawson.

"Yeah," Drake replied, as he thought about putting on his basketball uniform one last time.

"I've heard through the grapevine that Coach Harshman is going to be here scouting the big kid from Timberline," Mr. Dawson added. "If you have a good game, maybe he'll put you on his list of recruits."

Don't let me down.

"Yeah," Drake said, as he turned and walked toward the open door, muttering under his breath. "Too bad I'm leaving."

That night, in his final basketball game, Drake led his team to an upset of top-ranked Timberline High School from Lacey. He battled the burly red-haired, six foot eight inch mountain of a center from the Trailblazers to a statistical draw, holding him to a season low ten points. Drake always measured his success on the basketball court by his defensive prowess. In the locker room, his teammates showered him with hugs, high-fives, and the feeling of camaraderie he once knew with his brothers.

"You were awesome, Drake!" shouted one of his teammates.

"Thanks," Drake responded with a reddening face.

"Hey kid," announced a gruff voice emerging from behind his team. A gray-haired man with a gold tweed sports jacket and a purple and gold, diagonal striped tie approached Drake with his right hand outstretched. Drake responded by shaking the man's hand. The handshake was firm and meaningful. "Coach Harshman, and you're Fraser. Drake Fraser. Helluva good defensive game tonight, kid. You completely shut their big kid down. We value defense at Washington, Fraser. I think you should consider playing for me when you graduate. I'll be watching how your team does from here on in, and you, Fraser. Helluva game."

Drake stood in disbelief as he watched Marv Harshman walk away into the crowd of merrymakers. He was sure he'd just been recruited by the head coach at the University of Washington. The shock slowly wore off as he emptied out his locker and turned in his sweaty uniform, shooting shirt, and warm-up pants. The reality of the night pressed on him. It was his last game for his team. In fact it wasn't his team anymore, now that it was over. Hollowness filled him as he pushed his belongings into his duffle bag. Silently he slipped away from the happy team and faded into the darkness outside the school and his long walk home.

On Friday morning, the Frasers took one last nostalgic walk through their empty house before climbing into the family vehicles to make the drive south to the Vancouver suburb of Hazel Dell and their new home off NW 21st Avenue. Dad and Mom had driven down the packed U-Haul truck, their car, and the family van with Martin the day before. Martin did not come back up with them. On this final trip, Mark drove his car with Dennis riding along, and Dad drove the van with Mom, Drake, and Albert riding inside, pulling the travel trailer behind.

The gray December sky mirrored the somber feelings of the family as they headed east on Highway 12 out of Aberdeen. They had moved around a lot during the 1960s and early 1970s but had resided in the same general area for nearly ten years. Change was not something the Fraser's sought out, but change is what they were getting, like it or not.

Mark drove behind his parents since he didn't know how to get to their new house. He was exceptionally bitter about leaving and hoped driving over a hundred miles on the highway would help him cleanse those feelings. Mark loved driving, working on cars, and especially doing both with his car. His sense of value and pride was tied to his blue 1964 Chevrolet Impala. Dennis sat in the front seat cross from him, trying to mimic what his older brother was doing. The sense of value and pride for Dennis was in being cool like his older brothers, and moving up the pecking order to become the number one son. So far that had not worked out real well for him, but he was confident that it would someday all be exactly as he imagined.

"What're you doing butthead?" Mark asked Dennis, as he watched him move his arms in the same motions that Mark himself had made. "Are you mocking me?"

"No," Dennis immediately retorted, as he stopped moving and sat perfectly still. "Course not."

"Sometimes you're such a dillhole," Mark commented as he shook his head.

"I didn't think you were ever going to use that word again," Dennis mused as he recalled Mark shunning the word back in the summer at their grandparents' house after their fight with the treacherous mordgeists.

"There are always special circumstances, Dennis," Mark replied. "And you're the biggest special circumstance I know."

"Thanks," Dennis said, as he smiled to his older brother. "That's cool man."

Albert and Drake sat in the back of the van as the miles rolled by. They turned south at Elma, staying on Highway 12 toward southbound Interstate 5. Albert fidgeted and looked out the window. He was a ball of constant motion. His feet tapped, his legs wiggled, his fingers moved, or he just repositioned his body as he tired of sitting. Drake shook his head as he watched his baby brother squirm next to him. Sitting on Drake's lap was Monique, the white miniature poodle with a severe under bite that Drake had grown to love nearly as unconditionally as she loved him. Sometimes at night or at school in a boring class, Drake would analyze his life and conclude that Monique was his only true friend.

"Lemme hold the dog," Albert announced to Drake as he reached over to grab her.

"No!" Drake snapped as he pulled her away from him. "She's still scared of you because you dress her up and stuff."

"No she's not," Albert retorted. "'Sides, how do you know? Did she tell you?"

"Yes," Drake replied, as Albert chuckled loudly.

"Nuh-uh," Albert answered. "Dogs can't talk, stupid."

"Yeah they can, stupid head," Drake argued.

"Prove it," Albert stated. "Prove Mo can talk, right now."

"Mo doesn't want to," Drake reasoned with a shake of his head. "Besides, I didn't say she could talk here, but I imagine there is a place somewhere, in our reality or another, where all intelligent creatures can verbalize their thoughts and communicate, like we do."

"Huh?" Albert questioned with his eyebrows raised and knotted. "That didn't make any sense at all. Verbalize their communication through intelligence creatures. Sometimes I think you just make stuff up, Drake."

"I said I think there's a place where she can talk," Drake answered. He turned away from his brother and moved Monique further away from him. "I just don't know where or how to get there."

"That sounds completely made up," Albert replied, as he stuck out his tongue. Drake was done arguing. He silently looked out the driver's side windows while Albert slowly started to fidget again as he looked out the windows behind Mom.

About an hour later they were nearing the Kelso-Longview area and Drake tuned into what his parents were talking about in the front of the van.

"The boys'll do great," Mom stated quietly.

"Dennis and Albert will be fine, they are still young. But Mark and Drake, do we even know what Columbia River High School has to offer them?" Dad questioned, as Drake's attention shifted more intently on their conversation. In the distance, to the east, Drake saw the nearly perfect conical snow-covered peak of Mount Saint Helens dancing through breaks in the evergreens, or gaps in the rolling hills as they sped southward. A premonition began to manifest itself inside his mind.

"Columbia River has an auto shop class," Mom responded. "And Drake can play basketball for them, maybe even run for class president next year. Trust me dear, they will be perfectly fine in Vancouver. In fact, I think this is the best thing for them."

"I worry about them," Dad added, as he turned to look at Mom. Tears had begun to form at the bottom of his eyes, the moisture welling up. "Especially Drake, you know I never got to take him to the Highland Games, or expose him to the Clan Fraser, or our tartan."

"Drake needs to grow up," Mom replied in a very quiet tone. "Moving will make him do that. He's got to stop being such a baby, and you have to stop thinking he's any different than his brothers."

"What!" Drake interrupted, as he moved forward in his seat toward his parents. "Do you even know anything about me? Do you know how much effort it took me to run for class president? I could only do that because lots of people knew me, and because of Rachel. Do you even know anything about basketball? You have only come to one of my games, one game. During my freshman year, and that's it. Did you know that Marv Harshman, the head coach for the University of Washington was at my last game, and he came up to me afterwards and told me how well I played and that he was going to be watching me, and that he wanted me to come to Washington and play basketball for him? How's that going to happen playing basketball down here, for a new team, with players I don't know, and on a team he doesn't know I'm on!"

"Drake!" Mom snapped, as she turned in her seat to face him. "Stop yelling at me. You have no right to be this way, to treat me like this. We're moving to Vancouver to keep the family together, to do what's best for all of us."

"Mom," Drake continued as his face reddened, "I was blossoming, and now you've pulled up my roots. There isn't any guarantee Columbia River's going to be better. What if it's worse Mom, did you ever think of that? What if no one likes me? What if I can't make the basketball team? Forget class president, that took Rachel. She's gone, now I'm gone, that part of my life is over, damn it."

Mom flashed an angry look at Dad.

"Drake," Dad grumbled. "Apologize to your mother."

"No," Drake complained.

"Drake, don't make me stop this van," Dad added with a scowl.

"Fine," Drake conceded. "I'm sorry. I'm sorry I yelled at you. I'm sorry you don't understand my life. And I'm sorry you're moving us all down by that mountain over there that's going to erupt!"

"Drake!" Dad growled.

"Sorry Dad, I didn't mean it," Drake apologized, as he gazed off to the east. The vision of the pristine cone of Mount Saint Helens dazzled him, and yet he was unsure why he had announced that the mountain was going to erupt.

"Is it really a volcano?" Albert questioned. "I don't want to live by a volcano."

"That's great Drake, now you scared your brother." Mom scolded, as she looked over her shoulder toward the boys. "It isn't going to erupt, Albert. You're brother was just trying to scare you. Drake, tell Albert you are sorry for saying that."

"Fine," Drake conceded with a sigh. "Sorry Albert, I didn't mean to scare you… but it is going to erupt."

The eyes of the Fraser's turned and gazed upon Mount Saint Helens before it disappeared again behind a hillside covered in Douglas-firs. That majestic mountain was a thing of beauty, not a thing of fear or dread. But something lingered in Drake that made him look back toward the mountain and feel dread like he had seen a ticking time bomb tied to a busload of people.

6

DAEMON COUNTESS

THE BROTHERHOOD OF OLYMPUS
AND THE TOWER OF DREAMS

A Plot Revealed
Chapter Six
December 14, 1979
The Palace of Knowledge, Gehenna

Standing tall on the steep mountainous peaks of the craggy barrens of this netherworld frontier stood the sheer, blood-red stone walls of the Palace of Knowledge, the fortress that housed the legendary Grand Library of Gehenna, and home to the daemon Countess Furfur. Below the fortress the rocky outcroppings were so prominent and jagged that it seemed nearly impossible to climb up to the structure from the deep valleys that stretched out to the horizons. The imposing outer walls stood nearly five hundred feet tall between the higher battlements and turrets of the glistening crimson towers. Above the walls crackling amber lightning flashed across the burnt orange-hued sky, thick with dark rolling clouds of noxious gases. There was no sun in the sky. The illumination radiated from low on the horizon, three-hundred-sixty degrees around the mountains that were home to the palace. The hot dry air was heavily laden with the stench of sulfur. Gehenna wasn't a hospitable place for man or beast.

At the heart of the fortress, behind four concentric interior walls each with massive black metal gates, stood the pinnacled spires of the Grand Library carved from the stone of the craggy mountain. Nearly a hundred wickedly sharp points atop the spires challenged the violent storm clouds that rumbled and churned around the center of the blackened sky like boiling molasses.

In the tallest, most massive spire a radiant yellow light

pierced the walls through a series of circular windows bringing a false sense of warmth to the structure. Within it, the throne of Furfur sat on a raised golden dais that was also the source of the light. Before the intricately carved throne a series of lower couches and overstuffed chairs ringed the decorative marble floor. The room was bustling with movement, as lesser beings waited on more important creatures, who were in turn guarded by well-equipped warriors.

"Please," Aeon stated with a graceful hand gesture. His hand was long and shriveled with tight flesh clinging to the bones. He had a long, gray beard and huge bushy eyebrows that hid his bright eyes in deep shadows. His garments were black, layered and flowing, and he clutched a massive curved scythe in his left hand. "Have a seat with the rest of us, Succorbenoth. You make me nervous standing there like that."

"What care do I have of your feelings old one?" snapped back the sinewy daemon. Succorbenoth stood over seven feet tall. A thick fiery red mane of unkempt hair covered his head, and his thick, charred skin pulled taut across his body like it was two sizes too small for him. A smoky purplish aura radiated from him, escaping in thin wisps of dissipating ammonia gas. Neither his muscular form, wild hair, nor magic aura was the feature that dominated his presence—it was his daemonic face. His red eyes were lit with an internal fire, and his mouth was pulled back into a perpetual smile, showing interlocking razor-sharp fangs. Nearly a hundred of these pearly white teeth, each a stark contrast to his ravaged skin, lined his upper and lower jaws. "You've outlived your usefulness."

"Surely you must be jesting," Aeon responded with a light chuckle. A white light began to glow along the blade of the oversized scythe, flooding the room with the odor of burnt ozone. "Many of your ilk have tried to lay me low over the eons, but none have succeeded. One of the banes of being a god of time is that I can see all that lies before me, for good or ill, and I know my demise will not come from a daemon lap dog such as you. But you, my friend, will be most thankful when your time does come."

"Bah," Succorbenoth replied with his ever-present smile. "You're not my god, nor do I believe in your power. As a daemon, I can't be truly destroyed in battle, unless that battle took place in my home, the Abyss."

"So true, my friend," Aeon responded with a smile. "Or within the nexus of worlds, and sadly you have placed a mark of revenge upon yourself by attacking the Fraser's."

"Stop calling me your friend, because I'm not," the daemon demanded with a flash of his eyes.

"Fair enough, daemon spawn, you are not my friend," the god answered. "But take heed of the dogs of war, and be careful of thy gift of opening gates, of traversing the nexus between worlds, that will be your undoing when facing the Erlking unleashed."

"Riddles and nonsense," Succorbenoth snapped back. "The Erlking's no more. I am a warrior, bred for battle, and you were never more than a second-rate god. Now you are nothing but a decrepit has-been."

"Don't doubt me," Aeon stated as he tightened his grip upon the long handle of the scythe. "I have reaped many of your kind, and would not mind paying a visit to the Abyss to make that reaping permanent."

Succorbenoth's fiery hair bristled with the coursing ammonia charged energy of his aura. His eyes flared and he readied to launch himself upon the seated god.

"Gentlemen, please control yourselves," interrupted an elegant woman seated to Aeon's right. She was an ancient goddess of primordial chaos, long since banished to the nether reaches, and similarly removed from most of popular human history. Tiamat exuded a pheromone-enhanced beauty that heightened her exotic charms. Her wide set crystal-blue eyes, under jewel hued eye shadow, balanced her moist and plump ruby-red lips. Her facial beauty was betrayed by her red-scaled reptilian body and sharp talon fingers and toes. She wore a white toga-like robe that covered her torso, but not her constantly moving barbed tail. "Don't make me have to decide who I like least between you."

"Goddess, forgive me," Succorbenoth quickly apologized with a low bowing gesture. "I'm uncertain why we're here?"

"Because we were invited," Tiamat replied, as she batted her thick black eyelashes and smiled. "The least you could do is be gracious to our hostess. She is, after all, a very knowledgeable resource, who could aid our cause. As is the old one you want to fight to prove your machismo."

"Forgive me," Succorbenoth bent lower before the goddess.

"I think you need to train your pet better, Lady Tiamat," Aeon stated with a chuckle and a flash of his eyes from under his thick bushy eyebrows.

"Be thankful I keep him on a short leash, ancient one," Tiamat cooed with sensual deadliness. "You and I are kin, and we should get along much better than this, Aeon."

"Your charms will not work on me, my lady," Aeon rebuffed the pheromone driven attention.

"No, it would seem not," Tiamat continued with a flutter of her long lashes. "A pity really, my allies and I could use your insights. But, when it came to humanity, you never really were relevant nor did you have much sway or following. What pantheon are you from again, does anyone even remember, do you remember? I'm surprised you are still in existence, quite frankly."

"Tiamat," echoed a clarion voice from the raised golden dais. Standing before the ornate throne was the Countess Furfur. Librarian and supreme ruler of Grand Library, matriarch of the third plane of Gehenna, Countess of Hell with twenty-six legions of demons at her command, and a daemon with intense fascination with humans that some of her kind thought bordered on an obsession. She was curvy and tall, over six feet in height due to her stiletto heeled black sandals. She wore a long and provocatively tight black leather and golden rivet lattice dress that covered much of her but left some of her red skin visible in the open diamond patterns between the lattices. Her long barbed tail swayed behind her. She wore her dark hair partially up in a loose bun. Her eyes were an entrancing brown, with dark smoky hues upon the lids, and her lips were a glistening ebon black. Two horns protruded from her forehead along her hairline and curled slightly into her raven hair before turning up into sharp points tipped in bejeweled golden caps. Her black leathery wings were fully extended behind her, making her appear much larger and more menacing than her physical stature alone might indicate. "Don't bother my guests, for I invited each of you here for a reason."

"Countess," Tiamat responded, as she did a graceful but shallow bow to her host, and directed a sharp glare to Succorbenoth who followed her lead.

"Aeon is of particular use to me," Furfur continued as she folded up her wings behind her. Once they closed they seemed to disappear. "I had hoped you might see the benefit of his counsel."

"Why have you called us here? You're a known lover of humans, and didn't side with us at the Council of Retribution," questioned Succorbenoth as he began to pace once again along the tiled floor.

"Your goals and mine aren't that far apart, really," Furfur answered as she slowly sashayed to the throne and gracefully sat. "I seek one human. I've looked for him for generation upon generation, and after many centuries I have found him, thanks in part to Aeon and his foresight. I seek only his protection, he's the key to my desire, and the rest can roast in the pits of Hell for eternity."

"The pits of Hell are good for humans," Succorbenoth agreed with a stiff nod.

"You could easily protect this one human, Countess," Tiamat added with a sudden shift of her dragon body. "Why call upon us?"

"Well, Lady Tiamat," Furfur answered as she looked upon the pacing form of Succorbenoth, "the human I seek to protect is one of the brothers who defeated the mighty Succorbenoth when he attempted to crush them through his deadliest game attack."

"A Fraser!" Succorbenoth exclaimed with a wild motion. "You desire a Fraser? This is folly!"

"Why do you desire this boy?" questioned Tiamat with a calculating glare.

"My reasons are my own," Furfur responded with a steely look. "But, suffice it to say, he is the key to all my desires, and I won't allow him to be hurt."

"The Fraser's are now the new Brotherhood of Olympus," Succorbenoth spat in rage. "The very same group who thwarted every attempt we made at creating our dominion on Earth before the Covenant of Reason was enacted. And now they're the Fraser's, they're our enemies, Countess, and I'll not grant any enemy respite from my wrath!"

"Should you set aside your wrath, pet of Tiamat, it might grant you a longer existence," Aeon spoke with a wry chuckle and a raised brow.

"Speak of me again as a pet and I shall be your death, old one!" Succorbenoth snapped with a sudden turn toward the old god.

"I cannot condone the safety of the Fraser's, Countess. Succorbenoth speaks true, they have become our enemies," Tiamat stated coolly.

"I don't seek the protection of all the Fraser's, Lady Tiamat. Quite the contrary, I only want their success to come to the point that I can secure the one I desire. He has much to learn before that time comes to pass. But, I can do my best to divert their attention elsewhere. In fact, that is why I asked you here Succorbenoth. You are a daemon of gates, a greater daemon who could be worshipped as a god, and you can easily travel between planes of existence," Furfur explained to her guests.

"Except Earth, the Covenant binds me as it does all others. I can't completely travel there without being conjured or summoned by a human, or by using a magical talisman," Succorbenoth replied as he quickly forgot his rage and bent to the compliment given by the Countess.

"Could you deliver a small object?" Furfur questioned.

"How small?" responded the standing daemon.

"A key," Furfur answered, as she pulled an ornate skeleton key with a bronze chain from her delicate waist. "This key. I need it delivered to one of the Fraser's. It will allow him to open the door into a special room of my Library. And through that room, I may be able to persuade him to break up the Brotherhood."

"You would do that?" queried Tiamat with a raised eyebrow.

"Perhaps," Furfur replied. "If he was removed from your list of adversaries and if it fit my needs, of course."

"Of course," Tiamat stated, as she glanced toward Succorbenoth and fluttered her eyelashes at him.

"I don't work for you Furfur," Succorbenoth announced, as his words erupted with a wet spittle of rage. "And I will not spare your precious Fraser for you, *all* the Fraser's shall die by my hand! I want the pleasure of watching each of their life-forces slipping from their fragile bodies as they die. I will not listen to any more of your traitorous rabble, Furfur!"

Succorbenoth turned and stomped off toward the darkened doorways behind the shelves of ancient books that ringed the tiled floor of the throne room.

"So seals the fate of the great daemon of gates," Aeon chuckled to himself.

"Countess, I cannot support your folly, the time for petty desires has passed. It is now time to ally yourself with your own kind. I should not tell you this, but our agents are set to launch an attack on a scale other gods have long feared. It will be ushered in by a sign of epic proportions so the humans will see the coming of the end, and their world will be rocked by the cataclysmic change," Tiamat stated as she rose from the cushioned chair. "Your desires take you dangerously close to those who sit above in their smugness and try to judge us. I hope for your sake you see the error in your ways before we meet again."

"Thank you, Lady Tiamat," Furfur responded graciously. "I appreciate your time, and wish you well in the days to come. I had hoped that you would see the power of my conviction and grant me my request. I doubt we shall meet again in such a civil manner. Fair thee well."

Tiamat followed Succorbenoth from the throne room, and was accompanied by four of the well equipped demon guards of the Grand Library to assure her safety. When all traces of their presence had left, another figure moved out from behind the shelves of books. He was a round-faced man with unkempt black hair. His face was a weathered brown with bright inquisitive eyes, and his clothes were simple buckskin leather and adorned with feathers, flowers, trinkets, and other things of bright colors.

"I can deliver the key, Countess," spoke the newcomer.

"Raven," Furfur cooed with a smile as she seductively crossed her legs. "I'm pleased you joined us."

"My lady," Raven responded with a bow. "Only a fool would resist your charms."

"Please take this key, brother Raven," Furfur added as she held the key out for him. "And deliver it to young Drake Fraser."

"As you wish, my lady," Raven stated, as he approached her, bent forward to take the key from her hand and placed a quick kiss upon the back of her hand. He just as quickly vanished in a cloud of black dust and small feathers.

"Now," Furfur began, as she shifted her focus back to the ancient Aeon sitting quietly in his chair. "Tell me, what must I do to guarantee Rachel Finnegan, that pesky leprechaun witch, will not foil my plans."

"As long as she has hope she will defeat you, that much is certain," Aeon responded. "And should she become aware of her heritage she will be nearly impossible to defeat."

"Then I must strike first and with great force," Furfur sternly stated, as she moved further back on the throne. "And remove all of her hope for anything but the darkness of her own death."

"Drake will not let you harm her," Aeon added. "He will never accept you if he knew you hurt her in anyway."

"Well," Furfur began, "I've been making sure he will never remember her, or any other woman, as soon as I found out he was the one I sought. I cast a spell upon him that makes him forget about girls outside of his daily life. If they're apart for any length of time, his memory of them fades."

"Will it work?" questioned Aeon.

"It already has," Furfur answered with a smile. "I overheard them talking, he couldn't remember that she was with him in the second grade. Now that I have made sure they are apart for good, she is off living in Iowa, and he has moved to Vancouver, soon he will forget about her completely. So, you see, I don't have to worry about him accepting me. He will."

"You must also remember the prophecy that led you to him also stated that he will love the one he kisses first," Aeon stated. "And that may not be as simple as it seems, since he clings so to the power of words, especially those from his Uncle Wally."

"It will be easy enough with Rachel gone," Furfur replied. "I will just have to make sure I am there when he is older and begins to look for a mate."

"I believe the term is 'look for love,' Countess," Aeon chuckled.

"What do I care of love? It is of no purpose to any of our kind," Furfur stated, as she moved her hands up her legs and over her breasts. "I have created the archetype of his desire in him, and it is me."

"Yes, you have influenced what he finds desirable, that is undeniable. But Rachel Finnegan will not give up hope, I have foreseen that," Aeon added. "She will come looking for him when she is able, and unfortunately she also saw your influence."

"Wait, there's another way? She just needs to lose hope?" Furfur questioned.

"All hope, complete and utter despair," Aeon answered. "The time-stream is very consistent in this regard Countess. Your adversary, should she grow to maturity with any hope she can be with young Fraser, will be your undoing. Your only chance of success is to crush all hope from her. You cannot kill her, or Drake will turn against you despite all your magic because on some deeper level Drake and Rachel are connected. Even if he doesn't know it right now, someday he will. And should she be killed he will know that loss and seek vengeance against you."

"Very well, wise one," Furfur contemplated, as she tapped the long black polished nails of her right hand against the tight black lattice of leather over the smooth red skin of her thigh. "I must crush all hope from her. I know such a way. I will send some minions to ruin her life."

"Taking the tactics of the Council of Retribution?" questioned Aeon. "Mordgeists I assume, they are easily bought, and are relatively loyal."

"They would not work for what I have in mind," Furfur smiled. "I intend to drive her to despair, perhaps even suicide, which would be deliciously wicked. Then I will be free of any guilt and she will be gone. I will send daevas and have them possess people close to her. I'll have them abuse her, despise her, treat her like the scum she is, or better yet, I will command them to rape and molest her. My daevas are so viciously deviant that will enjoy this assignment. Yes, I will force her over the cliff of hopelessness. She will have no reason to live, she will have failed her true love and will never seek him out because she will know he would never love her being damaged as badly as she will be. It's a plan of such perfection and simple beauty."

"It would be more humane to kill the girl," Aeon stated

with a frown. "I cannot be part of this plan, Countess. Such cruelty is beneath me. Should you go through with it, I cannot continue to advise you in these matters."

"Answer two questions before you decide," Furfur asked with an intoxicating smile.

"Very well," Aeon responded.

"What did Tiamat mean with her reference to an attack and a catastrophic sign?" Furfur questioned.

"There is a plan underway to seize the Tower of Dreams, and from what I have seen it will be successful," Aeon began.

"What? With the Tower of Dreams, the Dark Council will have a mode to access the Earth. None of the elder gods, daemons, or spirits have ever attempted to take a Tower. It's forbidden," Furfur rationalized.

"As she stated, they have agents set to accomplish this task," Aeon answered.

"This cannot be allowed," Furfur interrupted. "Such an action would tip the balance of power, and make my long maturing plot die on the vine. I cannot allow it. What is the sign?"

"The eruption of a mountain in the Cascade range," Aeon replied with the look of deep thought upon his tired face. "It was originally set to be Mount Rainier, but since the Brotherhood moves south, so to does the target. It is now Mount Saint Helens that will be the sign of the fall of the Tower of Dreams."

"I must get word to Drake and the Brotherhood," Furfur announced as she stood up quickly. Her black dress hugged tightly to her feminine form as she began to walk away from her throne, the clicking of her stiletto heels echoed through the massive room.

"What is your second question?" asked Aeon.

"Tell me about the time-streams, why are they so fluid before you now? You used to be able to see precisely when an event would come to pass. And now you can only estimate within a range of possibilities. Why is that?" Furfur queried, as she turned to face Aeon.

"Well, I believe it is the change of the dynamic of the Brotherhood of Olympus," Aeon responded, as he pondered the question. "Once, we all knew Walter Reuss was destined to lead the Brotherhood, but the Dark Council killed him and sent the time-stream into chaos. Drake Fraser is a variable that masks the future. I cannot see all possible outcomes, or even the most probable in many things involving him. It is like he makes his own destiny, writing the future as he goes, though there are some things he will do in all possibilities, like kill you if you killed Rachel. But, I cannot clearly see the future around the Brotherhood of Olympus anymore."

"Then that answers my question I did not ask," Furfur replied as she began to walk away. Aeon could not help but notice a thin black line running up the back of her legs as she strutted away. "What do I need your advice for if you cannot see the future anymore? You have become useless to me, Aeon. Be gone, and don't worry yourself over my actions any more."

Aeon stood from the comfortable chair and began to walk up to the raised dais to follow the Countess to ask her to reconsider her diabolical plot. He was met by six quickly moving demon guards and their drawn weapons.

"Saurva! Aesma! Come to me my daevas! I have a job for you!" Furfur shouted as she walked below a large archway and into the room beyond. "Saurva! Aesma! Your particular set of skills are needed for this most succulently wicked duty I desire of you."

Aeon began to move closer to the demon guards in his pursuit of the Countess. He wanted to reason with her before she went down this dark path. He'd heard of both Aesma and Saurva. Their devious reputations were well earned, and they were certainly capable of pushing young Rachel Finnegan into the abyss of hopelessness.

"You shall not pass," the demon guards uttered in unison, their voices made a hollow monotone sound like it was from a singular source spread over different speakers. "Another step and we shall dispatch you."

"Who said I wanted to pass?" Aeon replied, as he gripped the handle of his overly large scythe and with a swift movement that caught the armored demons unaware, the curved silver blade spun and cleaved the heads off all the gathered guards in one single stroke. The sound of their skulls hitting the floor was like a series of gourds falling from a table onto the cobblestones in a marketplace, followed quickly by their lifeless bodies in a loud clamor. "Why do these infernal daemons and demons insist that I am useless and unable to protect myself? This will not be the last the Countess hears from me, I assure you. But first I must go tell Woden and the others of what I have learned here this day. And perhaps something can be done to help that poor Finnegan girl."

Aeon walked away toward the doorway Tiamat and Succorbenoth had exited through. He paused for a moment, turned and walked back along the wall to a closed door and took his bloodied scythe and cut a crude symbol into the floor along the stone wall in front of the door. It was a pentacle with a cross over it. The old god then bent and put his wrinkled hand to the freshly carved stone. A blue fire leapt from his hand and flowed into the pentacle and cross igniting it in a low flame.

"Be still flame," Aeon spoke as if in a trance. "Be silent, and be unseen. When touched by the grandson of Martin the Nameless, empower him, protect him, keep his possessions guarded, and guide him to the knowledge he seeks."

Aeon stood up and continued walking toward the doorway, leaving the unseen carving on the floor and the slumped bodies of six headless demons behind him.

"It has been a good day," Aeon said to himself with a smile as he exited the grand throne room and left Gehenna behind.

7

COLUMBIA RIVER CHIEFTAINS

THE BROTHERHOOD OF OLYMPUS
AND THE TOWER OF DREAMS

One Step Forward, Infinite Steps Backward
Chapter Seven
January 4, 1980
Hazel Dell, Washington

It was a cold morning outside the Fraser house. Thick white ice crystals covered the world in wild hexagonal patterns. The freeze had brought a change to the fragrance of a Washington winter, and Mark couldn't help but think that it smelled a bit stale, like the inside of the walk-in freezer at Danny's where he worked.

"Drake," Mark announced, as he handed his brother the ice scraper from inside his car. His breath was hot and steamy in the cold air. "Scrape the windshield so we can go."

Drake silently forced the plastic blade of the scraper over the white glass. A pile of ice fragments was forming above the windshield wipers. Mark sat in the car, the engine running, with the heater turned up as high as it would go.

"Hurry up or we're gonna be late," Mark said, as he opened his door. Drake put more leverage in his motion and quickened his pace. He finished the windshield and went to work on the driver's side door window, then the back glass, and finally the passenger's side door. With a solid pat of the scraper against his right leg, dislodging the ice shavings stuck to the plastic, Drake opened the door and climbed into the warm car tossing the scraper on the floorboard in front of him.

"It's our first day, we don't want to make a bad impression by being late," Mark stated with a sarcastic chuckle. He was still unhappy with the move to Vancouver during his senior year of high school. In many ways he looked at the situation as a joke, and was only going through the motions because he had to. He wanted to be the first in his family to graduate and go off to school. He knew he couldn't do that without finishing his senior year, even if it was at this new school, with no one he knew except Drake.

Mark backed his car out of the driveway and into the road. The street was a bit slippery due to the icy conditions. He cautiously began the drive to school.

"What time's your basketball practice over?" Mark questioned.

"The coach's letter said it lasts two hours after school," Drake responded. He knew Mark was unhappy with the move, the new school, and the whole situation. But he knew Mark would be okay, because his brother never had problems making friends. He worried about his own social shortcomings. He dreaded new things, unknown people, and had worked so hard on breaking through the barrier that had been his shyness at their old school. He'd convinced himself that he was going to try and be cool, like Mark, and just go with the flow. He'd meet some new people, and maybe even talk to them.

"Is it a try-out?" Mark asked.

"No," Drake replied. "The letter was from the head coach. A guy named Arthaud. Mom told the principal I played basketball when she registered us. The principal told the coach I was coming, and the coach had heard of me and wanted me to join the varsity team. Being on their varsity's cool, I guess. But I don't know what their record is."

"Does it matter?" Mark stated rhetorically. "Listen Drake, I know how shy you can be, and I know you have a hard time making friends. This move is a step forward for all of us, really. It's all about your confidence, you know. But think of it this way, you get to be on the varsity team, that's like ten new friends for you right there."

"I guess so," Drake answered.

"I've seen you play," Mark added. "The whole team's going to be happy to have you. You work hard, you're nice, and you're pretty good at the game."

"Yeah, that's true, I guess," Drake agreed. If it were that simple, he could do that, and he liked what Mark said about having ten new friends. But he had a nagging feeling in his gut that it wasn't going to be that simple.

Mark's car crested a hill on 99th Street and they saw their new school appear on the left. It was a huge, multi-storied cement building with few windows on the front. At the top a series of large diamond shapes defined the roof line. The diamonds were alternating purple and yellow in color. In front of the main doors in a small grassy area stood a giant boulder painted yellow with the purple number '80' boldly upon it. Mark saw where all the cars were pulling into what appeared to be the student parking lot, and quickly determined that the lot was nearly full. With a sudden turn to the right that brought the car into a bit if a slide, Mark turned onto NW 9th Avenue and pulled off to the side of the road.

"I think we'll just park here, little brother," Mark stated as he shut off the car. "Come on. Don't make me have to pull you out of the car."

"I'm coming," Drake replied, remembering the story their mother liked to tell about Drake's first day of school. How he grabbed hold of the car seat and wouldn't let go as she pulled on him to get him out of the car. As his hands slipped off the seat he grabbed the dashboard, then the door jam, then the school chain-link fence, and so on to the front door of the school. She'd say, 'he held on like a spider monkey.' Drake always wondered how she knew how a spider monkey would hold on to make such a comparison.

Drake and Mark stood and waited for a break in the traffic down the hill on 99th before they took off across the icy road, making sure they slowed down before reaching the other side and crashing headlong into the curb.

"I'll be right where we parked after school," Mark panted, as they crossed the bus loop and student drop-off area heading toward the main doors.

"Don't you work today?" Drake questioned, as he

followed his brother to the big glass doors.

"No," Mark replied. "I'm off, and I'll be here after your practice to take you home."

With a rush of warm air the two Fraser brothers stepped inside Columbia River High School for the first time.

"There's the office," Drake said with a directional nod of his head. "We need to get our schedules."

"Yeah," Mark replied, as they headed toward and then into the office.

"May I help you?" asked a lady with big poufy brown hair and large eyeglasses.

"This is our first day of school here," Mark answered. "And we need schedules, and maybe a map."

Drake nodded, the high school was way more massive then their old school.

"And your names are?" the office lady questioned, as she looked through some paperwork on the desk in front of her.

"Fraser," Mark replied. "Mark and Drake Fraser."

"Of course," the office lady remarked with thin smile. "Here are your schedules. Mark, and Drake."

Drake looked at the schedule she had handed him. It had senior classes on it, and Advanced Auto Shop. He nudged Mark, who looked at his schedule and saw it had a bunch of hard classes and art on it. He handed it to Drake, and the brothers exchanged the schedules.

"I'm Mark," stated Mark. "And this is my little brother Drake."

"I'm sorry," the office lady said. "He's taller so I thought he was older. Oh and here are maps of the school. Lemme see if there's someone who can show you to your first class."

Mark and Drake looked at each other and managed a smile in the sea of uncertainty. The office lady was looking around to see if anyone was around who she could trust with this special job, and also be late to their own first period class.

"Stacey," the office lady called out, as she waved her left arm. "Stacey, I've got a job for you."

The brothers turned and saw a blonde girl step into the office from the foyer. She stood about five feet-seven inches tall, with feathered hair somewhat reminiscent of Farrah Fawcett. Her blue eyes were wide and slightly almond shaped. She had a pixyish face that sparked of enthusiasm. She wore a white blouse under a thick purple sweater, a knee-length golden floral-patterned skirt, and black high heeled ankle-boots with a fur lining.

"Sure," Stacey eagerly agreed with sparkling eyes. "What do you want me to do?"

"Show these new boys to their first period classes," the office lady said with a broad smile, almost like she had become infected by Stacey's enthusiasm.

"That sounds like fun, can I get a pass so I can be late to my first period?" Stacey said as she approached the desk. The office lady scribbled something on a yellow slip of paper and handed it to the girl. Stacey smiled to the office lady and then turned to the boys. "Let's see your schedules."

Mark handed her his schedule and took Drake's from him before handing it to her as well.

"So you're Mark Fraser?" Stacey asked, as she looked up from Mark's schedule, and offered him her right hand. "I'm Stacey. Stacey Jansen."

Mark shook her hand.

"Where are you from?" Stacey questioned.

"My mother," Mark joked with a smirk. Stacey smiled and laughed, disarming Mark's sarcasm. "We just moved here from Hoquiam."

"Oakland? I've been to San Francisco, but not Oakland," Stacey replied.

"No, Hoquiam," Mark corrected, taking special caution to enunciate. Stacey shook her head. Mark wasn't sure she knew where Hoquiam was. "By Aberdeen, up on the coast. And this is my little brother Drake."

Stacey offered her hand to Drake who didn't accept the offer for a polite handshake.

"He's kind of big for a little brother," Stacey said, as she began to walk out of the office past the towering form of Drake. Mark turned to follow and realized Drake was not moving, so he slapped his shoulder as he passed him nudging him into motion.

"And he's very quiet," added Stacey.

"Sometimes I think he's a mute," Mark joked as he moved up along side Stacey. Drake followed behind them.

In his mind Drake was kicking himself for clamming up when Stacey had offered to shake his hand. He was doing it again, the social ineptness was crashing over him like a tidal wave and he was drowning in the near panic-driven shyness that coursed through his body. He struggled to speak, to say something like Mark had, to be cool and calm, and not be the shy dorky kid again.

Mark and Stacey were talking and laughing as they walked around the school with Drake in tow. Stacey decided to show them where all there classes were.

"What's back there?" Mark asked, as they stood outside the auto shop. "It looks like a gazebo."

"That's the student smoking area," Stacey replied. "Are you guys smokers?"

"I might be," Mark answered. "Are you, Stacey?"

"No," Stacey responded quickly.

"Neither is Drake," Mark stated. "He's a basketball star, and a bit of a goody-two-shoe."

Stacey turned and looked back at Drake. She smiled at him and he felt his temperature rise. Mark walked over to the doors leading to the smoking area and peered out at the gazebo and the students hanging out with cigarettes in their hands.

Stacey led them through the second half of their schedules after she showed them the cafeteria, and explained how the two lunches worked. Drake had first lunch and Mark had second, so they would not be able to eat together. Stacey was excited to share with Drake that they had biology together after lunch.

"So this is your first period class again, Mark," Stacey

said as they came to one of the first classrooms they visited on their long tour of the school.

"Thank you Stacey," Mark said with a smile. "Maybe I'll see you around."

"Maybe," Stacey responded with a grin, as she turned and started walking off toward Drake's first period class. Drake looked at Mark who made a head motion in the direction of Stacey and silently mouthed the word 'go' to his brother. Drake quickly followed the blonde girl.

"Let me know how your day's going this afternoon, Drake," Stacey said as she came to his first class. It was his English class. She looked at him, puzzled by his timid behavior, and waited. Finally he realized he needed to speak to end the awkwardness of the moment.

"Okay," he muttered.

"I hope you like Columbia River," she said with a smile, as she turned, her heels clicking on the tile floor as she began to walk away. "It's way better than Fort, or Evergreen, and especially Bay."

Drake watched her walk away for a moment and he pondered his nearly photographic memory. Stacey made him think of a girl he once knew, another blonde girl, her features just out of his mind, her name escaped him, and he felt an oddness to it all that he couldn't remember her. How could his memory fail him in such a way? He began to do a mental diagnosis of his memory as he opened the door to his English class and was lost in the sea of being the new kid in an established classroom. Twenty-eight pairs of eyes analyzed him, classified him, and determined within moments that he was most likely weird and not worth their time to get to know him.

The morning went by slowly for Drake, shuffling from one new class to another. Sometimes being introduced with the title 'new kid' and sometimes just blending into the back of the class somewhere, both ways left him feeling a level of despair he had not known since early middle school when his family had moved from Central Park to Hoquiam. At lunch, he had to go back to the office to get his free lunch ticket before getting his tray of cafeteria food. Of course, he found this out after he had waited in line first.

Once he had his tray of warm food—some kind of gravy with meatballs in it over mashed potatoes, a piece of buttered bread, some green beans, a cup of red gelatin, and a milk carton—he stood and looked for an open seat. As he scanned the cafeteria, he noticed Stacey at a table with a bunch of other girls, most of whom were the popular girls he'd observed in his morning classes. Stacey waved to him, the other girls shook their heads, and Drake looked away. He saw a largely open table at the other end of the lunch room and headed toward it. It was a social outcast table. Most of the kids eating there were pale, sickly looking, or looked like they hadn't bathed in a number of days. Sitting next to a smaller kid who had a dark moustache was the exception to the scrawniness at the table. This kid looked big. Not fat, more like rotund. He was so thick it did not appear as though he had a neck. He had wild, black hair that stood straight out from his head and a somber look upon his face. His skin was darker than Drake's, a caramel color. He wore an overly large crew neck sweatshirt with a Chieftain head profile, the school mascot, upon it.

Drake approached the table and a few of the nerdy boys moved down opening up a few more seats for Drake. He sat down and looked around. Drake didn't like to eat when others watched so he was making sure all of his new table-mates were busy eating before he picked up his fork and began to eat his mystery meat gravy and potatoes. He looked over at the big kid. His ethnicity puzzled Drake. As a person who classified everyone he encountered, or attempted to understand as much as possible about them, this kid perplexed him.

"Take a picture," the big kid said. "It lasts longer, freak."

Drake looked down at his tray and finished his lunch without looking up again. He missed seeing Stacey waving to him again as she threw her garbage away before heading off to her locker near the end of lunch time. When the bell rang he quietly got up and cleared away his tray on the counter where he saw other students putting their empty trays.

He made his way to his biology class. The teacher was late so the students stood noisily in the hallway outside the door. Finally, after what seemed like ten minutes, the biology teacher arrived. He was an older man with receding gray hair and thick black glasses. He wore a gray tweed sports coat with felt elbow patches. His breath was thick with the fragrance of peanuts. He apologized for being late. Stacey sought him out as she entered the room and talked to him amid the bustle of the students coming in and taking their seats behind the black topped science tables.

"Take a seat, Mr. Fraser," the teacher said, as he pointed to the back of the room. "And thank you Ms. Jansen for volunteering to be his lab partner."

Drake walked past Stacey and some of the girls she sat with at lunch and went to an open table at the back of the class.

"Stacey," one of the popular girls said, "what're you doing?"

"He's new," Stacey answered. "He needs a lab partner, and there are three of us here."

"But he's weird," the other girl said with a look of dismay on her face.

"He's quiet," Stacey corrected her friend.

"My mom always said, be careful of the quiet boys, Stacey," the first girl stated with a serious look. "They're dangerous."

"And he's kinda cute," Stacey said with a smile.

"So was Jack the Ripper," the first girl remarked. "But seriously Stacey, you saw who he sat with at lunch. The losers and dorks."

"He plays basketball," Stacey continued, as she gathered her things. "And I think he could use a friend."

"Being his friend will damage your popularity," the

second girl stated. Stacey continued to put her things into a single stack and grabbed her purse from the back of the chair where it had been hanging.

"Stacey, don't go," her friends said in unison.

She didn't listen to them as she rose from her seat and walked to the back of the room and sat down next to Drake.

"Hiya Drake," Stacey said with a smile. "I'm your new lab partner.

After school Drake walked past the smoking area on his way to the gym locker room. He noticed Mark standing out there with a group of guys. Mark had probably already made friends with all of them. He shook his head as he kept walking to the gym. Once inside the locker room door he made his way past row upon row of purple lockers until he came to an open office door with a bearded man sitting inside changing his clothes. The man became wide-eyed and stood up, pulling his athletic shorts up in one fluid motion.

"You must be Drake Fraser?" the coach questioned, as Drake nodded. "I've heard a lot about you from your old coach. And if you're half as good as he said you were we can definitely use you, son."

The coach stuck out his hand and Drake responded with a strong handshake. The coach went stronger and nearly crushed Drake's bones.

"You can call me coach," the bearded man said, as he released Drake's hand from his vice-like grip. He was nearly six feet tall, his hair was dark brown and speckled with gray. His beard was full and untrimmed, reminding Drake of a mountain man. "Coach Arthaud."

"Thank you coach," Drake replied. He was determined to make basketball his sanctuary away from the awkwardness of the new school.

"Go find a locker and get yourself changed," Coach Arthaud said. "I'll have one of my assistants, coach Healy, get you your uniforms and practice jersey out in the gym. Hustle up Fraser, we don't have all day!"

Drake made his way past a number of other boys. There were a lot of basketball players changing for practice. A freshman team, a C-team, a junior varsity, and a varsity squad all bustled about in various stages of nakedness, putting their school clothes in the big athletic lockers and putting their gym shorts and t-shirts on, before lacing up their court shoes. Drake determined who was the junior varsity and varsity because they were bigger and because they had reversible purple and white jerseys—the practice gear Coach Arthaud had mentioned to him most likely. Drake found an empty locker at the far side of the massive locker room, set his duffle bag down, and began to take out his shoes and gym clothes.

"Hey," an older boy said from nearby. "You're the new kid? The forward from the harbor?"

"Yeah," Drake replied as he put his school clothes in the locker and pulled his gym short up his legs as quickly as possible.

"Coach said you were coming," the older boy added. Drake turned his head and looked at him. He was a tanned looking boy, with straight, long black hair. He looked Hispanic like Drake and Mark, though Drake thought that he was most likely an Indian. Some of his friends at his old school had been from the Quinault reservation, and he was often grouped with them in school—especially in their Washington State History class when the teacher sent all of the Indian students to the library for a week while they studied the Christian Missionary period of the history of the territory before it became a state. The teacher said he didn't want to offend any of the Indian kids. Drake had protested, claiming to not be an Indian, but the teacher was relentless and said, 'Drake you're too dark not to be an Indian, go to the library.'

"I'm George," the older kid added. "George Kalama."

"You're named after the town?" Drake asked, as he bent to pull his socks up to just below his knees.

"No," George replied. "The town's named after a dude

who was like a cousin of my great-grandfather, he came here from Hawaii."

"Cool," Drake responded. He loved history, and liked to learn about everything he could. "What position do you play?"

"I'm a center," George answered, as he finished dressing by pulling the purple practice jersey over his head. He took a rubber band and pulled his long hair into a ponytail on the back of his head. He was nearly as tall as Drake, about six feet four inches, and was much thicker around the waist. He didn't look overly athletic.

"What team are you on?" Drake inquired, as he began to lace up his shoes.

"Varsity," George replied. Drake wondered if all of the varsity team was as athletic looking as George.

"Do you start?" Drake asked.

"Nah," George answered. "I don't play much in games, unless Jimmy's in foul trouble or we're way ahead. It's my senior year and I'm just glad I made the team."

"Oh," Drake responded, as he finished tying his Converse high top shoes.

"Come on," George said, as he turned and jogged out of the locker room. "Coach is gonna be mad."

Drake quickly followed, but he slowed as he passed a door near the entrance of the gym that said 'Weight Room' on a sign. Inside he heard a rhythmic banging and grunting. It was different than the noises that filter out of a weight room full of football players, it was as if a single person was in there.

"Fraser!" Coach Arthaud shouted jarring Drake from his silent observation of the weight room. "Hustle son, practice has started!"

Drake ran onto the court. Washed in hues of purple and yellow, a stylized chieftain head emblazoned the center of the court. The squeaking of shoes on the shiny wood floor reverberated throughout the gym. The forty-some players were running laps around the gym. Drake immediately sized up his new teammates. One kid was taller than him, maybe six feet seven, another was about his height, but the rest were shorter than George. Columbia River had a player taller than him, so he wouldn't have to play center, at least.

After they had finished their laps, they gathered in lines to stretch out. Five varsity players led the lines at half court. After the stretching they jogged back to the baseline under the main basket, and made eight nearly even lines. Drake joined one on the far side of the gym, near the end of it. They dribbled down the court, one from each line, doing jump stops along the way. After the first jump stop, the next player in line started down the court, and so on, until they all made it down to the other baseline. They returned the length of the court doing a jump stop and pivot step. The balance lines went on for a number of minutes. Finally they broke up and used the four side baskets to do the lay-in drill Drake knew as the daily dozen.

Drake noticed the five coaches were all watching him. Three of them—including Coach Arthaud—stood side by side and pointed or nodded. They watched as Drake laid the ball in with his hand high above the rim.

"Fraser, can you dunk?" one of the assistants yelled to him.

Drake nodded.

"Do it next time," the assistant instructed with a stare.

On Drake's next lay-in attempt he pulled the ball up and turned it below his hand and attempted to drive it through the rim. The ball hit the backside of the rim and shot off above him. The coaches turned to Arthaud and raised their eyebrows or nodded.

"You missed it son," Arthaud announced and Drake nodded. Arthaud blew his whistle. "Frosh and C-team, you're off to the auxiliary gym, varsity and JV you're in here. Let's go gentlemen!"

Over half of the players took off for the auxiliary gym with two of the coaches following behind. Arthaud moved over to one side of the gym floor, and talked to one of his assistants. The assistant picked up a purple practice jersey and went toward Drake.

"Fraser," Coach Healy stated, as he tossed the jersey to Drake. "Put this on, and get over with the varsity by Coach Arthaud."

Drake quickly pulled the reversible jersey over his head and hustled over to the ten players standing around the head coach. Drake moved into the loose circle next to George.

"Coach!" Arthaud yelled toward the assistant on the far side of the gym. "Get your JV ready, we're going to scrimmage for a bit."

The JV players all turned their practice jerseys to the white side and gathered around their coach.

"Okay gentlemen," Arthaud began. "We need to improve our defense if we are going to beat Bay this week. They have a bunch of scorers who're also good athletes. Ya think you guys can do it?"

"Yes coach!" the players shouted in unison.

"That's what I like to hear," Arthaud continued, as he began to point at players around the circle. "Washington, Johnson, Bean, Helms, and Caine are starting."

"As usual," George said under his breath.

A blonde-haired kid who was thickly built, wide at the waist, and a couple inches shorter than Drake put his hand into the circle. The rest followed.

"Defense on three," the blonde kid said. "One, Two, Three."

"Defense!" shouted the team as they broke their circle and the five boys who the coach named hustled out onto the court. The tallest boy lined up in the center circle opposite the tallest kid on the JV team. The assistant, Coach Healy, who had given Drake his jersey, tossed the ball up, and the varsity team controlled the tip as the shortest player on the team got the ball and advanced up the court yelling "UCLA! UCLA!"

Drake sat on the bleacher bench with the other five players on the varsity. George sat next to him.

"Who's who?" Drake quietly asked George.

"Number one, with the ball, that's Reggie Washington, our point guard," George said, as he pointed to the six foot tall extremely dark-skinned player. Reggie was an athletic kid, lean and well muscled, and a wizard with the ball. He dribbled it in ways Drake could never hope to. "He's a junior and the older brother of Otis, Little O, number three down there at the other end of the bench."

Drake looked down at Little O. He was the shortest kid on the varsity team. He was a whole foot shorter than Drake, but made up for some of it by the big afro he sported. His older brother kept his hair trimmed short so it didn't slow him down on the court. Little O smiled at him.

"Little O is a freshman, by the way," George continued, as he pointed out on the floor to another player. "Jimmy Bean, number fifty-five, is our six-seven center. He's a junior, and I back him up."

Drake looked at the thin form of Jimmy Bean. He was mostly arm and leg, even thinner and ganglier than Drake was. His face was pale and heavily freckled, his nose was a bit of a pug, and his hair was a messy tussle of dirty blonde with a hint of red.

"Thirty-five," George went on, "that's Steve Johnson, he's our best athlete and leading scorer. He's a junior forward and best friend of Reggie."

Drake looked at Steve. He was not as dark as Reggie, but had his hair in an afro that was nearly as big as Little O's. He was long and lean, his leg muscles were well defined, and he had big hops. He played his game high off the backboard. He was the same height as Drake. This was a kid Drake looked forward to playing basketball with. Steve's raw athleticism was better than anyone he had on his old team.

"See thirty-three?" George questioned with a point to the skinniest player on the varsity team. "That's Downtown Danny Helms, he's our shooter. He plays off-guard and is streaky as hell. Probably the most competitive guy on our team, too."

Drake looked at Danny. The sophomore guard was about six feet one inch, and might have weighed one hundred-thirty pounds dripping wet. He had a wild tuft of straight dark brown hair that stuck mostly upward and added to his height, steely blue-eyes, and a razor sharp focus on the ball.

"And that," George went on, "number twenty-four, is Moose Caine, our team captain. He's the only other senior on the team besides me. He thinks he's pretty good, but I think he only leads the team in fouls and attitude. Be careful around him, if you know what's good for ya."

Drake studied Moose. He was the six foot three inch, blonde guy, who had led the team in their circle before the start of the scrimmage. He was thick, and not overly well defined, but had the largest arms on the team. Drake determined that was because of a thick layer of fat that he watched jiggle as Moose jogged up and down the court. His blue eyes were small and set tight by his nose, almost too tight to be human, Drake concluded.

"The other guys on the team over here with us are," George continued, "fourteen's Bobby Jones. He's a backup forward-center who plays more than me even though he's only a sophomore like you. And number five is Chuck Newcomb. He's a junior off-guard who plays more when Downtown isn't on his game. And number twenty-three is Ryan Healy. He's the other freshman who made varsity. He's a forward who backs up Moose and only plays if Moose fouls out or if Bobby or Steve's in foul trouble or tired."

Drake looked down the bench. Bobby was a dark blonde boy, who was six feet three inches, and a bit thicker than Drake. He had a prominent mole or birthmark on his right cheek. Chuck was a six foot tall, pale boy with severe acne. His red hair was curled in a tight permanent that looked like an afro. Ryan was a six feet two inch boy with reddish-blonde hair that was cut short. He was thick in the torso, a bit out of shape, and he didn't push himself much during practice. He was a gym rat that would hang out after practice with Danny and shoot trick shots until the coaches were ready to lock up, since his dad was the varsity assistant coach.

The scoreboard horn sounded. The varsity was up ten to four, with four minutes played into the first period.

"Everyone out," Arthaud announced. "Next five in, Little O, Newcomb, Jones, Healy, and Fraser! Sorry Kalama, I'll get you in later."

The starters jogged off the court and headed to the drinking fountains.

The five replacements huddled around Coach Arthaud.

"Get the ball to Fraser on the wing, I want to see him drive it on them," Arthaud instructed. "And Fraser, I want you to dunk it on them, got it?"

"Yes coach," Drake responded. His pulse echoing loudly in his head, he could dunk the ball, but he hadn't learned to do it off the dribble and had almost always bounced it off the back rim like he did earlier during the daily dozen drill. He didn't want to fail again.

The five guys put their hands in. The chant again was 'defense on three.'

"Defense!" shouted the players in unison before they took to the court.

Drake matched up in the man-to-man defense against the JV power forward, Ryan took their center, and Bobby took their small forward. Ryan tipped an errant pass and grabbed the turnover. He passed the ball out to Little O and both teams sprinted up the court. Little O and Chuck worked the ball around the perimeter. Drake popped out to the wing on the right side, when Bobby set a screen on his man. Little O passed the ball to Drake, who ripped through clearing his man, and began to dribble drive to the basket. Near the block he elevated and glided high up above the rim with the ball in his right hand. The arc of his jump brought him down short of the rim and the ball hit hard off the front of it and shot back out of bounds with a loud clang. Drake felt his confidence crush itself into his already damaged heart from all of his experiences during the first day at his new school.

"Fraser!" Arthaud yelled. "You're out, Kalama get in there for him."

Drake jogged off the court and took a seat at the end of the bench next to Steve. He cradled his head in his hands.

"Hey man," Steve said, as he put his hand on Drake's shoulder. "Don't worry about it, it's your first day, it'll get better."

"Hey Fraser," Moose interrupted as he leaned forward and looked down the bench at Drake. "Stop crying, and learn to play basketball. You're a freaking joke, you pansy."

Mark was true to his word, he waited for Drake on the corner of NW 9th Avenue. Drake was late getting out from basketball. It was nearly quarter to six when he walked out of the dark to the passenger's side door of Mark's car.

"How'd it go, little brother?" Mark asked, as Drake plopped heavily on to the seat.

"It sucked," Drake announced. "I hate this school. I hate the team."

"What?" Mark questioned as he shifted the car into first gear and pulled away from the corner. "Why's that?"

"The team captain called me a pansy, and the coach benched me. It just sucks! I hate it all!" Drake answered with tears forming in his eyes. If he were capable of crying he would have.

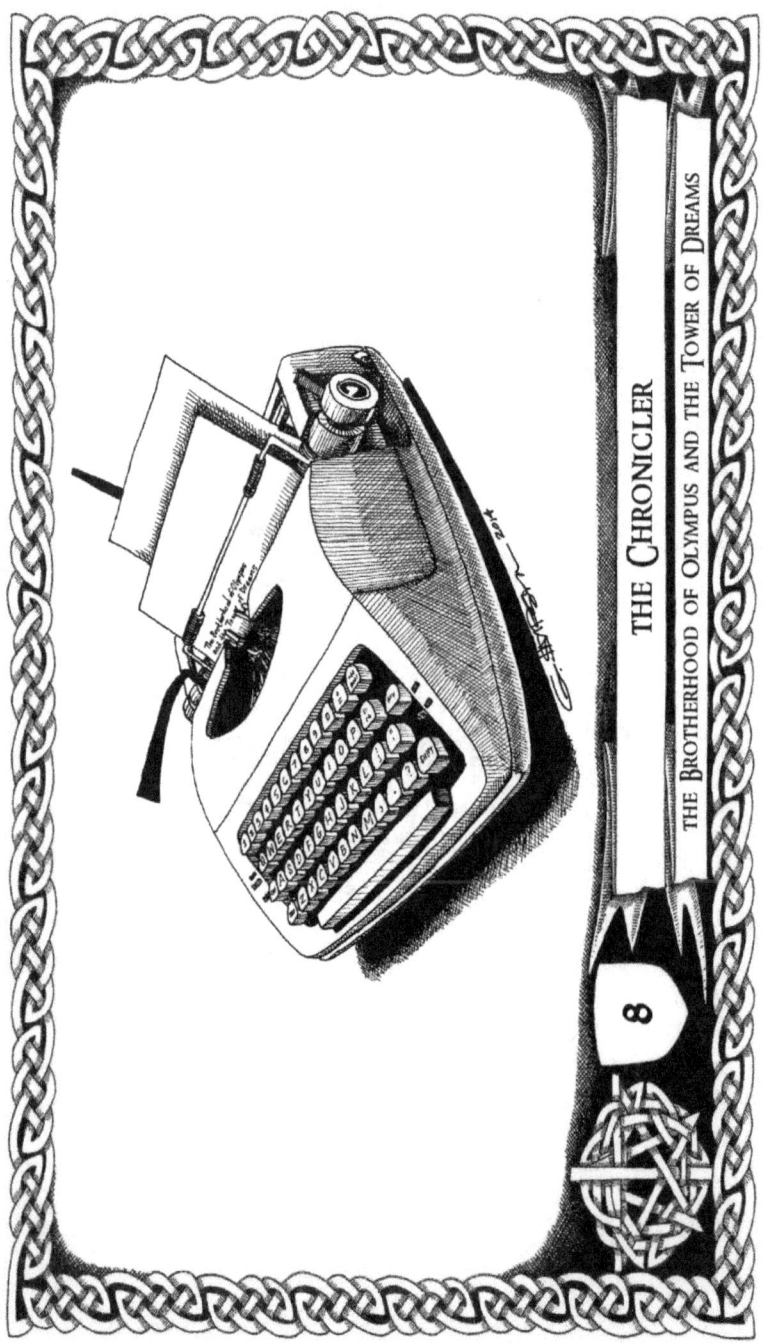

THE CHRONICLER

THE BROTHERHOOD OF OLYMPUS AND THE TOWER OF DREAMS

**Chronicler
Chapter Eight
January 6, 1980
Hazel Dell, Washington**

Drake had spent the last couple of days in a depressive funk. He replayed the events of his first day of school all weekend, and couldn't get the feeling of utter failure out of his head. Saturday turned into Sunday and he continued to wallow in the pain. He began to wish he had an illness, chicken-pox again, or the measles maybe, which he thought might be slightly worse than chicken-pox, something, or anything that would allow him to not go to school.

The cool gray January sky outside broke through the small gap between the thick brown woven curtains like a single vertical beam of light that moved across the dark bedroom illuminating a different area as the day passed. Drake could tell by the makeshift sundial that it was in the early afternoon. That fact, and that Monday would soon be there added to the anxiety he was already feeling.

A series of thumps echoed through the door as someone came up the stairs. A new louder thumping followed.

"Drake," a muffled voice through the door announced.

It was one of his brothers. He didn't move off his blue chenille bedspread.

The thumping came again.

"Drake," repeated the muffled voice.

Maybe if he laid there his brother would just go away.

The thumping returned, louder this time. His patience was normally one of his greatest virtues, but today he had virtually none. He was irritated by the insistence of his brother outside his room.

"Drake," the muffled voice continued.

"Whaaaaaat!" shouted Drake in an overly dramatic manner. The door opened with an audible pop and a flood of incandescent light.

"Hey, little brother, are you okay?" Martin questioned as he stepped into the dark room.

"Yeah," Drake responded as he sat up, swinging his feet off the bed.

"Mom said you've been in here all weekend," Martin added, as he walked over to the window and opened the curtains filling the room with gray light. He was carrying a large case that resembled a fat hard-sided suitcase.

"So," Drake mumbled, as he ran his fingers through his messed up hair. "Can't a guy even hang out in his room anymore?"

"I guess," Martin said as he set the case down and sat at the foot of Drake's bed. "But I wanted to talk to you about Brotherhood of Olympus stuff."

"I guess so," Drake responded. "What about?"

"A couple of things, really," Martin replied. Drake turned to face Martin. "You remember how I changed jobs in the Air Force when I got transferred to the 125th Special Tactics Squadron, and I said I couldn't tell you about it because it was top secret?"

"Something you made up," Drake replied casually. "Why would the Air Force put you in a top secret job?"

"It's real, Drake," Martin snapped back. "Listen to me. I need to tell you this. But you can't tell anyone else about what I'm going to tell you, got it?"

"Uh huh, sure," Drake responded.

"I'm serious, Drake," Martin continued with a stern look upon his face. "This is very important for both of us."

"Okay, okay, I promise," Drake answered.

"I was recruited to be a psychic spy," Martin stated with an odd panic in his voice. He looked around the room, like he expected to see someone standing in the shadows. "It's a top secret unit of the Air Force known as Project North Star."

"Uh huh, you're a psychic spy," Drake replied sarcastically. "And I'm next in line to be King of England."

"I'm serious," Martin excitedly. "I wanted to tell you right away, but I couldn't until I knew I could protect you from the prying eyes of my teammates. What they're capable of is amazing and downright scary too. It took me some time to figure it out."

"Wait," Drake said, as he held up his right hand. "You're really serious."

"Yeah," Martin responded. "That's what I said, I'm serious. What I'm telling you is the truth."

"Go on," Drake added, as he shifted his attention to the details his brother was sharing with him.

"Last month I was sent to New York City, to meet and be trained by a guy named Ingo Swann." Martin began to explain. "Manhattan was crazy, so many buildings, so many people, it was like organized chaos. I met Ingo at a delicatessen off Broadway, and he was kind of a crazy guy. He was paranoid as hell that there were aliens following him."

"Aliens?" Drake interrupted.

"Yeah," Martin continued. "He called them grays—big-headed, black almond eyes, and gray skinned aliens right out of *Close Encounters*. He said they're after him because he can see them through their disguises and as a psychic he's one of the few people who can stop them. Anyway, I spent ten days with him learning to sharpen my skills, to become the psychic I was meant to be. He was way out there, weirder than weird, but my god his mind was so complex and well disciplined. I was pretty good at reading minds then, but I couldn't get anywhere he wouldn't allow me to go. He told me that he decided to train me, because of what I'd be capable of."

"What do you mean?" Drake asked.

"Well," Martin began to explain, "remember when we were using the *Spirit* board and the mordgeists were trying to come through from the ethereal plane? I forced them back with my mind, like a powerful burst of energy that they couldn't fight. Ingo knew about that when he first met me, and he knew I was coming to him. He said I've got latent telekinetic ability on a massive scale. He also told me that I would easily surpass him as I learned to master my abilities. That was something I didn't tell my C.O., Captain Spenser, when I got back. Ingo's training allowed me to be able to move beyond the other members of my unit, even my C.O. who's a top-level grade three psychic."

"Why do you need to be able to protect me from your teammates?" Drake questioned.

"Well," Martin answered, "one of the techniques I've learned is called CRV—Controlled Remote Viewing, and it involves a viewer who travels across time and space to a location to see all that can be seen, or heard, or smelled, or tasted at that location. Most of my teammates are quite good at it and could easily find me here with you, if they wanted to. Anyway, one of the things a viewer tends to do is blindly draw on a tablet while they experience this distant location. When I first saw this it made me think of something. It made me think of you, Drake."

"Me?" Drake questioned. "Why?"

"Because," Martin answered, as he got up and looked for one of Drake's sketchbooks. He quickly found one and flipped it open, turning pages until he came to a rough sketch of a massive black tower. "You have been doing this CRV stuff for a long time. See this Drake? This black monolith is known as the Tower of Dreams. It's a practice target for my unit to view, because it seems to move around time and space. And you've been drawing it for a couple of years, usually when we are talking about other things. I think you have been seeing it remotely this whole time."

"What?" Drake remarked. "Are you serious?"

"I think you might be even better at CRV then me," Martin added, "if you were trained, and I think I can do that for you now."

"Really? Drake asked with renewed attention. "I figured

you were our team psychic, not me."

"I am," Martin responded with a smile. "From what I've seen, Drake, you're the perfect leader of the Brotherhood because you're the next best at every other skill set on the team, and the smartest. But, within your psychic skill set, CRV is something you'll excel at because it comes naturally to you."

"Cool," Drake said with a smile of his own, the first one he had in nearly three days. "What about this Tower of Dreams? Why is it something I keep seeing? Is it like Devil's Tower in *Close Encounters*, or what?"

"Kinda, yeah," Martin answered. "It's a tower of legendary origin. From what I've learned it was created by a very ancient race that came before the gods of myth and legends. There are supposedly other towers too, but I've never seen them, only this one. I've heard the voice of the Keeper of the tower, a dude named Addraemyr, but I've not gotten inside the tower yet. The Keeper has told me a little bit about the tower and why it's important. And he also told me about the Brotherhood of Olympus, and some of the same things you shared about a medieval order of knights with the same name. Kind of verified all that stuff for me. Anyway, the Keeper said I had to keep you safe, that you possessed the key to what's to come."

"What's to come?" Drake questioned. "Did he say anything more specific?"

"Yeah, a little," Martin replied. "There's a dimensional war on the horizon. Powerful forces that will seek dominion over the Earth are lining up on multiple fronts, but the Keeper warned me that it will be difficult to tell allies from enemies. But, get this, he said that the Brotherhood of Olympus would be at the center of it all, and we'll play a very crucial role in deciding the outcome of the war. But it'll be a deadly fight that we might not all emerge from."

"That's what the gods above Olympus showed me," Drake stated, as he remembered the dream-like encounter he had at Hurricane Ridge during the summer of 1978. "The fate of the world would be dependent on whether or not we acted, united as the team we were chosen to be."

"Yeah," Martin replied. "I remember you saying that after we burned the *Spirit* board, but I wasn't sure you were telling the truth or if you had just dreamt or imagined the whole god thing. I mean the whole Staff of Orkan was pretty good evidence, but seriously, ancient gods talking to you was a bit of a stretch."

"I know this whole thing has altered my perception of reality," Drake said. "None of this is in any encyclopedia I've ever read, or in any class I've ever taken in school. The concept of other dimensions, though scientifically plausible, isn't even up for conjecture among most rational scientists. Then you factor in magic that can defy the laws of physics and nature, and compound that with the existence of these ancient creatures humans once worshipped as gods or worse, it completely rocked my world-view and made me do a lot of soul searching about what I thought was true, or just fantasy. Now I'm not sure I believe all the myths and legends, but I'm way more open minded to the possibility that all of them might be rooted in at least some layer of truth."

"Me too," Martin agreed. "My time with Ingo blew the lid off my mind. I can now see things in a whole new light."

"So if this war is inevitable for us," Drake began, "and it's going to be deadly, then I think we need to keep both Dennis and Albert out of it. They are the least prepared, and would be our weakest links. I would hate to see them die."

"I agree," Martin concurred somberly, as he thought of the illicit information that he and Aunt Carmen had gotten from the *Spirit* board when they used it on Uncle Wally's grave—deaths it foretold among other things—things it had been eerily correct on. It had predicted that both he and Drake would die in 1984 in a war with old gods. "We'll need to replace them in the Brotherhood, the sooner the better. I'm just not sure who with?"

"We should start looking," Drake said with a puzzled look. "Although, I doubt I'll be much good at that task since

I don't have any friends here and I don't foresee me getting any in the near future, either."

"I can look at some of the people in my unit," Martin added, "though I can't be sure I can trust any of them with this information."

"So what's with the case you brought in?" Drake questioned, as he thought about the thick, oddly shaped, hard sided suitcase Martin had carried into his room.

"It's a present," Martin answered with a warm smile, as he got up and retrieved the case. "For you."

"What is it?" Drake inquired. Martin unlatched the two metal clasps that held the case closed and began to open it, revealing the contents. "A typewriter?"

"Yep," Martin responded. "Military surplus, we just got new typewriters in our unit headquarters and the old ones were being surplused. I thought of you, and your desire to write about the Brotherhood and the history of dimensions and the occult. So I asked my C.O. if I could get one to take home and he said, 'sure.' Now I'm giving it to you."

"Cool," Drake replied with a grin, popping his dimples out. "Is it electric?"

"Yep, it's an electric typewriter," Martin answered. "Now all you need is some paper and you can start typing your manuscript, chronicling the Brotherhood of Olympus."

"I've a lot of notes in my spiral notebooks I can start to make into a cohesive document," Drake added. "I've got a new title, I'm now the Chronicler of the Brotherhood of Olympus."

Both brothers chuckled at the name Drake had chosen. Drake moved the typewriter over to him and lightly pressed upon some of the keys, watching the typebars move up near black ribbon and the cylindrical platen.

"I've been dreaming of the tower," Drake stated, as he looked at Martin and continued to softly press the typewriter keys. "Some of my dream makes more sense now that we've talked."

"Really," Martin replied. "Why is that?"

"Well," Drake answered, "for one thing, neither Dennis nor Albert has been in any of my dreams, so we must have replaced them. And there are other people with us."

"Really, who?" Martin asked.

"One is an older guy with long black hair and glasses," Drake replied. "He is usually in the tower, but I'm not sure how he gets inside it. Another is a muscle-bound guy who I think is black. He's usually in the car with us in my dream. Does either of those guys sound like someone you work with?"

"Hmmmm..." Martin thought to himself about his teammates in his unit, and the support staff on the air base. "No, not really, I don't think there's anyone who fits either description. What about Mark?"

Drake had not thought about the absence of Mark in his dream until that moment. Mark and Drake had always been partners in nearly everything they did from a very early age. In fact, Drake was dependent on the inner strength Mark always seemed to possess in his times of struggle or hardship. Mark had always been his rock. Why then, was Mark absent in his dream? And why had he not realized it until this moment?

"I'm not sure where Mark was, but I think Beth was with us," Drake added with a raised eyebrow.

"Beth?" Martin questioned in disbelief. "My wife? I don't think that's going to happen. She didn't want to listen to me when I started telling her about my new job as a psychic spy. She tends to think that all metaphysical stuff's made up, or delusional fantasy. I didn't know that about her when we met, or got engaged."

"You didn't tell her about the Brotherhood?" Drake asked. "You were going on a date with her on June twenty-seventh, when we faced off with Succorbenoth and Grandpa and Grandma's house last year, how did you not manage to tell her about it? Even I told a girl at school. Some blonde girl, hmmmm... whose name I can't remember right now, but I do remember telling her about it."

"Whenever I've tried to bring it up, Beth has shot it down so quickly and changed the subject," Martin responded. "I just figured it was pretty pointless to bring it up anymore. So, if you have seen her in your dream, I can guarantee you that she wouldn't be with us and therefore your dream's flawed."

"Okay," Drake stated, unsure of his brother's claim, but very sure of the red-haired woman he had been seeing in his dream since before he knew who Beth was. "If you say so, but we do need to start looking for these new members of the Brotherhood, whoever they are."

"Agreed," Martin said.

Drake couldn't shake the realization that Mark had been absent from his dream and he began to ponder what that meant. He hoped to God that it didn't mean the deadly aspect of the coming war would claim his brother as its victim. He hadn't ever recovered from the death of their uncle Wally, and losing the brother that was the closest to him shook his soul at its fibers. That was a reality he was not prepared for.

River Rising, Fraser Falling
Chapter Nine
January 16, 1980
Hazel Dell, Washington

The last seven days at Columbia River High School had been an exercise at being invisible for Drake. He attended his classes without volunteering to answer a single question, and had only been called on once in his biology class because of Stacey, his lab partner, and her bubbly demeanor. He continued to sit at the table with the outcasts and losers during lunch, and even went out of his way not to agitate the big dark kid who sat at the far end of the table by not bothering to look in his direction at all. At basketball practice he did his best to blend in with the rest of the bench players on the varsity team. He liked some of his teammates, including Ryan, Little O, Steve, and George—who he thought looked something like the older guy with the long hair and glasses in his dream, though he knew it couldn't have been him. During the three basketball games they played, Drake got in one of the games as a deep bench player going in with George when they were twenty-some points behind with a few minutes to play in the fourth quarter and no chance of winning.

Mark had introduced Drake to a new song he had recorded onto a cassette tape, which he played on repeat as they drove to school. It was from Red Geoff, *Another Piece of Straw,* and the haunting lyrics began to echo in his mind as he walked through his life, numb and invisible.

I don't need your attention,

On this particular Wednesday, being invisible was not

139

going to be an option anymore. Drake was about to make a name for himself at his new school.

It started at lunch. Drake sat at the end of the table quietly eating his tray of cafeteria food, not exactly sure what it might have been, or what it was supposed to be. The big kid he had been avoiding arrived late and approached him.

"Hey freak," the kid stated, as he stood across the table from Drake. "I'm talking to you."

Drake looked up at the thick form of the boy in front of him. The boy was considerably shorter than Drake, maybe five feet ten inches at best, and wore huge baggy clothes. Drake took note that he walked with the slow, forced gait of someone severely overweight. His arms tended to stick out at a greater angle than most people, like his torso was so large that his arms could no longer rest easily at his sides.

"Do you ever talk?" the kid questioned. "Can I sit here with you? Those pencil-necked geeks took my seat down there."

Drake had not even noticed that the sickly, pale boys who normally sat between the big kid and him were all crowded at the other end of the table. He took a quick glance, and then nodded to the big kid, who took that as an invitation and sat down across from him.

"My name's James Kirk," the big kid stated. "But, I ain't all into that *Star Trek* stuff, so don't even mention it. Got it?"

"Drake," responded Drake out of politeness. "Drake Fraser."

James nodded to Drake in acceptance and began to devour his lunch. Drake was fascinated by the crudeness of James' eating technique, it reminded him of his little brother Albert and how he ate fried chicken.

"Oh," James interjected with a full mouth of sandwich. "This don't mean we're friends, either, got it Fraser?"

Drake nodded and returned to his lunch.

I don't need your fake concern,

Soon afterward, in biology, Drake sat in the back of the room by Stacey, his always perky lab partner. Mr. Ferris was teaching a lesson about genetics, referring to Gregor Mendel, Punnett Squares, and dominant and recessive traits. Drake was paying close attention to what his teacher was droning on about.

"Drake, what kind of music do you like? Don't you think Tommy Shaw, the guitarist for Styx, is kind of dreamy?" Stacey whispered to Drake, who just shrugged his shoulders, unsure how to answer her questions.

"We can see, through a pedigree chart, that certain traits are recessive while others are clearly dominant," Mr. Ferris lectured. Stacey raised her hand and Mr. Ferris pointed to her.

"How can we be sure that it's not just random chance?" Stacey questioned. "I mean, I get the whole brown-eyed parents make brown-eyed babies, but how do we know all of this stuff?"

"Well Miss Jansen," Mr. Ferris pondered, "organisms have genes, not like the kind you buy and wear from the Bon Marché, but little microscopic things in the nucleus of their cells that determine things such as eye color, hair color, or any number of traits or abilities."

Wait a minute, Drake thought. He had never examined it in that way before. Abilities being genetic made perfect sense. He was intrigued. He raised his hand.

"Yes," Mr. Ferris stated, as he pointed to Drake. "Mr. Fraser, how delightful to have you participate in the discussion."

"So, you're saying there is a spot in our deoxyribonucleic acid that accounts for all the abilities we have as organisms?" Drake questioned.

"Ummm…" Mr. Ferris replied, as he thought of a solid response. No student had ever come into his class knowing anything about such things before. "Yes, it has been stated within scientific circles that the deoxyribonucleic acid, or DNA, in the cells of organisms would be the source of all genetic material, traits, behaviors, and abilities."

"So we all possess these abilities," Drake clarified.

"Yes," Mr. Ferris answered, thoroughly enjoying the higher level of discussion. "But, not all of them manifest in the organism because they may be latent recessive traits. Kind of like they're a light switch that has been turned off, there isn't any light, but the switch is still there."

"Could these switches or abilities be turned on?" Drake asked.

"Hypothetically," Mr. Ferris responded. "Yes, if we could see the DNA, understand it, and work with it. I do believe that at some point in our future, scientists will be able to genetically manipulate organisms, make hybrids, or cure all manner of diseases through genetics."

"What about things like psychic abilities?" Drake continued. Many of his peers turned and looked back at him when he asked that question.

"You mean like spoon bending or mind reading? Or full on *Carrie* status?" Mr. Ferris replied.

"Both," Drake asked, taking notice of his peers looking at him. "Do you think those things are real?"

"Well," Mr. Ferris stated, as he loosened his tie a bit. "Many do think psychic abilities are the province of side-shows, or charlatan palm readers, but, it has long been speculated that our very government has been doing research into this field to try and use the knowledge against the Soviets. We always hear that the Soviets are way ahead of us in such research, and how we need to do things to catch up. But, I think, things like that are hypothetically possible. Many scientists will quickly claim we only use ten percent of our brain's true capacity. It's just that it's so hard to scientifically prove because of the nature of psychic abilities. They can't be easily replicated in a controlled environment, among other things. I think, now this is completely off the record, that there are many things modern science has not quantified, UFO's, bigfoot, other dimensions, or psychic abilities that will someday be found to exist in one form or another once we have the technology or ability to truly investigate them."

"If there are other dimensions, could organisms there

crossbreed with organisms here?" Drake queried.

"Mr. Fraser," Mr. Ferris responded with a chuckle, "that's a bit of a stretch, and yes I do enjoy intellectual discussions, but I also have a lesson plan to follow. You won't be getting your class out of homework by continuing to ask hypothetical questions."

Drake looked down, feeling ashamed. Stacey shook her head at her friends, the popular girls sitting toward the front of the class, who were all looking back at the two of them.

"Now, make sure you all do the assignments at the bottom of page two hundred sixty-one, and include a series of Punnett Squares for all of your answers," Mr. Ferris announced. "And because Mr. Fraser is so curious, I want you all to research crossbreeding of species, such as the lion and tiger, or the horse and the donkey, and write a one page paper on the limitations of such a genetic union."

Paper balls flew at Drake from around the classroom.

"Thanks a lot, new kid," came a chorus of similar statements from many of his peers.

The bell rang and the classroom emptied out in a rush of commotion and an orchestra of chairs sliding upon the tile floor, tempered with an eruption of student voices. Many of the voices still dripped with sarcasm directed in Drake's direction.

Stacey quickly and quietly moved out of the room without even saying 'see you later,' like she had every day since Drake first arrived at Columbia River. Drake slowly shuffled toward the door. His life couldn't get much worse than what it had become.

I certainly don't need no teachers,
Tellin' me it'll all be good,

"Fraser," Mr. Ferris stated with a raised hand. "Thanks for the good questions, sorry about the extra work. Oh, and mythology's ripe of examples of beings from one dimension crossbreeding with beings from Earth—they were called demigods."

Drake turned and left the room.

Get a clue, it ain't ever gonna be good,
Its all just another piece of straw,
And the camel's back can't hold anymore straw,

Before basketball practice, Drake once again heard the sounds of the mysterious person working out all by himself in the weight room. He was curious, but never had a chance to open the door, because Coach Arthaud was always yelling at him to hustle out on to the court and start practice. Drake had given himself extra time today to peer inside the door.

His hand quickly found the knob of the door as he slowly strolled toward the court. With a sudden turn, Drake began to pull the door open.

"Hey pansy!" Moose yelled from behind Drake. "You're so scrawny that you need to go into the weight room. You're freaking ridiculous and shouldn't even be on my team."

Drake hated paying basketball with this team. He hated Columbia River High School and wished he could go back in time and fix things so he wouldn't have to be there.

The team started practice, running, balance lines, and the daily dozen, just like every other day. Then the freshman and C-Teams broke off for the auxiliary gym. Coach Arthaud took the varsity and had them scrimmage against each other, going through situational drills, before finally letting them play five-on-five while the JV worked on something else on the other half of the court.

The starters—Jimmy, Danny, Steve, Reggie, and Moose—were schooling the bench players. Drake watched from the sideline near Coach Arthaud, as the starters continued to work the ball around the perimeter to either an open Downtown Danny who would fearlessly drain a long jumper, or to the athletic Steve who posted up either Bobby or the slow footed George and would easily score on either of them. The only solace Drake got in watching them scrimmage was that Moose was constantly being shut down by Ryan, the freshman gym rat.

In the games they'd played since Drake had moved there, this was always the case. The offense revolved around the very vocal senior forward, who constantly demanded the ball from his teammates, even if they'd a better look at the basket. Only Danny and Steve took their shots regardless of Moose's barking. But, neither of those kids took as many shot attempts as Moose. It was quite easy for Drake to see why the team was struggling. It was Moose, it was his team, and he was driving them right into the ground.

The bench players had the ball, down by twelve, and Ryan posted up the thicker Moose. Little O found him with a bounce pass.

"Ball! Ball! Ball!" screamed Moose, as he moved to block Ryan. The freshman did a quick head fake and jab step, convincing Moose that he was going off the block and into the paint. Just as quickly Ryan spun on his pivot foot and went baseline for an easy lay-in.

"Get it together, Caine!" shouted Coach Arthaud. "Or Healy will move up and you'll move down!"

The starters took the ball up the court, Reggie easily getting past the pressure applied by his brother Little O. The ball went out to Jimmy, drawing George out of the key and opening up the lane for Moose or Steve. Moose immediately started to yell.

"I'm open!" Caine bellowed. "Pass it to me, Jimmy!"

Back halfway between to the top of the key and midcourt, Downtown Danny had popped out and gotten complete separation from Chuck. Jimmy saw him and passed the ball to the open shooter. Without hesitation, Danny squared his feet and hoisted a thirty foot rainbow that hit nothing but net.

SWISH.

"ABA baby," Danny said as he turned and strutted back down the court. As a youngster, Danny longed to play in the now defunct American Basketball Association, where they always had a three-point line. His shot would've clearly been worth three points.

Chuck and Little O advanced the ball. Chuck found George open down low with a bounce pass. Moose moved over to help Jimmy cover George, giving George the opportunity to hit Ryan with a quick pass and an easy lay-in, but Moose was angered at being taken advantage of again and hit Ryan hard with his slashing right hand.

Moose raked Ryan's face, drawing blood from his nose. Coach Healy blew his whistle, and Ryan got first aid attention, keeping the blood flow to a minimum.

"Fraser," Coach Arthaud barked. "Get in there for Healy!"

I don't need your attention,

Drake sprinted onto the court. The game continued. Moose began pushing and slugging Drake, taking full advantage of Coach Healy being off taking care of his son. No fouls were going to be called. On defense, Drake was catching the thick meaty elbows of Moose to his body, neck, and occasionally the head. Drake's temper was rising, he knew he could play basketball at a higher level, he just had not shown it yet.

As a freshman last year, his old coach had him scrimmage against two big offensive lineman from the football team. Those two guys pushed him, bumped him, bruised him, and beat him, until one day when Drake had finally had enough. Drake began to push back, and used his height and athleticism to his advantage. That day was the day Drake began playing varsity basketball at his old school.

The next time down the court Moose called for the ball.

"I'm open!" Caine yelled. "Pass me the ball, the pansy can't stop me!"

The ball came into Moose who took it to the hoop for an easy lay-in. Out of nowhere the right hand of Drake pinned the ball to the backboard, blocking the shot.

Drake recovered the ball and passed it out to Bobby.

At the other end, the ball worked around the perimeter before going into George. George took a dribble and turned to the basket. Jimmy fell for his pump fake and the shot went up. Moose went for the block, like Drake had, but he missed the ball by about a foot. With a clank, the ball bounced off the far side of the rim, and into the outstretched hands of Drake. Moose quickly recovered and went hard into Drake's body. Drake dropped into a power dribble and shot upward, the ball in both hands and clearing the rim by nearly a foot before slamming the ball through the rim with authority over the top of the flailing Moose.

"Yes!" Coach Arthaud shouted. "That's what I've wanted to see from you, Fraser! Thatta boy!"

The rest of the practice was at the same pace, with Drake going hard against Moose, blocking every shot he attempted, clearing rebounds with ease, and driving home powerful two-handed dunks over the top of the angered Moose and the excited Steve. The final score of the scrimmage had the bench players ahead, forty-four to thirty-six, and they all high fived Drake, except for Moose.

"Bring it in!" Coach Arthaud shouted. "Great practice today, gentlemen. Coach Healy, is Ryan going to be okay?"

"Yeah," Coach Healy replied. "He'll be fine, his nose isn't broken."

"Today we saw the transformation to our new team, fellas," Coach Arthaud stated. "From now on, if he continues to play like he did today, Fraser's starting ahead of Caine. And I believe we can challenge the rest of the schools in our league with him, Downtown, and Steve. Hell, we might be the most under the radar team in the state, if we can pull it together and make districts, maybe even get to state if we're lucky. The River's rising gentlemen!"

The team was giddy about the possibility. Only Drake, who was still off in his basketball zone, and the brewing Moose seemed somber.

"Fraser on three!" Coach Arthaud shouted as the team put their hands in.

"One! Two! Three! Fraser!"

The team poured into the locker room. Moose followed them in, stopping for a moment to pound on the weight room door.

"Fraser," Coach Arthaud called out to Drake before he

had gotten too far away from him. Drake turned to face the coach. "Where's that been, son? I heard you were capable of playing at a higher level from your old coach. But I didn't think that was true after how soft you played these last few weeks. Anyway, I want you to know, I'm serious about you starting ahead of Caine tomorrow against Evergreen. The position's yours to keep, or lose. Just do what you did today, and it'll be yours until you graduate."

"Thank you, coach," Drake muttered as he turned and jogged into the locker room.

"Did I not tell you he was good?" Coach Arthaud said with a big smile upon his face to Coach Healy next to him. "I really do think we can compete for a district spot, I wasn't just blowing smoke up their asses when I said that. With three scorers and Fraser's defense, I think we make the playoffs, and who knows from there, who knows from there…"

Drake quickly got to the back of the locker room and opened up his locker and began changing clothes. He wiped the sweat from his body with a thick blue towel he brought from home. As he stood buttoning his shirt, some of the guys on the team approached him offering him high fives.

"Way to go Drake," Steve said in an excited tone. "You got me all wound up about how good we can be if defenses need to cover you down low too, that'll open me up for more open looks, and you can just clean the boards."

"Thanks Steve," Drake replied, as Steve patted him on the shoulder before disappearing somewhere else in the labyrinth of purple lockers that reeked of teenage body odor and overused cologne.

Drake began to notice a group of guys standing in a loose semicircle around him, a mixture of the varsity and JV teams. Between Jimmy and Bobby emerged the red-faced form of Moose.

I don't need your fake concern,

"Hey pansy!" Moose bellowed at Drake, pointing an accusing finger at him. "What the hell makes you think you can do that?"

"Yeah pansy," Jimmy concurred. "What the hell!"

"This is my team, you faggot," Moose continued, a trickle of spittle moved from his upper lip to his lower lip as he ranted. "You're not going to take my spot! Do you hear me, dickhead?"

Drake continued slowly buttoning his shirt, his heart bounding in his chest. Nearly twenty boys stood in a tight line, trapping him by his locker, and only Moose was inside the circle with him.

"Hey faggot," Jimmy added. "Did'ja hear Moose?"

Drake avoided eye contact, and put the rest of his stuff in his duffle bag, including his school shoes he needed to wear to leave the gym.

"I think he's retarded or something, guys," Moose stated, as he turned to face his teammates with a dorky smile on his face.

"Hey, Moose!" Ryan shouted through the crowd. "Leave Drake alone!"

"Shut up, freshman!" Moose retaliated, pointing out toward Ryan. "Or you'll get what he's getting."

Bobby pushed Ryan into the row of lockers knocking most of the defiance out of him.

"You better shut your trap, freshman," Chuck demanded, as he stuck a ruddy finger against Ryan's chest. "And don't run to your daddy either, got it?"

Ryan stood against the lockers, unsure of himself.

"Beat the dick up, Moose!" Jimmy shouted with a raised fist.

"Fight!" started a chant. "Fight! Fight!"

"Hear that, dick? They want me to beat some sense into you," Moose said raising his arms into a flexed position. He kissed his right bicep.

"Hey brotha Moose," Downtown Danny interrupted, as he stepped out of the circle of sweaty boys in front of Moose and Drake. Downtown did a funky moon-walk like dance move, and waved his hands like a rippling wave. "Fraser's coolio."

"Shut up, Downtown!" Moose snapped. He turned and pointed at the dancing Helms. "This ain't your fight! And why the hell do ya think you're black? You're the whitest kid on the team, dumbass!"

A dejected Downtown Danny faded back into the crowd, choosing to disappear rather than making this his fight.

"Fight!" the chant continued.

Drake zipped his duffle bag.

"Fight!"

"Dick, you ain't leaving yet!" Moose shouted. With a sudden movement he pushed Drake into the lockers. Drake hit the metal doors hard, denting the locker next to his, before sliding to the floor.

"Fight!"

Drake slowly got up, straightened his shirt, and closed his locker.

"Didn't ya hear me, dick, you ain't leaving yet!" Moose exclaimed, as he punched Drake in the abdomen buckling him over.

Moose turned and raised his arms to the crowd again, flexing and kissing both his right and left biceps.

"Fight!"

"Leave him alone!" George yelled at Moose from behind the wall of kids.

"Shut the hell up, Injun George!" Moose blurted back. "What're you gonna do, you pathetic piece of Indian crap?"

George looked around, what could he do? He was alone behind a throng of excited boys feverishly waiting to see Moose beat Drake up. George did nothing more.

Fear flooded the senses of Drake. A fear fueled by pain and failure.

I certainly don't need no teachers,
Tellin' me it'll all be good,

Moose turned to face Drake again. He hit him with his left fist in the shoulder. His right fist hit his lower ribs, once, then twice more in quick succession.

"All coach said was this kid, Drake Fraser, was gonna be good, help us get in districts," Moose went on. "Drake Fraser this, Drake Fraser that! To hell with Drake Fraser, from now on your name ain't Drake Fraser! Your name's Dick! Dick Faggot!"

"Faggot!" erupted a cheer from the assembled boys.

Drake rose up again, straightening his shirt, and grabbed his duffle bag. He knew the fight was pointless. Striking back would only justify the cause Moose sought to win. He just wanted to leave, to go home—all the way back home to Hoquiam.

"Faggot, where do ya think you're goin?" Moose shouted as a shower of spittle sprayed over Drake. Moose hit him fully on the left side of his face. Drake nearly blacked out from the force of the impact, but somehow remained standing. Moose closed in on him and began slugging him in his belly and ribs. He grabbed hold of Drake by his shirt, pulling him back into range, tearing the shirt and popping the buttons from the front.

"Come on, Dick Faggot," Moose said, as he clenched Drake's torn shirt. "You wanna leave? Tell the team what your name is! Tell 'em!"

Drake pulled his shirt free from Moose, his fight or flight instinct was welling up inside of him. He had stood and fought demons from the ethereal plane the summer before in his grandparents house, and knew he could beat Moose if he wanted to, but the rest of the team was another story. It was far better to flee at this point than engage them all.

"Come on, Faggot!" Moose said, as he hit Drake on the right side of his head, stinging his ear. "Tell 'em your name! You're name's Dick Faggot!"

Moose hit him again, and again.

"Tell 'em your name!" Moose shouted in a frenzy.

"My name is D..." Drake began, rising one more time before Moose, wiping a trickle of blood from his mouth. "Drake Fraser, the son of Drake Fraser before me."

Moose wasn't pleased and erupted in a frenzy of hitting. Drake covered his head with his duffle bag.

"Gerald!" yelled a deep booming voice from the back of the circle. "Let him go now, you pencil-necked, pea-brained, butterball!"

A massively large figure emerged through the circle of boys. Gone were the oversized sweatshirts and baggy pants, all that remained was a skin tight tank top, blue shorts, and tennis shoes. But what everyone noticed most was the muscle. Rippling muscle with corded, thick veins covered his glistening body. His skin was caramel, and his hair was black and wild. He had muscles on top of muscles. He had muscles where people don't normally have muscles. He was angry, his dark eyes glossed over in fury.

"Let him go now, Gerald!" James Kirk shouted.

"Don't even go there, you fat nigger!" Moose yelled back before he turned to see the approaching muscle-bound figure. Moose had always teased and tormented James since he was a little boy. James was obese as a toddler, and that carried over when he started school. James had been wearing large baggy clothes since elementary school to cover his fat and his insecurity. Moose hadn't seen what James had become after all these years of working out daily in the weight room—until that moment. "Dude, what the hell happened to you man?"

"Let him go!" the fury in James grew, as he advanced on Moose.

"Hey Captain Kirk," Moose said with a forced grin, raising his hands in front of him. The fear Drake had just possessed found a new home in the heart of Gerald Caine. "You and me, we're all good."

James Kirk did not like *Star Trek*, and he did not like being called Captain Kirk. With a titanic force he erupted into the taller Gerald Caine, knocking him backwards and upwards into the row of lockers behind him. As he slid down it was clear for all present to see that there was a body-sized dent across three lockers. Moose was unconscious when he hit the dirty cement floor. James bent down, grabbed

Moose's collar with his large left hand, and lifted him up. Upward Moose rose in the left hand of James, until Moose's feet no longer touched the ground. A wild, barbaric frenzy radiated from James' eyes and he slowly smiled. His right hand pulled back into a massive clenched fist, the muscles of his arm dwarfing those of anyone Drake had ever seen. With quick reasoning, Drake surmised that such a punch to a knocked out opponent like Moose might result in death. He acted, not to save Moose, but to save James.

"James, no!" Drake shouted. "He's not worth it."

James held his fist. Pondering Drake's words before he let Moose fall to the floor.

"You tell him," James said as he turned to the assembled boys, "if Gerald ever does anything like this again, I'll destroy him."

The boys nodded their heads not wanting to anger the behemoth that was James Kirk. James flexed his rippling muscles and let out a bellowing howl. The basketball team fled into the labyrinth of the locker room, except for Jimmy, Bobby, and Chuck who hung back and waited for James and Drake to leave so they could help Moose.

"Come on," Drake said, straightening his torn shirt one more time. "Let's get out of here."

"Don't think this means we're friends or anything like that," James said, as they walked for the door together. "Hey Drake, you okay? You look a little beat up."

"I'm good," Drake replied as they exited the locker room. "I mean, I have seen better days, but I'm okay. Oh, and James, thanks for helping me."

In the distance, Coach Arthaud began yelling at the boys to break it up.

"What's going on in here?" Coach Arthaud shouted, glad he had given the boys on his team time to work out their differences.

Get a clue, it ain't ever gonna be good,
It's all just another piece of straw,
And the camel's back can't hold anymore straw.

STAR WARS LUNCHBOX

THE BROTHERHOOD OF OLYMPUS AND THE TOWER OF DREAMS

10

To Seek Out New Life
Chapter Ten
February 7, 1980
Hazel Dell, Washington

A curious thing began to happen inside Columbia River High School. Over the next few weeks after the fight in the locker room people began to give Drake a wider berth as he negotiated the halls, sat in class, or helped the basketball team go on a winning streak that vaulted them into the District Four tournament—with the winning team earning a berth in the State Championships. The only constant was lunch time. Drake continued to sit at the geek table along with the thick form of James Kirk, who was still not his friend.

Drake was determined to know more about the mysterious James. Who was this guy that saved him? Why was he so much of an outsider? It became his quest, his search for knowledge, and he was only limited by the lack of information about the hulking boy. By February fourth, the day before the boy's basketball team would win its fifth straight game—Drake had found a source of information, a fellow student named Robert Cowan.

Robert was a short, pudgy sophomore with the thickest eyebrows Drake had ever seen, and a dark mock-afro for hair. He kind of shuffled as he walked, and didn't have many friends, but did count James Kirk as his dearest friend. His most notable feature was his bushy mustache, which was a full-on cookie-duster. He had the most facial hair of anyone in the entire tenth grade. Robert had been sitting next to James at the loser table every day for lunch but Drake just hadn't noticed him, beyond his eyebrows and very obvious mustache.

"Hey Robert," Drake said as he sat down across from the mustachioed boy. "I'm Drake, Drake Fraser."

"I know you," Robert replied, as he looked up from his lunch toward Drake. "You're in my English and Biology classes, and Scrappy has told me about you."

"Oh yeah, that's right," Drake stated, realizing that he did indeed have Robert in a couple of his classes. He chewed and swallowed a bite of his lunch. "Who's Scrappy?"

"You don't know who Scrappy is?" Robert queried with his thick right eyebrow raised. "I thought you two were buds now? You're all he ever talks about any more."

Drake's mind raced through the logical sequence of people he had met since moving to Vancouver. Not one reference emerged with a connection to anyone named Scrappy. The only outlier in his mental search that popped up was the television reference to the annoying little Great Dane puppy on the newer versions of *Scooby-Doo* cartoons— Scrappy-Doo.

Robert looked at Drake and he wondered what the tall lanky kid was thinking about so intently, but soon lost interest in watching him.

"Scrappy?" Robert questioned with both hands raised. "The big black kid everyone thinks is a fat freak? Doesn't like *Star Trek*, but suffers the ultimate irony of being named James Kirk?"

"James?" Drake asked.

"Guess you aren't his friend after all," Robert remarked with a boastful chuckle. "But guess what? I am. In fact, I'm probably his best friend."

"Why's he called Scrappy?" Drake questioned. "Is he here today?"

"Naw, he's not here. Only his friends call him Scrappy, so don't do it." Robert replied with a serious glint in his eyes. "He's takin' care of his mom. Whenever he misses school it's cause he's takin' care of his mom."

"Is she sick?" Drake inquired.

"She's got a drinking problem, son," Robert responded with a chuckle. "Not water, or soda, mind you. I'm talkin' about hooch! Ya know what hooch is don't ya?"

"Alcohol, of course," Drake answered in a rather monotone fashion. "Hooch is a colloquial term with unclear origins usually associated with the Prohibition Period in American history. Now more commonly used in the Southeastern region of the country and it's curious that you use the term, yet you lack most of the mannerisms associated with its residents, and you certainly don't possess the dialectic accent."

"How do ya know all that junk?" Robert questioned with another chuckle. "You're down-right freaky, almost like you're an encyclopedia, or like Mister Spock!"

Drake smiled and ate more of his lunch. He liked being referred to as an encyclopedia, almost as much as he liked being called Spock. Mister Spock had been a role model and personal hero of Drake's for many, many years.

"Don't tell Scrap I used a *Star Trek* reference, okay?" Robert pleaded. "He seriously doesn't like that TV show. He hates it."

"How long have you known James?" Drake asked.

"Since before Kindergarten, son," Robert responded. "Back when he started to get fat. You know how fat he is?"

"I know he's not fat," Drake replied. "I've seen him without his baggy sweats. Most of the basketball team saw him when he knocked Moose out, he doesn't have to hide behind what he used to be anymore."

Robert swallowed hard. Scrappy had hidden in his 'fatness' for years. It made him feel safe. Few people interacted with him, and most had stopped teasing him because they had thought he had just gotten pathetic. He worried about what his friend would have to do now if everyone knew he wasn't fat anymore.

"So," Robert began, hoping to change the subject away from his friend who wasn't here to defend himself, "I heard from a friend of a friend of Stacey Jansen—who is seriously cute, by the way. This friend said that Stacey said you are a drawer. Is that true?"

"Yeah," Drake replied. Of all his skills and talents, he possessed the most confidence in his artistic abilities. At his old school he was widely regarded as the best artist there. "I'm probably the best illustrator at this school, but I haven't had time to check out all the competition yet."

"Prove it," Robert announced with another chuckle.

Drake turned and opened his duffle bag and fumbled through it for one of his art tablets. He found one, pulled it out and flipped it open looking at the picture it landed on.

"Whoa!" Robert exclaimed. "That's awes!"

"Thanks," Drake replied.

"Is it a Ringwraith?" Robert queried excitedly.

"No," Drake answered.

"What book is it from then?" Robert hurriedly asked.

"It's not from a book," Drake began to explain. "It's a mordgeist. A death spirit, from the ethereal plane. I researched them a couple years ago, out of some books my brother Mark permanently checked out of the Hoquiam Public Library. So I guess it's from a book, and I'm kinda writing a narrative history, another book, about what they did to my brothers and me."

Robert was lost in the details of the illustration. The intricate cross-hatching Drake used to shade the robes were layer upon layer of different lines of black ink.

"So you're sayin' that's real?" Robert questioned.

"Yes," Drake replied. "Very real, I've seen them."

"Na-uh," Robert responded, after nearly choking on his sandwich. "That's crazy, son. Got anymore drawings?"

"Sure," Drake stated, as he began to flip a few more pages looking for something to show Robert. Drake wasn't sure why Robert, a fellow sophomore who might be a year, or maybe two years older at the most kept referring to him as 'son,' but it was beginning to irritate him. He stopped on a picture he had drawn of a thickly muscled barbarian with a blood splattered double-bladed battleaxe. He turned the tablet to show Robert.

"Oh my god!" Robert exclaimed, spitting out some milk from his mouth. "That's freaking awes! You have to show that picture to Scrap, he'll love it."

"Absolutely," Drake replied with a smile. The rest of the lunch was rather quiet with the exception of Robert going on and on about how awesome of a drawer Drake was.

On February fifth, Drake carried his lunch tray toward his accustomed seat at the loser table. At the other end of the table, Robert and James sat side-by-side. The moment Robert saw Drake, it began.

"Drake! Drake!" Robert practically squealed, waving his hand above his head. "Come sit with us."

Drake turned and headed toward that end of the table. The geeky unclean boys in the middle shifted down to let Drake have more room on the opposite side of the table from Robert and James.

"Have a seat," Robert instructed with a smile, barely visible beneath his thick mustache. Drake set his tray on the table and sat down. James didn't look up. He was eating his hot lunch rather crudely, almost like he was starving.

"Scrappy," Robert began, "this is Drake, Drake this is Scrappy."

"James," interjected James with a rumble. "Only my friends call me Scrappy, and you aren't my friend."

"Come on Scrap," Robert pleaded with a chuckle. "Drake's cool, and he's the best drawer ever. Show him the barbarian drawing Drake, show him."

Drake turned and opened his duffle bag, quickly found the art tablet and flipped pages until he came to the illustration in question. He turned the other pages on the spiral spine and revealed the drawing to James and Robert on the other side of the table.

"Awes!" James shouted with a big toothy smile. "That's so awes! Robert you were right, that's amazing. What's his name? That axe is killer. He kinda looks like a monster though, maybe a villain for Conan to fight. Is he from a Conan story?"

"Thanks, James," Drake replied with a smile that made his dimples pop out.

"Scrappy," James quickly responded. "All my friends call me Scrappy."

"Thanks, Scrappy," Drake added. "He's not from a Conan story and I don't know his name yet, but I know he's evil. In my dream he killed a good guy and took his axe."

"Have you read any Robert E. Howard?" Robert asked.

"I've read a few stories, compilations mostly," Drake answered. "*The People of the Black Circle, The Hour of the Dragon, Red Nails*, and a couple more, but I also have read a number of the pulp Conan comics Marvel has published."

"I've always loved Conan," Scrappy added.

Drake liked the raw adventure and fantasy settings that Howard created in his Conan adventures, but he preferred the elegant prose, wordy descriptions, and epic fantasy of Tolkien. Drake decided trying to make that distinction wasn't important with Scrappy.

"Did ya know they are making a Conan movie?" Scrappy announced. "With Arnold Schwarzenegger, he's an awesome body builder, three-time Mister Universe, and seven-time Mister Olympia."

"That's pretty cool," Drake said. "But can he act?"

"I don't care, it's a Conan movie," Scrappy replied with a smile. "My ultimate dream has been to fight Conan, to the death."

"Isn't he a good guy though?" Robert questioned.

"Yeah, kinda," Scrappy answered. "He's a barbarian, they aren't necessarily good, but sometimes they do what's right. So maybe, my ultimate dream should be to fight that barbarian monster you drew Drake, to the death."

"In my dream he was pretty badass," Drake added, as he chewed some of the oddly flavored school lunch. It smelled like hamburger, but tasted more like processed fish.

"Okay," Scrappy said with a wide smile. "My new

ultimate dream is to fight both your monster barbarian and Conan to the death. Just not at the same time, because that wouldn't be fair."

"Scrap," Robert stated with concern for his friend. "Dreaming about fighting some fictional character to the death isn't a good life goal. I worry about you, son."

"Worry about me?" Scrappy responded, as he smiled and patted Robert on the shoulder. "I said it wouldn't be fair to fight them both at the same time, and it wouldn't be, for them."

On Wednesday, February sixth, the buzz at Columbia River High School was all about the boy's basketball team and how they won their fifth straight game the night before. Statistically, if they won one more game they could qualify for their first trip to the playoffs in years. Much of the victory was being credited to the stellar play of Drake Fraser. He scored twenty points and grabbed fourteen rebounds, and he also managed to block six shots down the stretch to seal the win. As students passed the loser table they made comments like, "Great game Fraser," or "Go River!" Even the geeky boys at the other end of the table seemed to be enjoying the popularity that came from sitting near Drake.

"Sometimes I think Mr. Ferris is just making things up as he goes," Robert droned on. "I mean that whole numerical sequence that exists in nature? I think that is a case of too many eggheads sitting around trying to figure out how a puzzle is put together but not having any idea what picture the puzzle is supposed to make."

"Fibonacci," Drake added. "The number sequence does appear a lot in nature. It's pretty cool, the sequence is: zero, one, one, two, three, five, eight, thirteen, twenty-one, thirty-four…"

"My god, Spock," Robert interrupted, as Scrappy nudged him for using a *Star Trek* reference. "Knock that crap off."

"It's easy," Drake explained. "The next number is always the sum of the previous two. Zero plus one is one,

one plus one is two, and one plus two is three, and so on."

"Well, that makes way more sense," Robert stated, as he rubbed the soreness from his shoulder from the brute force of Scrappy's nudge.

"So these things you draw," Scrappy changed the subject, as he came up for air from his lunch. "They're all real?"

"Yeah," Drake responded. "Mostly, I mean, they all come from myth and legend, and most of them have at least some measure of truth to them. And some I have seen in my dreams."

"Cool," Scrappy said.

"I see lots of things in my dreams, that don't mean they're real," Robert argued.

"Well," Drake added after he swallowed some of his lunch, "I've been informed that my dreams are more reliable than the outcomes of some of the government's ultra-covert psychic spies."

Robert nearly choked on his food.

"Government psychic spies?" Robert pondered, as he caught his breath. "Is that why you asked Ferris about psychic abilities a couple weeks ago, Drake?"

"Maybe," Drake replied with a curt smile.

"So this badass barbarian," Scrappy continued, "you think he's real?"

"Probably," Drake said, as he thought about how many times he had dreamt about the barbarian and the clarity of the dreams.

"Then I want to fight him," Scrappy added with a smile. "I'm just sayin'."

"Listen son," Robert began with a chuckle, "Conan, that barbarian Drake drew, *the Lord of the Rings*, Bigfoot, and the Loch Ness Monster all have one thing in common—they're all f-i-c-t-i-o-n, fiction."

"May I sit here, brother?" a deep voice questioned from behind Drake.

Drake turned to see the large form of George Kalama,

wearing a green plaid shirt, and old blue jeans. He held a worn paper sack in his hand. Drake turned and looked toward Robert and Scrappy. Both boys kind of shrugged. Drake took that as a yes.

"Sure," Drake said, as he moved down to give George more room. The geeky boys at the other end of the table clustered tighter together.

"Why'd you call Drake your brother?" Robert asked. "Are you both Indians?"

"Drake is my basketball brother," George replied. "He brings honor to our team, and has been my friend."

"Wait a minute," Scrappy interjected, as he looked up at George for the first time. "I thought Indians did the whole blood-brother thing, does that mean you guys cut your hands and shared each other's blood?"

"That is true," George said, as he pulled a sandwich out of his brown paper bag. It was wrapped in an old newspaper and he took his time opening it up, folding each piece of paper back out of the way. Robert stared at him. "Indians still do blood-brothers, but that's a deeper bond, like you're now part of each other's families. Drake and I are basketball brothers, we're on the same team, we face the same foes, and that makes us brothers."

"That's awes!" Scrappy said with a smile. "I like that a lot. I've never had a brother. I'd like to have a battle brother."

George said something very quietly and raised his face upward toward the ceiling, and then he grabbed his peanut butter sandwich and began to eat it.

"What the hell was that?" Robert asked with a chuckle and a raised bushy eyebrow. "Did you just pray to eat a peanut butter sammich? Are you a priest? Do ya want to be a priest? Or maybe a monk? Hey, aren't monks all brothers?"

Scrappy rolled his eyes and Drake shook his head.

"No," George replied once he finished chewing his bite of sandwich and swallowed it. "I'm not a priest, and I don't wanna be one. That wasn't a prayer, it was more like a thank you to the great spirits for providing me with the food I was about to eat."

"That's pretty cool," Scrappy stated.

"So George," Robert began with a chuckle. "You don't mind me calling you George, do ya?"

George shook his head.

"So George," Robert continued, "you're like an athlete, a senior, and an Indian. You can sit anywhere in the cafeteria, so why sit here?"

"Well," George responded, "after the fight in the locker room, I felt bad because I couldn't do more to help my brother Drake. My uncle Freeman took me to a sweat lodge and I asked the great spirits what I could do to fix it, and I was told to be better. That's what I'm going to do. I'm going to be a better person, a better friend, and a better brother."

"You asked the great spirits? Okay," Robert stated, as he thought of how to proceed. "When you walked up here, the three of us guys were talking about fictional creatures, characters from stories, monsters, myths, and legends. As an Indian spirit talker, what do you believe, are things like that real?"

"The customs of my people say that all things possess a spirit," George answered between bites of his sandwich. "There are many stories of the great changer who traveled around changing things—people into rivers or mountains, wolves into the Quileute tribe—or stories of brother bear, or Raven the trickster. There are even tales of the Sasquatch."

"Robert," Drake said, before he took a quick drink of his milk, "the world is a big place, and there are many things we haven't officially discovered or quantified because scientists haven't been able to do empirical studies on them."

"What was the tallest mountain in the world before Mount Everest was discovered, my friend?" George questioned Robert.

"How would I know, I wasn't alive back then," Robert replied with a chuckle. "Mount Fuji, or one of the Alps? I don't know, hey, help me out Mister Spock."

Drake acknowledged Robert, but was trying to finish chewing before he answered. Scrappy nudged Robert with his big forearm because of the *Star Trek* reference.

"Ooww," Robert responded.

"Mount Everest was still the tallest," George answered his own question. "Just because humans hadn't ever seen it, didn't mean it never existed. It was always there, since it was first created, long before humans."

"There are lots of cases like that," Drake added. "For instance, in the upper Congo jungle there were legends of a hairy wild-man who lived in the mountainous regions. Scientists discredited the whole legend, until 1902, when the mountain gorilla was first documented by modern science."

"So you're telling me that things like Sasquatch are out there wandering around, like a freaking gorilla?" Robert responded with a loud chuckle. He turned to the geeky boys at the other end of the table. "What'd ya think of that guys? Welcome to the weird-ass loser table!"

The next day, Robert, Scrappy, Drake, and George sat at the far end of the loser table as they had the day before. The students who passed by said things like, "Good luck tonight Fraser," or "Go River!" The geeky boys began to say thank you to the well-wishers who wandered by.

"I'm just sayin' some things are called that for a reason," Robert said with both his bushy eyebrows raised. "Fic-tion, the barbarian from your dream, Drake, is just that—from a dream."

"I'm gonna fight him," Scrappy stated with a wry smile. "To the death."

Robert shook his head and chuckled.

"Scrap," Drake began with a smile, "where did the nickname come from? I could see you being called Conan, or something barbarian-like."

"I don't like to talk about it," Scrappy replied somberly. "But since you're my friends, my lunch table brothers, I guess

I can tell you."

Scrappy and George high-fived across the table, he really liked the concept of brotherhood.

"My dad's black and my mom's white. I'm what's called a mulatto." Scrappy stated. "I know that word because I was called it so many times when I was little by my dad that I thought it was my name. Anyway, my dad didn't like being a dad. There's too much responsibility and crap like that, so he up and left. I haven't seen him since I was four. Before he left he used to get so mad if I made noise, so I learned how to live in silence. Ever hear that song from Simon and Garfunkel, *the Sound of Silence*? That became my song, silence was my best friend."

Robert shook his head and frowned. Drake and George looked at Scrappy mournfully.

"Anyway," Scrappy continued, as he wiped his eye, "after my dad left, my mom started drinking and I got fatter and fatter. The bigger I got the more I got teased and tormented. To cope with it all I ate, and ate. So I got bigger and fatter, but on the inside I got smaller and smaller. Almost insignificant, but I loved reading about warriors and high adventure and dreaming that some day I could do that, but I knew the truth—I was a fat nobody. Then one day, I'm watching TV and I see this new little dog on *Scooby-Doo*. He's so small and insignificant, but when everyone else runs away from the monster of the week he stands up to it, because he has heart and courage. And I thought, I want to be like that, to be like *Scrappy-Doo*, to be like Conan. So I began to work out, and I have lifted weights everyday since."

"Now you're Scrappy the Barbarian," Drake stated with a smile.

"Hell yeah, I am," Scrappy replied with a wide smile. "And your battle brother against a common foe, Gerald Caine."

Drake and Scrappy high-fived across the table and the boys turned back to their lunches. Another basketball player approached the table carrying a *Star Wars* metal lunchbox.

"Hey," Ryan Healy said, as the four boys at the end of the table turned to look at him. "Can I sit here with you?"

"Aren't you a freshman?" Robert questioned with a raised eyebrow. He pointed down to the other end of the table. "No freshmen allowed at this end, you can go sit down there with those guys."

"Ryan's also my basketball brother," George stated. "And he stood up against Moose, so he has the same common foe as Drake and Scrappy."

Scrappy looked at Drake and George, he shrugged his shoulders and returned to his lunch.

"Have a seat," Drake said.

"Geez," Robert whined. "Are you kidding me? Since when do we accept outcasts at the loser table, son?"

Drake, George, and Scrappy all looked at Robert, and he immediately realized the absurdity of his question. Ryan sat down and set his lunch box on the table before him.

"Nice lunchbox, did ya steal that from a second grader this morning on the bus, son?" Robert questioned with a chuckle. "Where have you been sitting at lunch all year freshman? I mean its kind of late in the year to up and change seats."

"Over there," Ryan replied as he turned and pointed to a table occupied by well dressed boys. "With my friend Houston."

"Say what son?" Robert asked rhetorically. Ryan wondered why Robert kept calling him son, because he obviously wasn't his son. "You're friends with that preppy snob, the rich kid with the big eyebrows?"

Scrappy turned and looked at Robert in disbelief.

"Kid with the big eyebrows!" George interjected, almost choking on his food. "Well that's one of the best examples of the pot calling the kettle black I've ever heard."

"You're just jealous cause I've got hair enough for three sweet mustaches on my face, and you got nothing," Robert quipped with a chuckle.

"Did you use to talk this much before we started sitting

here, Robert?" Drake asked.

"Yeah, all the time. You've heard of the fountain of youth? Well I'm the fountain of truth, and it'd be a crime if I didn't share it with you, son, " Robert nodded. Scrappy shook his head. "Hey George, how far does this brother stuff go? I mean, aren't we all brothers in some sense, based on your rules?"

"Only if you looked for a common foe all humanity fought," George replied.

"Like taxes," Robert remarked with a chuckle.

"Or death," Scrappy added.

"Brotherhood's more than a common foe, guys," Ryan interjected.

"The freshman speaks," Robert quipped.

"We've been reading the *Odyssey* in Mrs. Mulkey's class, and she's been going over a lot of the origins of Greek words," Ryan continued, doing his best to fit in. "The Greeks had a word for brotherhood, *Philia*."

"Brotherly love," Drake interjected. "Delphi meant city, so Philadelphia is literally the city of brotherly love."

"Mrs. Mulkey said that the Greeks were smart to split love up into four different words, *Agápe*, *Éros*, *Philia*, and the other one. I keep forgetting the other one," Ryan added.

"We all had Mrs. Mulkey for freshman English, son," Robert said with a chuckle. "We've heard her whole 'Choose Love' lecture she does, and it would make a lot of sense if everyone did it."

"But they don't," Scrappy added. "Just look at Gerald Caine. You think that pinch-eyed butterball loves anyone but his own ugly self?"

"True that, son," Robert remarked in agreement.

"You keep using that word," Ryan stated in confusion. "I don't think you're using it correctly. James isn't your son, and I know I ain't your son."

"It's just kinda my thing, freshman," Robert replied with a chuckle. "It's like how in some old movies the guys are always calling each other Mac, or Joe, or some other name. I just use son."

"I think it sounds kinda stupid," Ryan rationalized. "It's like you're trying to be cool, using some hip vocabulary, but it isn't working very well."

"I was curious about that too," Drake added with a smile.

"Shut up Spock," Robert quickly replied with a smile.

All five of the boys at the end of the table laughed. The geeky boys at the other end took notice and joined in their laughter.

"What are you guys laughing about?" Robert said loudly, as he pointed down at the other end of the table, and then laughed harder himself.

"You know," George began philosophically, "I think Ryan brought up a good point."

"That I sound stupid saying son?" Robert remarked.

"Well, yeah, but I meant the whole choosing love thing," George added. "I think *Agápe* love—unconditional love—can be even more powerful when combined with *Philia* love, or *Éros* love. I'd forgotten about Mulkey's love lecture. That was like three years ago, man."

"Really?" Ryan questioned enthusiastically.

"Yeah," George stated. "Choosing to love each other unconditionally makes the bond of brotherhood stronger."

"I like that," Scrappy added, as he finished his lunch.

Ryan looked at each of the boys, gauging the thought racing in his mind. George looked the most at ease with the subject.

"I love you, George," Ryan announced with a smile.

"I love you too," George replied.

"I love you, Drake," Ryan continued.

"I know," Drake stated without emotion.

The other boys at the table laughed again.

REJECTED

THE BROTHERHOOD OF OLYMPUS
AND THE TOWER OF DREAMS

Go River
Chapter Eleven
February 29, 1980
Hazel Dell, Washington

Thursday, February seventh, the Columbia River boy's basketball team won their sixth straight game and mathematically qualified for the district playoffs. They finished their season strong, winning the rest of their games, even beating league favorite Fort Vancouver at home in front of a thunderous crowd of River supporters and students.

As February drew to a close they entered the district playoffs as a low seed and drew a tough opening game against Kelso. Downtown Danny led the team with thirty-five points, Steve added twenty-eight, and Drake contributed twenty-four, as the Chieftains rolled over the higher seeded Hilanders. The following Thursday, Columbia River played Hudson's Bay for the third time, and beat the Eagles convincingly 73-38. On Saturday, they faced off against Evergreen with a chance to play for a state bid if they won.

The Plainsmen were a difficult team to match up with for the Chieftains, but the athleticism of Steve and Drake ultimately won the game 59-58. The school had gone crazy. One more win and they were in the state championship tournament, but the best team in their league, the Fort Vancouver Trappers, awaited them.

On February twenty-ninth, they played for the district championship. With two minutes to go in the game, River was up by four, 45-41, and Steve Johnson was called with his fifth foul and was out of the game. Moose went into the game for him.

The Trappers made both free throws, bringing them within two, 45-43. Reggie brought up the ball methodically.

"Run the clock!" Coach Arthaud yelled. "Pass the ball!"

The ball went out to Downtown Danny, who passed it to Drake who passed it back to Reggie. The clock was down to just over a minute left in the game. The Chieftain bench was about to explode. With a minute left the ball went to Jimmy. Moose had posted up on the right block and began calling for the ball.

"Ball! Ball! Ball!" Moose yelled, as he fought and pushed the Trapper guarding him. Jimmy looked to make the pass to his friend.

"Pass it around, Jimmy!" Coach Healy yelled from the bench.

Jimmy listened and passed to ball back out to Downtown Danny who put up a long shot that hit nothing but net. A whistle blew from below the basket as the shot went up, however.

"All ABA baby, all ABA!" Downtown Danny shouted, as he flicked his hand mimicking the shot.

The baseline official came out on to the court waiving off the shot.

"Offensive foul on two-four, purple!" the official yelled to the scoring table, as he held up two fingers then four fingers. Moose Caine was called with the offensive foul and the turnover.

"What!" yelled Coach Arthaud, as he came off the sideline and approached the official. "The basket counts! The basket counts!"

"Your man was pushing, and I warned him twice, then he threw an elbow against their man," the official explained.

"Moose!" Coach Arthaud bellowed. "Get your head out of your ass, son!"

Fort Vancouver got the ball. Fifty-eight seconds remained in the game. They worked the ball up the court under the pressure applied by Reggie and Downtown Danny. With forty-three seconds to go they worked the ball around the perimeter, looking for an opening down low. The clock was running down.

"No fouls!" Coach Arthaud shouted to his team.

With twenty-two seconds remaining the ball went in to the Trapper center, who got Jimmy out of position and put up a soft floater toward the rim. Drake came out of nowhere to emphatically block the shot out of bounds. Drake wagged his finger silently saying, 'no, no, no,' as the Chieftain bench all stood up and cheered. Steve waved a towel over his head.

"Great block son," the baseline official said to Drake, as he walked up to him. "But, this is your warning, any more taunting and I'll call a technical on you, got it?"

Drake nodded and got set up in the half court defense, they were still in man-to-man. The Chieftains raised their arms and prepared for the inbounds play.

The Trappers passed in the ball, and ran the clock some more looking for something their coach had pointed out along the sideline as they set their inbounds play. With five seconds to go, they found it—the Chieftains had been switching defenders down low because Moose was slow, and with the last switch Moose was in man coverage on their center. The ball went into their big man, who did a power dribble and put up a shot. Moose hit him hard across the arm as the shot went up, hoping to make him miss. Both Drake and Jimmy were too far out of the key to do anything. The shot rolled on the rim twice, and fell in. The official called the foul with the obvious 'count the basket' arm motion. With no time on the clock, the Trapper center took a free throw. The ball hit the front of the rim and bounced high in the air before falling through the rim. Fort Vancouver had won 46-45, and punched their ticket to the state basketball tournament. The miraculous season was over for the Chieftains. Some things in life are just not meant to be, but some could argue at times that the ride along the way is more important than the destination.

On the first day of March, following the loss in the

district championship game, there were many students who passed Drake in the halls or at lunch who said things like, "Great season, Fraser," "Better luck next year," or "Go River!" Lunch at the loser table now included Robert, Scrappy, Drake, George, and Ryan. Some of the geeky boys even sported Columbia River spirit wear.

Drake thought how horrible Moose must feel knowing he was personally responsible for a five point swing in the last two minutes that cost them the game. Losing like that in your last game of your senior year would be tough.

"All I have to say," George stated, "is that my senior season was the most memorable I ever had. We made the playoffs and we're two points from making state, all because of my brother Drake Fraser."

Drake blushed.

"I can't wait to see what we can do next year with you for a whole season," Ryan chipped in with a smile. "I'll miss our senior though, love you George."

"I love you, too," George replied with a smile. Robert rolled his eyes.

"I love you, Drake," Ryan added.

"I know," Drake responded.

"I just want you to know how creepy and wrong that sounds for a bunch of guys to be saying they love each other," Robert stated with both bushy eyebrows raised.

Two boys approached and sat at the table with them. Steve Johnson sat on the side next to Robert, and Downtown Danny Helms sat down on the side with Ryan, Drake, and George.

"You don't mind if we join you, do you?" Steve said. Robert shook his head quickly. Steve Johnson was one of the most popular boys in school. Having him sit next to Robert probably raised Robert's cool rating by at least fifty points or more among his peers, and certainly way more than that among the girls.

"Hey, that's a sweet mustache, son," Downtown Danny stated, with a quirky smile and a side-to-side head move.

"How long did it take you to grow it?"

"It just grows," Robert replied with a smile. "I've had it since fourth grade."

"Yeah, he has," Scrappy added, before changing the subject. "This isn't exactly the cool table, so why'd you guys join us?"

"Just the other day," Downtown Danny answered with and exaggerated hand movement, "I was telling my bud, Steve here, that this table was beginning to corner nearly all of the coolio factor in the school, and it sports quite the brain trust, with all the brainiacs over here."

Steve nodded his head.

"Now, we could've just hung out over there with the other jocks," Downtown Danny continued, "or we could shift the seismic scales a bit and rock the world for the common folk! So, my man Steve and I decided to stroll over here and make this the epicenter of cool, if ya'all can handle my radiant glow?"

"You both are my basketball brothers, and are welcome here," George stated, Drake, Scrappy, Robert, and Ryan nodded their heads in agreement.

"I love you, Downtown," Ryan added with a goofy smile.

"Whoa!" Downtown Danny exclaimed, as he stood up and brushed his clothes. "My coolness makes all the ladies love me, but I don't play for the other team, son!"

The boys laughed.

"He meant like how brothers, or family members, love each other," Drake clarified, Downtown Danny smiled and sat back down.

"It's cool," Downtown Danny responded with a smile and his side-to-side head movement. "I knew that, brotha Drake. We all are one big happy family, am I right?"

No one answered because Jimmy, Bobby, Chuck, and Moose began to move past the table.

"Hey Dick," Moose yelled at Drake. "Thanks for costing us the game. You couldn't get over and help on defense? Couldn't help out your teammate? No blocked shot? You're a freaking joke, Dick Faggot!"

Scrappy's eyes turned wild, the table began to shake as he started down the short path to eruption.

"Scrap!" Drake exclaimed, as he put his hand on Scrappy's clenched fist. "He's not worth it."

"Hey Moose," Steve said, as he stood up to look eye-to-eye with the senior. George, Ryan, Downtown Danny, Robert, and the entire group of geeky boys stood to support Steve. "You need to figure it out, man. You're wasting all of our oxygen over here with all of your huffin' and puffin'. So you don't like Drake, we all get it, now get over it. A lot of us do, and you're making lots of people not like you. Is that truly how you want your senior year to end? Your last lingering memory of high school will be how big a douche-bag everyone thought you were? Stop being a waste of human flesh, man."

Moose looked at the assembled group of boys before him, he looked to his friends on either side of him, and then to the massive form of James Kirk clenching the table and cracking the wood in his hands.

"Come on guys," Moose announced, as he turned and walked away. "This isn't over, Dick."

"Hey Gerald!" Ryan shouted. "Be better! Choose love!"

Moose flipped Ryan off over his shoulder as he walked away.

RAVEN AND THE KEY

THE BROTHERHOOD OF OLYMPUS AND THE TOWER OF DREAMS

12

Raven and the Key
Chapter Twelve
March 16, 1980
Hazel Dell, Washington

School went on, and the boys at the new cool table stayed together at lunch every day. Drake was beginning to feel roots being planted. He started doing more things with his mom again, repairing the bridges that were broken the previous year. He volunteered to accompany his mom on her weekly excursion to get groceries, something he used to do a lot of when he was younger because he loved spending time with his mother, and she always used to get him a treat or two at the store. In fact, that was how he got each of the three books of *the Lord of the Rings*.

At home he was typing more of his notes into what he called his manuscript. He had typed so much, counting pages with mistakes that he couldn't fix and had to throw away, that he needed to get more typing paper soon.

The parking lot at the Fred Meyer on Pacific Highway, old Highway 99, wasn't too full for a Sunday morning when Drake and his mom pulled the family van in. Usually on a Sunday the parking options were slim, but today they were able to park right up in front of the store.

"Most people are either outside," Mom stated, as she shut the motor off, "or they're at church, so this shouldn't take too long." She was referring to the unseasonably sunny and warm, nearly spring day. Drake knew that if he had stayed home his dad would've given him a list of chores to do outside.

Drake unbuckled his seat belt and climbed out of the

van. He walked around the front and joined his mother as they approached the automatic doors of the store. Above them the red stylized Fred Meyer sign's lights went out as they passed underneath. That happens a lot, Drake thought.

This store was one of the things Drake immediately liked about their new home. It had everything—groceries, toys, clothes, electronics, auto supplies, camping gear, home improvement supplies, and of course his favorite—books and stationery. He loved the smell of new books, and loved looking at pens, pencils, paper, tablets, and art supplies.

"Drake," Mom said, as she separated one of the shopping carts from the long line of other carts, "can you go get a box of crayons for Albert?"

Drake nodded.

"Just a box of twelve or twenty-four, not one of the big ones," Mom clarified, as she started to push the cart through the interior set of automatic doors.

Drake set off in the direction of the stationary and art supplies, but he didn't see his mom smile as he left. She also knew how much he loved that section of the store, and was glad to have her son reconnecting with her.

He quickly found the crayons, and compared the boxes available. Albert needed the crayons as a replacement for the ones he got at the beginning of the school year. He held up the box of twenty-four and the box of twelve, looking at the color options in each. He thought about how this would've been different if he were still in elementary school and needed new crayons.

He looked at the cheaper boxes of eight crayons hanging above the shelf. That's all he would've gotten back then. Albert was so spoiled, he thought.

Drake looked at the unit price of each box, and finally chose the box of twenty-four because the price per crayon was cheaper. He turned to go find his mom, and saw paper at the other end of the aisle. He casually walked over and looked at the assorted typing paper available. He needed more typing paper.

There was onion skin paper, carbon paper, fancier papers in smaller quantities, and two different kinds of white typing paper in reams. Drake picked up one of the reams, and he looked at the price of both types. One was three cents cheaper for five hundred sheets. Not much of a savings, but a savings none the less.

Drake put down the wrapped ream of paper he was holding and grabbed one of the other, cheaper reams of paper in its off-white wrapper, from the middle of the stack and pulled it carefully out so the whole pile didn't collapse.

He casually walked the rest of the stationery aisle before heading off to find his mom, somewhere in the grocery section.

Drake systematically walked the end of the aisles, looking down each that he passed until he found his mom in the cereal aisle. He casually turned and approached her cart, and slyly attempted to put the ream of paper in before she noticed.

"I got these crayons for Albert," Drake said, as he attempted to draw his mother's attention momentarily away from the cart. "They should last him the rest of the school year."

"Thanks son," Mom said, as she turned and put two large bags of puffed wheat cereal in the cart. "I'm sure he'll appreciate them."

"How much do you have left to get?" Drake asked.

"Drake, you know I go up and down each aisle," Mom replied. "The cereal aisle isn't even half way."

"Okay," Drake stated. "I was just curious."

"Hey," Mom said, as she found the ream of paper in the cart while putting a big box of *Corn Chex* in the cart. "What's this doing in here?"

"What's what doing in there? The cereal? You just put it in there, Mom, my brothers have to eat," Drake responded with a smile.

"You know what I mean," Mom replied, as she lifted up the ream of paper. "We don't need more paper. Go put it back."

"But Mom," Drake began to plead. "I'm almost out of the typing paper Martin got for me. I've been typing a lot recently now that basketball is over."

"Drake," Mom said with her scolding voice.

"Mom," Drake interrupted her. "Writing's what I enjoy, that and drawing. It keeps me out of trouble. I could be using the money to buy cigarettes like Mark if you'd rather have me do that."

"Fine," Mom relented. "But next time ask first. Don't just surprise me by putting things in my cart."

"Okay," Drake said as he walked past the cart, sliding a box of instant oatmeal next to the assorted cereal inside it. He smiled a wide smile, popping out his dimples. "I'll ask first next time."

Later, after they had stopped and gotten ice cream cones for the ride home, Mom and Drake arrived back at the house. Drake helped carry the groceries in, and found the ream of paper in one of the brown paper shopping bags. When all the groceries were brought in he bounded upstairs with his loot.

His room was a bit stuffy. The sun had been shining through his window all morning. He went over and opened the sliding window about halfway and glanced out at the majestic view of Mt. St. Helens some thirty miles away.

Living in Vancouver wasn't so bad, he thought. He had Fred Meyer, he had friends who were now his brothers—that made him smile, and there was this awesome mountain to look at from his bedroom window.

With a smile on his face he walked over to the desk area he had with the electric typewriter on it. He set down the ream of paper, moved the paper he had left out of the tray, put the ream in the tray, and then placed the extra paper on top of it.

Out of the corner of his eye he noticed movement on the ledge of the open window. Slowly he turned and was startled to see a very large black bird sitting on the window ledge inside his room. The bird was completely black, bigger than a crow, maybe twice the size of the biggest crow Drake had ever seen.

The big bird ruffled its feathers and beat its wings once, and Drake noticed it was carrying something with its right foot. It was something metallic, a cylinder of some sort with some protrusions on it, on what appeared to be a silver chain.

Drake immediately wondered what would make a large bird fly into his room. He had read stories of animals doing odd things, usually as a precursor to a natural disaster. Or maybe the bird was sick, or dangerous.

"Hey mister bird," Drake said as he started to move away from his desk. He scanned his room for his sword, Hikari, or the Staff of Orkan, both of the weapons were safely hidden in his closet. "Dang it."

Drake slowly walked toward the closet. The bird watched him intently, and hopped up on its left foot, making the metallic object it carried hit the ledge of the window with a clang. Drake reached the closet and slowly slid the wooden door open. Without taking his eyes off the bird, he reached in for the sword, but found the wrapped shape of the staff instead. He grabbed it and began to pull it out. The blanket around it began to fall away from it as he moved it out.

"Everything's just fine mister bird," Drake said in a comforting tone. The staff lit up in his hand, blue light coursed through the runic inscriptions along the length of Orkan.

"Aw Caaa!" the bird blurted. It started to flap its wings and puff up its feathers looking even bigger than before. "Aww Caaaa! Fine way to treat a guest! Pull a weapon on him! Aw Caaa!"

Drake took a step back. The bird looked like a big crow or raven maybe, but it spoke like a parrot. And it wasn't just random things either, its words made contextual sense. This was no normal bird.

"What're you doing in my room?" Drake questioned as he pointed the staff toward the bird.

"Aw Caa!" the bird replied with a fluster of feathers. "Settle down, Grandson of Martin the Nameless! I was there when you got that stick! Got that stick! Aw Caaa!"

"What're you talking about, bird?" Drake asked, as he took a step forward and leveled the tip of the staff toward the bird's head. Blue fire smoldered over the metal tip of the Staff of Orkan.

"Aw Caaa!" the bird responded. "Easy! Easy! Don't point that at me, it's dangerous! Dangerous! Aw Caa!"

"Who are you, and what do you want?" Drake demanded without moving the seething staff.

"Aw Caa!" the bird answered. "My people call me Raven! But I've many names! I, Raven, bring you a gift! A token from a friend! Aw Caaa!"

Raven bounded over to Drake's bed, dropping the metallic cylinder on the chain, then hopped back to the window.

"Aw Caaa!" Raven stated, as he raised his wings. "Be careful of the gift! The giver expects much from you! Keep it hidden! Aw Caaa! Aw Caa!"

Raven jumped out the window and took to the sky. Drake moved over to his bed to look at the gift, when suddenly Raven reappeared in his window.

"Aw Caaaa! Aw Caa!" Raven exclaimed. "Be cautious young Fraser! If I can find you, they can find you! You're not safe anymore doing nothing! Prepare! Prepare! War comes!"

Raven bolted out his window again, screeching "Prepare!" over and over again until he just kind of disappeared in a smoky black cloud about one hundred yards away in the sky.

Drake closed the window, locking it shut. He turned back to the gift on his bed. It was a key, an archaic skeleton key. He had seen one like it before in the possession of Miss Furfur, the librarian. He grabbed the chain and lifted the key from his blue bed covering. It fell into his hand as the chain slid through his fingers. Something moved to his left and he turned suddenly, with the Staff of Orkan raised defensively before him.

Along the wall between his window and the closet was a door. It was the same ancient looking wooden door with brass fittings that he had first seen in the basement of the Hoquiam Public Library. The secret Archive Room lay behind that door then. Drake had no idea what might be behind it now. Through the wall, there should be a plum tree and then the neighbors' fence below it. Perhaps this door would just give him a view into his neighbors' yard.

Drake moved up to the door, slid the key into the lock, and turned it. A click sounded and the door was free, moving gracefully on its heavy brass hinges. Slowly Drake pulled it open. Inside was the library Archive Room. He saw the well-tooled table, the book shelves, and the single hanging light bulb on a chain. Sitting on the table was a single sheet of paper. Drake propped the door open with one of his converse basketball shoes.

Cautiously he stepped inside the room, a room that shouldn't be there. In all rights he should be stepping out high over the yard below and into the branches of the plum tree. But the room was solid stone. He felt its structure beneath his feet. He took another step in and caught a whiff of something floral. He approached the table and looked at the paper. It was a handwritten note. It was addressed to him.

My Dearest Drake,

I am sorry I couldn't deliver this note in person. I cannot begin to tell you how much you mean to me. I will always be at your side, I am your one true love, and I will wait for you for as long as it takes. The gift, the key, is very important and very valuable. It will open this room wherever you need it, and as long as you keep the key, this room is yours.
Danger approaches you, but always remember that I will always love you…

Your Lady Forever,
Veronica Furfur
*Ps. You can return the books now, and keep them safely in
here. And thank you for the kind note when you 'checked'
them out.* ♥

Drake lifted the paper to his nose and the heady
fragrance of roses wafted around him.

It was a love note! To him! Drake had never gotten
anything ever from a girl, although part of that seemed a bit
wrong in his mind, but he knew it was true. A girl liked him,
and this wasn't just any girl, this was Miss Furfur, the older
librarian. She was a complete evolutionary step above girls.
Drake felt his heart beating faster.

He smelled the note again.

"Hey dillhole!" Albert shouted at Drake from the door
into his bedroom. "Mom and Dad are gonna be pissed you
put a door in their wall!"

"Do you not know how to knock?" Drake yelled back,
folding the note and sliding it into his shirt pocket.

"Whoa!" Albert said as he approached and peered into
the Archive Room. "How does this work? Did you build it?
Where's the tree? Can you fall through the floor? Is it safe?"

"Can you shut up?" Drake answered all of his baby
brother's questions.

"Tell me, or I'm gonna yell for Mom and get you in
trouble," Albert threatened. Drake knew Albert would do
such a thing. He had been doing it for years to get attention
from his older brothers. Once he had even hit himself and
told their parents that Drake had done it, just to get his
brother in trouble.

"Alright," Drake responded. "But only if you help me
experiment with it for a minute or two."

"Sure," Albert said with a wide grin.

"Okay," Drake replied, as he stepped out of the room.
"The first thing we need to see is whether or not it stays here
all the time."

"How do we do that, Drake?" Albert asked. He stood right next to his older brother.

"Well, let's just step outside the door and close it and see what happens," Drake explained. He and Albert did just that. They closed the door, Drake still held the key in his hand, and then he quickly opened the door back up. The archive door was still on his wall.

"Maybe it's like the light in the fridge, Drake?" Albert questioned. Drake pondered his question, and assumed it was a fair question.

"So, I need you to sit here on my bed and watch the door," Drake stated, as he walked to his bedroom door again. "And I will go back outside my room with the key, and you will let me know if the door stays there. Just like if the light stays on in the fridge after the door closes."

"Cool," Albert said, a flash of fear ran over his face. "But if you're gonna leave me alone in here can I hold your staff?"

"Um, okay," Drake replied. He handed the staff to his brother, who smiled at him.

"Okay," Albert announced. "Ready!"

Drake stepped outside and closed the door. Inside the room, Albert shrieked, and Drake quickly opened the door. Albert still sat on the bed and the archive door was still on his wall.

"What are you screaming about?" Drake asked.

"The door!" Albert frantically exclaimed. "It just kind of faded away."

"So possession of the key is literally the key," Drake added. "Come here, let's try something else."

Albert got up, holding the staff, and followed his brother.

"Watch the door one more time, I want to see what happens if I go over into Mark's room with the key," Drake said. Albert nodded.

Drake closed the door again. Albert resisted the urge to scream again as the solid wood and brass of the archive door slowly faded to nothingness, leaving the off-white plaster wall of his brother's room just like it had always been, before today.

From across the hall Albert heard Drake calling for him, through the bedroom door. Albert opened the door and stepped across the landing at the top of the stairs, past the bathroom and into Mark's open bedroom.

"Mark's gonna be pissed you're in here when he's gone," Albert informed his brother, as he stepped into his older brother's room.

"Look!" Drake exclaimed excitedly. "The door!"

Albert saw the archive door, its dark wood and heavy brass fittings on Mark's far wall.

"Whoa!" Albert shouted. He was stunned. "It moved rooms, that's cool, where does it open to in Mark's room?"

"Good question, little brother, let's find out," Drake answered, as he stepped up to the door and unlocked it with the key. It clicked and Drake slowly swung it open.

"It's exactly the same!" Albert excitedly announced.

"Maybe it is, we'll have to check," Drake explained, he grabbed one of Mark's matchbox cars off of one of his shelves and stepped into the Archive Room. He placed it on the table. He stepped back out, and walked to the bedroom door. "Come on. Let's go see if it's the same in my room."

Both boys left the room, and Albert closed Mark's door. They walked the short distance across the landing and into Drake's room.

"It's not there!" Albert yelled. "Mark's gonna be pissed that you lost his car!"

"Wait," Drake said, as he thought about the conundrum. "It has to work. I know, I think we left the door open in Mark's room. Go close it."

"I'm not goin' in there to close a magic door by myself," Albert stated, as he shook his head from side-to-side.

"I'll do it," Drake replied. He quickly left his room and headed back to Mark's room. Sure enough the Archive Room door was still on Mark's wall and open and the matchbox car was still on the table. Drake closed the door. He walked back out, closing Mark's door and walked back into his bedroom. Albert turned to look at him. "There, I closed it."

"Look, its back," Albert said excitedly, as he pointed to the heavy wooden door on the far wall.

"Now let's see what's inside it," Drake explained, as he walked to the door and pulled on the handle. It was unlocked and swung open with ease. Inside the room, the matchbox car sat on the table. "There it is! It's the same room, exactly the same!"

"That's so cool!" Albert shared in the excitement of the discovery with his brother. "Now what?"

"Well, now we need to see what happens with living tissue," Drake added from a very scientific perspective.

"Okay," Albert said in agreement. "Where are we getting' that?"

"Well, you're alive Albert," Drake replied. It took a moment before Albert realized what Drake had just said.

"No way, I'm not gonna do it," Albert said, as he started walking for the bedroom door. "Use the dog, Mo is alive too, ya know."

"That's true, but I can't ask her what she felt in the room with the door closed now can I?" Drake explained. Albert stopped and listened to his brother. That did make sense. "Besides, I'd do it myself, to be the first human to travel through a portal like that. It would be like Neil Armstrong, first stepping on the moon. But, I can't be sure you'd open the door, I know you too well, Albert. I'd step into the room and someone would call for you and you'd forget to let me out. The safest way is for you to go inside, and me staying out here to make sure you're safe."

Albert shook his head.

"I'll let you hold my staff," Drake added. "And I'll make sure to write your name in my manuscript as the first to travel through the mystic room. You'll be famous."

"Okay," Albert replied. "But I also want Mark's car, to

keep."

"Deal," Drake said, knowing that he could easily just tell Mark that Albert took the little car afterwards when he noticed it missing. He helped Albert into the room, and then he took one of his wooden chairs and put it in the Archive Room with Albert so he could sit down. "Okay, so just sit in here and I'll close the door, and step outside, then back in here. We know the room comes right back."

"Okay," Albert responded, as he took the little car and put it in his pocket. "Ready."

Drake gave him a thumbs-up, Albert responded with a thumbs-up of his own, and then Drake closed the door. He quickly opened the door to make sure Albert was still okay.

"Wow," Albert stated. "That was really fast, almost like you just opened it right back up."

"I did," Drake said. "Now I'm going to do what I said. Try to be aware of everything you can."

"Roger," Albert replied with a thumbs-up.

Drake closed the door. He walked out of his bedroom door, closed it, put the key in his pocket, and then opened the bedroom door again. The archive door was gone, with Albert inside it. He pulled out the key from his pocket, and the door was on the far wall once again. Drake walked over and opened the door.

"That wasn't as quick," Albert explained. "Am I still in your room or Mark's?"

"Mine," Drake answered. "That's next. You ready?"

"Ready," Albert said with another thumbs up and a toothy smile.

Drake closed the archive door, walked out of his room, closing the door. He quickly walked in Mark's room and pulled out the key. The Archive Room door appeared on the far wall, just like it had before.

Drake approached the door, pulling it open, but Albert wasn't there. His eyes opened wide, and his pulse thumped in his head. He closed the door and ran across to his room. The Archive Room door appeared and he quickly opened it,

Albert wasn't there either. Once again, he closed the door and ran across to Mark's room. Frantically he went to the Archive Room door as it appeared, but before he got to it, the door swung open by itself. Out stepped Albert.

"What took you so long?" Albert questioned.

Drake grabbed him in a big hug.

"What happened?" Drake asked. "Where were you?"

"Well," Albert answered. "I waited a minute but you didn't open the door, so I did, and you weren't there, neither was your room, or Mark's room. It was like an old building like a big church with books and junk. I rolled Mark's car on the floor and it went under a shelf so I stepped out to get it, but I couldn't reach it. Then I got back into the room and closed the door, but when I opened it, it didn't go anywhere. So I closed it again, and then opened it again, and presto I'm in Mark's room."

"Wow," Drake said. "I'm just glad you're safe."

"Let's do it again," Albert added with a smile. "But I need another one of Mark's cars cause I lost that one."

"I think that's enough for now," Drake answered. "I need to document what we already learned. Besides, there will be another time when we can experiment more and see where you went when you weren't here."

"Okay," Albert replied. "But we need to get Mark's car back too. I don't want him mad at you for losing it."

"I didn't lose it, you did," Drake clarified.

"That's not how I 'member it," Albert said. "Maybe I need another car to help me 'member it better."

Drake smiled at his conniving little brother and grabbed another matchbox car off Mark's shelf and gave it to Albert.

"Thank you," Albert stated with a smile.

13

DRAKE VERSUS QUATYL

THE BROTHERHOOD OF OLYMPUS
AND THE TOWER OF DREAMS

The Adventures of Dennis & Albert
Chapter Thirteen
March 20, 1980
Hazel Dell, Washington

Albert had tried to explain to Dennis, nearly every moment they were together the past four days, about what he did in Drake's room. He was excited about going through space from Drake's room to Mark's room, and he wanted Dennis to see it for himself.

Dennis for the most part didn't believe his brother and thought that Albert was probably up to something to try and get him in trouble with Drake. But, he also humored his brother because he knew that Drake might be up to something secret, just not anything as fantastic as what Albert had tried to explain.

"What makes you think you know how to do it?" Dennis inquired skeptically. He wore their dad's welding goggles on the top of his head. He thought he might need eye protection if what Albert said was true and they were going to be travelling through space and time.

"Duh," Albert replied, as they headed up the stairs toward Drake's room. "Don't be a dillhole, course I know how it works, I was there, 'member? All we need is the key."

"And what makes you think Drake doesn't have the key with him?" Dennis questioned his taller little brother, as they neared the landing at the top of the stairs.

"Geez, Dennis," Albert answered, as he cautiously opened Drake's bedroom door. "All clear."

Dennis followed Albert into Drake's room.

"Drake keeps it in the little metal box, the one he painted

red and blue," Albert added, as he headed toward the closet door. "He puts all of his good junk in this corner of his closet, under other things."

"How long's he supposed to be gone?" Dennis asked. "I don't want him to come in and find us in his stuff."

"Mom said he was staying a couple hours after school today," Albert answered, as he found and opened the red and blue metal box. The key was residing under a folded piece of paper that smelled funny.

"Let me see it," Dennis demanded. Albert shook his head, looked at the folded paper, held it up to his nose, and smelled it. He wrinkled his nose. "Ick, it smells like girl junk."

Dennis leaned in and smelled the paper.

"Perfume," Dennis clarified. "What is it?"

"Don't know," Albert said, as he unfolded it. Together the brothers read the note. They looked at each other.

"Ewwww!"

"Drake's got a girlfriend!" Dennis squealed with a smile. "Quick, put it away, he'd get pissed if he knew we saw it."

Albert refolded the paper, put it back in the box, and then pulled out the skeleton key on its long silver chain.

"How does it work?" Dennis asked.

"Look," Albert answered, as he pointed to the wall outside the closet. Both boys stepped out and saw the heavy wood brass-trimmed door, securely installed on the wall between the closet and the adjacent wall with the window.

"Whoa!" Dennis excitedly exclaimed. "That's so cool, show me how it works."

"Okay," Albert responded. He approached the door, slid the key into the lock and opened it. The door unlatched and easily swung open. Inside was the Archive Room, just as it was the other day. Drake's extra wooden chair was still sitting inside it. Albert quickly went back into the closet and re-emerged with the Staff of Orkan. "I need this too."

Albert handed Dennis the key, and then he stepped inside the Archive Room.

"Okay, this is what you need to do," Albert instructed, as he sat on Drake's chair. "You're gonna close the door, then leave Drake's room with the key and go into Mark's room. Once you do, open the door in there, and I'll be there."

"You're sure about this?" Dennis questioned.

"Yeah," Albert responded with a smile. "I did it a couple of times with Drake, just trust me."

Dennis closed the door. He shook his head. This wasn't going to work, or end well, or some combination of the two. He walked out of Drake's room, went over to Mark's room and was amazed to see the Archive Room door on Mark's bedroom wall, too. He approached the door and slid the key into the lock. It clicked and then the door easily opened for him.

"Boo!" Albert shouted, as he jumped out of the Archive Room.

"Ahhhhh!" Dennis screamed, as he ran in a circle. Albert laughed. "What the hell, Albert! That's not cool at all, damn it!"

"That was so funny," Albert wheezed.

"How did you get over here, is there a passage way?" Dennis questioned.

"No," Albert said. "I just sat on the chair and waited, and then when I heard the door unlocking I got up to scare you."

"What if it wasn't me?" Dennis asked. "What if it was someone from the church place you talked about, dillhole? Did you think about that?"

"No," Albert replied. "Do it again, close the door and go find me in Drake's room."

Dennis closed the door, making sure he had the key, and then left Mark's bedroom. He went into Drake's room and there was the Archive Room door again.

"This is crazy," Dennis said, as he approached the door. He slid the key into the lock, but the door was already unlocked, and Albert stepped out of the room.

"Maybe we should try it a different way," Albert stated.

"Like close the door here, and then take the key down to our bedroom. That'd be cool, kinda like an elevator."

"Okay," Dennis responded. "But it's my turn. Give me the staff!"

"No!" Albert refused loudly.

The boys struggled over the staff and tumbled into the Archive Room. As they wrestled on the cobbled stone floor, Albert kicked the open Archive Room door, dislodging the key from the lock. The boys couldn't hear it as it hit the carpeted floor of Drake's bedroom. They rolled into the table in the center of the room, pushing it into the single chair. They didn't see the motion of the door that originally started with the kick, which had opened it completely and now it was slowly closing.

"Give me the staff, dillhole!" Dennis shouted.

"No! Drake gave it to me," Albert argued, as they rolled on the floor all four of their hands on the staff. "It's mine!"

There was an audible click behind them. The door had closed. At that moment they both realized what had happened. Dennis let go of the staff and stood up. He brought the welding goggles down over his eyes and flipped up the darkened lenses. Albert got up and moved the table over a little bit so he could sit in the chair.

"This probably isn't good," Albert said.

"No duh, dillhole," Dennis replied. "If the room moved with me when I had the key, but only appeared if one of us was holding the key, then where are we now? No one's out there with the key."

"Where's the key?" Albert questioned.

"I left it in the lock, before you started fighting me," Dennis responded.

"Well if it's still in the lock then we should still be in Drake's room," Albert said. He all of a sudden sounded pretty smart to Dennis.

"Okay," Dennis said. "Then open the door."

"You open it," Albert snapped back.

"I'm not gonna open it," Dennis retorted. "You open

it!"

"You open it, you're older," Albert stated, as he held onto the staff tightly.

Dennis saw the apprehension on the face of his little brother and he thought what Mark or Drake would do for him. They would open the door of course.

"Okay, I'll open it," Dennis announced. He stepped closer to the door, flipped down the darkened lenses over his eyes effectively making him blind in the little amount of light inside the Archive Room. He opened the door. As it swung open he heard his brother behind him.

"Uh oh," Albert said.

"What?" Dennis responded. He turned and flipped up the dark lenses. "Uh oh what, Albert?"

Albert pointed outside the room. Dennis turned and looked. They weren't in Drake's bedroom anymore, or Mark's either. Both boys stood in the doorway and looked at where they were. The space outside the Archive Room was vast and open. It was simply enormous, like a cathedral that was constructed of red and gray stone. Pillars rose up high to the arched ceiling above. On the ceiling were painted images of men, gods, dragons, devils, and some things neither boy had ever seen before. Between some of the pillars and against the walls were high shelves filled with books and curios. Jars filled with all manner of organisms, odd little skeletons or skulls, a few things that looked like locked boxes, and a couple metal devices that resembled weapons occupied the spaces between the books. Beyond the shelves, there was a wide open space that had a series of chairs in what appeared to be a semi-circle facing a raised platform. On the platforms sat a gilded gold throne that from a distance looked like it had skeletal features adorning it.

"Close the door," Albert said. "We can just wait for Drake to come home and find us."

Dennis reached out and grabbed the door, and slowly began to close it.

"Wait!" Albert shouted. "We should go find Mark's car.

I rolled it out there. It went under one of the shelves."

"That's not a good idea, Albert," Dennis replied. "We're safer just waiting right here, with the door closed."

"But look," Albert said, as he stood in the doorway and pushed the door open again. "It's like a church out there. Nothing bad ever happens in a church, right?"

Dennis nodded.

"Besides," Albert stated, "if we have to wait a couple hours for Drake to come home, we might as well explore a little bit, or at least take something back into the room more exciting than just a bunch of books to pass the time with."

Exploring a little bit couldn't get them in any more trouble then they were already in, Dennis rationalized. Besides, Albert was right, there were lots of things to look at out in the cathedral.

"Okay," Dennis agreed. "We'll find the car, and then look around just for a little bit."

"Deal," Albert said with a smile. He walked out into the bigger room. "Close the door so Drake can come get us if he gets home early."

"Won't the door go away if we close it? Neither of us have the key," Dennis asked.

"No," Albert responded. "It's always here. When I was here the other day I opened it once and there was just a wall, but I think that's when Drake was looking in there and I wasn't in it."

"Oh, okay," Dennis stated, as he stepped out and closed the door. He stood and waited for it to disappear, fully expecting Albert to be wrong. It never did.

"Dennis!" Albert yelled from around a couple shelves. "Come over here!"

The boys lost track of time as the wandered through the massive expanse of what they referred to as the cathedral. They found many fascinating things as they explored, Dennis was completely in awe of some of the organisms in jars. Many of them were things he could recognize, like fish, chickens, or rabbits, but occasionally he came across something that should have been in a freak show. Something that had too many arms, legs, or heads, or something that seemed to be a mutated version of an animal he vaguely recognized. Albert, too, was amazed by what he saw. He sat on the throne for a bit, ordering Dennis to do things—which of course he didn't do. He also had to check every single one of the locked boxes he found to see if they were locked or if they weren't what might be inside them.

Suddenly they heard voices moving their direction. They crouched down and looked for their way back to the Archive Room door. It was on the far side of the vast cathedral. To get there they would either have to cut across the large open space with the semi-circle of chairs in front of the throne, or circle all the way around along the wall. The shortest distance was straight across, so that was what they attempted.

Slowly they moved as quietly as they could manage through the rows of shelves, before Dennis extended his arm to stop Albert from moving any further.

People, or rather creatures, were moving down the center of the cathedral toward the throne. A couple looked vaguely human, some looked like some of the monsters Drake was fond of drawing, and behind them two very bright balls of light followed.

"Are those bright ones angels?" Albert asked in a nearly silent whisper. "Maybe they captured the monsters in front and are bringing them here."

That was very logical for his little brother, Dennis thought. He stared toward the two balls of intense light. It hurt his eyes to look too long. Then he remembered the welding goggles. He re-adjusted the goggles over his eyes and then flipped the dark lenses down. The cathedral was now dark, except when he turned to look at the two glowing 'angels.'

"Those aren't angels," Dennis whispered to Albert. He saw the source of the illumination. There were creatures moving inside each of the bright lights. One had legs that were like the hind legs of a horse, the torso of a heavily muscled man, huge feathered wings attached to his shoulders, and he had a large head that looked like a goat. It appeared as though the light from him was a fire that surrounded him. The second one was snake-like. It slithered across the floor on massive serpentine coils. Its body was long and slender but had four arms—two on each side. It too had wings, but its wings were more bat-like. Its head was a slobbering, fang infested lizard-head with large protruding horns along the skull turning into smaller barbs along the jaw. Its light just seemed to glow from its body.

"What are they?" Albert whispered.

"I don't know, but they don't look like any angels I ever heard of," Dennis responded.

Something moved up from behind the throne, and it had massive black wings. Dennis and Albert listened to the voices and attempted to see who was talking.

"Greetings," a feminine voice announced. "It's an honor to welcome you here, my Lord."

"The pleasure is mine, Countess. I seldom get out to see the netherworlds anymore. Most of my time is tied up with bureaucracy or settling the disputes of our fellow nobles," a melodic voice stated from the light with the goat-man in it.

"Let me assemble a proper welcome. A feast, or perhaps an orgy for you, my Lord?" the Countess replied.

"I would be honored to taste your hospitality Countess, in time, but first the matter that bade me visit you today," the lord responded.

"Of course," the Countess answered. Albert strained to try and see more of the Countess, but all he could see was part of her long red feminine leg, and her foot in a slinky high-heeled shoe.

"Lady Tiamat informed me of her visit to see you," the lord began. "The Council of Retribution is poised to strike the first blow for our independence and our right to rule humanity as we see fit. You and some others need to be made very aware of our position. If you choose to not ally yourself with us, you will not reap the full benefit of our victory."

"That's a steep price to pay," the Countess said. "Assuming you are victorious."

"We will be Countess," the lord replied. "But furthermore, Lady Tiamat shared your interest in one of the Brotherhood, a Fraser boy."

Dennis and Albert looked at each other with raised eyebrows.

"Lady Tiamat was correct, my Lord," the Countess added. "I do desire the well-being of one of the Fraser's, and I will make a deal that guarantees his safety."

"Unfortunately," the lord responded, "I cannot make such a deal, all the Frasers are enemies of the Council. But here is a deal I am willing to make with you, Countess."

"Go on, my Lord," the Countess cooed. Albert could see that she crossed her legs revealing more of her reddish thigh.

"If you agree to not interfere with our agents and our strike on the Tower of Dreams, then I'm willing to count you as an ally when we divide the rewards of our victory," the lord explained.

"That's not fair!" blurted another voice. Dennis assumed it came from the glowing snake.

"Be still, Quatyl," the lord responded, his voice similar to a sing-song enchantment. "You do not have a seat amongst the nobility here."

"I'm a god!" Quatyl furiously barked, as his burning aura expanded brightly.

"A minor god," the lord chimed, "with no leverage amongst the royalty of the netherworlds, so be still and you may yet join the ranks of the rulers of Hell."

"Deal," the Countess announced. "I accept those terms, my Lord. But I would ask for one condition, that any Frasers captured be first brought here so I can inspect them for what I seek."

"I think that can be arranged," the lord replied. "The rivers of Hell will soon be red with the blood of Frasers."

Albert didn't want to lose any of his blood, so naturally he let out a gasp. Actually it sounded more like he squeaked. Dennis shushed him, holding up his index finger in front of his mouth. The monsters that preceded the glowing lord and Quatyl into the Grand Library spread out looking for the source of the odd noise.

"We have to go," Dennis whispered. He motioned Albert to follow him.

They moved quietly down one of the aisles of shelves, away from the center of the cathedral. Dennis motioned the way they needed to go to get back to the Archive Room. Albert nodded and they moved around the end of the shelf and right into the waiting arms of a large demonic guard.

The demon grabbed both boys by their necks and lifted them up off the floor. Albert flailed the staff around trying to hit the monster.

Another of the demons arrived from behind them, then another. They looked at the two boys hungrily.

"Humans!" shouted one of the demons, looking at the struggling boys. As the demon holding them gripped them harder, their air flow decreased, and their grip on consciousness loosened. The bright form of Quatyl was before them, his nostrils flaring, sniffing their essence.

"They are Frasers!" Quatyl screamed. "You have Frasers lurking in your throne room, Countess!"

"Bring them forward," the lord commanded. Albert and Dennis were close to blacking out. They saw little of what happened next.

The demon holding them dropped them hard on the stone floor between the glowing lord and the Countess. Albert could see her red toes in her black strappy sandals. The lord moved closer to them, and they could feel the heat of his aura. A delicate hand touched their faces.

"These two are of no use to me," the Countess said. "You may have them."

"They possess the Staff of Orkan, my Lord," Quatyl added with glee. "I sent one of your guards, Countess, to retrieve something to wrap it in so we can touch it. It is a fine weapon to take off the field of battle without a fight, or any casualties. For us, that is, and these two pathetic humans are already dead."

"Guard them, Quatyl, I will be back shortly," the lord stated as he and the Countess began to walk away. "This has been a fine day. Nearly half of our greatest foes are captured, we have their mightiest weapon, and the Countess and I have agreed to a pact. Now let me sample this feast, and, of course, your orgy."

"Yes, my Lord," the Countess cooed, as they walked away. "I will have all of my finest assembled for your pleasure, Lucifer."

When Drake arrived home from school he found that his mom was nearly frantic. She had been looking for Dennis and Albert for over an hour and couldn't find either of them anywhere.

"Drake," Mom pleaded on the verge of tears. Her La Madrid instincts were going wild within her. "I need you to help me find your brothers, they aren't in the house, and I've got a terrible feeling they're in trouble."

"Okay Mom," Drake responded. "Let me put my stuff away first then I will go outside and start looking for them."

"Thanks Drake," Mom said with her car keys in her hand. "I'm going to drive down to the store and see if they walked there."

Drake nodded then he turned and went up the stairs to his room. Monique ran up the stairs with him. He heard the front door close downstairs as he approached his bedroom. His door was opened, which wasn't the way it should have been. Perhaps Mom had left it open when she was looking for his brothers earlier.

He entered his room, followed by the white poodle, and set his school stuff and duffle bag on his bed. Monique was parading around at the foot of his bed, and then she started to bark.

"Did you miss me Mo?" Drake asked, as he finished putting his stuff on the bed. She barked again, but held it longer until it turned almost into a howl. "What's all that about, girl?"

Monique did not respond to him. She began the scratch at the wall past the foot of his bed.

"What are you after, Mo?" Drake questioned. He walked over to the wall and saw the poodle standing on her hind legs, scratching on the plaster wall with her front feet. She howled again. "What are you doing?"

Drake bent down to pick her up, to calm her, and saw the skeleton key and its long silver chain lying on the floor. His pulse began to throb in his head and a feeling of dread overcame him.

"Oh no!" Drake exclaimed. He went to his opened closet and saw that the neatly wrapped Staff of Orkan was missing, and only the blanket he wrapped it in remained. "What did they do?"

Drake came back out and looked at Monique.

"Where are they Mo? Where are Dennis and Albert?" Drake asked.

Monique looked at him, turned her head slightly sideways, and then went back to scratching at the wall and howling. Drake bent down and picked up the key and the heavy wood and brass Archive Room door appeared on the wall in front of Monique. She barked at it.

"They went in there, didn't they?" Drake said to the dog. Monique danced on her hind legs, begging with her front legs, moving them up and down together. She howled again.

Drake put the key into the lock and opened the door. Inside he found neither Dennis nor Albert, but the matchbox car Albert lost a few days ago was sitting on the table among a few locked boxes, and a couple of jars of weird pickled organisms.

"They took the Staff," Drake began. "And went through the Archive Room, but somehow the key was left behind, so they weren't able to come back here. To come back here, someone's got to have the key on this side."

Monique looked at him as if she wanted to speak but couldn't.

"I need to go rescue them, but I can't take the key," Drake reasoned. He quickly turned to his desk and grabbed a sheet of typing paper and scribbled a fast note to Mark.

> Mark,
> Please pick up this key and open the archive door in my room—it's the same room that was at the Hoquiam library. I went to save Dennis & Albert.
> Your brother,
> Drake

He took the note and the key and set them on the floor right inside his door. He went into the closet and unwrapped the present he had gotten from his grandfather, the master crafted sword Hikari—*the light*. He buckled the scabbard belt around his waist. He looked down at Monique and she wagged her stubby tail.

"I need you to stay and let Mark know about the note," Drake said, as he picked Monique up, kissed her head and set her outside his room. He closed the door and walked toward the open Archive Room. Monique barked outside his bedroom.

Drake grabbed the Archive Room door and pulled it closed behind him as he stepped into it. He heard Monique bark and then nothing. He stood there quietly for a few moments and then went to open the door.

He was amazed to see the massive expanse of the Grand Library of Gehenna before him where just a moment before his bedroom had been. Albert had failed to do the massive chamber justice when he tried to describe it to his brother. Drake wasn't sure where to begin, but felt that he didn't have a lot of time to waste. He stepped outside the Archive Room and instinctively touched the hand made charm that hung around his neck. It was the rose and lilac wood medallion in the shape of a pentacle and a cross, with a three-banded Celtic weave around it, and in that moment he remembered a blonde girl. Her face flashed into his mind. Rachel Finnegan, he knew her, he liked her, maybe more than that, and she was connected to him. The ambrosia of love coursed through his veins, and the floor below him lit up with a blue fire in the shape of the star-cross hanging from his neck. He had to find his brothers. The medallion felt like it was pulling him to the left. Unquestioning, he followed.

He took an immediate left turn out of the grand throne room and into a corridor lined with doorways. The star-cross urged him forward. At the end of the hall, a room opened before him. He cautiously scanned the room. A large scaly creature that resembled a dragon moved out of the room on the far side, as if it was compelled to leave. Behind the exiting creature he saw two forms struggling in tight, neck-to-ankle cording or rope. From this distance they looked like they were spools wrapped completely in thread. They had to be his wayward brothers.

Drake advanced cautiously toward his brothers along the wall of the great room. He reached the edge of the nook that held Dennis and Albert.

"Dennis, Albert," Drake uttered, his voice barely above a whisper. "Dennis, Albert. It's Drake, I've come to rescue you."

"Drake!" Albert squealed.

"Shut up, dillhole!" Dennis yelled at Albert. "It's your squealing that got us in this trouble, and now you're gonna let 'em all know he's here."

Drake moved in and went to hug his brothers. He began to lift up Dennis and nearly threw him up to the ceiling. His brother was almost lighter than air in his hands.

"Whoa!" Drake exclaimed. "How's that possible?"

"We discovered it after we got tied up," Albert stated sarcastically. He stood up on his toes and rapidly went down, and back up in a bounding shot, up nearly to the ceiling of the nook of a room they were being held in. "Otherwise we would've put a tag-team beat down on 'em. Instead, now we're just jumpin' beans... Dennis thought the gravity was less here, making us stronger or something."

"Like *John Carter of Mars*," Dennis said. "We're stronger here, almost like superhero strong."

"Good to know," Drake stated, as he pulled Hikari from its scabbard. A faint blue glow radiated from the blade. "I'll have to do more experiments later when we aren't in danger."

"Whoa!" Dennis exclaimed with wide eyes. "Your sword is glowing like it has a light in it."

"Like *the Hobbit* swords!" Albert exclaimed. "You know, like in the cartoon movie we saw."

Drake and his brothers stared at the blade of the sword.

"That must be why it's called the light," Drake pondered.

"That's kind of a dumb name for a sword," Albert remarked.

"Yeah," Dennis added, "light isn't cool like Sting, or Glamdring, or Orcrist."

Drake shushed his brothers then used the blade of Hikari to cut part of the cords off Dennis so he could get the rest off himself, before turning to do the same for Albert.

"Hurry," Drake stated, as he looked around the nook. "Get all of the rope off, we need to move fast. Where's the staff?"

"The glowing snake-guy, Quatyl, took it," Dennis answered.

"And where is he?" Drake asked.

"Last I saw of him," Dennis replied, as he finished removing the ropes from himself and went to help Albert, "he was goin' in a room across the big cathedral we started in."

"Okay," Drake said, motioning his brothers to come with him. "Show me where he's at, we absolutely need that staff back."

Dennis shook his head.

"Drake," Dennis began, "you don't understand, he's a

glowing snake-guy. He also said he was a god. And he said he was going to kill all the Frasers. That's all of us. All of us. We're too young to die Drake, I mean Albert and me, we're just kids."

"Dennis, I get it, trust me I get it, but you don't understand," Drake replied sternly. "We need that staff back or we may all die anyway. So show me where he went. I'll get it back while you and Albert stay in the Archive Room."

Dennis and Albert nodded in agreement. The boys quietly walked back toward the Archive Room. Once they reached the grand throne room, Dennis started pointing to the far side of the room.

"He was over there," Dennis said.

"Okay," Drake replied. "Both of you, get over to the Archive Room and get inside it, but keep the door open for me. Got it?"

"Yep," Albert said.

"We got it, Drake," Dennis added. "Oh, Drake! You might need these to see the snake-guy Quatyl, he's pretty bright, but you can see him inside the glow with the goggles."

Drake took the welding goggles from Dennis and started off across the room, quickly and silently. The star-cross guided him. Left, around a shelf, another left, then he slowed down as heard talking on the other side of the shelf he was walking past.

"The Countess is a fool," a gravelly voice stated.

"She should stand with 'er own kind," a second voice added.

"Lucky Quatyl was 'ere to show 'er how to treat humans. Those Fraser brats' flesh sure'll taste good," the first voice continued.

"Yauhhh, we eat well tonight," the second one responded with a guttural chuckle.

Both of them laughed, the sound was like a deep chortling snarl that echoed down the aisles of the vast library.

Drake stood silently. He already didn't like this Quatyl person, or god, or whatever he was, nor did he particularly like his minions who were talking about eating his brothers. In his mind he saw Moose. He felt the shame of being pummeled by him in the locker room. Drake had experienced too much bullying in his life, and couldn't move past these two talking about his brothers that way. It was one thing to pick on him, but don't ever pick on his brothers. He didn't realize until it was too late that he had moved from behind the shelf. He was standing behind the two large demons, their barbed tails swishing in the air as they slowly walked away from him. Drake could have just let it go, but something inside of him changed. He felt the ambrosia of love in him, he felt the blue-fire, and he felt the confidence of being 'superhero' strong.

"Hey!" Drake announced defiantly. "What're you two butt-uglies gonna do to my brothers?"

The demons turned and jumped from the startle. Their faces were reptilian, their eyes glowing yellow, their mouths filled with jagged teeth, torsos heavily muscled, and covered in coarse tufts of hair. In their hands they carried weapons—long handled spear-like things with wickedly-sharp long blades at the end—halberds, Drake concluded. They bellowed and lunged at Drake.

The demons never expected him to move and committed themselves to their lunge attack. The star-cross blazed on his neck as he jumped up toward the shelf on his right. He went up at least ten feet, put his right foot on the towering shelf and pushed himself into the larger demons. Hikari erupted in a blue fire, completely covering the blade, and with a downward slashing motion Drake cut deeply into their hairy chests spraying surging black demon ichor in the sword's wake. The cuts were deep and severe. One was fatal as a demon buckled completely to the floor. The second demon staggered on its feet, holding its open chest with its left hand, and then it turned and launched itself at Drake.

Drake was in a crouch, the flaming Hikari in his right hand parallel to the stone floor. When he saw the motion toward him from the lumbering demon, he reacted. He sprang low out of his crouch and swung Hikari through both of the advancing demon's goat-like legs below the knee. The demon slammed to the floor with a loud crash. Drake stood above the demon and plunged Hikari into its back.

"No one's gonna eat my brothers," Drake said, as he walked away from the carnage he never knew he was capable of inflicting. Hikari blazed as the black demon blood sizzled off the blade. Drake had not drawn first blood in the coming war, the mordgeists had achieved that when they killed Uncle Wally, and that fact was not lost on the young Fraser boy. "They drew first blood."

The star-cross guided him forward.

In the distance behind him, Drake heard yelling, guttural and angry. The clash with the demons undoubtedly alerted other demons to his presence, or to Dennis and Albert's escape.

The star-cross burned bright and led him to the left. An archway stood between him and a room that appeared to have a miniature sun inside it. Drake put on the welding goggles and advanced into the next room.

There in front of Drake, in the intense glow of Quatyl's fiery aura, stood the snake-god. Behind the god and his leathery wings appeared to be the staff, partially wrapped in a heavy cloak. The illumination from Quatyl was so intense that Drake could only see anything in the room at all because of the dark goggles.

"What are you doing here, human?" Quatyl shouted in a commanding voice. "Kneel before me, human!"

Drake felt a tremor to comply with the demand, like a psychological impulse, but resisted it.

"You have something of mine, snake-guy!" Drake yelled back.

"I am Quatyl, god of the night sky, reaper of souls!" Quatyl decreed. His reptilian head rose up and his radiance burned brighter. Spittle dribbled off his chin. Drake could see the form of the god inside the growing fire. The heat of the aura began to intensify. Even with the goggles, the light was getting too bright. "I am not 'snake-guy!'"

"Give me back my staff, and no more of your minions will get hurt," Drake stated defiantly. He moved Hikari into view and its blue flames burned into the fiery aura of the god, struggling with the bright aura but slowly overcoming it.

"What is that you hold, human?" Quatyl questioned. The blue-fire consumed more and more of the aura as it spread out like tendrils away from Drake.

In his mind, Drake heard Uncle Wally.

"I am with you, always."

Drake's heart welled up inside him as power and courage surged through him. Uncle Wally's ashes were part of the sword.

"Give me that weapon too," Quatyl stated, as he pointed one of his arms at Hikari. "And I'll let you leave in one piece, human."

Quatyl advanced. As he neared Drake, he inhaled the essence of his adversary. His nostrils flared, and his reptilian eyes bulged in excitement.

"What is this? Blessed be me, what luck to find three in one day, a third Fraser!" Quatyl screamed. "All Frasers must die! Die!"

Quatyl moved slowly, deliberately around Drake, his slithering body coiled upon itself as he put himself in front of the doorway and the only way out of the room. With a rush of motion his two left arms feinted an attack toward Drake, followed by his two right arms with deadly aim. Drake had dodged, but not quickly enough as he crumpled to the floor from the impact.

If not for Drake's augmented abilities, the slashing blow could have been fatal. Drake looked down, his shirt was slashed and there was a trickle of blood upon his chest. The wounds stung and his muscles ached from the force of the blow. Without moving his head, he looked back up at the god. Hikari flamed in his right hand.

"Is that all you got, snake-guy?" Drake taunted—a skill he had learned from playing basketball. He stood back up to face the god.

Quatyl coiled and slithered, then launched another frenzied attack. Drake had analyzed the pattern from the first attack, and was able to easily dodge the second. Infuriated, Quatyl attacked again, and again, but each time Drake avoided his feint and lunge. The god moved side-to-side in front of the doorway, and the spines along his body flared making him seem larger.

Suddenly the long serpentine tail of the god wrapped around Drake's left leg and pulled him over. The god sprung upwards and began to drop on to Drake from above, his wings pulled back and all four hands showing deadly talons at the end of each gnarled finger extended for the death stroke.

Drake moved with great dexterity. There was no thought, just raw adrenaline and unknown instinct. He rose up, the snake-like tail of Quatyl still wrapped around his left leg, and he responded like he was scrambling for a loose basketball on the floor, except this time he slashed Hikari through the tail of the god, severing it from his body. The sudden pain radiated in Quatyl's body causing a spasm that made his deadly attack miss, wide to the left. One of Quatyl's talons tore through Drake's left shoulder, ripping fabric and flesh. Drake felt the god's talon hit his bone, knocking him to his knees. Blood sprayed from his deep wound as the talon tore free.

Drake rolled on the cobbled floor away from the god. He felt like he was going to throw up, but he also knew that the snake-guy would quickly finish the job if he didn't move fast. Drake was losing a lot of blood from his deltoid. Instinctively he took Hikari and placed the burning blue-fire inside the wound to cauterize it. Drake screamed in pain. The blood loss stopped, but so to had the functional use of his left arm.

The god writhed on the floor before Drake. Quatyl had never felt pain like that before. He wouldn't have been able to describe what pain was until that moment, because he had never truly been hurt, he was a god, after all. He held his severed tail in three of his four hands, the other pointed menacingly at Drake.

"What have you done Fraser?" Quatyl screamed. "No human can do such things to a god! How can you even see where to strike through my radiance?"

"Apparently," Drake said through the searing pain in his shoulder, "you're wrong. And as far as being able to see you, you can thank my little brother. Remember, you met him earlier and you told him you were going to kill him. He lent me his goggles, so I can see all of you, snake-guy."

Quatyl looked at the goggles covering Drake's eyes. Of course, why had he not thought of that, all he needed to do was remove the goggles from the human and he would no longer be able to see him.

Through the welding goggles Drake saw that Quatyl was recovering and staring intently at him, and plotting his next move. Drake knew he couldn't survive another attack like the last one. He had to become offensive and take the attack to the winged serpent. Without a pause to think about probabilities or measures of success, he attacked. He took Hikari high in his right hand and stepped into the god with his left foot, and ripped through, like he had been taught to do with a basketball. The motion brought the burning blade clean through the body of the god, cleaving him between his sets of flailing arms. Fire erupted from the mortally wounded god.

"I am immortal!" Quatyl screamed. He saw his body was cut in two. "This cannot be! I cannot die! No human can do such things!"

The fire from his wound engulfed the god and he screamed a blood-curling scream that would forever haunt Drake's dreams.

Drake moved behind the burning Quatyl and grabbed the wrapped staff. He wedged it under his damaged left arm, and then he looked at the god engulfed in the flames of death and moved sideways against the wall to exit the room.

"I'm not just a human!" Drake shouted at the burning

mass. "My name is Drake! Drake Fraser, snake-guy!"

Drake had killed a god. He didn't even know if that was even possible, but he did it. He quickly flipped up the welding goggles and sprinted back across the throne room to his waiting brothers on the other side.

Three monstrous demons, like the first two he fought, fell into pursuit behind him. They were nowhere nearly as fast as Drake and his augmented strength.

"Here he comes!" Albert shouted, as he turned back and looked at Dennis sitting on the chair inside the Archive Room. "And he's being chased by monsters!"

"Get ready to close the door!" Dennis screamed.

"Not until he's inside!" Albert yelled back.

Drake ran into the room and slammed into the shelves at the back. He turned to see the advancing demons in pursuit.

Albert slammed the door shut.

"Now what?" Dennis questioned. "Who's on the other side to save us?"

"I left a note for Mark," Drake said.

"You're hurt!" Albert screamed, as he looked at Drake's slashed and bloodied shirt.

Drake felt the pain of the deep wound again. He set down the staff, slid Hikari back into its scabbard, and then looked at his shoulder. It looked bad. What would he tell Mom? He moved his slashed shirt away from his skin, unsure if he could stomach looking at his own bone. Fortunately, Hikari's blue-fire had apparently stopped the bleeding. Cautiously, Drake peeled back the shirt. He nearly passed out as he looked at the severity of his cut arm, and the wound was charred from the fire. His deltoid was deeply cut, but not to the bone as he first feared, and would undoubtedly require medical attention, definitely stitches, when they got home.

"Whoa!" Dennis exclaimed. "That looks like it hurts, Mom's gonna be pissed at you."

"It does hurt," Drake responded. "I think I'm going to have to go to the hospital. Luckily my sword was able to stop the bleeding."

"That's a cool sword," Albert said. "Can we get swords like that to?"

"Yeah that'd be cool," Dennis agreed.

"Why, so you guys can hurt each other?" Drake responded. "How'd you guys manage to both get in the Archive Room without the key?"

Dennis and Albert looked at each other sheepishly and shrugged their shoulders in unison.

"Are we still in the cathedral?" Dennis asked, completely changing the subject. Albert shrugged his shoulders and opened the door. Outside the door, the three demons paced, unable to get to the door because of the flaming star-cross cut into the floor.

"Yep," Albert stated. "We're still there, and so are those monsters!"

"We have 'em trapped!" the boys heard from outside the Archive Room. "They won't get away!"

"This isn't good," Dennis said. "We're gonna die."

"No we're not," Drake replied. "Mark will get us, trust me."

Outside, the room became quiet again. Albert cracked the door open and quickly closed it.

"They're still there," Albert announced. "And they don't look happy."

"How can you tell if they look happy?" Dennis argued. "They all looked mad all the time."

"No they didn't, 'member how that one nasty green one looked like it was smiling all the time," Albert responded. "I think that one was happy."

"No it wasn't," Dennis replied. "It looked like that because it didn't have any lips, dillhole!"

"Guys," Drake said. "Stop it! Listen, its quiet outside. Let's check the door."

Albert peeked out the door, and then pushed open the door, revealing Drake's bedroom.

"We made it back!" Dennis shouted.

"Thank you, Mark!" Albert screamed.

Mark was nowhere to be seen. Drake was confused. He stepped out of the Archive Room and looked for the note and the key. They shouldn't be back unless someone was in the room with the key in their hand. In front of the slightly open door, sat the note, with the key on top of it, and on top of the key was the right front foot of Monique.

"Mo saved us!" Drake shouted. Monique barked as the three boys shouted and yelled in happiness. Albert excitedly slapped both Dennis and Drake on the arm, unfortunately for Drake it was his wounded left arm.

"Owwwww!" Drake moaned. The pain in his arm was now coming to life, it hurt, and it hurt badly. Drake sat on the edge of his bed and passed out backwards.

"I think Mom needs to know about his arm," Albert said.

"But I think we should wait and make sure our stories are all the same," Dennis reasoned. "Or Mom will never let any of us out of her sight again."

On Thursday, March twentieth, a magnitude 4.2 Earthquake just north of the summit of Mt. St. Helens triggered a series of avalanches on the face of the mountain. The forces of the Council of Retribution had begun their siege of the Tower of Dreams.

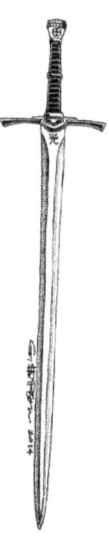

14

ADDRAEMYR

THE BROTHERHOOD OF OLYMPUS
AND THE TOWER OF DREAMS

To See Addraemyr
Chapter Fourteen
March 27, 1980
Hazel Dell, Washington

Drake's left arm required fifty-five stitches, twenty of which were made of dissolving thread sewn inside the deep cut. He told his mother that he cut it on a piece of jagged metal on a fence he climbed over to find his little brothers. Both Dennis and Albert backed up his story. Unfortunately for Drake, a cut from jagged metal meant getting a tetanus shot on top of all the other treatment—and he'd rather have been cut again than be poked with a needle.

Going back to school after killing demons and a god was an odd juxtaposition of realities for Drake. In the mythic world of Gehenna, he had fought and defeated monsters guided by an internal fire and the spirit of his dead uncle, exuding a confidence beyond even the level that he only possessed on the basketball court. Back in the mundane world of school, he was still a borderline outcast, supported by his new friendships, but severely lacking that bold confidence he harbored somewhere deep inside himself. He still avoided Moose Caine, or backed down from the bully in a way that many around him thought was kind of submissive of him. Drake pretended not to care, but he heard the snide comments and the names they called him. He thought of the old English adage, 'Sticks and stones may break my bones, but words will never hurt me,' and knew it wasn't true. Those cheap words, sissy, pussy, faggot, and the like laid an oppressive weight upon his soul. The cut in his arm was healing—sure it was still sore and the stitches had started to itch—but it was getting better. However, the wounds caused by those words would never go completely away.

Drake was equally somber at home. He had spent much of the week since the rescue of his brothers trying to type more of his notes into his growing manuscript. That endeavor was a challenge with his very sore left shoulder, but he methodically pecked away on the typewriter hoping to record the details of the fight in the Library of Gehenna while it was all still fresh in his mind.

Dennis and Albert hadn't volunteered to come into his bedroom, nor had they wanted to talk much about their experiences. They seemed to have been pretty shaken by the whole thing. Dennis had actually started to try and convince Albert that the whole thing was kind of like a hallucinogenic drug trip and that it never really happened.

Mark was busy all the time with school, working on friends cars, and working at the restaurant. He had been distancing himself from Drake and the others since they moved to Vancouver. Mark had started looking at what he was going to do after he graduated in June. Two of those options—joining the Army, and going to Arizona to a leading mechanics school—both meant moving away. Mark hated good-byes. He preferred to push people away to the point that it didn't hurt to leave.

Drake arrived home from school later than usual. He had been walking for nearly a month since Mark had stopped giving him rides home.

"Hey little brother," Martin stated from across the living room. He was sitting in one of the high backed stools that lined the kitchen counter. "Are you always this late?"

"No," Drake replied, as he started up the stairs to his room.

"Mom said you hurt your arm?" Martin questioned.

"Yep," Drake responded. He kept walking up the stairs.

"Fifty-five stitches?" Martin probed. He got up from the stool and started to follow his brother upstairs.

"Yep," Drake answered, as he neared his bedroom door.

"You cut yourself on a fence?" Martin asked, as he walked up the stairs.

"Something like that," Drake replied. He turned to face Martin, who was still below him on the stairs. "Why did Mom send you fishing for answers? She asked me like a thousand times what happened."

"She did ask me," Martin responded, "to see if you'd tell me anything more than what she already got from you, but honestly, even with my psychic abilities, your mind is still out of my reach."

"Good," Drake stated. He opened his door and stepped into his room. He didn't close the door. "Besides, there are some things that no one would believe if you told them anyway. You know that just as well as I do."

"Yes," Martin answered, as he entered Drake's room. "I understand that, and I wouldn't try to explain some things to Mom. She's just worried about you. She said the cut was pretty deep, and it could've ended badly if you hadn't gotten to the hospital right away."

"Yeah," Drake replied, as he sat down at his desk and turned to face the typewriter. "I know, the doctors told me all about how lucky I was. You really want to know the truth?"

"Yes," Martin responded.

"First," Drake began, as he loaded a sheet of paper into the typewriter and turned the platen to get it set to type, "you have to swear as a member of the Brotherhood that you won't tell anyone else outside the Brotherhood."

"I swear," Martin said.

"Second," Drake continued, as he adjusted the top margin of his paper, "I'm not going back there, at least until I've healed, and I've done some more experiments to guarantee my safety."

"Okay," Martin stated.

"Good," Drake replied. "Close the door and I'll tell you, but you better not tell Mom any of this. Got it?"

"Yeah, I got it," Martin said, as he closed the door.

Drake told Martin the story of Dennis and Albert's adventure into the Grand Library of Gehenna, complete with the details of the augmented strength, his fights with the burly demons, and his brush with death against the god Quatyl.

"Wait," Martin finally stated. "You're not just making this up are you? You're serious aren't you?"

"Yes," Drake answered. "I told you. Not very many people would believe it. It's all true. It all happened. But its not like I can go around telling people I fought and killed a snake god, I'd get locked up in a mental hospital or something."

"You know what, little brother," Martin responded with a wide smile, "I believe you, and I'm really happy we're on the same team."

"Thanks Martin," Drake replied. "It's good to be able to tell someone the whole story. Mark hasn't been around much and I haven't been able to talk to any of my friends at school about it."

"Is the key safe?" Martin asked. "We don't need Dennis and Albert going on any more adventures."

"Yeah," Drake answered. He started to type something on the typewriter, scowled, and then grabbed the paper and pulled it out of the machine, crumpling it up and tossing it into his waste basket. "I have secured my room and my gear so I shouldn't have any repeats. So what are you going to tell Mom? I know she is going to ask what you found out from me."

"That you got cut on a fence," Martin said with a smile. "Besides, I came here to see you for another reason."

"Oh really?" Drake questioned, as he grabbed the ream of typing paper he had convinced their Mom to buy for him. He tore the white wrapper off the stack of paper, and set the stack into his makeshift paper tray. "What's that?"

"Well," Martin answered, "you remember that stuff I was telling you about my job, the top secret CRV?"

"Coordinate remote viewing," Drake replied. He looked at the stack of new paper, and ran his thumb up the corner of the stack. It hit something more rigid than typing paper about halfway up. He ran his thumb up the stack of paper a second time and got the same result. He leaned over to look closer at the paper.

"Yeah," Martin responded. He noticed Drake was becoming pre-occupied with the stack of typing paper. "I want to do it with you. I think you have a gift for it, with all the drawings you do of things you've never seen."

Drake nodded and looked at the paper. One single sheet seemed to be thicker, almost like cardstock, and was placed nearly in the middle of five hundred sheets of typing paper. He had no idea what it was doing there. The probability of a sheet of cardstock being packaged with was virtually non-existent. But there it was.

"What is it?" Martin asked.

"There's a single sheet of thicker paper in this ream of typing paper," Drake explained. He lifted the typing paper up off of it and pulled out the thicker paper. Handwritten in pencil across the middle of the paper was the statement:

Place the numbers numerically

"There's something written on this sheet of paper," Drake announced, as he turned it to show his brother. "It says, 'place the numbers numerically'."

"You just opened that package of paper," Martin responded. "I watched you. How's there a note written on a sheet of paper inside the package? Where did the paper come from? Who got it for you?"

"I don't know," Drake replied. "It's kind of weird, isn't it? Mom bought it for me at Fred Meyer."

"Mom picked that particular one out for you?" Martin questioned.

"Yes," Drake answered. "No, wait a minute, I got it from the shelf, but I almost got another one. But I chose this one, and then I convinced Mom to buy it for me."

"That, little brother," Martin reasoned with a wry smile,

"is a pretty big coincidence, it's almost like someone *wanted* you to get that message. I think it's a clue."

"Now you sound like we're part of the *Scooby-Doo* Gang," Drake responded with a chuckle.

"Either way, I think it's important," Martin added.

Drake placed the paper with the clue on his desk.

"Of course it is," Drake laughed. "So tell me about this CRV thing you want me to do."

"Well," Martin began, "it's simple in a lot of ways, and you do it already when you doodle and talk. How many times have you drawn that black tower without thinking about it?"

"The Tower of Dreams?" Drake asked. "I don't know, twenty or thirty times, but I've only kept a few of them."

"I want to see if we can get you closer to it," Martin added. "You were in touch with it long before I started doing CRV, so I think you can get more information about it, and why we are being pulled to it."

"Okay," Drake said. "What do I have to do?"

"You need a tablet to draw on," Martin replied. "And you need to clear your mind."

"Okay," Drake responded, as he pulled a tablet of college ruled paper from out of his desk and grabbed a black felt-tipped pen from the board beside his desk with sixty-four holes drilled into it, allowing it to function as a pen and pencil organizer. "Now what?"

"Take a deep, cleansing breath," Martin instructed as he pulled a piece of paper from his pants pocket and unfolded it. "And take another deep breath. Close your eyes, and relax. One more deep cleansing breath, and push everything from your mind, don't think of anything, your mind should just be idle."

Drake was following the instructions, and appeared to be nearly asleep.

"When you are completely at peace," Martin added, "I'm going to give you a set of coordinates, and I want you to just go to those coordinates, and tell me what you see. You may also draw what you see. Nod if you understand."

Drake nodded.

"Good," Martin continued. "The coordinates are forty-six point two and one-hundred twenty-two point two, focus on those numbers, focus on that point and when you're ready you can tell me what you see."

Drake's head turned slightly to the side like he was trying to make sense of what he was seeing with his eyes closed.

"I see a mountain," Drake stated without opening his eyes. He began to doodle in quick scribbles as he talked. "But there's something else there. An obelisk, no a tower, a massive black tower that stretches up into the sky and doesn't seem to end. I'm being pulled inside the tower. The tower is filled with rooms and long hallways. There are many people and places within the tower."

"Good," Martin said encouragingly. "What else do you see?"

"I hear death, or dying, but its not here yet," Drake added. "I smell the color gray, and I can taste it. Something gray is here. Wait, I'm in a big room, filled with machines of some sort, it's like the bridge on *Star Trek*, and there are lots of flashing lights."

"What's gray?" Martin questioned.

"A person," Drake replied, as he turned his head again, trying to see more clearly. "He's nearly as tall as me, his skin is gray, he's bald and he's wearing a long black robe that goes down to his feet. I can't see his feet."

"Which way is he facing?" Martin inquired.

"Away from me," Drake answered, as his right hand quickly doodled. "He's raising a hand, and his fingers are really long. I don't think he's human."

"What's he doing?" Martin asked.

"Waiting for us," Drake responded.

"Good," Martin stated, as he walked over and sat down on Drake's bed. "I'm going to relax and join you in your mind Drake, I need you to stay where you are, don't leave the place you are, and don't fight me as I visit your mind."

"Okay," Drake replied. "He's waited a long time for us,

Martin. He wants to talk to us."

Drake became aware of Martin's presence in his mind, and it quickly manifested as him standing next to Drake inside the tower.

"I'm here," Martin stated. "I can see all that you can see, little brother. I've never made it this far inside the tower before. You are doing an awesome job."

"My name is Addraemyr, I am the guizor, Lord of the huisum who reside here," the gray humanoid stated with a hollow sounding voice that echoed in the brothers' minds. Addraemyr turned to face them. He had a large head, with a small nose centrally placed, framed by two large almond shaped black eyes, and a small lip-less mouth above a sharp pointed chin. "Welcome, brothers Fraser, to my keep. I seldom entertain humans, so your understanding of my phraseology might be suspect."

"So we aren't actually speaking the same language, my Lord?" Drake questioned. He was careful to try and use a dignified tone and honor the guizor.

"You of all humans shall have no need to address me as lord, Drake, son of Drake," Addraemyr replied with a slight bow. "It is not untrue that we communicate in languages unlike each other. You will find as you travel to other planes that languages are assembled within your understanding. It was a gift of the ancient ones, who came before the Elder gods, to those who travel, so it was passed on to us the curators of that knowledge."

"You know us?" Martin asked. "How?"

"You are the brothers Fraser," Addraemyr replied, his hands slowly swaying to the beat of his voice. "The guardians of the Brotherhood of Olympus, you have been chosen by many powers greater than yourselves to do something that you may not be able to achieve, because there are as many, if not more, who wish you to fail."

"What about the rest of our brothers?" Drake questioned.

"I have only sought you two, for now," Addraemyr

answered. "The mind-manipulator, and the leader, who is now known as the demon-slayer, and the god-slayer, both titles have never been given to a single human before. Many have made war against demons, but none have ever felled a god. But be cautious, Drake, son of Drake, in your actions you have forged a powerful enemy."

"The snake-guy, Quatyl?" Drake inquired.

"Death is not all you suspect it is," Addraemyr replied. "It has many possibilities—redemption, damnation, rebirth, and the outcomes are different when one encounters death away from their plane of existence."

Drake was trying to assimilate all that Addraemyr was telling them within his understanding of reality.

"Why have you been trying to talk to us?" Martin asked.

"You are my only hope," Addraemyr responded. "I am the keeper of this tower. It has been my duty, as guizor, to oversee it since long before humans walked upon the Earth. This is one of the Towers of Ominous Power. Long have we stood as neutral observers to the history of all the realities. But there are agents of the Council of Retribution, the dark gods, who are prepared to take my tower by force. In fact, they have already begun their attack."

"How are we your only hope?" Drake inquired.

"The gods cannot directly interfere with any of the great towers," Addraemyr began with a series of blinks. Neither Drake nor Martin had suspected that he had eyelids. "Since my tower travels through all realities, many see it, but few ever understand what they have been witness to. But, the Tower of Dreams is never truly far from your world, because humans have such a rich dreamscape. Only those who reside on the prime plane of Earth may help us in our hour of need, since we do not have an army ourselves, and we can no longer get word to the Tower of Might for assistance. Those of us in the Tower of Dreams are pacifists. We shall not make war, or raise a weapon to fight anyone."

"Wait," Drake interrupted. "So you'll just let these evil agents take your tower, and kill you, and you'll do nothing to defend yourself?"

"They will not kill all of us," Addraemyr responded. "None of them know how the tower works, so they will attempt to torture us to get that information first."

"No offense," Drake interjected, "but that sounds stupid. You'll let yourself be captured and tortured instead of fighting back, not defending yourself and what's yours."

"I never stated we will be defenseless," Addraemyr remarked. "The tower has many defenses of its own, and then we also have the Brotherhood of Olympus to come to our aid, if you will choose such a path."

"How can we do that?" Drake questioned. "We're only here right now because of a mental link. We're not really here, so we can't really defend you or your tower."

"Good observation, god-slayer," Addraemyr responded. "The tower will cycle through to your world on a date known to us. It is an anagram of January thirteenth, a date you both know too well, and will be more than six months hence for you. Fortunately, you will have time to prepare and ready yourselves for the battle ahead of you inside the tower. You must liberate us."

"Your people, the huisum, will be getting tortured and dying for the next six months?" Drake queried. His sense of justice was being perplexed. "We have to come sooner."

"Your compassion is well placed, god-slayer," Addraemyr stated with another slight bow. "My brother Ranthalion, Keeper of the Tower of Infinity, has informed me of your place in many prophecies that will soon come to pass. I am honored to address you and your concern over the wellbeing of my people. But, do not worry your thought process. Time within this tower does not function as it does on your Earth. You will arrive at the precise time to liberate us, should you choose to act."

"How will we find you or this tower on this anagram day, six months from now?" Martin asked.

"Many riddles have yet to be uttered," Addraemyr replied. "And many allies have yet to join you, do not worry about what will come to pass, instead worry whether you will be ready for the challenge that awaits you. This duty you have earned will mark a new direction for the Brotherhood. From this point forward your battles will take on new meaning, and your battlefields shall be in worlds new to you, but your cause will always be one of justice and freedom for your people and your world. Mine as well. But worry not, mind-manipulator, the tower will find you."

"Why us?" Drake questioned. "I mean, why do these gods and demons even care about humans?"

"God-slayer, it is not up to us to determine the worth of a person, or of a people," Addraemyr answered. "Humans possess many qualities sought after, or coveted by those you speak of, gods, daemons, demons, and spirits. All humans are capable of being greater than they suspect, the brothers Fraser are just further along or more open to the possibilities of their genetics. We do not measure the value of a person by their outward appearance, rank, or species, rather by the sum of the agápe in their heart. Your value in the cosmos is greater than precious metals or even the rarest of jewels. Humans have the potential to take us all into a period of great enlightenment, or to our ruin. The choice will ultimately be yours."

"What do we need to know?" Drake asked. He was starting to assemble a plan in his head and knew he might not get a chance to have another conversation with the Keeper.

"To the point, god-slayer," Addraemyr responded, "you must train. The fight ahead will test your courage, your spirit, your strength, and your love of each other. You must choose new allies to complete your ranks, and they will be easy choices. You must be prepared for what you will see and encounter within my tower, it is the Tower of Dreams, and all realities exist within it, or are accessible from within it. Some will shock you. Some may try to terminate you, and some you may not want to ever leave. But, if you truly have chosen to be the champions of our liberty, you must not forget your task."

"That's a lot to do," Martin reasoned.

"Anything else we need to know?" Drake questioned.

"Seek the clues," Addraemyr replied. "When the user of magic finds you, accept him for verily this is his quest as well, for he will assist you greatly in the gathering of needs. The war has begun with the attack upon my tower. Should you fail in liberating us, darkness will cover all of your world and many others, and all of humanity shall suffer."

"We shall not fail you, or your people, my Lord," Drake said with a bow of his spectral form. "We accept your request, and shall liberate your tower and your people."

"I am humbled by your words, Drake, son of Drake," Addraemyr answered with a deeper bow and a flutter of his eyelids. "We, the huisum, have long been neutral, but in the perilous days ahead we may seek an alliance for the first time. And should that come to pass, you and your people, the Brotherhood of Olympus, shall be most welcome within our towers, and whatever aid we may give would be yours."

"I don't know if we are worthy of such an alliance, Addraemyr, but we will do our best," Drake responded. "There'll be justice served for the attack upon your tower, and any injury or damage inflicted by them will be avenged by the Brotherhood of Olympus. This I solemnly swear to you."

"The fabled power of vengeance from the Brotherhood is great, god-slayer," Addraemyr replied. "And in this very moment I feel true pity for your foes."

A loud explosion rocked the room they were standing in.

"I must now go, brothers Fraser," Addraemyr stated, as he placed his long spindly fingers upon their shoulders. "The agents of doom have breached the outer wall, and I must prepare for my capture."

"Wait," Martin interjected. "We need to know more. What should we be cautious of? What dangers will we face?"

"The future is unwritten before the Brotherhood of Olympus," Addraemyr responded. "Follow your hearts, and trust the agápe you all possess for each other. That is all I can tell you from this point forward. Be well, brothers

Fraser. Train, and take the next step in becoming what you were meant to be. If the great wheel in the sky is willing I will see you again, soon."

Drake bowed once again to the keeper. He swooshed his spectral arm through Martin, intending only to nudge him to follow his lead in showing respect to the gray man.

"You have my word, Addraemyr," Drake added.

"Your word may very well be the gospel of humanity as you rise up into the stars, should you survive and emerge from the darkness being assembled before us all," Addraemyr stated, as he walked away from the brothers.

The clarity of the control room they stood in began to fade. Suddenly it shifted to just a snow-capped mountain. Drake knew this mountain, it was outside his window. It was the nearly perfectly symmetrical cone of Mount Saint Helens.

Then they were back in Drake's bedroom. They both sat silently for what seemed like minutes.

Drake began to feel his memories opening inside his mind.

"Get out of my head, butthole!" Drake exclaimed. The presence of his brother in his mind was nearly unbearable. Drake focused on Martin and forcibly ejected him from his consciousness.

"Ouch!" Martin yelled. He rubbed his head. "You could have waited and let me leave, instead of kicking me out. Now my head hurts. Damn it."

"I don't want you snooping around in my mind, Martin," Drake replied. "What'd you think you're doing looking around in there?"

"Nothing," Martin said. "I wasn't looking for anything."

"Uh huh, right," Drake stated. "We have bigger problems ahead of us Martin. I suggest you and I find a way to get along better. To trust each other."

"Okay, fair enough," Martin responded as he rubbed his head. "What did the keeper mean, what's agápe?"

"Agápe is Greek for unconditional love," Drake answered.

"Oh, I guess we all need that right?" Martin replied. "But right now, I really need some aspirin for my headache."

On Thursday, March twenty-seventh, a hole in the summit ice cap on top of Mt. St. Helens appeared, followed by a loud boom, ash, and smoke. The boom signaled a 4.7 magnitude earthquake. The ash and smoke formed a 7,000 foot tall black plume. Following the explosion, a 200 foot wide crater was left on the top of the mountain. The agents of the Council of Retribution had breached the outer wall of the Tower of Dreams.

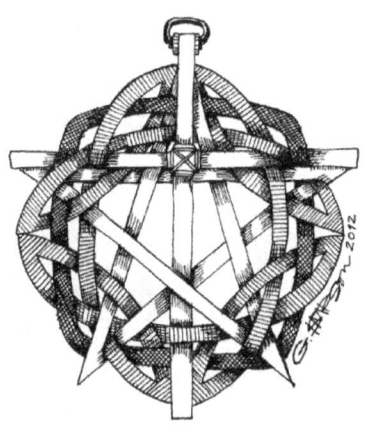

15

AEON, GOD OF TIME

THE BROTHERHOOD OF OLYMPUS
AND THE TOWER OF DREAMS

Devotion to a Dream
Chapter Fifteen
April 29, 1980
Dorchester, Iowa

Rachel didn't mind living in Iowa. In fact, she rather enjoyed being around some of her extended family when they first arrived from Hoquiam after Thanksgiving. It got cold as November turned into December, and she was excited to finally have a white Christmas.

Dorchester was not much of a town, it only had two streets, Main Street, and Back Street—which was actually more of an alley behind the buildings along the north side of Main Street. It also had a bar with a pool table, a county shop for storing road maintenance equipment, an old Methodist church on one side of town, a larger Catholic Rectory at the far end of Main Street, a small grocery store, and an old elementary school. About four hundred people lived in the valley and the surrounding countryside. Rachel's dad had gotten a job as a long haul truck driver and was gone for many days at a time. Her mom worked off and on at a local café along the state highway.

Rachel rode the bus seventeen plus miles into Waukon everyday for school. The bus ride, with all the stops along the way, took over an hour. Since she was not one to get motion sickness, the long bus trip gave her time to do homework. School was easy, and she quickly fit in with the band and drama kids.

Life for Rachel took an ominous turn in mid December. She began to experience a series of unfortunate events. The first occurred on a trip back from Decorah with her Mom.

The roads were icy, with a thick pile of slushy snow along the shoulders from being recently plowed.

"Why can't you take home-economics?" Mom asked, as she slowed down to turn up the winding hill through to the back side of Dorchester. "You don't need to take chemistry, Rachel. You can meet a pig farmer, or a truck driver, and settle down and be happy right here. A medical examiner's a man's job."

"But Mom," Rachel pleaded. She sat on the far side of the bench seat next to the passenger side door. She already knew who she was going to marry—Drake Fraser. "I don't wanna marry a pig farmer, and I've always wanted to be a doctor."

"Honey, the school said you can't take chemistry," Mom said, as she drove quickly up the hill, barely avoiding the slushy border of the road. Driving into that much slush would cause her to quickly lose control of the car. "Even doctors need to know how to cook, and clean, and balance a checkbook."

"I know how to cook, Mom," Rachel replied. Rachel had been doing most of the household chores for her family for quite some time. Her mother had occasional flighty episodes, where she wasn't sure she wanted to be a wife and mother, and didn't understand how to balance a checkbook herself. "Maybe you should take home-ec for me."

"Rachel!" Mom scolded, as she turned late into the biggest corner on the hill, nearly losing the passenger's side into the snow bank.

Rachel saw the door click open next to her as the car started to turn the other way. She felt something, like a cold hand on her ribs, and she was pushed from the car.

"You need to apologize for that, Rachel!" Mom snapped, as she struggled to control the car in the turn. "Do you hear me? Rachel? Rachel?"

Mom looked over to where her daughter had just been and saw an empty seat. The passenger's side door was swinging back and forth. She immediately slammed on her brakes, bringing the car into a spinning slide into the snow bank on the far side of the road.

Rachel felt the cold air slap her face as she was pushed from the car, followed almost immediately by the jarring impact past the slushy edge of the road. She tumbled, head over heels, through bramble and woody brush down the hillside. Her thick coat was torn and tattered from the fall, and she finally came to a stop nearly two hundred feet down the bank against a barbed wire fence. The thick snow may have saved her life as it cushioned the impact of her fall.

Rachel saw light, down a long dark tunnel, radiating like some sort of halo. In the light she saw an old man with a long white beard, and a long curved scythe. He was like Father Time, or the Grim Reaper. Her grasp on consciousness was fading.

"You shall not perish here," Father Time said in a booming voice.

Rachel closed her eyes and remembered no more.

By early January Rachel had recovered from her fall out of the moving car. Remarkably, she hadn't broken any bones. According to her, she was sure she was pushed out of the car, and since it was only her and her mom in the car, her mom must've pushed her out. That festering accusation tore a deep hole in the already weakened relationship with her mother.

Rachel was spending more time at her maternal grandmother and step-grandfather's house in Waukon so she didn't have the long bus ride to and from school. Her grandmother was a strict Lithuanian, with short gray hair and a pinched face from too many years of worrying. She had divorced Rachel's grandfather before any of her grandchildren were born, because he had been an alcoholic and abusive to their children. Her step-grandfather was a friendly old guy in town, who everyone called Raymond. He was Nordic, with neatly combed gray hair, bright blue eyes, a quick smile, and a bit of a problem with alcohol himself.

Raymond was often dropped off at home by the police late in the evening, after they picked him up stumbling on his way home from a bar.

Rachel was frequently down in the basement, among the old appliances and boxes of old things. She had made a safe place to sit behind the musty boxes and an old refrigerator, where she could write notes in her journal, or read science books she had checked out from the library without being bothered by her younger brothers or cousins.

The basement door opened with a loud creak.

"Are you down there Rachel?" Raymond questioned with a bit of a slur from the top of the stairs.

"Yeah!" Rachel shouted back. She closed her journal, and put her library books on top of it.

The stairs creaked under the weight of her step-grandfather. He stumbled at the bottom of the steps and crashed into the stack of boxes.

"Are you okay, Grandpa?" Rachel asked, as a sense of concern for the wellbeing of her step-grandfather rushed through her. She got up and came toward the stairs to find him leaning against the boxes, half asleep. "Grandpa, are you okay?"

"What?" Raymond questioned. He stood up straight, swaying a bit from side to side. He smiled at Rachel. "You know, you're a damn fine, pretty girl."

"Thanks Grandpa," Rachel replied with a smile.

"You got a boyfriend?" Raymond asked.

"No, not here," Rachel responded rather whimsically. "But there's a boy back in Washington."

"Bah," Raymond interrupted. "You don't need a boy. Hell, you're a damn fine woman! You need a man!"

Rachel was flustered by where this discussion might be going. She had heard all about the local pig farmers, and was not interested in any of them.

"Wait a minute," Raymond stated, as he adjusted his crotch. "I have a dress I got in Texas last summer, in a box down here. You'll look ravish, ravish, ravishing in it Rachel.

Help me find it. The box says Texas on the top. Come on, come on, and help your old grandpa."

Rachel began looking through the boxes as Raymond leaned against the wall and watched her climb up on the boxes and bend over to read what was written on them. She finally found a box with Texas written across the top and pulled it out of the pile.

"Found it Grandpa," Rachel announced.

"Good, good," Raymond replied. "Open it up, the dress is a red Mexican dress, one they use for their sexy dancin' and it should fit you fine."

Rachel opened the box, not sure how to take her step-grandfather talking about her being ravishing and sexy. She saw folded red fabric and reached in to grab it. Rachel didn't see the light brown arachnid next to the dress. Its large pinchers opened and closed, its coiled tail rose up to strike.

"That's it, girl!" Raymond shouted excitedly.

Rachel looked over her shoulder at her step-grandfather. He was re-adjusting his crotch again. That's just so gross, she thought. And then there was a sudden stabbing pain on the back of her right hand near her ring finger.

"Owwwww!" Rachel screamed. She looked down, thinking she poked herself on something sharp in the box. She was shocked when she stared down at the scorpion preparing to sting her again. "It's a scorpion! It got me! It got me!"

Rachel dropped the dress and ran toward the stairs past her drunken step-grandfather.

Her hand was already beginning to throb by the time she reached the top of the stairs.

"Grandma! Grandma!" Rachel screamed, as she raced through the house looking for her grandmother.

"What is it, child?" Grandma asked, as she stood up from her chair where she was knitting. "What did Grandpa do now?"

"He didn't do anything!" Rachel yelled. Tears began to freely flow down her cheeks. "Owwie! Owwie! Owwie! My hand hurts! A scorpion stung me on my hand!"

"We don't have any scorpions here, Rachel," Grandma replied. "Let me see it."

Rachel showed her hand to her grandmother. The sting was swollen, and her hand was becoming discolored, like a massive bruise. Rachel could feel her heart beating faster, and it felt like her lungs were getting smaller.

"Oh no, get your coat dear," Grandma stated, as she quickly grabbed her purse and her coat. "Raymond! I'm taking our granddaughter to the hospital! I suggest you sober up and kill any damn scorpions you have down there before we get back!"

Grandma helped Rachel get her coat on, and then helped her into the car, before they sped off toward the hospital. Rachel felt her world collapsing around her. She couldn't hear her grandmother anymore, but could faintly see her talking. Her vision began to fade, and she experienced the same light at the end of the tunnel from her tumble out of the car. Father Time was there again.

"You still have much to accomplish, Miss Finnegan," Father Time stated, as Rachel lost consciousness.

She had no recollection of the struggle at the hospital emergency room to revive her, how blue her skin turned, the multiple shots of epinephrine, or the crying over her life ending so tragically. And then her heart began to beat with a regular rhythm, and her color began to return.

Scorpions don't live in Iowa, and if they did they wouldn't be out in January. Rachel's scorpion attack was officially classified as a freak accident. She recovered from the toxin and her allergic reaction within a week, and got a job at Gus and Tony's Pizza and Steak House as a waitress so she could start saving money to go off to college when she graduated from high school. The job in Waukon meant that she had officially moved in with her grandparents.

By February, her siblings Junior, Patrick, and Maddy were spending more time at their grandparents' house too, since their mom was working more at the café. Rachel would often come home from working late at Gus and Tony's to find her brothers and sister asleep somewhere in the house. Maddy usually found her way into Rachel's bed. Rachel would just move her over, and climb into bed next to her baby sister. She'd cover her head with the blankets and pray to God that she'd fall asleep before her step-grandfather came home from the bar. She was numb to him, but was also terrified of what he had said he'd do to her sister and her father if she didn't cooperate. Most nights he didn't care if she was asleep already, and would just force himself on her. Rachel had looked up the definition of rape in the dictionary at the library, and that word didn't describe the revolt and pain inflicted upon her by her step-grandfather.

On Sundays after church, the family would gather at Grandma's house. Rachel felt safer with all the people over, but would still go down into the basement, to her safe place. After the scorpion attack, Raymond had not gone back down there.

"Sis!" Junior shouted, as he thumped down the creaky stairs. "Hide me!"

"What are you doing Junior?" Rachel asked from inside her corner.

"Playin' hide'n seek!" Junior squealed. "Ya gotta help hide me!"

"There's not a lot of hiding places down here, Junior," Rachel replied.

"Come on Sis," Junior whined, as he looked around the cluttered basement. It was mostly boxes and a few old appliances. "I don't wanna to get found. I always get found."

"Where would you like to hide?" Rachel asked. She felt sorry for her brother always losing at this game with their cousins and some neighbor kids.

"What about in there?" Junior questioned, as he pointed to a large discolored refrigerator. "No one would look in there, if you told 'em I wasn't down here, that's for sure."

GUY T. SIMPSON, JR.

"I don't think that's safe, Junior," Rachel responded.

Junior tried to open the refrigerator door. The rubber seal around the door was old and cracking, but the locking latch held it tight.

"Help me, please, Sis!" Junior pleaded, as he did a little dance with his feet in front of the refrigerator.

"Okay," Rachel replied, as she got up and forced the old appliance open. The inside was musty, and completely empty. All of the shelves were missing. "Get in."

"Uh uh," Junior said, violently shaking his head. "What if it's dark and scary in there once the door closes?"

"It won't be dark and scary," Rachel answered. "Besides I'll be right here, and I'll let you out as soon as you win."

"Ya know I'm scared of the dark, Sis," Junior clarified. "You get in first and lemme know how scary it is."

Rachel shook her head.

"Come on Sis!" Junior exclaimed. "They're lookin' for me by now!"

Rachel shook her head again.

"Please," Junior pleaded. "I'll let ya right back out."

Rachel shook her head one more time.

"Please," Junior begged, as he started to cry. "I always get found."

"Fine," Rachel relented, as she stepped inside the open appliance. "But you need to open it right back up, no running off, got it?"

"Yeah, yeah," Junior said excitedly. "I got it."

Junior closed the door and the latch locked tight with a metallic click. Junior waited, unsure how much time his sister would need to determine if it was dark and scary inside the refrigerator. He figured she probably had enough time by now and reached up for the handle.

"Junior!" Patrick screamed from the top of the basement stairs. "Grandpa's gettin' us ice cream! Come on!"

Ice cream! Junior loved ice cream. He quickly turned and ran for the stairs.

"I love ice cream!" Junior shouted as he bounded up the

creaky old stairs. Patrick looked for Rachel in the basement, and didn't see her in her corner, so he flicked off the light switch.

Inside the refrigerator Rachel waited patiently, thinking that the lack of stimuli was probably why it had seemed longer than a few minutes since Junior had closed the door. Finally, she was sure that Junior had forgotten to open the door and began to bang on the inside of the door.

"Junior!" Rachel yelled. "Let me out!"

She leveraged her feet against the door and pushed, to no avail. Time passed slowly in the dark recess of the refrigerator. She had no idea how long she had been inside the appliance, it could have been minutes, hours, or even days. She wished Drake were there, he'd surely save her, like a knight in shining armor. But as her thoughts began to drift into dream-like concepts, she realized that she was struggling to breathe. The door was sealed tight and there was no source of fresh oxygen. In her logical mind it was a pretty easy path to her eventual suffocation if she couldn't get out of the fridge. Frantically she scratched at the door, clawing for her life. Over and over she scratched the inside of the door. Her fingernails broke and bled on the texture of the door, and she continued to scratch. Deep in her mind, she saw the smiling image of Drake, his dimples showing, and she thought, 'I'm sorry Drake.' She felt the presence of two smiling faces, but these weren't Drake, nor were they smiling for her. They were smiling because the time had come, within the small space of the closed refrigerator there was no more oxygen. Her last memory was of the evil that was inside there with her.

Clancy Finnegan got to his in-laws house about two o'clock that Sunday afternoon. He had brought home gifts for each of his children from his two-week long road trip. It made him happy to bring things home for his kids, seeing their smiling faces as they tore into the packaging of the toys and trinkets he gave them. By quarter after two, he had given everything he had brought home away, except for the books and records he brought back for Rachel.

"Where's Rachel?" Clancy asked his mother-in-law.

"Haven't seen her since church, Clancy," Grandma responded. "That girl behaves mighty strange sometimes, hiding out in the basement all day."

Clancy nodded and scowled at the same time. He walked to the basement door. The old door creaked open. Down below in the dark basement nothing stirred.

"Rachel!" Clancy yelled. "You down there, big girl?"

A sudden feeling of dread overwhelmed the cheery heart of Clancy. He flicked the light switch on and thundered down the old wooden stairs.

"Rachel!" Clancy shouted, as he frantically looked around the basement. He squinted his eyes, and saw a faint golden glow around the door of a large old refrigerator. He raced to the appliance and busted open the door. Rachel tumbled out, her skin cold and blue, her fingers bloodied and torn, and her eyes were rolled back in her head showing nothing but bloodshot white. "No! No! No!"

"What's all the shoutin' about down here, Clancy?" Grandma yelled from the top of the stairs. She saw her son-in-law on the floor leaning over and holding her granddaughter's lifeless body. She started down the stairs. She saw a light glowing in front of Clancy, a diffused full spectrum of light that separated into a rainbow and seemed to arc from father to daughter.

"Come on, big girl!" Clancy sobbed. Tears streaked his face. The rainbow intensified. "Come on Rachel!"

Rachel saw the light at the end of the long tunnel again, except this time she was on the other side standing with Father Time.

"Miss Finnegan," Father Time stated. "My name is Aeon, and I have been watching over you. You have many allies who have yet to reveal themselves, including your father. You are the key to everything. Without you, well, I don't like to think about the world without you. Your destiny lies elsewhere, not here, so it's time you go back."

"So am I dead?" Rachel asked.

"No my dear," Aeon replied as he placed his gnarled old hand upon her shoulder. "Even now your father is trying to bring you back. See the rainbow of light coming toward you? It's time for you to go back."

"Okie dokey Loki," Rachel said in her sing song voice. "You know, up close you kinda look like that wizard, Gandalf."

Aeon smiled and sent her back across the divide.

Rachel fluttered and opened her eyes. Clancy hugged his daughter tightly.

"Hullo Daddy," Rachel said in a parched, barely audible voice.

"Don't ever do that again big girl," Clancy cried as he held onto Rachel.

By late April, the weather had gotten unseasonably warm. Rachel was concerned that Drake had not yet written back to her. She had been sending him at least one letter a week since Christmas time. Not hearing back from Drake was the hardest thing she had to deal with. She knew that he loved her, but he just hadn't realized it yet.

The family sought refuge from the heat at the public pool in Spring Grove, Minnesota. It normally didn't open until after Memorial Day, but the week of summer-like temperatures were supposed to last at least into May, forcing the city to open it up early.

Rachel wasn't happy to go to the pool. She had listened too many times to her step-grandfather saying how skinny and sexy she was. She rationalized that if she wasn't skinny anymore, then her step-grandfather would lose interest in her and leave her alone. She willfully began to overeat. On days she worked at the restaurant she ate everything she could. Eating brought her solace. It brought her hope. But it also brought her despair. She had gained over forty pounds since she had started her job. All she ever saw in the mirror was a fat girl looking back at her, and she wondered where the real

Rachel had gone. Despite her weight gain, the molestation continued. And in her mind she concluded she just had to get fatter.

Being fatter and going to the public pool did not go hand-in-hand. Rachel was embarrassed to put on her swimming suit that was too small for her because it was from last summer. Mom gave her one of her old one-piece suits to put on. That didn't help her confidence at all.

The heat was overwhelming, so she quickly exited the changing room and plunged into the cool water. Once in the pool, none of her friends or family could see how large she had gotten.

"Hey Rachel," Laurie said from the middle of the crowded pool. Most of the kids were in the shallow end. Very few people were in the deeper end.

"Hey Laurie," Rachel stated, as she wiped the water from her face and pulled her hair back behind her head. Laurie was a very petite brunette, one of the three band kids from Dorchester, who Rachel made fast friends with soon after moving to Iowa. The other two, Michelle, a tomboyish blonde, and Dawn, a short pudgy girl with enormous breasts, thick black eyebrows, and peroxide blonde hair, were nearby. "Hi Mich, hi Dawn."

"Let's go into the deep end away from all the babies," Michelle announced, as she turned and swam off toward the deeper water.

Laurie quickly followed. Rachel was apprehensive because she really didn't like being in water where she couldn't touch the bottom.

"Come on Rachel," Dawn prodded, as she swam into the deep end. "Don't be such a scaredy-cat."

Rachel swam out to her friends. Laurie and Michelle were diving down under the water when she arrived out in the middle of the deep end of the pool, it was marked twelve feet deep.

"Let's see if you can touch the bottom," Dawn announced with a laugh.

Rachel shook her head.

"Come on, Rachel," Dawn said, as she prepared to duck under the water. "It's not like you have to worry about not floating, as fat as you are, don't you know? Fat floats!"

Dawn dived under the water with a loud splash and a thrashing leg kick. Rachel wiped the water from her face. When she looked at Dawn she saw an ugly girl who was mean to her, a lot. But, she was also her friend, and Rachel knew that she'd gained a lot of weight, and was very self-conscious of it. Maybe Dawn was right. Maybe the mirror was right. Maybe all she was anymore was a fat girl. Drake wouldn't even notice her anymore. In her mind she realized that in trying to protect herself from her wicked step-grandfather she might have lost her one true love.

She felt a tug on her left leg. She kicked back, thinking Dawn was pulling on her. Michelle and Laurie broke the surface with gasps for air, followed soon by Dawn.

The tug happened again, Rachel wasn't sure who would be doing that since all her friends had just surfaced. She looked and saw her brothers at the other end of the pool. Then she looked down. An unseen hand grabbed her leg and pulled her under. She didn't have time to take a breath and immediately started to struggle for air. She thrashed upward, nearing the surface, and was pulled violently down again. Above her she saw the legs of her friends kicking and the light above them. She pushed upward once again, cresting the surface, and gasping for air before being pulled under once again. This time a hand pushed her down from above as well. She struggled and fought for her life.

Above the water, her friends wondered what she was doing. Rachel seemed in distress when she came up for air.

"I think she needs help," Laurie said.

"She's just playin' us," Dawn laughed.

"No, I think she might be drowning," Michelle announced, as she and Laurie dived back under the water to help Rachel.

"Drama queen," Dawn responded, as she shook her

head.

Under the water, Rachel fought against her unseen attackers. The hand pushing her down was attached to her left shoulder. She grabbed its wrist and pulled. More hands grabbed her from above. She fought against them too. Upward the new hands pulled, causing Rachel to stop fighting because she knew upward meant rescue. Suddenly a larger presence emerged in the deep end of the pool. It was to large to fit in the water and it splashed up like a massive five fingered hand and crashed back into the water. The water hand passed through the girls and crashed into the unseen assailants pulling them to the bottom of the pool, crushing them until they slipped into the ether.

Together all three girls emerged from beneath the water. Rachel coughed violently. Michelle held onto her with one arm under Rachel's right arm and across her chest.

"Get out of the water!" Laurie exclaimed to her friends. "Get her out of the water!"

"Did you see that splash?" Dawn questioned. "It came out of nowhere, all of sudden, just wooosh!"

At the other end of the pool people were staring at the commotion being made by the girls.

The four girls got to the ladder on the deep end of the pool and helped each other out. Laurie quickly ran and got towels. The girls made it over to a bench and sat down. Rachel still coughed, trying to get the water from her lungs.

"What was that?" Michelle asked Rachel and Laurie in a hushed tone. She didn't want to draw any more attention to them than they already had.

"What was what?" Dawn interrupted. "The splash?"

"That thing," Michelle stated, as she pointed to the pool. "That thing that was pulling you down, Rachel, what was it?"

"I don't know," Rachel cried. "It grabbed me and pulled."

"I saw it," Laurie said in a hushed tone, as she began to cry. "It was like it was invisible, except, it had mass and it displaced the water. I saw glassy eyes."

"How can you see an invisible thing?" Dawn questioned. "Did they cause the splash? It kind of looked like a hand, it was weird."

"We didn't see a splash, Dawn, we were down there, with whatever that was," Michelle responded. "I felt its hand on her shoulder, and I kicked its head, or at least it felt like a head."

"Why would invisible monsters, if they even existed, want to drown Rachel?" Dawn asked. "I mean get real, girls, invisible monsters? Can you say, drama queen?"

"It's a long story," Rachel sobbed. "It started back in Washington, when I met this boy in second grade, and I'm not sure you want to hear about it, or if you did, if you'd even believe it."

"Rachel," Laurie began. "Trust me, Mich and I just got totally freaked out by whatever that was under the water. But, you're our friend, and friends stick together."

"And," Michelle added, "after fighting whatever that was, there's not much you can tell me that I wouldn't believe."

Dawn shook her head, but refused to walk away.

Rachel shared her story, her love of Drake, the powers of the daemon Miss Furfur, the plight that Drake and his brothers faced, her study of herbology and witchcraft, and the series of unfortunate events that had plagued her since she moved to Iowa. The only thing she left out was her step-grandfather, because she knew that he'd hurt those that she loved if she ever revealed what he was doing to her.

At the end of her story, the girls sat and stared silently at each other.

"Don't witches usually work together in a pack?" Michelle broke the silence with a question.

"Not a pack, a coven," Dawn clarified.

"Then we need to be a coven," Laurie added, "the four of us, to make sure no one gets Rachel anymore."

"And that she gets her dreamy guy in the end," Michelle said with a giggle.

"Are you sure?" Rachel questioned. "Studying magic isn't fun, and it doesn't make you very popular."

"We're not very popular now, in case you didn't notice," Michelle responded as she motioned around them.

"So whatta we got to lose?" Laurie asked.

"Our sanity, most likely," Dawn chirped.

The girls smiled at each other and hugged, even Dawn.

That very night, when Rachel was hiding under her blanket pretending to be asleep, she heard the door open and she began to cry. Raymond approached the side of the bed.

"Why is she crying?" Raymond questioned. "We don't know, do you know Raymond?"

Raymond began to have a conversation with himself.

"Maybe it's cause we almost drowns her?"

"No, I think it has to do with that boy?"

"Fraser? Why do you think that, Raymond?"

"I'll show you," Raymond said before he left the room. Rachel pulled back the blanket and hoped that he was gone for the night. She heard the floorboards creak outside her room and knew he was coming back.

"Wakey, wakey, sleeping beauty," Raymond said as he stumbled into the room and stood over the side of the bed.

"Please Grandpa," Rachel begged with tears in her eyes. "Don't do this anymore."

"You don't love your dear old grandpa anymore, is that what I'm hearing, baby girl?" Raymond questioned with an angry slur in his voice.

"Course she doesn't love us, Raymond, she loves that boy."

"That boy doesn't love her back!" Raymond snapped, as he threw a stack of opened letters at Rachel's face. "Look, all of your pathetic love letters, marked return to sender. The boy moved on. You got no one else to love now, my beauty. I have to do this, so you understand how to take care of a real man. You do want to be loved, don't you baby girl?"

Rachel looked frantically at the letters. They were all

stamped 'Return to Sender' just as her step-grandfather had said. Her tears began to flow.

"Now roll over and get ready for us."

"Yeah, girl, let me see your lovely fat ass," Raymond said.

Rachel began to cry uncontrollably. Maybe Drake never loved her. Maybe she had just imagined it all. Maybe she deserved what her step-grandfather was about to do to her. She felt his cold calloused hands on her hips, smelt the reek of alcohol on his breath, and tried to shut her mind off.

"Aesma, let's make her pregnant."

"We can't do that, Saurva, Furfur gave us orders. We must make her die, not make her have demon babies."

"Will you guys shut up!" Raymond snapped, as he climbed on the bed. "I need to get me some of this sweetness."

She wasn't certain why there were three voices coming from her step-grandfather, she wasn't mistaken, each voice was different, and that made no sense to her. But she knew one of those names they said—Furfur, and she'd not give up her dreams and let that daemon win. Part of her soul hardened. Thankfully, Rachel was able to shut off her senses, but not before she marked those three names in her memory. Aesma, Saurva, and of course, Furfur. She'd survive this ordeal. She'd get stronger through the help of her friends, her new coven. She'd get out of here, this hell she found herself in. She would become a doctor. And she would go find Drake.

In her logical mind she flashed ahead to June 1982, her graduation from high school. The math came easy— approximately 763 more days, or 18,312 hours, or 109 weeks. 109 was the smallest number, so she resolved she'd count the weeks, then she'd be gone, and then these demons were going to get their asses handed to them. She made that promise to herself, and she fully intended to keep it.

On Tuesday, April twenty-ninth, after the crater on the

top of the mountain had grown to over 1,500 feet and the north flank of the mountain bulged outward, U.S. government authorities imposed a red and blue zone around Mt. St. Helens, limiting human access to the mountain. It moved up to a state of emergency. The official closing of the area prompted local legend and Spirit Lake Lodge owner Harry Truman to say, "I think the whole damn thing is over-exaggerated. Spirit Lake and Mt. St. Helens are my life. You couldn't pull me out of here with a mule team." Inside the Tower of Dreams a battle raged.

16

BRIGID TUATHA DE DANANN

THE BROTHERHOOD OF OLYMPUS
AND THE TOWER OF DREAMS

Council of Olympus
Chapter Sixteen
May 18, 1980
Hazel Dell, Washington

On Friday, May sixteenth, Drake sat with his friends having lunch, and he decided he was going to test the waters a little bit more. Not being able to tell any of his friends about the time in the Grand Library or fighting the demons and gods was eating him up inside. Telling it all to Martin helped a lot, but he needed someone else he could confide in.

"See, that's the difference between you and me, son," Downtown Danny said to Robert. "Well, that and your sweet mustache."

Robert chuckled and stroked his mustache.

"You guys just talk to amuse yourselves, I swear," Steve stated with a smile.

Drake slyly pulled out one of his drawing tablets.

"You got more drawings to show us, brother?" Scrappy said with a wide smile.

"I have this one I'm working on," Drake responded, as he flipped pages looking for his most recent drawing. He stopped when he found it, and flipped all of the other pages over on the spiral so they were out of the way. He turned it to show Scrappy, Robert, and Steve. It was a pencil drawing of a man who kind of looked like Drake, with a blazing sword in his right hand. Wrapped around his left leg was the tail of a large snake-like creature that had four arms and two bat-like wings. The snake monster looked to be attacking the guy.

"Whoa!" the three boys across the table said in unison.

"Let me see," Ryan demanded.

"Me too, brotha," Downtown Danny chimed in.

Drake turned it so the boys sitting on his side of the table could see the drawing.

"That's so awes!" Robert exclaimed.

"Is that supposed to be you, Drake?" George asked because of the obvious similarity.

"Yeah, I guess so," Drake answered.

"I want to fight him too," Scrappy announced.

"To the death, Scrap?" Robert inquired with both his bushy eyebrows raised.

"Yep," Scrappy replied. "Me and that snake-guy are going to get the smack down happening."

"Was this in one of your dreams or something, Drake?" Ryan asked. "Cause its kind of scary to think what I'd do in your place."

"Oh come on, Healy," Downtown Danny added with one of his patented head movements. "Ya know the first thing you'd do's crap your whitey-tighties, son."

The boys laughed.

"Yeah," Drake continued deliberately. "Looking back on it, I can see where it looks pretty scary. But when it happened I was so amped up with adrenaline and the need to save my brothers, so I didn't even think about it, I guess."

Steve looked at Drake, expecting him to laugh because he was joking. Robert and Scrap stared at him too, Robert started shaking his head, and Scrappy just started to smile. George just kept eating. Ryan's eyes opened wide as he thought about what Drake had said. And Downtown Danny never even looked up from his lunch, but started to laugh.

"You had us all going there for a minute, son," Downtown Danny broke the silence. "That's pretty funny. Hey, you think that would work on babes? I can tell 'em I had to fight some big nasty snake-guy to save them. They'll think I'm their hero."

"You're joking, right Drake?" Steve asked. "Cause if your not, you're kind of freaking me out, and you might need to go see a head-shrinker."

Drake evaluated his friends one more time. Steve was out, George was out, Downtown Danny never took anything seriously, and Ryan was too young. That left Robert and Scrap. He knew Robert was almost always with Scrappy, so he'd have to tell them both. Robert seemed way more skeptical than Scrappy, and Drake realized he'd have to temper his story with enough reality checks to keep Robert from imploding it all for Scrappy.

"Steve," Drake finally responded, "of course I'm joking, things like that snake-guy only exist in stories and junk like that, duh."

The boys laughed and returned to their lunches.

"But seriously," Robert added, "that drawing is so awes!"

"Two words," Scrappy explained with a wide toothy smile. "To the death."

"Good job brainiac," Robert chirped with both bushy eyebrows raised. "That's three words!"

Drake spent the rest of the day thinking about how he'd approach the subject again with just Scrappy and Robert. He got home late from school and spent the evening up in his room typing. Saturday was much like Friday evening. Drake pecked away at the typewriter most of the day, except for when he came down for food.

By Saturday night, Drake was tired and feeling kind of brain-dead from typing most of the day. He knew he could probably type faster if he took a typing class in school, but didn't want to because those classes were typically filled with lots of girls and few boys. He didn't need any other fuel to be added to any discussions about his perceived sexuality.

He came down and watched the end of the local news on KGW Channel 8. At eleven thirty, *Saturday Night Live* started. Steve Martin was announced as the host of the *Not Ready For Primetime Players*. Drake remembered back to his odd interaction with Bill Murray in the bleachers of Olympic Stadium, he had no idea who the man was back in the summer of 1978.

"You need to follow your dreams too Drake. Go after 'em. Don't let your life rush by until one day when you stop and look back and say, man I wish I would've, or I should've, or I could've. Seize the day kid. Be the best you that you can be, and don't ever let anyone tell you that you can't be what you want to be. Even if that's a pro ball player, or a comedian," he told Drake.

He thought of how he probably blew it, by not asking him for his address, or phone number, not like they would've ever become friends or anything, but still weirder things did happen. Drake smiled and settled down to watch the show.

Steve Martin's opening monologue was about what he believed, and it was a bit different than what Drake had seen from Steve Martin in the past.

"What I believe," Steve Martin stated with a single spot light upon him and the rest of the stage completely dark, as somber music played in the background. "I believe in rainbows and puppy dogs and fairy tales. And I believe in family, Mom and Dad and Grandma... and Uncle Tom, who waves his penis."

Drake sat up. He wasn't sure he had ever heard that word on television before. He looked over at Dennis and Albert, who were both half asleep, or in Albert's case mostly asleep, because of the string of drool connected to his chest.

"Did you hear that?" Drake asked his brothers.

"Albert snores," Dennis mumbled.

Drake shook his head and went back to watching the television show. Steve Martin and the absurdity of the sketches performed kept Drake awake for the next ninety minutes. He stretched and turned off the TV, covered each of his brothers with a blanket, picked up Monique from where she was sleeping on the couch, and then headed up the stairs to his bed.

Sleep came easily for Drake. Rest, however, did not. He tossed and turned for much of the night. As morning neared Drake finally began to dream.

He was standing outside his window, on the roof of the

house. In the distance Mt. St. Helens rumbled and shook. A huge blast blew out the north side of the mountain and a massive column of steam and ash stretched up into the sky before becoming a mushroom cloud at the top. Drake was in awe over the spectacle of nature. From out of nowhere he felt a pull upon his torso, and he began to rise up off the roof. Drake had experienced numerous flying dreams in his life, so he wasn't scared or even startled really. Rapidly upward he rose, nearly to the height of the mushroom cloud churning out of the distant mountain. Suddenly, with a flash of blue light, he was being pulled north and the erupting peak fell behind him. Drake saw Mt. Rainier off to the right, Puget Sound appeared below him, and he turned slightly to the west as he rocketed northward. Before him rose the Olympic Mountains. Drake knew where he was going. He'd been there once before during a dream when he and his family were camping below Hurricane Ridge during the summer of 1978. As he approached the four peaks of Mt. Olympus he climbed in altitude. The air smelled fresh and fragrant with a mixture of evergreen trees and rainfall. Electrified clouds swirled and clashed in brilliant flashes of lightning above the mountain. The moisture of the water vapor in the clouds dampened his skin as he flew upward into them.

A bright flash blinded him, and he stopped moving. He felt the solid base below him as he sat cross-legged on a pedestal. It was the same as before. In front of him, approximately fifteen feet away from the disc he occupied and beyond the gap in the floor that illuminated the tumultuous clouds in the night sky far below, rose a half-circle platform like a judicial panel on a raised white dais. On top of the dais, many beings were moving in the bright white light and rolling mist that blinded Drake. The bright light did not hurt his eyes, but it just made it difficult to see. The fragrance of the moisture in the clouds was replaced by a jumble of aromas, many of which were reminiscent of incense. Missing was the distinctively heady aroma of roses that flooded his senses the last time he sat here.

"Welcome," a warm feminine voice lilted through the air. "Drake, son of Drake, son of Martin the Nameless."

"It is the hour of our greatest need," spoke a booming masculine voice from the middle of the dais. Drake saw the god emerge from the white mist. He wore a broad chest plate of golden armor. His large, thick shoulders were covered in a dark cape. He held a long golden spear in his right hand that oozed electrical energy. He had a patch covering one eye, and a long white, braided beard. He knew this god from his interactions with him before. This was Woden, the All-Father from the Norse pantheon of gods. "The dark gods will shortly gain control of one of the great towers, and we need our champions to be able to strike a blow for its liberty, and ours."

"Mr. Woden," Drake stated respectfully. "It's a pleasure to see you again, sir."

"Please," Woden responded with a booming echo. "You may address me as simply Woden, or Odin if you would prefer, or simply as All-Father. I don't think I have ever been called mister before."

The All-Father laughed like deep rolling thunder.

Another masculine figure emerged from the white light and mist. He was a tall, well-muscled man with a squared off beard. He wore virtually no clothes, and his lower body was surrounded by a loose cylinder of turbulent water. His head was adorned with a crown of jeweled coral, and in his hand he held a massive golden trident.

"Drake, son of Drake," the water god began. Drake could smell sea salt on the air. From the look of the god, he guessed a Greek origin, and that would make him Poseidon. "My uncle, Aeon, has spoken highly of you."

"Thank you, Mr. Poseidon," Drake replied. He knew the pedigree chart of the Greek pantheon, Aeon—also known as Khronos—was one of the primordial gods, brother of Gaia, the grandmother of the big three, Zeus, Hades, and Poseidon. That solidified his guess, and made him confident to address the god by name.

"What does this title 'mister' mean, Drake, son of Drake?" Poseidon queried, as he stroked his beard with his left hand.

"It's a term of respect given to male elders, like teachers, or fathers," Drake tried to explain.

"Most humans have addressed my kin as lords, ladies, or highnesses," Poseidon replied. "But times have changed, so I accept the respect of your title so given unto me."

Drake bowed his head.

"As you recall, my boy," Woden began, "the old gods of men, some of us are gathered here of course, were banned from influencing humanity over five hundred years ago. By agreeing to the Covenant of Reason, we can no longer walk the Earth as we once did. Many of us have slipped into antiquity or sought out new adventures elsewhere. But, there were those of us who still watched over the world of mankind, both for good and ill, I'm afraid. We are the Council of Olympus, and you have accepted our offer to be our champions. Our adversaries, the Council of Retribution, or the Dark Council, has champions of their own. They have set upon a plan to take the Earth through one of the Towers of Ominous Power."

"I'm aware of this plan, All-Father," Drake replied. "I have spoken to Addraemyr, the guizor of the Tower of Dreams. But, I want to know why exactly gods and daemons even care about what we do on Earth?"

There was a commotion upon the dais that included lots of whispered tones that Drake couldn't discern.

"You seek knowledge," a tall blue-skinned god said, as he stepped forward from the light. Upon his head was a bejeweled turban adorned with two massive feathers that made him appear even taller. He had thick black outlines around his almond eyes. Drake instantly perceived him to be Egyptian. "I have watched your development for quite sometime, Drake, son of Drake. Allow me to introduce myself, I am known as Amun, or Amun-Ra. I began my duties as the god of knowledge within my pantheon, and over time became the god of the sun and sky, but I have always held the search for knowledge to be the highest calling of both man and god. As for your question, gods and daemons—who are in reality minor deities in their own right—are so interested in humans because they possess something in their life-force that is unobtainable elsewhere. Some crave that power within the souls of humanity, and they yearn to harvest it through fear, enslavement, torture, and ultimately the death of all humans. Others fear it. And some of us hope that in the future, when humans begin to reach their full potential that they will freely choose to be our friends and allies."

"Pardon me, Drake, son of Drake," a radiantly beautiful woman with distinctly Asian features interrupted. As she moved forward, Drake could see that her lower torso was serpentine. He immediately flashed back to his encounter with Quatyl and prepared to defend himself. "We have heard rumors, unsubstantiated of course, that you have gained much power since we last saw you. There are even those that have bestowed the unheard of title of god-slayer upon you, are these rumors true?"

"I'm sorry, my Lady," Drake responded diplomatically. He quickly thought how to best reply to this question. What if Quatyl was her relative? This might not end well. "If Quatyl was any relation to anyone here, he left me no options. I just wanted to get the Staff of Orkan back. It was a gift from this very Council and it's extremely important to me."

Drake could hear, 'oohs' and 'aahs' amongst the assembled deities.

"My dear boy," the beautiful snake-lady replied, "allow me to introduce myself, I am known as Nu Kua, and Quatyl was no relation of mine. I am pleased you retrieved the staff, but I am fearful that you have already made a powerful enemy. The war to come is still in its infancy. Therefore, I believe it is imperative that we act in your behalf by assisting you and your brothers as you liberate the Tower."

"Thank you, my Lady Nu Kua," Drake responded with a head bow.

"This news distresses me," Amun stated. "If the agents of our adversaries have discovered our champions, and they will soon have the Tower of Dreams to stage their attacks from. None of the brothers Fraser may be safe. These are no simple foes. They can sense the essence of our champions, and should they find them they will do everything in their power to extinguish the flames of the Frasers."

"We must act to support our champions if we have any hope for victory in the coming war," Nu Kua added.

"What do you propose, Lady Nu Kua?" Woden inquired.

"First, our champions must be hidden. Their essence must be disguised," Nu Kua answered with a fluttering of her eyelids. "And then I believe we must become more involved. Some of us still have the ability to influence the mortal world. Raven can still travel there. Poseidon's uncle still travels through the streams of time, why, even Poseidon himself still possesses some ability within the element of water."

"Is this correct, brother Poseidon?" Woden asked.

"'Tis true," Poseidon replied. "I have been assisting my uncle. He has decreed that there is a human girl that has become a target of a daemon. According to his insight, without this girl all we may attempt might eventually unravel. But I can say no more lest I alter the future that lies ahead of us."

"I see," Woden responded. "How have you assisted her?"

"The daemon has sent daevas after her," Poseidon answered. Many of the assembled deities shook their heads when they heard about the daevas. "And I can still reach out through the waters of Earth with some effort."

"Those are ill tidings, brother Poseidon," Woden remarked. "Daevas can bring down a godling, that bodes not well for this human girl. These are Ill tidings indeed... It is imperative, as Lady Nu Kua suggested that we find a way to assist the Brotherhood."

"There are some amongst the Fraser bloodline who have the power to cloak the essence of our champions," Amun added, as he deliberated a plan. "Both a grandmother, and the mother's sister, are powerful in aura manipulation. Is there one amongst us who can deliver a message to either of them and ask for their assistance for the safety of our young charges?"

There was movement on the dais and a slightly disheveled man emerged. He had long black hair adorned with feathers of many shapes and colors, mismatched hand-stitched clothing, and shiny baubles and trinkets around his neck, wrists, and ankles.

"I might be so able," the disheveled man said, as he winked at Drake and waved to him. "Hope you like the key, Master Drake. These gifted ladies you speak of, Lord Amun, are hidden from even our eyes, but I might find them, with a little luck."

"Thank you, brother Raven," Amun stated.

"Yes, thank you brother Raven," Woden added. "Now then, what would you have us do to assist our champions, Lady Nu Kua?"

"We need to make sure they have the skills and tools they need to stand up to the enemies who lay in wait upon their path," Nu Kua answered thoughtfully, "and those who will now seek vengeance upon them for the blood already shed. I do not believe we have prepared them to face gods in battle, and that is what they will encounter, I now fear."

"Wise words, as ever, my Lady," Woden added.

"The timeline of our champions' growth has been pushed forward and our adversaries have many allies already in place on the field of battle," another goddess stated, as she emerged from the white mist and light. She was a statuesque woman with piecing blue eyes, long flowing auburn hair, and a simmering fire that burned close to her head. Drake searched his memory for any conceptual links to the mythologies he knew, but came up empty.

"Your insight is most welcome, Lady Brigid," Woden

stated with a slight bow.

"Like our brother Poseidon," Brigid continued, "I still have some connection to the mortal world. Worship of me was incorporated into the church of the one God, when his dogma spread to Celtic lands. I was never officially banished from Earth for that reason. I will assist Poseidon and Aeon and grant aid to our champions."

Nu Kua smiled and bowed to Brigid, then nodded to Woden who returned the nod.

"I look forward to tutoring you and your warriors, god-slayer," Brigid said with a warm smile. "And aiding you however I may in the days to come. It has been a long time since I have had such a charge. It is surely a challenge that makes my heart beat anew."

"So it shall be!" Woden decreed with a mighty roar. "I bid you all to search your armories and return with a most formidable weapon that might be used by our champions. We will choose the best and place them where they may be best utilized, with the help of Brigid, of course."

"Of course, All-Father," Brigid replied with a bow.

"Now we must part once again, my boy," Woden stated with a sweeping hand gesture.

"Wait, All-Father," Drake interjected. "This war's too dangerous for my younger brothers and I'm glad Mr. Amun has suggested hiding our essences, but I've been told to find new members of the Brotherhood. How will I seek them out? How will I know who to recruit? I want to make sure I choose correctly."

"The wisdom you seek already resides within you," Woden replied with a smile. "The conviction of a man is measured through his heart and the love that resides within it. You will know your brothers when you meet them, and they will, of course, rise to the challenge of your bidding. Do not fret over such things, my boy. Those you seek will be great and noble warriors for our cause. And one might say that they have been searching for you and what you offer for their entire lives."

"Thank you All-Father," Drake responded with a bow of his head.

"Now be off, for the hour is at hand," Woden announced. "The Tower of Dreams falls!"

Drake began to fade into nothingness. Before he vanished, Poseidon appeared by his side.

"Drake Fraser," Poseidon quickly and quietly said. "Be it known to you, that my uncle and I shall look after Miss Finnegan. Though there is not much water in the landlocked realm of Iowa, I will protect her."

Drake smiled as he vanished. In that moment he remembered who Rachel Finnegan was and he was glad that Poseidon was going to be protecting her in the upcoming war. Rachel was very special to him, but he couldn't remember why, and the more he thought of her the less he knew of her, until he was completely enveloped in a swirling mist steeped in the fragrance of roses.

"Drake! Drake!" Dennis shouted from the window side of his bed. Dennis pulled open the draperies revealing the blue morning sky. "Look! Look!"

"Okay, okay," Drake said, as he rolled over and got up out of bed. Monique was equally excited as she leapt up and down by the wall like she was trying to see out the window. Drake bent over and picked her up.

"The mountain's erupting!" Dennis exclaimed. "Just like you said it would to Albert when we were moving down here. You're like Nostradamus, Drake, that's just freaky."

Albert came crashing into Drake's room behind them and joined them by the window.

"Holy spumoni!" Albert exclaimed with wide eyes and a gaping mouth.

Together the four of them stood and looked at the spectacle of nature unfolding before their eyes. Only Monique broke the silence as she barked at what she saw. Drake had just seen this reality moments before in his dream. He was in awe of the sheer power of the eruption.

On Sunday, May eighteenth at 8:32 AM, a massive Earthquake beneath Mt. St. Helens triggered the largest landslide in American history as the north face of the mountain collapsed and was immediately followed by a catastrophic lateral blast that leveled a blast zone within fifteen miles of the north face of the mountain. Gone were the evergreen trees, the reflective waters of Spirit Lake, the thousands and thousands of animals that lived in the wilderness, and the fifty-seven people who were trapped near the mountain. Geologist David Johnston, five miles north of the mountain at the time of the eruption, radioed to the U.S.G.S. field office, "Vancouver! Vancouver! This is it!" and was never heard from again. By 8:47 AM, a churning column of boiling ash and steam rose up into a mushroom cloud twelve miles above the decapitated mountain. The eruption generated its own lightning storm within the ash cloud. Addraemyr and the huisum of the Tower of Dreams had either been killed or taken captive by the invaders of the dark gods. The Tower of Dreams had fallen, and so, too, had the hope of all humanity.

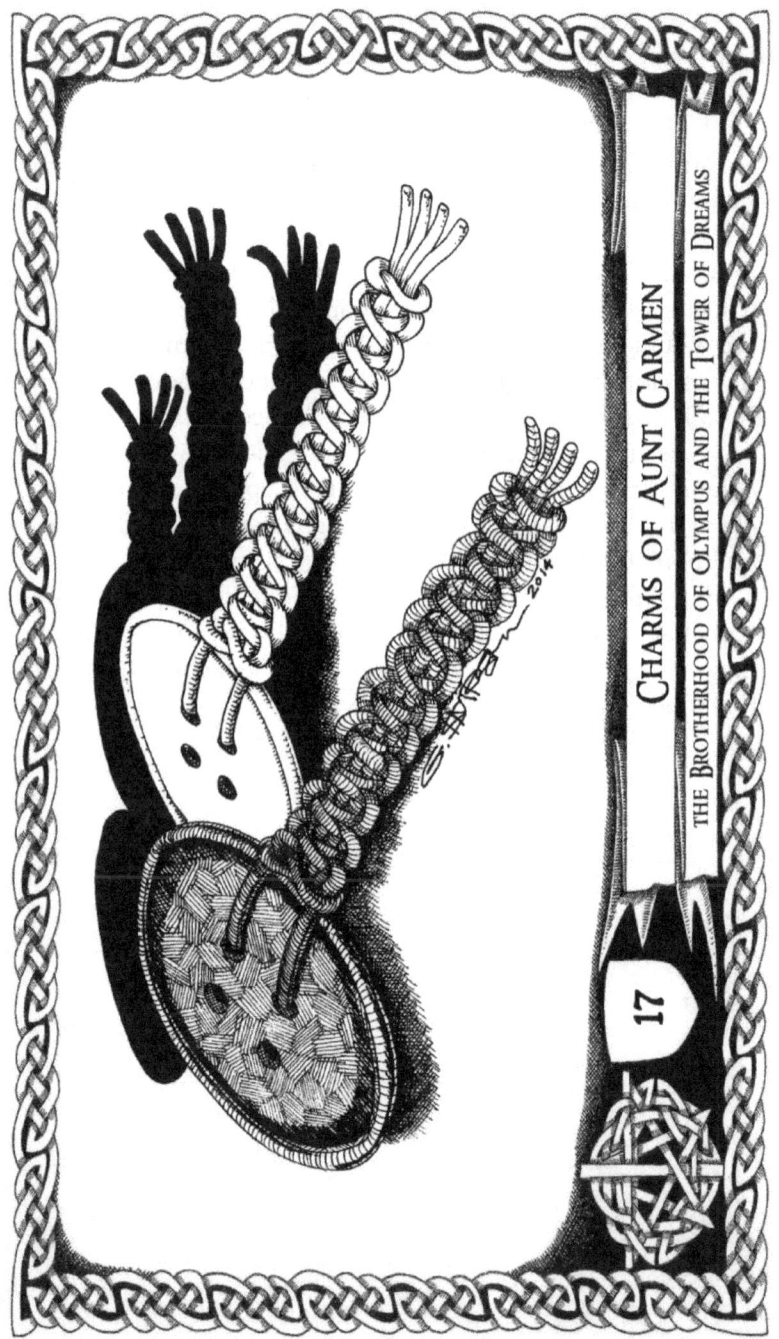

CHARMS OF AUNT CARMEN

THE BROTHERHOOD OF OLYMPUS AND THE TOWER OF DREAMS

17

Aunt Carmen
Chapter Seventeen
June 14, 1980
Hazel Dell, Washington

Drake carried a lot of pent up information in his mind as he went through the motions during the last few weeks of school. He tried many times to isolate Scrappy from Robert to talk to him about the truly weird experiences that had been happening. Each time he thought he might have pulled it off, Robert would suddenly appear and pop into the conversation with a, "whatcha doin' son?" kind of expression. Drake hadn't even gotten to talk to Martin about his dream the morning of the eruption of Mt. St. Helens.

On May twenty-fifth, the mountain erupted again, but this time the winds blew out of the Northeast and carried the ash cloud over Southwest Washington and into Oregon. The Memorial Day weekend turned into a five day mini-vacation, since the buses couldn't run until they were all cleaned and prepped to handle the ash that churned up from the roadway. Ash getting into the carburetor would be heated and turn to glass, like glaze on pottery in a kiln when it's fired. Such a thing would ruin the engine of the vehicle. The precaution to avoid it was to affix a secondary air filter to the outside of the vehicle with a finer mesh to catch the ash. The hybrid buses were ready to roll by the twenty-eighth of May and school returned to normal in the Vancouver District.

The volcano and the coming end of the year made the routines of school a bit off. However, a few things remained the same. For instance, Drake still avoided Moose Caine, and continued to put up with the teasing and ridicule for backing down to the bully. He saw less and less of Stacey, who started dating a tuba player in the school band who also claimed to be either a friend or relative of Tommy Shaw. Drake doubted the validity of that assertion, but gave the guy credit for using it to date the popular girl.

Mark graduated from Columbia River High School on the first Friday of June. He celebrated by going to work. Mark's focus had shifted completely toward making money, and he hadn't been talking much with any of his family since the move to Vancouver.

The last day of school was on Tuesday, June tenth. Drake hurried home, tossed his duffle bag in the closet, and sat down to work on his manuscript. He spun in his chair and turned on his radio. He missed KISW from Seattle, but had found KGON 92.3 the Defenders of Rock from Portland to fill its place. Fittingly, the song they were playing was *No More School* by Sandy Campbell. Drake began to sing along as he opened a spiral notebook to type from, grabbed a sheet of white paper and worked it into the typewriter.

Summer time, summer time,
The bell finally rang,
We're free, we're free, the kids all sang,

Free of the dirty looks of his fellow students or rude comments about his sexuality because he wouldn't fight Moose Caine.

No more bullies,
No more fights,
Never goin' back, no more school nights,

Drake concluded he'd be okay with never going back, he already knew more than most adults because of his voracious thirst for knowledge.

No more school,
Or the teacher's rules,
No more school,
Till maybe September comes,

Yeah, Sandy Campbell got it right in that song. There's something about the start of summer vacation that fuels the mind of a boy with the hope and aspiration of freedom and fun. Lost were the feelings of dread over the whole Tower of Dreams war, worries about friendships, or even confidants.

Drake smiled. He was going to make it a good summer.

On Friday, June thirteenth, those hopes would come crashing down. The occurrence of a Friday aligning with the thirteenth day of the month, had taken new significance since the untimely death of Uncle Wally in 1978, on the first Friday the thirteenth of that year.

Everyone was at the house for an almost lost tradition—the family dinner. It was a week after Mom's thirty-eighth birthday, and even her younger sister Carmen had come to visit. Mom and Carmen had made a salad and were in the kitchen catching up on their busy lives and preparing the last parts of two big pots of pasta. Spaghetti had long been a staple of their working-class poor family of seven, and it had become the food of choice for big gatherings.

Carmen's husband Steve and their nine-month old son Jebediah were in the living room with the rest of the boys and Beth. Dad sat in his recliner centered on the television near the front window. Steve was on the end of the couch nearest to Dad, and was joined by Mark, Beth, and Martin on the printed floral sofa. Beth delightfully held the baby. Drake, Dennis, and Albert were sprawled out in oversized beanbag chairs on the floor beyond the long coffee table.

"Any plans for the summer, boys?" Steve asked.

"Just to continue to cost me money to clothe and feed them," Dad remarked with a sly smile. "Have you seen how big they're all getting, Steve? Here's my advice to you, enjoy him while he's small, and while you only have one."

"Thanks Dad," Mark snapped. "All of us, who weren't born first, appreciate the love of our father."

The living room erupted in laughter.

"Any big plans now that you've graduated, Mark?" Steve inquired. Mark liked his Uncle Steve. After he got out of the Navy at the end of the Viet Nam conflict, Steve had worked his way up doing road work for the logging companies in Grays Harbor, learned to operate a backhoe, and then bought one himself and started his own contracting company. His success allowed them to purchase the large tract of land south of Brooklyn, where they were building their house. Mark admired that.

"I'm gonna work a lot," Mark replied. "Save up as much money as possible."

"What about long term? Are you going to go to school?" Steve questioned. "Or join the military like your brother?"

"I don't really know yet," Mark answered. "There's a school in Phoenix, Universal Technical Institute, that's supposedly the best mechanic school in the country. One of their reps came to the high school a few months ago. It was pretty impressive."

"Mechanics is good," Steve said.

"Arizona is pretty hot," Martin added. "I spent part of a summer in Texas, and I wouldn't want to do that again. Washington weather is perfect."

"He's so adorable," Beth announced, as she made faces at the baby. "But he's got an awful big name for such a little guy."

"We call him Jeb, for short," Steve remarked with a smile. "But, I think he'll grow into his name."

"You two made any plans for making me a great-uncle yet?" Steve asked with a chuckle.

"Hell," Dad interjected, "Martin couldn't take care of a dog. He's not ready for a baby."

"Thanks Dad," Martin responded. "You've got company over and you start lighting us up. Nice."

"My house," Dad said with a wry smile. "My rules."

Over time the boys had grown to appreciate the berating humor their father would use on them. He was kind of like the comedian Don Rickles, except he never called any of them a 'hockey puck.' Drake in particular appreciated his dad's dry humor, having spent that evening with him at his lowest point last year made him reflect on the resilience of his father. He'd tease, torment, and at times come across as a bit of a tyrant, but in his heart he loved his boys unconditionally. He'd also stand at the very gates of Hell to defend them if he needed to. He was a model of agápe that Drake strived to be more like.

Drake smiled.

"I hope so," Beth chirped with a giggle. She turned her head to look at Martin. "I love babies, and look forward so much to being a mommy. What do you think, dear?"

"You heard my dad," Martin replied, as he tickled little Jeb. "I can't even take care of a dog."

Beth slapped his shoulder.

"Drake," Steve said, "what about you, any plans for the summer? You playing any basketball?"

"Nah," Drake responded as he thought of his summer of freedom. "I think I'm just gonna draw and write."

"Can you make a living doing that?" Steve asked. "I don't know how many artists or writers there are in the world who actually make money, least while they're alive."

"The hell you are, Drake," Dad announced. "You think you're just gonna hang out all summer and write? This is what I know about writing. No one who ever wrote anything just sat around and wrote. They had to pay bills, buy food, and pay rent. They needed money. No one's going to come knocking at our door asking if there's a kid here who writes that wants to make lots of money for writing something no one ever heard of. The world doesn't work that way. If you want something you have to do something about it, not sit there and wait for it to happen for you. Carpe Diem, seize the day. You want to be a writer, great, but you need a real job first."

"Your dad's right," Steve added. "Most people start off working odd jobs before they settle into a career."

"Did I just hear you correctly Steve?" Carmen questioned as she stepped into the living room behind Dad's recliner. "Did you actually say Drake's right? Not the young one, the dad? This one right here?"

Steve laughed.

"Don't try and start something with me," Dad replied. "Just because I never believed in all your hippie mojo crap."

"Hey," Carmen interrupted with a smile. "I was never a 'hippie' so let's get that straight. I just grew up in a troubled time, with the war and the counter-culture movement, and I embraced parts of both of them. My husband was in Southeast Asia, remember? Besides, my mojo has nothing to do with hippies. It's a family thing, most likely it's genetic. Got it?"

"My, you're feisty Carmen," Dad chuckled. "Are all hippies that feisty?"

Carmen lightly punched Dad in the shoulder, and they laughed together.

"Hey Mark," Dad began. "Are they hiring at the restaurant?"

"Dad," Mark responded, "it's a twenty-four hour restaurant, we go through like two or three guys a week in the dish pit or busboys since most of them are high schoolers. If he was eighteen I could get him into the kitchen with me. But I could get him a job tomorrow, if he wanted it."

Drake shook his head.

"Done," Dad stated. "Take him down there to fill out an application and talk to your manager."

"Oly, Mr. Olsen," Mark added, "will be there after three. I work at four, so I can take him when I go."

Drake shook his head again. He had plans, a summer of freedom to draw and write.

"He'll just need some brown pants and some white shirts," Mark continued.

Drake shook his head some more.

"Hey, I came in here to tell you dinner's ready," Carmen stated. Dennis and Albert launched themselves out of their beanbags and raced to the dinner table. Mom had set up a card table at the end of the dining room table to accommodate everyone at one table. Everyone else rose and meandered into the dining room. Carmen took Jeb from Beth and walked back through the dining room and into the kitchen. Beth looked at Martin as they walked.

"You really don't want kids?" Beth asked her husband in a hushed tone.

"Yeah, I do, I just don't know if we're ready for that," Martin quietly answered. "We can talk about it later."

"Okay," Beth replied. She longed to be a mother, and it made her sad and a little bit upset to think her husband might not want kids.

"Come on everyone, get a seat, dinner's on the table," Mom announced. Aside from Dennis and Albert, who already sat in their usual seats, the other boys were waiting to see where people were going to sit. Once Dad sat down, everyone else fell into place around the table.

Dinner was good. Mom's tomato paste and fried hamburger chunk sauce allowed Drake and several others to add Ketchup to their spaghetti to bring out the flavor. The discussion around the table was light and lively. Drake hoped it would allow Dad and Mark to forget about that whole 'him getting a job' idea.

After dinner, Carmen asked all of her nephews to step outside with her for a few minutes. She said she had something for them. The boys followed her out to her car. In the back of their white 1977 Toyota Land Cruiser she pulled out a small wooden box.

Inside the box were five buttons from assorted garments. One was red, one was silver, two more were black, and the last one was yellow. Attached to each button through the holes in the middle was a macramé dangle of yarn about four inches long.

"What are those?" Dennis asked.

"Are they for us?" Albert inquired.

"They're buttons, dillholes," Mark stated.

"Yes, they are, Mark," Carmen replied. "But they're more than that."

"What do you mean?" Martin questioned.

275

"You all remember the whole *Spirit* board incident?" Carmen responded. "And yes, Dennis, it really happened."

"How does she do that?" Dennis exclaimed. He had just been thinking that the whole haunting and fight to burn the game was just a bad dream.

"I have my ways," Carmen added. "Anyway, it seems as though there are forces out there that would want to hurt my nephews."

"How do you know that?" Drake asked. He knew he wasn't thinking about his fight with the god or anything like that for her to read his mind. Oh crap, he just thought about it.

"I'm perceptive," Carmen replied, with a wide smile. "Besides, I know a lot of things that were foretold by that game have already happened, and some of the things it talked about that have yet to occur involved you guys. And you need to be careful."

"There were some bad things the *Spirit* board predicted for us," Martin agreed.

"And on top of all of that," Carmen continued, "I had a visitor. A large black bird who brought me a message."

"Whoa," Albert uttered.

"That's crazy," Mark added. "Was it a carrier pigeon?"

"No, nephew," Carmen replied with a bit of attitude. "He wasn't a carrier pigeon. Most people would probably call him a native spirit, or maybe a god. Raven visited me, bringing me a warning and a request. He warned me of your safety in the coming months, because things like those mordgeists that haunted you are going to be looking for you."

"I don't like that, Aunt Carmen," Albert said. "Those things were scary."

"Yes they are, Albert," Carmen responded.

"What was the request?" Martin asked.

"He asked me to help you, in the name of some old gods," Carmen stated. "Now boys, I want you to know, I'm not real big on mythology, and I believe in God. But, I also know that the *Spirit* board had said there was going to be a war with the 'old gods' that you were going to have to fight in. And that message from the bird scared me. I will do whatever I can to protect you, I love you all."

"So you brought us buttons?" Mark questioned. "I'm not big on this whole spectral mojo crap. I know what we saw last year. I know what we did, but that doesn't mean I have to know anything more about that stuff. I just want to be a mechanic, not a wizard or some crap like that."

"I hear ya, Mark," Carmen replied. "These aren't just buttons, either. I made them. They're charms that your grandmother and I have put some of ourselves in, a little bit of our auras, to give you some protection."

"Cool," Dennis remarked. "I want the silver one!"

"How do they work?" Drake inquired. Of all his brothers, he understood the need the most, since he was there when the 'old gods' talked about all of this.

"Well," Carmen responded, "they're kind of like a cloaking device, or shield. You each possess an aura that spectral things or people with gifts can see. Each of your auras is unique to you, but there's a common element in them that links you as brothers, that marks you as Frasers. So these buttons emit a generic aura, a very powerful generic aura that will mask you and hide you from prying eyes. You need to keep them with you, in your pocket, when you leave the house. I will blanket the house before I leave. It's a bit easier to do since it's tied to property and can recharge itself from the living things on the land."

"That kinda sounds like the Force," Martin stated. "Obi-Wan said, 'The Force's what gives a Jedi his power, it's an energy field created by all living things, it surrounds us and penetrates us, it binds the universe together.' Master Yoda talked a lot more about it in the *Empire Strikes Back*."

Mark shook his head.

"So I need to carry a button around to make everyone feel better?" Mark asked. Carmen nodded, and then Albert and Dennis joined her by nodding. "I can do that, but I get the silver one."

Mark grabbed the silver one out of the box with lightning dexterity. Dennis pouted.

Martin and Drake looked at the remaining buttons. The yellow and red ones were bigger and looked like they may have come off from a girl's jacket.

"I think I'll take a black one," Martin stated.

"Me too," Drake said quickly. Both boys grabbed the black buttons.

"I'll take the red one, cause its like fire," Dennis announced.

"And I'll have the yellow one cause I'm like the sun," Albert added, one upping his brother. Dennis and Albert took their buttons and glared at each other.

"Promise me you'll be careful," Carmen said. "All of your possessions and anything that's in contact with your body will have residue of your aura on it, so don't leave it out where it can attract demons, or worse. And don't draw attention to yourself by talking a lot about this, or by using the names of the entities. Their names are powerful things that can be used to bind them and to summon them, so be very careful."

The boys all nodded in agreement.

"I'm not sure what else I can do," Carmen added. "This path is yours to take, not mine. If I can help you I will."

"Thank you, Aunt Carmen," the boys said in unison.

As they turned and walked back into the house, Mark thought to himself, I wonder if the button'll work in Arizona.

"Yes it will, Mark," Carmen stated as she closed the back door of her car.

At 2:00 PM, on Saturday the fourteenth, Mark came into Drake's room. Drake was sitting at his desk drawing.

"Dad said you need to be ready to leave by three," Mark announced. "You don't want to make him mad. I suggest you take a shower, brush your hair, and put on a nice shirt too. You don't want to go for a job interview looking like that."

"What!" Drake exclaimed. "I don't want a job!"

"I don't care what you want, Drake!" Mark yelled back. "Dad said you're doing it, and I'm not gonna make him mad at me. He's already talking about charging me rent now that I graduated from high school. So get your ass up, and get ready. I'm leaving a little after three and you better be ready to go."

Mark left Drake's room in a huff. All sort of possibilities raced through Drake's mind. What might happen if he didn't do this, if he just refused to go? Almost every single one that didn't involve him being hospitalized didn't have a good outcome. Maybe, if he went and just didn't do well during the interview, maybe then they wouldn't hire him. That would get Dad off his back, and let the whole thing die from natural causes. No yelling, no hospitalization. He liked that. Drake got up and headed to the bathroom to take a shower and get ready to go bomb an interview.

By three, Drake was showered and dressed. He wore a button-up shirt and the pair of blue dress pants Martin had dropped off for him in the morning. The pants smelled like starch. He sat in the living room and waited for Mark. This was going to be easy. He'd fill out the application, and then sit there and not say anything, maybe even drool. He smiled at his cleverness.

"Come on little brother," Mark said, as he headed out the front door to his car. "You got your button?"

Drake felt his pocket. He had forgotten. He turned and quickly darted upstairs and retrieved his button from beside his bed, then bounded down the stairs with a series of heavy thumps.

Hey!" Dad yelled. "Your mom's sleeping!"

"Sorry Dad," Drake said, as he closed the door and ran out to Mark's car.

Mark was inside his car, the engine idling, waiting for his brother.

"About time," Mark stated, as Drake climbed in the passengers side of his car. "I was getting tired of waiting for ya."

Mark shifted the car into reverse and backed out of the driveway, and off they went. Danny's was on NE 6th Avenue, by the corner of NE 78th Street, between the Ferryman Motel and a gas station. It sat right next to Exit Four from the Interstate Five freeway. Mark sped into the restaurant parking lot. An old yellow school bus was parked in the far corner of the lot. Mark drove over and parked next to it.

"The old bus's Eugene's," Mark said as he opened his door. "He's one of the cooks. He's cool. He's a drummer in a band."

"He drives a bus to work?" Drake asked, as he got out of the car.

"Yeah," Mark answered. "And he lives in it too, isn't that cool?"

Drake had to admit, that was pretty cool. Ever since he watched the television show S.W.A.T. he had thought vans were way cooler than cars because they could carry equipment and gear. An old school bus was kind of like the ultimate van.

Drake followed Mark around to the front of the building and through the big glass door. The entryway had two large glass doors separated by about ten feet of carpeting. Once inside the second door, Mark pointed to the counter to the left side of the building near where the sign that said 'Restrooms' hung. Drake sat in the first seat. Mark kept walking and went behind the counter and around a corner and into the back of the restaurant.

The wood in the restaurant was dark and richly grained, and the upholstery was a thick vinyl in two colors that repeated next to each other in a pattern throughout the building—pink and orange. The short carpeting enhanced those colors but included more earth tones in swirling browns and greens. The floor plan of the place was kind of an elongated 'u' with the bottom of it being the stretched part. There were four booth tables opposite of the counter

Drake sat at that made the aisle that led to the restrooms and the pay phones. At the end of the long counter that ran in front of the kitchen nearest them was the cash register. Opposite of the longer counter was most of the seating area in what appeared to be four main sections.

Drake couldn't help but absorb this new environment. Mark returned with a one page application.

"Fill this out," Mark instructed. "I'm going to get something to eat before I start, and I'll let Oly know you're here. When you're done with the application, let that waitress right there know. Her name's Debbie. She's Eugene's girlfriend. Oh, and here's a pen, I borrowed it from Debbie, so you can also give it back to her."

Drake nodded, as he looked at the application. It was pretty straightforward. It did want his Social Security number, so it was a good thing he put that card in his wallet. Mark disappeared into the back of the restaurant again.

Soft instrumental elevator music played through flush ceiling-mounted speakers. Drake had never heard *Hotel California* played in such a way before. It perplexed him.

It took him the better part of twenty minutes to fill out the application, mostly because he wasn't sure what to write for previous experience. Should he write that he held the position of demon-slayer? That would certainly not get him the job. But it would also probably result in a phone call home to his Dad. Not a good option. He did list that he had played two years of varsity basketball for the question about other activities or hobbies. He thought that would look better than saying he liked to draw and was writing a manuscript detailing a historical account of demonology. Once again, that wasn't a good option.

He looked around for the waitress that he was supposed to give the application and the pen to. She was a short woman, maybe in her early twenties. Her hair was cut shorter than Drake's, in kind of a boy cut, but poufy on the top. It was a dirty blonde color with more of a pronounced blonde at the tips. She wore bright red lipstick that certainly drew his attention. She was a bit thicker in her torso than most of the girls he knew at school, but that could have been because of the uniform dress that she wore. Her eyes were blue and welcoming. That's when he realized he was staring at her eyes, and she was standing right in front of him on the backside of the counter. He blushed.

"Are you done, sweetheart?" Debbie asked. "I can take this back and give it to Oly. Would you like a Coke?"

"Sure," Drake was able to mumble. "Thank you."

Debbie took the application and her pen and quickly returned with a glass of iced Coke.

"Here's a straw. Has anyone ever told you how cute you are?" Debbie cooed, as she batted her long heavily mascara darkened eyelashes at Drake. Drake wasn't sure what this waitress was doing to him because he was feeling all warm and flushed. He decided she must have some sort of occult powers.

Debbie disappeared. Drake sat and sipped some of his soda. An older man in a white shirt with a brown tie came out of the back of the restaurant. He had thinning brown hair, metal-framed glasses, and a stressed but friendly face. He looked like he could be a police officer—at least that was how Drake perceived him. Maybe it was because he was the authority figure in the business.

"Hi, you must be Drake?" Oly questioned, as he came out to sit next to Drake at the counter. He held the application in his left hand. He stuck out his right hand, Drake knew he needed to shake hands, and did so firmly. Oly sat down. "I'm Mr. Olsen, but everyone calls me Oly. Nice handshake, its funny how many guys your age think they need to try and crush my hand."

Drake sat quietly as Oly skimmed through his application.

"You're Mark's brother?" Oly asked.

"Yes," Drake answered. Oly nodded as he skimmed more.

"Basketball player too?" Oly inquired.

"Yep," Drake responded. He thought maybe now would be a good time to start to drool.

"Great," Oly said. "I'll have you start on Thursday, let's go take a look at the schedule and get the rest of your paperwork filled out. Welcome aboard."

Drake thought, what? Wait, what did he just say? He never got the chance to blow the interview.

Oly stood up and motioned for Drake to follow him into the back of the restaurant. Drake quickly complied.

Once behind the swinging door with a single porthole window in it, they passed by a stinky room on the left filled with mops and buckets, before walking by a stainless steel dish station that was filled with brown bus tubs overflowing with dirty dishes. There was a shelf above the dirty dishes that held green plastic racks filled with dirty glasses. Someone was behind the racks washing dishes, a boy with blonde hair, nearly Drake's height.

"This is the dish station, you'll be working there," Oly said as they walked past. A little farther up on the right, across from the dish station sinks was a big metal door that led into the walk-in refrigerator and the walk-in freezer further inside.

They walked to the intersection of the hallway. To the right the path went past a door on the left that was a closet and had the ladder to the roof. A little further to the right past a couple of small cork bulletin boards was the entrance to the long slender kitchen, and at the end of the hall, just past the kitchen, was another swinging door with a single window in it. This door was at the end of the longer counter out in the front of the restaurant.

Straight ahead was the break area. A small counter and three chairs lined the wall on the right. Beyond that was a door into the dry storage area. A cork bulletin board decorated with a minimum wage and worker's rights poster hung on the wall above the break table.

To the left was an ice machine, a couple of tall rolling racks of breads and buns, and the door out the back of the building. Opposite of the ice machine was the door into the little managers' office. Oly took out a key and opened the door. A smaller man, who looked to be in his fifties with gray hair, a blue shirt and a yellow tie was sitting at the desk counting stacks of money.

"Drake Fraser," Oly said. "This is Mr. Poteete, the general manager. Most people just call him Master Po. This is Mark's younger brother, and he's going to start on Thursday."

Mr. Poteete stopped counting money and reached out to shake Drake's hand.

"Nice handshake, Drake," Mr. Poteete stated. "Make sure to show him the schedule, and introduce him to who'll be training him."

"Will do, Master Po," Oly said, as he closed the door with a handful of other papers for Drake to fill out that had bold headings like 'W-4.' "Come here Drake, I'll show you the schedule."

They walked toward the kitchen. On the bulletin boards next to the kitchen were a number of weekly schedules—one for the hostesses, one for the waitresses and waiters, one for the cooks, and finally one for the dishwashers and busboys. The schedules were for the current week that ended on Wednesday and the next week that started on Thursday. On the second dishwasher schedule he noticed there was no name at the bottom, a blank spot and five days worth of shifts. Oly took a pencil and wrote "D. Fraser" in the blank spot.

"The schedule is by seniority," Oly explained. "Up at the top are the guys who've been here longest. So you're gonna start at the bottom. You said you played basketball, right? For Columbia River? We got a couple of guys from the team working here."

Drake nodded and looked at the schedule to see the names. Going up the roster he saw, 'B. Squire,' 'G. Kramer,' 'B. Jones,' and 'C. Newcomb,' those two could be Moose's pals Bobby and Chuck. Further up was 'J. Kirk,' Drake wondered if that could possibly be who he thought it was. If he was correct, working there might finally allow him the opportunity to talk to him without his friend Robert pestering them. Near the top he saw a name that Oly was pointing to, 'G. Caine.'

"Gerald's one of our best workers," Oly said, as he started walking back toward the dish station. Drake followed his new manager into the dish station. The large blonde kid had his back to them as they entered. He was using the stretchy ceiling mounted spray nozzle to rinse a rack full of dishes before he opened up the large cubical dishwasher releasing a seething cloud of hot steam. "Gerald, I got our new trainee here. I think you might know each other."

Gerald, who turned around and faced Drake, was the pinched-eyed bully who'd been harassing him since he first arrived in Vancouver.

"Yeah," Gerald stated with a wide smile. "We've met. I'm gonna look forward to training you."

"Thanks Gerald," Oly replied, as he began to walk out of the dish station. "Come on, Drake."

"Good to see you," Gerald added, as Drake began to turn to leave. Moose Caine silently mouthed 'Dick Faggot' toward Drake as he left.

Drake thought to himself that the benefits of the job included hanging out with Mark, possibly working with Scrappy, making some real money, and there were some cute older waitresses working there—like Debbie. The drawback, and it was a big one, was Moose Caine. But, Drake was done running and hiding from Moose and all his other fears. He'd have to face him to overcome this weight that hung on his soul like an albatross.

This was going to be an interesting summer.

18

CEDAR MASK OF THE SHAMAN

THE BROTHERHOOD OF OLYMPUS
AND THE TOWER OF DREAMS

Magic Man
Chapter Eighteen
July 2, 1980
Hazel Dell, Washington

"I'm glad I made it through my training, Scrap," Drake said to his friend who was sitting at the short counters near the restrooms. Drake was in his uniform, white button up shirt, brown polyester slacks, non-slip shoes, and a brown vinyl apron that tied in the back. "I wasn't sure I would, with the way Moose was treating me."

"Want me to kill him?" Scrappy replied. His thick black hair stood out in every direction from his head, almost like an afro, but not quite that neat and orderly.

"No," Drake chuckled. "He's not worth the trouble that would cause for you."

"I'm glad you made it too, brother," Scrappy added. He took a big swallow of the beverage in the glass before him. "And I wouldn't actually kill him. It's more a figure of speech."

Drake smiled at his friend.

Starting anything for the first time is never easy. For Drake, beginning his first job while being trained by the bully who had tormented him through the whole school year compounded it. His training week was hell. He was taunted, teased, ridiculed, and set up for failure.

Moose had plotted for Drake's training to go poorly, so that when he was placed on the schedule for real the following week he'd fail and get fired or quit. Unbeknownst to Moose, Drake had vowed to himself to persevere, to be polite, and to win this struggle with the bully. Every time

287

Drake smiled in response to a put down, although fake and extremely non-genuine, it infuriated the husky Moose, flushing his features with the oddest blotching of red that Drake, in the midst of being bullied somehow found amusing. In fact, Drake had noted that the red pattern on Moose's left cheek looked somewhat like the British Isles.

"You still riding your bike to work?" Scrappy asked. He took another drink, crashing the ice against his face. "Can you get me a refill? Coke."

Drake nodded and took the glass to the soda fountain to refill it. Two of the five days he worked that first week, he was able to ride with Mark because they had the same shift. The other three, Drake rode his ten-speed bike. The just over two mile ride took him about ten minutes, longer going home since there were hills to ride up on NW 82nd Street, at the end of NW 88th Street, and then up NW 21st Avenue in front of Lakeshore Elementary where Albert went to school. Out of precaution he had started carrying Hikari wrapped and under the thin, blue trench coat that he had gotten from Martin. He locked it securely to his bike with a chain, and kept his bike in the mop room when he worked.

"You need to buy a car," Scrappy added.

"I'm not sixteen yet, I can't drive to work," Drake responded. "I had to get a work permit to even work here."

"What's that wrapped thing you lock up to your bike, it looks like a stick or crowbar, or something?" Scrappy asked.

"It's my sword, Hikari," Drake answered in a hushed tone. "That's Japanese for light."

"Awes!" Scrappy exclaimed. "Let me see it."

"Let me check the bus tubs, then I'll go unlock it if you want to see it," Drake said. He walked off looking below the counter seeing if any of the brown plastic tubs were full of dishes that needed washed. He walked out to the center waitress station and checked the tubs there too. Then he scanned the level of ice in the bin, they were going to need more ice.

Drake walked back into the mop room where Scrappy

was waiting for him. He was like a kid on Christmas morning, waiting to see what surprise might be waiting to be unwrapped before him.

"Bout time," Scrappy stated.

Drake pulled the key from his pocket and unlocked the chain. He took his time undoing the crisscrossed chain, until he was able to draw the sword from its scabbard.

"That is freaking awes!" Scrappy exclaimed. "Can I hold it?"

Drake nodded and then turned the blade toward him and presented the hilt to Scrappy. He let go of the sword as Scrappy grabbed it.

"It's heavier than I thought," Scrappy stated. He moved the sword side to side in his hand. "But still pretty light. I think I'd need something beefier, bigger, and a bit more barbaric, if you know what I mean."

"Yeah," Drake replied. "I know what you mean."

"Has anyone seen Drake?" Debbie questioned, as she walked into the back of the restaurant, past the mop room. "We need ice out in the waitress station."

"I got to put it away and get ice," Drake said. Scrappy turned the sword and handed it to him in the same fashion that Drake had used to present it to him.

Drake put it back in the scabbard, wrapped it, and started crisscrossing the chain to it and the bike, until he was able to snuggly snap the paddle lock back onto the chain to secure it.

"Are you staying for a bit?" Drake asked. Scrappy nodded. "Good, I got something to talk to you about. But first I got to get ice so Debbie doesn't kill me."

Drake found Scrappy back out at the counter after he had filled all the ice bins and brought out silverware, glasses, plates, and exchanged a few half filled bus tubs with empty ones. Scrappy had ordered some food, a bacon cheeseburger with a side of barbeque sauce and French fries. It smelled good and the hickory of the sauce almost made Drake drool.

Another guy, an older looking fellow with long black hair

pulled back into a ponytail, was sitting at the far end of the counter near the cash register.

"So what did ya want to talk to me about?" Scrappy asked. He took a big bite of his hamburger. Scrappy enjoyed eating, and always smiled when he did.

"So remember all my pictures," Drake began, in a hushed tone so the guy at the other end of the counter wouldn't take notice, "and how I told you and Robert that all of that stuff was real?"

"Yeah," Scrappy stated, as he swallowed hard.

"Well," Drake said. "I'm serious about that stuff being real. Over the last couple years my brothers and I have experienced some pretty crazy things. Stuff I would've never believed existed before I saw it with my own eyes. And even then, it took being able to smell it, to touch it, or in some cases being touched by it, or hit by it pretty hard to make me believe it."

Scrappy nodded and ate.

"I found out we were champions of a group of special people," Drake added. He looked down at the older guy. The man was fiddling with something in his hands. "But my younger brothers are still just kids, and there's a war coming up. We need people who can fight. We need someone like you Scrap, someone who'll make a difference."

Scrappy continued to chew, smile, and nod.

"I was hoping you were willing to join us," Drake continued. "To be a member of the Brotherhood of Olympus, what do you think?"

"Do I get weapons?" Scrappy asked. Drake nodded. "And I get to fight monsters?"

"Yep," Drake replied. He pulled up his left sleeve to show the scar on his deltoid. "I could really use some help. Remember my stitches? This came from that snake-guy I drew the picture of. I'm pretty sure we could take someone like him a lot easier together. You're pretty buff. So what do you think?"

"Drake," Scrappy responded, as he wiped his mouth

with his white paper napkin, "I'm not sure what you're thinking."

Drake felt the pangs of disappointment welling in his heart. He was sure Scrappy was going to be his battle brother. In fact he even resembled the dark-skinned, muscle-bound guy that was in his dreams of the black tower.

"You had me when you first told me about this stuff back in school," Scrappy explained. "I've lived my whole life wanting to belong. To make a difference, to make a stand for others and be remembered for doing it, and then out of nowhere you drop into my life. And you talk about all this occult and freaky crap, but I see in your heart that you're serious. So when I saw what Gerald was doing I came to your aid. You're someone special in this world and apparently other worlds too, and if I can help you then I will."

Drake felt agápe, unconditional love surging in his chest. Scrappy truly was his brother, and like Woden had said, he'd know it when they met.

"You're my brother," Scrappy added. "I think I have been looking forward to finding you my whole life."

"Hey busboy?" the long haired man at the other end of the counter called out to Drake. "You got a minute?"

Drake nodded and walked over that end of the counter.

"Would you like a refill of your soda?" Drake asked. The man nodded.

"Thanks man," he said. He was manipulating something that looked like black plastic in his hands. "It's been a hella rough day."

"Why's that?" Drake inquired, as he returned the filled soda glass to the counter.

"I applied for a cook job here," the man said. The object in his hands appeared to be eyeglasses. "The manager said he'd love to hire me, if I cut my hair. I can't cut my hair, but I really need this job. I'm gonna lose my apartment, be homeless, and then my glasses broke in half, right in the temple. I might be able to put it back if I had some of those small screws."

"Why can't you cut your hair?" Drake asked. That seemed the easy solution to all of this guy's problems.

"I'm Quinault," he replied.

"Hi Quinault, my name's Drake."

"No, I'm a Quinault Indian," the man explained. "I'm a shaman, a magic man, and my hair is symbolic of my faith. I can't cut it."

"But you need the job?" Drake questioned.

"Yep," the man replied. "This one's my last option, besides living in my car."

"Cut your hair, or be homeless," Scrappy added from the other end of the counter. "Seems pretty simple to me."

"Easy for you to say," the man responded, as he turned toward Scrappy. "But look at your wild-ass hair, how are you able to work here? The man just wants to hold the Indian brother down."

"Hey," Scrappy remarked, "don't be pulling any of that racist crap on me, you have no idea what my life's been like either. So just back off bub, got it?"

"Yeah," the man said. "I got it, but I'm not sure why the three of us are getting all up in each other's faces. We're all minorities."

"I'm not getting in anyone's face," Drake replied.

"You brother is," the man added, pointing toward Scrappy.

"Is he still here?" Scrappy asked, as held up his hand right to block his view of the stranger. "Can't see him."

Drake shook his head.

"I get it," the man began. "Listen, I told you it's been a hella bad day, and I'm probably setting you guys off, so I'm sorry. I know you guys have had it rough too. The gorilla over there, he's fatherless and has been teased and tormented his whole life for how he looked and how much he weighed, and he's just looking for acceptance from the brother he never had. And you, you've got too many brothers and too many secrets. You had your heart crushed when your uncle died."

"Stop it!" Drake exclaimed. "Who are you? How do you know so much about us?"

"My name's Freeman," the man replied with a bow of his head and a sweeping open palmed gesture with his left hand. "Freeman Kalama, of the Quinault Tribe. I'm a shaman and magic man. It's my business to know things."

"I've heard that name before," Drake recalled. "Our friend George Kalama said he had an uncle named Freeman. He said his uncle took him to a sweat lodge."

"George Kalama's my nephew, he's a really nice guy, but he's a bit slow," the man stated. "I love him with all my heart, don't get me wrong."

"You're George's uncle?" Scrappy asked.

"Guilty as charged," Freeman responded. "Hey, listen, both of you, I'm really sorry I said what I did. I think we got off on the wrong foot. What'd ya say we start over from the beginning?"

"Hi," Drake said, as he extended his hand to Freeman. They shook hands. "My name's Drake, Drake Fraser, it's a pleasure to meet you."

"The pleasure's all mine, Mr. Fraser," Freeman replied. "My name is Freeman Kalama, shaman and magic man."

Freeman stood and went to shake hands with Scrappy.

"Hi, Freeman Kalama, shaman and magic man," he said, as he shook Scrappy's hand.

"James," Scrappy responded. He didn't want to explain the whole not liking *Star Trek* thing to this guy. "Just James."

"It's a pleasure to meet you, just James," Freeman chuckled.

"So why do you introduce yourself as a shaman and magic man?" Drake inquired.

"Because that's who I am," Freeman answered.

"Sounds like you're gonna have to add homeless to what you are, too," Scrappy added with a laugh.

"Very true, my friend," Freeman agreed.

"I'm not your friend," Scrappy replied.

"Here, let me see your glasses?" Drake asked. Freeman handed them over. Drake looked at the two pieces. He knew that his dad had some extra little screws and the small tipped tools to work on glasses. But those were at his house. He surveyed the pieces. The glasses were not fractured, just missing the screws that held the temple to the glasses. "I've got the parts to fix these at home. I can do it for you tomorrow, cause I'm not off work until eleven. I might be able to do something now though, just a second."

Drake turned and walked to the back of the restaurant.

"So how do you really know all that stuff about us?" Scrappy asked.

"I told you," Freeman replied. "I'm a shaman and magic man. Just like you're a barbarian, we each have our own calling, and if we are brothers, we complement each other's strengths and protect each other's weaknesses."

"I never said you're my brother," Scrappy remarked.

"I know you didn't," Freeman replied. "I'm just saying if we were."

"You kinda talk in a circle," Scrappy added.

"Many things in life are a circle," Freeman replied. "A great wheel in the sky, the circle of life, the cycles of elements through the environment, even circles of friendship and brotherhood."

"That's true," Scrappy stated. "But I'm not your friend."

Drake walked back out, and showed Freeman his glasses. The temple was re-attached to the frame with some white tape.

"This'll hold until tomorrow if you want me to fix it," Drake announced, as he handed the glasses back to Freeman.

"Thank you," Freeman said. "This means a lot to me, it really does."

"And while I was back there taping your glasses, I think I thought of a solution to your other problem," Drake added. "If you're interested?"

"Of course I am," Freeman answered.

"Good," Drake replied. "We can meet here at one

o'clock tomorrow, and get you ready to come back and get the job."

Freeman nodded.

Scrappy decided he needed to be there tomorrow with Drake just to make sure his brother was safe.

"Good," Drake announced "'cause I've got to get to work. I've got a pile of dishes to wash back there in the dish station."

"Tomorrow at one," Freeman confirmed.

Drake nodded and went off into the back. Scrappy finished his French fries and put his used napkin on the plate.

"I really do hope that you and I can be friends, James," Freeman added.

"We'll see," Scrappy replied. "But don't count on it."

The following day, July third, they met precisely at one o'clock in the afternoon. First Drake fixed Freeman's broken eyeglasses with two small screws and an equally small Phillips-head screwdriver. Drake and Scrappy rode in Freeman's car to the destination Drake had decided possessed the solution to Freeman's problem. They found what they were looking for. Drake made a few adjustments with some scissors he brought with them, then they headed back to the restaurant so that Freeman could talk to the manager again about the vacant cook job.

Drake and Scrappy sat at the short counter, waiting to see how Freeman's discussion with Mr. Poteete went.

"He's kinda weird," Scrappy said.

"So," Drake replied. "You and I are both kinda weird."

"True," Scrappy remarked. "He did say his calling is magic, maybe that means he gonna be a wizard or something? Could we use a wizard, against these demons and monsters?"

"If his magic was real," Drake answered. "And not just sleight-of-hand, or card trick kind of illusions. Maybe he was a real wizard like Gandalf was. Having him around helped out a lot in both *the Hobbit* and *the Lord of the Rings*."

"Maybe it's his calling?" Scrappy asked. "Kind of like

mine is to fight monsters, his is to be a wizard."

"Maybe," Drake replied.

Freeman suddenly re-appeared from the back of the restaurant, a wide smile upon his face.

"Gentlemen," Freeman stated with an exaggerated bow, "I'd like to introduce you to the newest cook here at Danny's."

Both boys looked at the short black hair upon his head as he dipped it below their eyes.

"Hey Freeman," Drake began with a wry smile.

"Yeah?" Freeman replied.

"Your hair's wiggin' out," Drake commented with a laugh. Scrappy joined him with a hearty chuckle. Even Freeman started to laugh.

They had gone to the thrift store to look for an old black wig. They had found one for a dollar, the only problem was that it was made for a woman and was almost as long as Freeman's own hair. Drake promptly gave it a hair cut with his scissors. With his new short hair, Freeman easily got offered the cook job from Mr. Poteete.

"Thank you," Freeman said, "both of you. Your help has meant a lot to me."

"You're welcome," Drake replied.

"Yeah," Scrappy added. "You're welcome."

"Say," Freeman began, as he sat at the counter next to his new friends, "you know that stuff you guys were talking about yesterday?"

Both Scrappy and Drake shook their heads.

"Come on," Freeman added. "The whole freaky things, and scars from fighting snake monsters? I want to offer you my service, out of gratitude for your help and your faith in me. I'm interested in being the shaman and magic man for the Brotherhood you guys were talking about yesterday."

Scrappy and Drake looked at each other, and kind of shrugged at the same time.

"What sign are you, Drake?" Freeman asked.

"A Libra," Drake responded.

"Me too," Freeman added. "What day?"

"September twenty-second, the same day as Bilbo and Frodo Baggins," Drake answered.

"Me too!" Freeman exclaimed. "That's pretty freaky. What year?"

"Sixty-four," Drake replied.

"Fifty-seven," Freeman continued. "We're exactly seven years apart. Seven is a mystic number, man. It's like destiny that brought us together."

Scrappy raised his eyebrows and shrugged again.

"This Brotherhood stuff won't be easy, Freeman," Drake added. "There are many dark and dangerous things out there waiting for us."

"Yeah," Scrappy agreed.

"It could be a deadly journey," Drake began, "and I can't promise anything about your safety. We have less than four months to train and prepare for a war of Biblical scale. Are you sure that's what you want to do?"

"Yes," Freeman answered. "My life has been spent studying arcane and forbidden knowledge. I've sought out the magic that exists in our world. It's what inspires me to go on, to get up each day. It's my destiny. And then I met you guys, and you talked about this opportunity to do something that most people wouldn't even believe existed if it hit them in the face like a gunny sack full of dead, wet kittens. This is my opportunity to see how far I can go, how much magic I truly possess, and I want in. Hell, I'm even willing to learn sword play with you guys, though I doubt I would be any good at it. Whatta ya say?"

"Dead wet kittens?" Scrappy questioned. "Man, that's sick. But I like it."

Drake thought about what Woden had said. Just as Scrappy had admitted yesterday, it was what he'd waited his whole life for. Unlike how this whole thing just kind of was forced on Drake and his brothers after the death of their uncle, both Scrappy and Freeman seemed to be answering a call to service. Drake couldn't help but think of the compulsion to go to Devil's Tower that multiple characters had in the movie *Close Encounters of the Third Kind*. Maybe that's what was going on with both of them. They were all brought together for a reason, and if that sort of divine providence was occurring he wouldn't want to mess it up.

"Okay," Drake responded. "You're in. We'll start training as soon as I talk to my brother Martin."

"Cool," Scrappy said.

"That's excellent," Freeman added.

The waitress covering the counter approached them.

"Would you gentleman like to order any food?" she asked with a slight British accent.

All three guys looked up at her. She was a tall woman, with long auburn hair pulled up in a thick bun on top of her head. She had piercing blue eyes and an angelic face. She filled out the short clinging dress of her waitress uniform better than any other waitress who worked there. Drake thought she seemed very familiar.

"Are you new here?" Scrappy questioned. He didn't recognize her, and he knew most of the waitresses.

"Yes, I am," she replied. "I just started right now."

"Today?" Freeman asked. "Me too!"

"No," she stated. "Right now. I just got here, and you're the first people I've talked to."

Drake was staring at the waitress, trying to jog his memory. He had found over the years that his memory of girls often failed him. There was something almost glowing around the head of the waitress.

"You're staring," she said to Drake.

"I'm sorry," Drake replied. "You're glowing."

Scrappy pushed Drake's shoulder.

"No," Drake clarified. "Around her head, it's like a golden aura."

"You're perceptive, Drake, son of Drake," she stated with her accent being more pronounced.

"Are you British?" Freeman asked.

"Yes," she answered. "Kind of, or maybe the British are

more me, than I am them."

"Great," Scrappy remarked. "Another person who talks in circles."

"Who are you?" Drake inquired. "I feel like I know you."

"Why, yes you do," she responded. "When last we met, I volunteered my service to train and tutor your brothers for the coming war, my name is Brigid, goddess of the sacred flame, and I'm here to help you."

The three guys looked at each other and grinned. Things were starting to look up for the Brotherhood of Olympus.

"Hey Brigid, goddess of the sacred flame," Scrappy stated with a wide smile. "Can you get me some waffles?"

At 7:35 PM, on July fourth, in a small non-descript office within the bowels of the Apostolic Library near the Tower of the Winds at the heart of Vatican City, a cloistered man entered. He wore black robes and sandals on his feet.

"Your eminence," the cloistered man stated to another far older man sitting at a desk lost in the pages of an archaic leather-bound book.

"Yes Father Gregorio," the cardinal replied. "What is it?"

"It has happened, your eminence," Father Gregorio answered. "Just as we have feared for over five hundred years."

"What are you saying, Gregorio?" the cardinal asked.

"The Covenant of Reason," Father Gregorio replied. "It is under attack. The eruption of Mt. St. Helens in the United States has signaled it. And some of our best agents believe that the Brotherhood of Olympus has been formed anew."

"This cannot be!" the cardinal stated, as he closed the thick book. "The Brotherhood of Olympus was extinguished by order of the Pope in 1469, Gregorio. They hold no charter with the papacy, and are considered heretics before the eyes of God."

Father Gregorio nodded.

"Alert the Hospitallers," the cardinal decreed. "Let's see what information we can recover before we bring this matter up to the Pope. And Gregario, keep me informed of anything they discover. I do not want any information coming in to be viewed as too trivial for me to see."

"Yes, your eminence," Father Gregorio replied with a bow.

"Gregorio," the cardinal stated with a scowl, "I'm not sure which news disturbs me more, the assault on the Covenant that has kept otherworldlies away for so long, or the existence of the Brotherhood of Olympus."

Risk
Chapter Nineteen
July 14, 1980
Vancouver, Washington

On Monday nights, one of the two Portland independent television stations played black-and-white Joe E. Brown movies. The evening crew at Danny's had started having Joe E. Brown parties, where the attendees would drink every time the actor did his signature wide, opened-mouth scream. It seemed to happen at least twenty times in any of the old films. Drake, Freeman, and Scrappy began to attend the festivities, except they tended to just group together and talk about paranormal topics rather than socialize with their peers.

Debbie was always the hostess of Joe E. Brown night and, to a minor degree, she was assisted by her boyfriend Eugene. What was unusual this evening was that for the first time both Brigid and Martin attended Joe E. Brown night. Drake sat in the middle of a short, well-used couch, with Freeman on his left and Debbie on his right.

"Do you guys need refills?" Debbie asked, as she got up from the sofa. The cushions were so worn that it was sometimes a challenge to escape to gravity of the couch. Both Drake and Freeman nodded.

"Man," Freeman stated, "that Joe E. Brown was one crazy cat. Why isn't he in any newer movies?"

"I believe his last movie was, *It's a Mad, Mad, Mad, Mad World* in the early 1960s," Drake answered. "You know, the one that had all the old comedians in it?"

"Yeah, I've seen it," Freeman replied. He smiled and readjusted his thick, black-framed glasses on the bridge of his nose. "Are you sure about that though? No movies since then at all, Drake?"

Drake sat silently as he shuffled through piles and piles of irrelevant knowledge stored within his mind. Freeman chuckled.

"You know," Freeman said, as he leaned closer to Drake, "I do enjoy your encyclopedic mind, my young friend. You know so much about so many different things, but struggle when I ask you something as trivial as this."

"I think he died in 1973," Drake finally answered. He vowed to himself that he'd acquire more knowledge about popular culture—the trivial, the mundane, and the obscure.

"Are you sure about that?" Freeman questioned with a wry smile.

Debbie returned with a cold bottle of *Lucky Lager* for Freeman and a blue plastic cup of soda for Drake. Both guys took their beverages with a polite 'thank you.' Freeman opened the bottle and began to study the rebus on the inside of the bottle cap, while Debbie put her left hand against her short skirt on the back of her thigh before she sat down next to Drake. When she sat down, she kind of fell into Drake and nearly spilled her beverage because of the soft cushion.

"Sorry Drake," Debbie giggled. She moved a little bit away from him, but had her leg fully against his. Her left hand came down upon his right thigh. Drake nearly jumped out of his skin from her touch. His eyes were open so wide they might have burst if he took too deep of a breath.

Freeman took notice of Drake's predicament, and shook his head. "My kingdom for your plight," Freeman muttered to himself with a wry smile.

The commercial break in the movie ended, and the party quieted down as the attendees waited for the next wide-mouthed holler from the star. As they watched the movie, Debbie's hand began to move on Drake's thigh, almost like she was lightly massaging above his knee. Drake had worn a slight hole in the faded denim of his blue jeans, and Debbie's soft fingers found the hole and his warm skin underneath.

Drake became rigid and couldn't move. He wondered if Debbie knew what she was doing, maybe she'd drank too much, perhaps she mistook him for her boyfriend Eugene, or maybe the most inconceivable option of all, she actually liked him? Drake swallowed hard. He looked down at her small hand. Her well manicured nails circled upon his exposed flesh and electricity surged inside him. He glanced at her. Debbie smiled, and her blue eyes twinkled in the light of the room. She had put on fresh red lipstick before coming back to the living room with their beverages, making her lips even more full and pouty.

"I love knees," Debbie cooed, as she fluttered her long eyelashes. "You have sexy knees, Drake."

Drake suddenly felt that he had to flee.

"Drake, Freeman," Brigid said, as she stepped in front of them. She wore a flowing summer dress covered in yellow and blue floral patterns. Her legs were well muscled and exposed to the thigh through the long slit in the front of her skirt. She was a goddess in many ways, Freeman had stated to the other guys after they had first met. Brigid held out her hand to Drake. "Come with me to the other room, your brothers await you."

Drake took her hand and rose up from the couch. He'd been somewhat skeptical of her when she first arrived out of nowhere. But there was something about her that wasn't like any other woman he'd ever met, except maybe Veronica Furfur, the librarian from Hoquiam. Brigid had been warmly accepted by her new work colleagues, even without any snide comments from some of the younger waitresses who tended to be territorial of their beauty. She worked every day Drake did, and most of the days Freeman was there, but Drake had never seen her name on the schedule. Drake had first thought that only he and his friends could see her, but he observed her interactions with their co-workers—they seemed to be able to talk with her, and he'd noticed that the lights inside the restaurant created shadows upon her. She also cast her own shadow, and he personally witnessed her reflection off the shiny stainless steel milk refrigerator. All things he concluded that she couldn't do if she wasn't a real flesh and blood person.

"Come on Freeman," Drake said, as he walked away with Brigid. Drake felt like he owed her for his rescue from his moment of fight or flight.

Freeman pulled himself up and began to follow Brigid and Drake. He leaned over toward Debbie, who was still sitting on the couch.

"He's only fifteen, my dear," Freeman stated quietly.

"Fifteen? Oh my God!" Debbie responded with a shock. "But he's so tall and handsome."

"You also have a boyfriend," Freeman added. "My brother Drake doesn't need that kind of drama."

"Oh my God, he's only fifteen?" Debbie continued to question. "Are you sure he's only fifteen?"

"Now, if you just have a need," Freeman said with a smile. "I'm twenty-two and know what to do."

Debbie slapped Freeman's across the right side of his face with her soft left hand.

"Hey Kalama!" Eugene shouted from across the room. "You botherin' my girl?"

"No," Freeman responded, as he walked into the other room behind Drake and Brigid. "Apparently I just told her a joke she didn't find amusing."

Eugene looked at him and broke out into a wide smile. He continued to tap his drumsticks on the ottoman in front of his chair.

Martin and Scrappy sat at the kitchen table. They had cleared a space at one end by pushing the party supplies all the way to the other side. Upon the table was a board game, already set up and ready to play.

"Your brothers desire to simulate domination of your world," Brigid said, as they walked up to the table, "using numerical cubes to determine the outcome of battles."

"Sweet," Freeman announced, as he sat down at the table. "You set up my *Risk* game."

Freeman carried this particular board game nearly everywhere he went. It was his favorite. He had gotten it at a garage sale a few years ago. It was a 1963 edition, with all wooden pieces.

"I'm red!" Freeman declared with a happy smile.

"I'm black," Scrappy stated with a laugh. "In more ways than one."

"Do you know how to play, Brigid?" Drake asked.

"I have read the instructions just now," Brigid replied. "It is a game of strategy, but the champion is determined not by strategy alone, but by the luck of the gaming cube roll."

"I don't think I've ever heard it described in such a lovely way before," Freeman added. "What color would you like to play, Lady Brigid?"

"You've chosen red, the color of my flame and the barbarian has chosen black," Brigid answered. "Martin favors yellow, the color of his departed uncle, and the noble Drake prefers blue, the color of his banner in campaigns yet to be. So I shall choose the color of the cherry blossom, pink, to represent the armies of Brigid upon this map."

The five of them sat at the kitchen table and played *Risk* well into the morning, laughing, taunting, and learning about each other. Debbie had fallen asleep on the couch. Eugene covered her with a blanket before he went to bed, letting the people still in the house know they were welcome to spend the night.

"Why can't your people, the other gods, I mean," Scrappy asked Brigid, as he waited for his turn, "why can't they just come here and stop all this war stuff before it happens?"

"Most of us, my barbarian friend," Brigid answered, "are bound to outer realms because of the Covenant of Reason. There are a few of us on both sides or firmly in the middle who still possess the ability to travel here."

"So how do demons get here?" Scrappy questioned. Drake turned in a set of *Risk* cards to collect seventy-five armies. "Like the one that Drake and his brothers fought?"

"Summoning mostly, my friend," Freeman added with a serious tone.

"Tis true," Brigid responded. "Possessing the knowledge of the name of my people, gods, daemons, and such, does give others the ability to summon or bind us. But, the same can be said of humans. When we know a human's name we can hunt them, or find them, and send those who can freely travel here to do our bidding."

"Like the mordgeists," Martin interjected.

"Precisely, Martin," Brigid continued. "The mordgeists are notoriously mercenary, and would do whatever their employer asked. Including killing your uncle, I'm afraid."

"But, if you and your people knew that, then why didn't you stop them?" Martin questioned.

"We knew many things were heading in a particular direction," Brigid replied, "mostly because some of my kin have the gift of foresight and prophecy. Sadly I do not. We knew the Brotherhood was nigh upon us, but did not see the attack against your uncle until it was too late. Only Aeon did warn us that such an attack might occur. The great Hecate and Amun advised us to stay the course, that the tapestry being woven would be stronger should such an attack happen. The tale of Walter Reuss is not done. He still has a part to play in the outcome of all of this."

"Really?" Martin asked.

"So, back to this name thing," Drake interrupted. Freeman was busy counting out his new armies after turning in a set of *Risk* cards. "I know your name, Brigid, so I can summon you?"

"To an extent," Brigid replied. "There is more to it than just saying a name, usually. Though with some minion-like creatures, that is all it takes. For instance, if you wrote and spoke the name of lesser demons over and over, it could call them enough to where they seek you out."

"The classic demonic possession seen in horror movies," Freeman added. "Like *the Exorcist*."

"And if some of these creatures knew your name, they

would hunt you," Brigid warned.

Martin looked at his watch.

"Crap," Martin said. "It's three-thirty, I need to call my wife and let her know I'm running late."

"So I'm the smart one," Scrappy said, "since I use an alias, and not my real name."

"Yes, dear barbarian," Brigid responded. "I have yet to even call you by your name, because it has not been given to me."

Scrappy smiled a wide toothy grin. Martin found the kitchen telephone mounted to the wall by the refrigerator. He picked up the olive green handset and spun the rotary dial one number at a time.

"What if I had a charm made to shield me from those who were out to find me?" Drake inquired, as he found the black button in his pocket.

"The charm you speak of does shield your aura, Drake," Brigid answered. "Your mother's sister is quite skilled, but should you continue to chronicle the events that are transpiring, I fear that it may not be enough to shield you from their eyes."

"I can't stop writing about it," Drake replied. "It's the history of the Brotherhood. If I don't write it down, it will only be a story told by the few of us who were there, and over time it would be lost. It needs to be recorded so it's not all lost in the vastness of history."

"If I cannot persuade you to stop your chronicling," Brigid added, "then at least take more precaution for your own safety, son of Drake."

"Hey," Martin said, as he turned away from the action around the kitchen table.

"Marty," Beth's voice cracked over the phone. "Is that you? It's so late, why didn't you call me sooner? Are you okay?"

"Beth, I'm sorry," Martin stated. "We watched some old movie, and then started playing *Risk*."

"Marty," Beth replied.

"Beth," Martin said. "Time just slipped by, I'm really sorry."

"You know you have to work in the morning, Marty," Beth added.

"I know, I know," Martin responded. "But we've been talking about the Brotherhood stuff all night."

"Marty," Beth stated. "You know I don't believe in that crap, why do you do that to me?"

"Beth," Martin answered. "It's important. There're big things coming. The eruption of the mountain signaled the start of it, we have to be ready."

"Ready for what Marty?"

"You don't want to hear about it, Beth, so I don't talk about it."

"That's the problem, Marty. Even when you're here, you're not all here. I feel so empty."

"Beth, that's not fair."

"Marty, I'm not gonna argue. You're always somewhere else, and our apartment isn't a home."

"Martin," Drake said from the kitchen table. "Hey Martin, it's your turn."

"Come on man," Freeman added. "It's getting' late, come take your turn so we can get this awesome game over with."

"Beth, I gotta go, they're calling me. It's my turn."

"Marty, if you don't start including me in your life, one of these days you'll come home and I'll be gone. My parents moved back to Alaska, and I'll just go live with them for a while."

"Come on Beth, that's not fair. You know how much I love you. It's just that you've never wanted to be a part of the darker side of my life. The psychic part."

"Marty, I can't do this anymore."

"Just a few more hours, Beth. Then I'll take Drake home, and come home to you."

"Not home to me Marty, so you can go to work. I can't do this. I can't be on the outside of your life anymore."

"Come on Martin," Scrappy said with a yawn. "I'm getting' tired here. Want me to take your turn?"

Martin waved off the suggestion.

"Come on guys," Martin stated with his hand over the receiver. "I'm almost done."

"Go play your game, Marty," Beth added over the phone. "Hang out with your boys. But this isn't going to happen anymore. I'm not gonna be left at home. I'm your wife Marty, your partner."

"I'm sorry Beth. I'm really sorry, but baby what can I do? They need me."

"Marty, have you thought that maybe I need you too?"

"Beth?"

"Good night Marty."

The click of the telephone line disconnecting happened as soon as she had finished saying 'Marty.' Martin hung up the phone and began a slow walk toward his empty seat at the kitchen table.

"It's about time, Martin," Scrappy announced. "So Brigid, when are we gonna start practicing fightin'?"

"Soon, my good barbarian," Brigid answered.

"Scrappy," Freeman stated with a smile, "be polite to our gracious ally and tell her your name."

"He does not have to share, Freeman," Brigid added. "He has been most gracious enough already."

"My name is James," Scrappy said with a dark blush raging across his cheeks. "James Kirk, but my friends call me Scrappy."

"Am I your friend, James Kirk?" Brigid questioned.

"Yes, of course you are," Scrappy answered. He assumed his body temperature must have raised nearly twenty degrees.

"Thank you, Scrappy," Brigid replied with a smile that could melt the hearts of men.

Martin sat down and began his turn.

"Everything okay?" Drake asked his brother. Martin shrugged.

"You seem perplexed, Martin," Brigid added. "Mayhaps I can assist you?"

"Not unless you can make my wife understand how important this stuff is," Martin answered. "She's telling me I have to make a choice, the Brotherhood or her."

"The simplest choice always lies the closest to you," Brigid stated.

"Talkin' in circles again," Scrappy said.

"She wants to be included in your life," Brigid continued. "This is part of your life. Include her. Show her why you must do this, bring her into the Brotherhood."

"Wait a minute," Scrappy interrupted. "You're saying bring a girl into the Brotherhood? Wouldn't that make it more of a sisterhood?"

"I think the term would be sibling-hood," Freeman corrected.

"My dear Scrappy," Brigid said, "the Brotherhood is not about gender. It is about the love between you. A female could easily join the Brotherhood and fight along side you for everything that was right and just in the world."

Drake pondered what Brigid had stated.

"Brigid's right," Drake added. "She's here with us, and I would gladly let her join us as a member of the Brotherhood. I think we are a lot stronger with a goddess on our team."

"What's this?" Freeman questioned, as his eyes opened widely. "Drake, of course, why didn't we think of that before? Brigid, will you join the Brotherhood?"

"My role is currently limited to being an advisor, I cannot fully join, but perhaps in time, if the invitation is still good, I would be honored to accept it," Brigid replied. "But for right now, I will do all I can to assure your success in the strife that looms before you and the campaigns to come."

"So where does that leave me?" Martin asked. "Beth's the ultimate skeptic, or more of a non-believer in anything paranormal. I don't think she just walks in here with us, and is good with everything."

"Then," Drake began, "as the leader of the Brotherhood,

I will officially ask her to join, to train with us, to prepare for the liberation of the Tower of Dreams."

"She won't agree to that," Martin replied. He shook his head. "It won't work."

"I believe it will, Martin," Brigid responded. "In all my years of observing humanity, I have seen the hearts of women hold true to those they love, beyond the limits of their own beliefs. She loves you more than she distrusts that which she cannot see."

"Great," Freeman stated. "The goddess thinks it's a good idea. Drake's for it, I'm in. Let's do it."

Scrappy nodded.

"Okay, I'll try," Martin agreed.

"Good," Freeman said. "Now can we finish the game?"

"Yes, please," Brigid added with her magnificent smile. "For all of Asia is about to fall to the cherry blossom warriors of Brigid, goddess of the sacred flame."

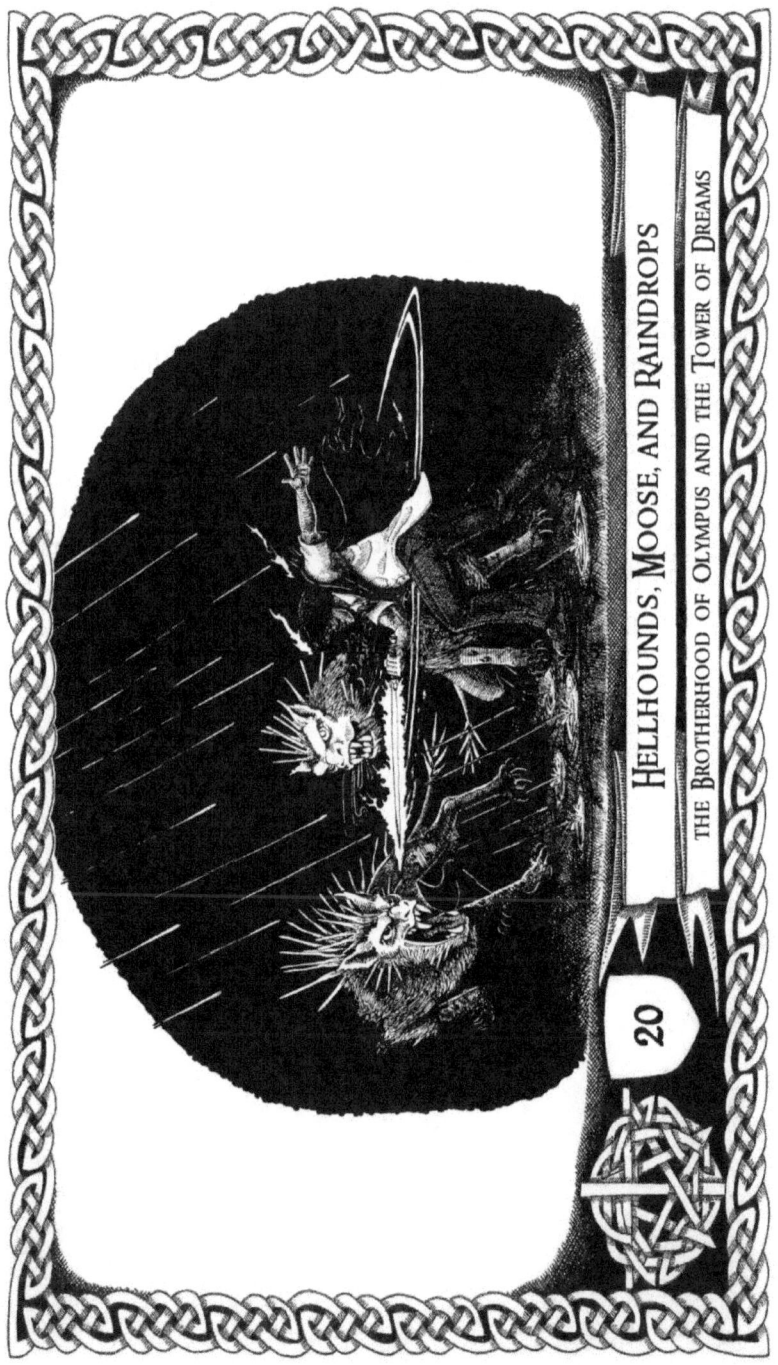

HELLHOUNDS, MOOSE, AND RAINDROPS

THE BROTHERHOOD OF OLYMPUS AND THE TOWER OF DREAMS

20

Moose Caine
Chapter Twenty
July 29, 1980
Vancouver, Washington

Beth had accepted the offer to join the Brotherhood as a skeptical observer. She thought the training the boys were doing was a bit outlandish, practicing with wooden swords, studying maps and old books, and then there were the things Freeman and her husband were doing under the tutelage of Brigid that began to alter some of her perceptions.

The self-proclaimed goddess was a very attractive lady, and Beth thought she should be upset that her husband was working so closely with her, but somehow she felt no jealousy at all. Martin practiced using his mind to influence things, people, and events. He also demonstrated his ability to move objects with his mind. When Beth first saw Martin lift and move the garbage cans outside the little house that Brigid was renting on Minnehaha Street, she walked down the road for nearly half a mile before she returned. She had to clear her head and think about what she really saw. However, after Brigid had started having Martin lift Beth and move her into the air, her tolerance for the metaphysical began to grow.

"Are you sure you want me to lift you that high, Beth?" Martin asked. "To the top of the trees is pretty high."

"Will I be safe, Brigid?" Beth questioned.

"Aye," Brigid replied with a nod. "I will make sure no ill befalls you."

"Do it, Marty!" Beth yelled. She lifted her arms up. "Lift me to the top of those trees!"

Martin looked at Brigid. She smiled at him and nodded.

Brigid gifted him some of her divine aura, boosting his telekinetic skill level and enabling him to do nearly impossible things. Martin concentrated on his task.

A cool wind swirled around Beth and she was lifted up off the ground. Upward she rose through the air, higher and higher.

"I'm flying Marty!" Beth screamed in excitement. She neared the top of the massive Douglas fir near the edge of the property. Martin focused and moved her slowly to the top of the tree. She reached out and plucked a small piece of fir bough from the tree. She smiled widely. Martin moved her away from the tree, and then suddenly she began to plunge toward the ground. With a blood-curling scream she fell.

Less than a second later, she was enveloped in a bright flame that did not burn, but it slowed her fall and lowered her gracefully to the ground.

"Dude!" Beth shouted, as she walked up to Martin. "We're not doing that again until you are way better at landing, got it?"

Martin nodded.

"Thank you Brigid," Beth said, as she walked toward the small house.

"My pleasure," Brigid replied.

Later that same day Beth watched Brigid work with the shaman. Freeman was kind of an Indian hippy, in her opinion, with his long hair and black unkempt clothes. But Brigid had been helping him learn to bend the will of plants, animals, and the weather among other things. She said it was channeling his mana, the magical spirit within all humans. Freeman called it his 'mojo.' Beth was highly skeptical of the whole endeavor, but was shocked when she got to witness living things responding to him, such as trees turning their limbs to touch him or to close a path behind them. She checked for invisible cords, or hidden strings afterwards and found none. The thing that seemed the most outlandish was that Freeman learned to alter the weather. He had brought rain to the normally dry, late July climate of the Columbia River valley, and she was at a complete loss to explain that.

"Great," Beth announced, as the large drops of rain fell hard on the corrugated fiberglass that covered the front patio of the house with a loud repeating 'thwack, thwack, thwack.'

"It's amazing, isn't it?" Freeman asked Beth with the smile of a young boy looking at a wondrous present sitting before him on his birthday.

"Well done, Freeman," Brigid added with a graceful bow of her head.

"Yeah, it's amazing," Beth replied shaking her head. "Except I have to take Drake to work today. He works at three, and now we probably need to go get him a jacket for his ride home after work."

"Oh," Freeman said. "Sorry about that Beth, I can take him."

"No," Beth responded, as she began to walk away and look for Drake. "It's okay Freeman, I like spending time with my brother-in-law."

"Are you working today too, Brigid?" Freeman asked. "You always seem to work when Drake does, but we've noticed that your name isn't even on the schedule."

"Freeman," Brigid replied with her disarming smile. "You flatter me. Drake has been my responsibility, which is why I have been at the restaurant every day he has been."

Freeman smiled.

"So I guess you'll be leaving soon, too?" Freeman questioned.

"Mayhaps, Drake has earned an evening free of my guardianship," Brigid answered. "Would you and your brothers like to continue training with me?"

"Of course we would, fair Brigid," Freeman replied with a bow. "Besides, if any one of us can take care of themselves it is probably our esteemed leader, the young Mister Drake."

The ride to his house was one of absolute quiet. Drake hurried in through the heavy rain to get his jacket. He hoped that the rainfall would subside before he was off work at eleven because he really didn't want to ride home in the monsoon.

"You don't talk very much, do you Drake?" Beth asked after she backed her car out of the driveway.

Drake shook his head.

"Although, I've seen you talk to your brother and the other guys a lot," Beth added, as she deduced her hypothesis. "So it's kind of just girls you don't talk to, isn't it?"

Drake kind of shrugged.

"You know," Beth continued with a smile, "we are related. You don't have to be scared of me. I really like you. Sometimes I even wish Martin were more like you. You're so calm, and smart, and talented, and dreamy."

Drake sat and processed what Beth had just said. Once again, he was slightly convinced that another older woman had just flirted with him. But this flirting thing was such a foreign concept to him and he'd no real tangible way to process it. The only thing Drake knew for certain that this was different because this time it was his sister-in-law. He wondered what kind of powers he might possess that would cause this, because he was pretty sure that he wasn't overly attractive. When he looked in the mirror every day all he saw looking back at him was a borderline ugly kid—not Elephant Man ugly by any means—but not movie star attractive either. In fact, in his memory, no one had ever really told him he wasn't ugly. So he'd just concluded that must be the case since he didn't have lots of friends like the other kids he knew in school—the popular kids like Steven and Downtown Danny. So this oddity of older women flirting with him perplexed him in ways he couldn't comprehend.

"But," Beth reasoned, "I've also seen you talk to Brigid too, so maybe its just human girls you're scared of?"

"I'm not scared," Drake replied.

"No?" Beth questioned. "It sure seems like it."

"I just don't know how to act," Drake said.

"Drake," Beth replied, "sweetie, you don't have to act.

Just be yourself, you already are pretty amazing."

Drake blushed. He was glad that they were pulling into the parking lot of the restaurant. Once they stopped he quickly jumped out and opened the back door to pull his ten-speed bicycle out. His sword was still wrapped in cloth and chained to the frame of the bike. He leaned in after closing the back door, the rain ran down his face and pooled on his back.

"Thanks for the ride Beth," Drake stated before he quickly closed the door and pushed his bike toward the front door of the restaurant.

Beth shook her head. Maybe she came on too strong for him. She didn't want to damage her relationship with him, but her husband's younger brother intrigued her in ways she couldn't understand. She turned up the radio and the swoosh, swoosh of the windshield wipers kept time to the music and she drove away with a smile.

Drake wasn't overly pleased to work that rainy night. He was the three-to-eleven dishwasher, and the two-to-ten busboy was none other than his personal nemesis, Moose Caine. After he put his bike in the mop room, Drake hung up his jacket and took some paper towels to dry off the water that clung to him.

"Come on, Dick!" Moose yelled, as he banged a bus tub full of dirty dishes onto the stainless steel shelf. "You got a lot of dishes to do, dickweed!"

Drake slowly made his way over to the dish station. There were stacks of full bus tubs, some on the rubber floor mats inside the dish station. Moose had not washed anything for the whole hour he was there by himself, and had left everything for Drake to do.

Frustration and anger fueled Drake as he worked his way through the mountain of dirty dishes. He was surprised that the restaurant hadn't run out of plates because he had so many to wash.

"Come on, faggot," Moose encouraged Drake, as he

leaned into the dish station to grab the rack of clean silverware to take to the front of the restaurant. "Seems like everyone's coming here to eat cause of the damned rain. Stop jerking off and get caught up, Dick!"

Drake shook his head. Moose was a complete waste of human flesh. He scrubbed and sprayed the dishes as he piled them onto the green plastic dish racks, staging them one-after-the-other in front of the large cubic dishwasher. As soon as the machine shut off, he quickly lifted the bar and opened it in a cloud of churning steam. Out came the hot clean dishes, and in went the next rack of dirty dishes. He pulled the arm down and started the machine, turned and stacked the clean dishes in piles, and quickly moved back to scrubbing and spraying the dishes on the next rack. The process was never ending.

"Come on, Drake," Oly stated, as he walked through the back of the restaurant. "Looks like your falling behind bud, maybe I should send Gerald back here to help you."

"I got it!" Drake snapped back to the manager.

"Okay," Oly said, as he walked away. "See that you do."

The night was busy all the way through nine o'clock, before it finally slowed down. That meant Drake would have at least another hour to get caught up and do the things he needed to do before the end of his shift.

Moose chuckled to himself as he watched Drake struggle. He could have easily made it less work for Drake by helping him out and by not flooding him with bus tubs when ever he thought he might be catching up. But somewhere inside of Moose, it made him happy to see the miserable look upon the face of Drake. It served Drake right for doing what he did to ruin his senior year, to take away his starting position on the basketball team, and for making some of his classmates despise him for the way he treated the new kid.

At ten o'clock, Moose gazed outside at the rain—it had begun to slow but was still coming down hard. He headed back into the break area to clock out. He pulled his timecard and wrote his out time as ten o'clock. He grabbed his jacket off the back of a chair and paused.

Moose knew Drake rode his bike to and from work. Sitting on the back of the chair next to his coat was the jacket Drake had worn when he arrived for work. Moose smiled.

He put Drake's jacket inside his own and walked toward the dish station.

"Hey faggot!" Moose called out to Drake. "Hey, no hard feelings. You worked your ass off tonight, enjoy your ride home."

Drake turned and looked at Moose, wondering why he'd give him any kind of compliment. Moose smiled at him, waved, and was gone.

Drake shook his head, it takes all kinds, he thought.

At eleven, he had accomplished all of his tasks and left the dish station almost completely under control. There were still massive stacks of clean dishes that needed to be taken out to the front, but otherwise Drake had pulled it out, despite the effort or lack of effort from Moose.

Drake clocked out and went to get his jacket from the chair. He couldn't find it. He looked on all the chairs, under all the other coats. He even thought that maybe he'd left it on his bike, or perhaps in one of the other rooms in the back of the restaurant. Finally, after fifteen minutes of looking, Drake decided he just wanted to go home. It would be about fifteen minutes of wet hell, riding in the illuminated darkness, with the rain soaking through his white button up shirt. He dreaded that thought most, he wasn't a fan of being wet and cold.

"Wait," Drake said to himself. He quickly went to the back door and grabbed one of the large black garbage bags they used for the big rolling trash cans in the restaurant. He went into the kitchen, nodded to Eugene, who was tapping the long yellow cutting board with his hands, keeping beat to a song he heard in his head. Drake grabbed one of the knives and spread out the unopened black bag. He cut a slice out of the closed bottom, and two more on opposite sides.

"Thanks Eugene!" Drake shouted to the bopping cook.

Eugene waved to him and kept jamming.

Drake got his bike and headed out the front door. Once outside, under the eave of the building, he took his modified garbage bag and pulled it over his head, popping his arms through the two holes on the side, and his head through the one he cut in the bottom. At least his shirt would stay dry on his torso, and the ride wouldn't be completely miserable.

Drake climbed aboard his bike and began to pedal down 6th Avenue. The smell of the water on the cool asphalt assaulted him like the fragrances and perfumes sprayed inside the department stores in the mall. He pedaled harder, shifting the gears on the bike as water sprayed off the back wheel up the middle of his back.

In the nearly empty parking lot of the J&M Plaza ahead of him, beneath one of the incandescent lights, was a car with a man on the roof. That was very odd—especially given the current weather. Drake was sure he had never seen such a thing before. He slowed his bike and wiped his already wet hair from his eyes.

Around the car circled a couple large dogs, they seemed very big actually, definitely larger than the St. Bernard's the Frasers used to have as pets, and they had things that looked like spikes sticking out of their backs.

The man on the roof of the car was frantic as the massive canines paced around him, nipping at his feet. Drake thought the guy looked familiar, but at this distance he wasn't sure. Then it hit him. It was Moose Caine.

Drake stopped his bike, reached down, and unlocked his sword. He pulled Hikari from its scabbard. Faint blue-fire glowed from the metal blade. He locked the chain back on the scabbard, and held the sword up.

"For Olympus!" Drake shouted as the street lights around him blinked off. He pushed hard on the pedals and sped toward the stranded Moose. As he drew nearer the scene, he could see that Moose's car was beaten. Huge dents lined the sides, its tires were torn out leaving it sitting on the metal rims, and its windows were shattered and broken—

every single one of them. The canine monstrosities didn't hear him approaching since they were so completely focused on the hapless Moose.

Moose swung a thick piece of fabric at the animals, attempting to shoo them away.

"Please go away, doggies!" Moose cried, as he swung at the creatures. "Shoo! Go home! I don't wanna die!"

With a flash, Drake was upon them. Hikari cut deeply into the dog in front spewing thick black blood across the cement. It yelped loudly in response and turned quickly away from its attacker.

The other dog circled around to see its partner licking the deep wound along its right front leg.

"Moose!" Drake shouted. "You gotta run! You're a sitting duck out here!"

"Run where?" Moose yelled back. A good question, Drake thought. He quickly looked around. The dumpster enclosure next to the Ferryman Motel was their best bet since it had three tall walls and a defensible front gate.

"To the dumpster!" Drake commanded. Moose froze, uncertain that running away from the dogs that had just destroyed his car was such a good idea. "Move it Moose, we need somewhere we can defend ourselves against them!"

The injured creature circled back toward Drake as the other one came from behind. Drake dismounted his bike and swung it with his left hand into the first animal buying some time, in his right hand, Hikari grazed the tips of the second dog's ears off. The lumbering dogs retreated once more.

"Now!" Drake shouted to Moose. "Run, damn it!"

Moose jumped from the roof of his car and sprinted faster than Drake had ever seen him move on the basketball court. Drake picked up his bike and mounted it quickly, pushing down hard on a pedal and moving rapidly behind Moose. Behind them, through the patter of the rain, they heard the hounds running after them.

Moose got to the dumpster enclosure and pushed on the metal doors to no avail, they were locked.

"Damn it Fraser!" Moose yelled in frustration. "It's locked! We're gonna die out here!"

"Moose!" Drake bellowed, as he turned his bike to a sliding stop in front of his nemesis. "It's got pins at the bottom, and the latch is in the middle, get it open!"

Moose looked at the metal doors. Sure enough, each door had a large curved steel pin holding it in place. He quickly bent down and pulled one of them up, as it cleared the cement he pulled the latch on the door and it swung outward. Moose darted inside and began to close the door.

The dogs attacked once more, pressing Drake backward toward the dumpster doors and Moose. Hikari lit up the rain-streaked sky like blue lightning as Drake slashed it between the animals. Once again they retreated, and Drake turned to enter the enclosure. Moose pulled the door shut behind them.

"What the hell are those things, Fraser?" Moose demanded. "They came out of no where and attacked my car!"

"Why are you still here?" Drake asked, as he tried to make sense of what was happening. "You got off work over an hour ago?"

"I took your coat," Moose admitted, as he held up the thick fabric he had been attempting to shoo the dogs away with. "I wanted to see you ride home in the rain. I was just sitting in my car waiting to see you ride home in the rain. I'm so sorry."

Drake looked at his jacket in Moose's hand. Parts of the sleeves were torn and missing. He liked that jacket and now it was ruined.

"Those dogs, Drake," Moose added, "they're like devils! They have human faces, and my God they destroyed my car! Did you see what they did to my car? What the hell are they?"

"Well, honestly," Drake explained, "I believe they're hellhounds, I've never actually seen one before, but they match all the descriptions I've read about."

"Hellhounds?" Moose asked almost rhetorically. He was scared to the point that he couldn't really question the validity of what Drake had just stated. "But why would they attack me?"

A loud thud of one of the beasts crashing into one of the metal doors echoed inside the enclosure as the door pushed inward, Moose frantically pushed it back, this was quickly followed by coarse steam billowing under the metal doors as the hellhounds sniffed for them.

Drake wondered. Why would hellhounds attack Moose? It was a fact that he was a royal pain in the ass, and probably deserved to be harassed by hellhounds more than anyone else in the whole world. But that was all figurative, not literally. No one truly deserved to be attacked by these beasts. Then it all made sense to him, he'd been warned about his essence being like a scent. Even Quatyl, the snake-god had muttered something about being able to smell him as a Fraser. Aunt Carmen had made the button charms to shield their Fraser essence, and he still carried his. But Moose had taken his jacket, a coat he had worn for over a year. It was sure to have some of his essence on it. They must've attacked Moose because they thought he was Drake. Unfortunately, Drake couldn't tell Moose that.

"I don't know," Drake finally replied. But he had already formulated a plan for their escape. "There are two of them, and I can't get both of them at once. I cut one of them badly and it's hurt. I need a diversion."

"Wait a minute," Moose said. "I'm not going back out there. I'll stay right here until the garbage truck comes and empties these dumpsters, thank you very much."

"Moose," Drake stated. "Listen to me, in a little bit the healthy one will probably jump over one of these walls. We don't have a lot of time here. They know I have a weapon, and you don't, except my coat."

"Yeah," Moose replied with wild eyes. "Which is exactly why I ain't going out there, Drake."

"Listen," Drake asked, the only noise from outside the

enclosure was the pitter-patter of rain upon the cement of the parking lot. "Do you hear that? They're quiet, which probably means they're planning their attack right now."

"You think they can make it over these walls?" Moose questioned fearfully.

"Remember what they did to your car?" Drake answered. Moose nodded.

"Okay, Drake, what's your plan?" Moose asked as the realization that they didn't have much time settled upon him.

Drake quickly explained it to him, and the hellhounds made their first attempt at jumping the wall. A hound hit hard against the top of the wall and fell back with a yelp.

"I think that was the hurt one," Drake explained. "Are you ready, Moose?"

"Yeah," Moose replied.

Drake opened the door and moved out, the hilt of Hikari in both hands. The hellhounds were back in the distance, separated, and began to approach him on opposite sides. Moose stepped out of the enclosure, swinging Drake's coat. The hellhounds were intelligent, and Drake had counted on that. They adjusted their attack to go after the one they thought was Drake—the guy with the swinging jacket. They bounded rapidly toward Moose. The first one leapt, its ravening maw open and spittle spewing from its row upon row of razor sharp teeth. Drake reacted in an instant—Hikari blazed blue as it swung downward. Drake had pivoted to his right and launched himself between Moose and the hellhound. Hikari cut true, severing the tufted neck from its sinewy body. The dead hellhound slammed into the cement right in front of Moose.

Moose closed his eyes from the scene that unfolded before him. Moving his left leg backward, Drake pivoted on it and swung Hikari into the remaining great beast. The blue-fire blade bit into the ribs of the hellhound. Drake's swing was forceful enough to cut the snake-god in half, but that was in Gehenna where his abilities were amplified. Here on Earth, he was just a normal athletic guy. And his swing was not enough to kill the monster.

Up rose the hellhound, and Drake tugged to free his sword from its side. The hellhound slobbered blood and spittle as an unearthly growl rumbled in its throat.

"Oh my God! Oh my God!" Moose shouted, as he ran back into the dumpster enclosure. The movement caught the eye of the hellhound.

It nipped at Drake, just missing his hand. Drake freed Hikari from its side as thick black blood spewed from the deep wound.

The hellhound turned and lunged at Moose, trying desperately to complete the kill. Drake responded once again, catching the beast with an uppercut swing in the center of its abdomen. Intestines and blood spilled out of the cut and the hellhound collapsed in front of the dumpster door.

Moose stared at Drake. He looked like he was crazed, like he had just lost his grip on his sanity.

"You did it," Moose said. "You saved me, Drake. But why? I've picked on you every day I've known you, you didn't have to save me, but you did. Why?"

"That's just it, Moose," Drake answered. "The difference between you and me, is that I honor my commitments, to my friends, my team, my brothers, and even my co-workers. Yeah, you've been a dick to me, but it's like Ryan said, what makes us better is our ability to love each other, to rise above the pettiness and become something stronger because of that love in our hearts. You've been my teammate and my co-worker, and those hellhounds were going to kill you. I couldn't just turn away and let a defenseless guy get eaten, not if I could prevent it. I had to help you, I had no options. That's what heroes are for."

Moose stared at him blankly. He shook in the cold rain, and Drake wondered how long he had been on the roof of his car being drenched in the downpour.

"Come on Moose," Drake said. "We need to get out of here. You need to get home and get dried off. Come on, let's go."

Moose handed Drake his jacket, and then walked back across the parking lot to his car. Drake went to his bike. The front wheel was bent a bit. He wiped Hikari off on his pant leg and unlocked the chain on the scabbard. Quickly he put the sword away and re-secured it to his bike. He pulled his torn jacket over the equally torn trash bag poncho he had made at work. The wet had soaked deeply into him and the torn jacket did little for him but seal a layer of moisture on him.

He heard the sound of metal scraping the cement and turned to see Moose's broken car with torn tires rolling away. Each revolution of the wheels scraped on the hard cement. Thick exhaust billowed out of the back of the car as it slowly moved out of the parking lot. Drake stood there on his bike and watched Moose turn right onto NE Hazel Dell Avenue. The grinding of his metal wheels along the pavement of the road echoed in the rain, before finally vanishing.

Drake looked at the carnage of the dead hellhounds, and decided he had better leave before someone arrived and began asking questions. He pushed off on his right pedal. The front wheel of the bike squeaked loudly against the stopper of the front brake. The bend in the wheel made the bike swerve a bit as he pedaled.

Drake crossed the road, looking far to the right to see a small trail of sparks coming from the metal of Moose's wheels on the pavement. Drake shook his head and hoped Moose was going to be okay. He wondered what he'd tell his friends and family about the battle fought outside the restaurant that night. Drake turned and rode up the hill on NE 82nd Street, and away from Moose.

No one Drake knew ever saw Moose again after that night. He never came in to work again, and Bobby had even said that he stopped by Moose's house but his mom said he didn't live there anymore. He just vanished. Drake somehow knew in his heart that might happen when he looked into the vacant eyes of Moose Caine. The hellhound attack had rocked his perception of reality and somewhere inside of him his world had been shaken beyond his ability to cope. Some people rise up in the face of unadulterated evil, some hide and hope it passes them by, and others break and flee. Moose Caine broke in the July rain that fateful night at J&M Plaza.

A week later in a small non-descript office within the bowels of the Apostolic Library near the Tower of the Winds at the heart of Vatican City, a cloistered man frantically entered. He wore black robes and sandals on his feet.

"Your eminence," the cloistered man stated to another far older man sitting at a desk flipping through the pages of an archaic leather-bound book. "You asked to be updated."

"Yes Father Gregorio," the cardinal replied. "What is it?"

"I have these," Father Gregorio stated. He held a couple of Polaroid photographs in his right hand. "And I know you're going to want to see them."

"Bring them here, Father," the cardinal asked with a wave of his hand.

Father Gregorio approached the cardinal and set the pictures down on the book he had been reading. The cardinal looked up at the Polaroids. He then frantically pulled them closer once he saw the subject of the pictures.

"Sweet Mother of God!" the cardinal exclaimed. "Where did you get photographs of these abominations, Gregorio?"

"One of our agents," Father Gregorio replied. "He got them from an Animal Control officer in Clark County, Washington, in the United States. Your eminence, it seems the officer brought the photographs in for confession. He was convinced it was a sign of his own sin, or of the end of days."

"These are dire times, Gregorio," the cardinal began with a frown. "Dire times indeed. These mangled beasts are hellhounds, and they are forbidden to walk upon the Earth.

And look here at the precision of these cuts, these beasts were not hacked to death. Only a skilled swordsman could have made these wounds."

The cardinal sat and shook his head. Gregorio crossed himself.

"Father," the cardinal added, "we need to get a detachment of Hospitallers on the ground there, post haste. Make sure they know the severity of the otherworldly incursion, and advise them that their greatest foe may well be this re-born Brotherhood of Olympus."

"Yes your eminence," Father Gregorio stated, as he backed away from the cardinal. "Right away, your eminence, it shall be done."

The cardinal sat in disbelief and looked upon the cut-up bodies of the hellhounds.

"May God protect us all and guide us to do what is right, Gregorio," the cardinal said somberly.

21

SAYING GOOD-BYE AND MOVING ON

THE BROTHERHOOD OF OLYMPUS AND THE TOWER OF DREAMS

Of Mark and Drake
Chapter Twenty-One
August 14, 1980
Hazel Dell, Washington

Brigid was markedly upset following the hellhound attack.

"I should have been there," Brigid rationalized. "It was pure folly of me to act otherwise, I am pledged to support Drake and see him through to the task that awaits."

Brigid stood upon the porch of the house she occupied, her aura burning brightly around her. Drake knew she couldn't go anywhere public like that or she'd attract a lot of unwanted attention. Drake and Freeman had brought her the news, and they stood there now beneath to green fiberglass roof.

"Hey," Freeman stated, as he placed his hand upon her arm, "none of us saw that possibility, that the oaf—Moose Caine would do such a thing and make himself a mark for the enemy."

"Tis true," Brigid replied. "Good Freeman, yet this does serve notice to the stakes the enemy has undertaken to destroy the Brotherhood. Sending hell spawn freely upon the Earth is a dire warning for us all. We shall not take this lightly, nor shall we feign ignorance to their tactics."

"What shall we do, Lady Brigid?" Drake asked.

"We must prepare," Brigid answered. "We must be vigilant, and I think it is time you brought your brother Mark back into the fold. He is quite courageous and strong and we could use his aid."

Drake nodded. He liked the idea of Mark becoming

involved with what the Brotherhood had become. He knew all of them, he worked with Scrappy and Freeman, and of course he knew Beth as well. Mark had even given him rides to Joe E. Brown night before, though that may have been more for the girls and beer. Brigid's suggestion rang true for him. Drake was all for bringing his closest brother back. It was a great idea, the only problem was how?

Over the next week or so, Drake casually brought up the subject to Mark numerous times. But each time he did, Mark deftly avoided it by changing the subject to another of Drake's passions—basketball, or more specifically the four Seattle sports teams, the Supersonics, the Mariners, the Seahawks, and the Sounders. Drake always fell for the bait, and Mark dodged the topic yet again.

On August seventh, Drake was in Danny's to check the newly posted schedule for the week of the fourteenth through the twentieth. He was working four days—a dayshift, two swings, and one graveyard shift. More hours meant more money, and Drake was saving money to buy a car so he didn't have to ride back and forth to work. The variable shift kind of schedule was common for most of the busboy/dishwashers employed there, but it didn't help with his sleep patterns. He glanced over at the cook schedule to see when his brother worked, in case they could carpool on one or more days.

Something was not right. The current cook schedule had 'M. Fraser' on the fifth line, with nine more names listed below him. The new schedule had only thirteen names on it. One was missing, and that one was his brother Mark.

Drake spent the next couple of days trying to arrange to talk to Mark to find out what was going on, but Mark avoided him like the plague. Finally Drake asked the manager why his brother wasn't on the schedule anymore.

"Oly," Drake began, as he stood in the office doorway, "I was looking at next week's schedule, and…"

"Something wrong with your hours, Drake?" Oly

interrupted.

"No," Drake answered. "Not my hours, my brother. Why isn't Mark on the schedule?"

"He put in his transfer papers," Oly replied. "Wait, you mean he didn't tell you? His own brother?"

Drake shook his head.

"Your brother's transferring," Oly stated. "Sorry to be the one to have to tell you that, kid. Now get back to work."

Drake went back to the dish station and somberly thought about what Mr. Olsen had just said. Mark was transferring. But transferring where? There were two other Danny's restaurants in the area, one out near Orchards and another at Jantzen Beach on Hayden Island in the Columbia River, just inside the Oregon border. Mark must have gotten offered more money to cook at one of those restaurants. In fact, Mark had spent a week in July working at the Oregon restaurant. That must have been when this all started to happen. It was an extra five miles away, but that wasn't too far if the money was better.

The next day, Drake found a note from Mark on his desk:

Drake,
Meet me in the J&M Plaza parking lot when you get off work tomorrow.
Mark

Finally Drake would get some answers, and Mark would get the offer to join them and help fight the evil that was brewing on the horizon.

The day passed dreadfully slow, but finally the time had come and Drake clocked out of work at three o'clock. He gathered his sweatshirt—his old basketball gray hooded one from 1978—since his jacket was not much of a jacket anymore. He thought of how his life had changed since he first wore that sweatshirt—the death of his uncle, the fight with the mordgeists over the *Spirit* board, the founding of the

Brotherhood, his dad's suicide attempt, their move south and all the struggles associated with that, but yet there was goodness there too. He had new friends, new brothers, and they had the guidance of a goddess to help them along their way.

He walked his bike out of the restaurant and rode off to meet his brother. Mark stood beside his car, near one of the lamp posts on the street side of the parking lot, not too far away from where Moose had been attacked.

"Hey Drake," Mark said, as his brother rode up to him.

"Hey," Drake replied, as he pulled his bike to a stop and leaned on his right leg.

"We have to talk, little brother," Mark began. Drake nodded. "You've always been the closest to me, and that made talking to you the hardest."

"What do you mean?" Drake asked.

"Ever since we moved, things have been different," Mark added. "Hell, Drake, ever since Wally died things have been different."

"Yeah, I know," Drake replied. "But that's part of what I've been trying to talk to you about. Mark, you have always been the strongest of us, the bravest one, or maybe the one who just didn't care what anyone else thought. This Brotherhood stuff is heating up. There are bad things out there hunting us, and we need you. I need you."

"Drake," Mark responded. "You know how I feel about all that paranormal crap. I can't believe in all that stuff. If I did, the world I know would make no sense at all."

"I know," Drake added. "Trust me, I've been there, done that. The foundation of my reality has been reshaped a million times since Wally died. But, damn it Mark, you were there with me. Only you and I could go back in and face Succorbenoth and the mordgeists. Only us. It was real."

"I don't know what was real anymore," Mark replied. "That day was like a bad dream to me, little brother. I can't live my life that way, I just can't. That's not my path, not my destiny."

"What are you saying?" Drake questioned. "We've always been together, side-by-side, friends to the end. Why aren't you on the schedule anymore at work? Oly said you're transferring? How much more money are they paying you to go work in Oregon, Mark?"

"Drake," Mark shook his head. He saw now that he was wrong in not talking to Drake earlier about his decisions. Of all of his family, Drake still was the most connected to him, and the most likely to be hurt by his actions. "I'm sorry I didn't tell you sooner, but I thought it would be easier this way."

"What's easier Mark?" Drake asked. "You still haven't answered my question, how much more money are you making to transfer to Jantzen Beach?"

"I'm not going to Jantzen Beach," Mark answered. "I'm transferring to Phoenix. I'm moving to Arizona to go the mechanics school."

Drake looked at Mark, who appeared a hundred percent sincere. Then he quickly glanced at his car. Mark's car was packed with boxes. Only the area around the driver's seat was free from boxes, and the entire backseat was crammed full.

"Wait," Drake began, as he realized what his brother was explaining. He felt like the ground had just opened beneath him and he was falling into a dark nothingness. "You're going to school in Arizona? The one you talked about a few months ago?"

Mark nodded.

"When are you leaving?" Drake asked.

"Today," Mark answered. "Right after I talked to you, technically I guess I've already done that, so I guess I'm leaving now."

"So that's it?" Drake questioned, anger and sadness welled up in him. The reality that his brothers would all eventually grow up and move away had always lingered in his mind. When Martin had gone through the process by joining the Air Force, it had been easier because they weren't on good terms at the time. But Mark was different, even when he was difficult he was still the brother that Drake had experienced most of his life with. And now, Mark was telling him that part of his life was over.

"Yeah, I guess so, little brother," Mark answered. He stepped over to Drake and hugged him, patting him on the back with his right hand, then pulled his taller brother's head down and kissed his forehead. "Stay out of trouble, and please be safe."

Mark's eyes watered and a trace of tears pooled at the bottom of Drake's eyes.

'Crying only makes it hurt worse,' boomed in Drake's head.

Mark climbed into his car and fired up the engine. He buckled his seat belt, adjusted his rear view mirror so he could see between the stacked boxes in the back seat, and turned on the radio. It was on KGON 92.3, the Defenders of Rock. *The Ballad of the Pure Knight*, by the Jacks blasted through his speakers as he shifted his car into drive, and began to pull away from his little brother still standing astride his bike beneath the lamp post.

In the field stands a banner of blue and gold,
Beneath it a single knight true and bold,

Mark looked into the mirror, Drake still stood there, shocked and dumbfounded, by his sudden departure.

He carries his honor upon his shield and blade,
Yet the pain of his duty is greater than is known,
Though his wounds may be grievous, he asks for no aid,
The battle that he wages is for glory and all his own,

Mark reached the corner of the parking lot. He looked up and Drake still stood there, behind him.

Yet in my sadness and sorrow,
I'll not stand with him on the morrow,
I'm off today, I'm going away,
But the pure knight and his valor are there to stay,

Tears began to streak down Mark's face as he looked back at his brother in the mirror. The image of them together in his car on their first day of school at Columbia River flashed in his mind.

"Is it a try-out?" Mark asked.

"No," Drake replied. "The letter was from the head coach. A guy named Arthaud. Mom told the principal I played basketball when she registered us. The principal told the coach I was coming, and the coach had heard of me and wanted me to join the varsity. Being on their varsity's cool, I guess. But, I don't know what their record is."

"Does it matter?" Mark stated rhetorically. "Listen Drake, I know how shy you can be, and I know you have a hard time making friends. This move is a step forward for all of us, really. It's all about your confidence, you know. But think of it this way, you get to be on the varsity team, that's like ten new friends for you right there."

"I guess so," Drake answered.

"I've seen you play," Mark added. "The whole team's going to be happy to have you. You work hard, you're nice, and you're pretty good at the game."

"Yeah, that's true, I guess," Drake agreed.

Mark saw his little brother, wounded, and still standing behind him, as he waited for the traffic on the road to clear so he could pull out and head toward the freeway south.

I promised my loyalty, I promised my love,
I promised that I'd be there always by your side,
I promised you everything, but now it seems like I lied,

Through the tears, Mark thought back to the day on the deck at their grandparent's house, when the two of them, assisted by Albert, were about to go back in the house to face the perils inside it together to save their brothers and their family.

"Good idea," Mark said. "Let's go, remember Albert, keep this door open."

"I got it," Albert answered. "I got it."

"Little brother," Mark stated as he turned to Drake, "I want you to know something before we go in there. You and I have always been together, I trust you with my life, and I think you feel the same. I love you. No matter what happens, I will always be there for you. You got that?"

"Ditto," Drake nodded since he was not good with statements of emotions.

"Me too!" exclaimed Albert as he prepared for his job.

Mark and Drake stepped in to the house.

Lie, lie, lie,

Lie, lie, lie,

Mark pulled out onto the road, and still Drake stood watching his brother leave for school in Arizona, and out of his life.

Mark thought of them together as elementary school kids, they were like eight or nine years old. They had been sent to bed early because Mark got caught smoking, and Drake had been with him and was guilty by association. It was the height of summer, and it would be daylight for many hours as they lay upon their beds looking out the window watching the world go by.

"You think bigfoot is gonna come down the road again?" Drake asked enthusiastically.

"Nah, I don't think he's comin' back. You know what, we should just run away, little brother," Mark stated. "We could live up in the woods together. I read a book called *My Side of the Mountain*, it was all about a kid living on his own in the woods, and I know you and I could do it."

"Yeah," Drake replied. He was an idealist and could see the justice in fleeing from the persecution they both felt at the moment.

"I'm serious," Mark added, as he looked out at the blue sky. "We're always gonna be brothers, best friends to the end, and when we escape to the woods we can make our own country with our own laws, and bed times, and you can draw our flag cause you'll make one way cooler than me."

I promised my loyalty, I promised my love,

I promised that I'd be there always by your side,

I promised you everything, but now it seems like I lied,

Mark reached the end of the road next to Danny's, then

flicked his turn signal to the right so he could get on 78th Street and double back to the interstate and his future. He looked back one final time. Drake still stood there, beneath the lamp post, watching him leave.

A very early memory flashed before his eyes. Drake was a toddler, and one of the kids at the park had teased him because he had such a big head.

"Stop it!" Mark shouted at the kid. "He's my brother!"

"Your brother's retarded! Look at his big bald head," the kid remarked. He was at least a foot taller than Mark, and wore a baseball cap with an 'NY' upon it. "What're you gonna do about, you're a baby too."

Mark was furious. No one attacked his baby brother, and no one dared calling him a baby. With a flurry of hitting and kicking Mark was upon the bigger kid. The baseball cap went flying, and the kid went down pummeled by punches, kicks, and bites. Uncle Wally and Cousin Ralph pulled Mark off the dirty and beaten kid. Mark had blood from the kid's nose upon his hands.

"Mark!" Wally exclaimed. "You can't go beating up kids at the park, or you'll go to jail."

"He started it," Mark replied. "He made fun of my brother, he's my brother! And no one's gonna hurt him!"

Lie, lie, lie,

Lie, lie, lie,

Mark wiped away the tears, turned out onto the roadway, and was gone from Drake's life.

22

A TRAP IS SET

THE BROTHERHOOD OF OLYMPUS
AND THE TOWER OF DREAMS

Flight to Home
Chapter Twenty-Two
September 14, 1980
Hazel Dell, Washington

It had been a month to the day since Mark had left for technical school in Phoenix. Drake was still in a somber mood, and seldom smiled or laughed at anything anymore. School had started again for both Scrappy and Drake, and neither boy took a lot of comfort in what was the beginning of their junior year of high school. The Brotherhood had trained religiously every opportunity they found. Scrappy was getting good at leaving welts and bruises upon all of his brothers with the wooden swords. Drake would sometimes prevail against him by sheer cunning against his superior strength, and Brigid was quick to point out that he needed to learn from what Drake did and counter it. She explained that the foes he'd face would be both strong and cunning. One stood undefeated against the massive barbarian, and that was none other than Beth.

She took pride in the fact that Scrappy had never beaten her during their melee practice. But everyone else who stood before the barbarian and traded blows with him knew she had achieved that accomplishment solely because he chose not to hit her very hard.

"If you didn't hold back against her, it would be far better for her training," Freeman explained to Scrappy when Beth had gone into the house. "None of our foes will be as kind to her."

"Freeman, my brother," Scrappy chuckled and patted him on the back, "if I wasn't holding back with all of ya, there'd be none of ya to fight any foes."

Freeman looked at the thick muscles of the barbarian and at his wide jovial smile.

"Point taken," Freeman replied. "However, you could just beat her once so the rest of us don't have to hear how pathetic we are at swordplay."

"As you say, point taken," Scrappy laughed.

Freeman had become even more eccentric, often telling people that he saw the spirits of his ancestors, or heard their spectral drumming in the forests calling out to him. Martin was very interested in his visions but only wanted to compare notes with the shaman. Scrappy quickly determined that the Indian was becoming a 'deranged coot,' only Drake encouraged him to pursue the knowledge that was out there before him, calling him. Drake knew that each of them had particular set of skills, and under the guidance of Brigid those skills were becoming enhanced or sharpened.

Freeman stood before them, gushing about the ghostly ancestors who stood in the trees outside the house. Martin opened his minds eye and searched the tree line for the apparitions.

"There's something there," Martin announced. "I feel them. They are benevolent and mean no harm."

"I must go to them," Freeman said, as he walked off the porch and toward the woods. "Greetings, my ancestors, may your journeys be fruitful, the sun bright on your path, and brother wind always at your back."

The mists among the trees congealed and formed loose humanoid shapes. One of the white shapes became more solid and moved from the forest. Everyone in the group—even Beth the wide-eyed skeptic—saw the apparition hover across the ground.

"Brother Kalama," the ghost whispered in a wind-like tone full of odd noises. He was an elder of a coastal tribe, dressed in white billowing cedar bark clothes, and had a beaded braid of glistening white hair that stretched to where his waist would have been if he still had one. "I bring you tidings. Should you seek the great magic's, your time here will be fleeting. Choose well your fate, for your brothers depend upon you."

"Thank you, elder," Freeman said.

"The Tower comes on a date you are ill prepared for, Brother Kalama. Look to the west on the eve of All Hallows."

"Thank you for your tidings, elder," Freeman stated with a bow. "May I make my ancestors proud upon the path I walk."

"Fear not, Brother Kalama," the apparition uttered. "Many songs will be sung of your deeds in all the hunting lands."

Freeman bowed low to the ghost and the spectral elder faded into the evening mist.

"Okay," Beth said. "That wasn't right. I mean, that was like a ghost and ghosts aren't real, right?"

Freeman, Drake, and Martin looked at her curiously.

"Neither are goddesses, right?" Scrappy added sarcastically. Beth looked at Brigid. The goddess tipped her head slightly to the side and smiled.

"What's that thing you guys say," Beth stated. "Point given, or earned, or something?"

All except Drake laughed with Beth.

"It's point taken," Drake remarked coolly.

The rest of the evening they discussed the coming of the Tower of Dreams. Addraemyr had told them it would come on the anagram of January thirteenth. They had naturally assumed it meant November third.

"Numbers are symbolic and possess power," Freeman stated. "January thirteenth has been marked by the dark gods."

"It wasn't that far of a stretch to see the clue as meaning November third," Martin added. "It's simply writing them out one-one-three, the only difference is where you put the dash to separate the month from the day. One dash one-three, January thirteenth and one-one dash three, November third."

"The eve of All Hallows is Halloween," Drake clarified. "And it, too, is an anagram, if you put the zero placeholder on the month of January. Zero-one one-three, flip each number set, and you get one-zero three-one, October thirty-first, Halloween."

"Thank god your ancestors came and told us," Martin rationalized. "We wouldn't have been prepared for that day because we thought it was the third."

"I don't think that would've ended well," Drake added.

Martin and Beth gave Drake and his bike a ride to work that night. It was Saturday evening and he worked the graveyard shift. Drake put his bike in the mop room and clocked in at ten fifty-nine. He got to be the busboy tonight, since there was a new dishwasher working with him. He was an older guy named Juan. He walked out into the front of the restaurant and saw the smiling face of Brigid.

"You're working tonight too?" Drake asked.

"Of course, dear Drake," Brigid replied with a smile. "You are now the keystone that holds the Brotherhood together, and I am pledged to see you safely through to your journey."

Drake shook his head. Sometimes, he wished he went away with Mark. Sometimes, usually when he was tired, he dreaded the whole thing and wondered what he had gotten involved with. Mordgeists, hellhounds, demons, daemons, gods, and goddesses, it was almost oppressive to think about. It seemed that they all spoke of him having choices, and that the future before them was unwritten, and yet it was like he had no real choice at all. He was simply cast to play this part, and he wasn't really sure he wanted to audition for it in the first place. It felt kind of like how he got his job at the restaurant, he really didn't have a choice, it just kind of happened.

"Does it really matter?" Drake asked.

"Of course it does," Brigid replied. "It is of grave importance to all creatures that cherish love, freedom and liberty."

"Okay, Brigid," Drake added as he shook his head slowly. "Sometimes I'm just not so sure. Maybe it would be different if Mark was still here."

"It is painfully clear that your brother is sorely missed by you, Drake Fraser," Brigid responded. "Would that I could change that, I would, verily."

Drake walked away and began to bus some tables. He knew that Saturday nights became exceptionally busy after two o'clock when all the bars closed. The bar rush was different from the dinner, lunch, or breakfast rushes he had worked because most of the patrons were somewhere between slightly and heavily intoxicated. Most of them were jovial and loud, but a few tended to be belligerent or mean spirited. Those customers were part of the reason the managers liked to hire high school basketball players as busboys. The taller than average busboys tended to act like bouncers to keep the peace in the front of the restaurant. Drake didn't mind that, it usually meant the waitresses would tip him better for playing that role and every dollar he was tipped added up to the total he needed to buy a car.

Everything was set and ready by two o'clock. By two fifteen, there was a line of people outside the door waiting to be seated.

Drake was kept busy running drinks out to customers, glasses of ice water mostly, and extra place settings. By two thirty, the restaurant was packed. One of the waitresses turned to Drake.

"Sweetie," Sandy said, "can you do me a huge favor and wait on my big top? They're being a bit to obnoxious for me."

"Sure," Drake replied. He had helped a few of the waitresses out like that in the past when they got too busy, were falling behind, or had a challenging customer.

"Great, here's what they ordered so far. I haven't gotten

the order from the other half of the table," Sandy stated, as she handed him the light green order book page.

"Okay," Drake added. "Can I borrow a pen?"

"Sure sweetie," Sandy replied. She handed him one of her ink pens.

Drake went off to finish getting the order.

"Hello, my name's Drake. Sandy asked if I could help her and finish taking your order," Drake announced to the loud table.

Some of the men at the table looked at the busboy wearing his brown vinyl apron and laughed.

"Were we too rowdy for her?"

"How old are you kid?"

"Are you the missing member of the *Beatles*?"

Drake just kept his forced smile and tolerated the comments.

"Guys, cut the kid some slack," a dark haired man with a rolled red bandana headband around his forehead said. He wore what appeared to be red leather pants, and a tight blue silk shirt. "My name's Mike and this is my band. We played a gig in Portland tonight and we're on our way back up to Vancouver, B.C. but we're hungry, so I hope you can help us out."

"Yeah," Drake replied. "I can do that, it looks like Sandy got the orders for seven of you, so she's only missing three?"

"Yeah," Mike answered, as he pointed to the smaller end of the two tables connected by folded leaves. "The roadies."

Drake quickly wrote down the remaining food orders and went to turn the ticket in to the kitchen. He hung it on the wheel with a click and spun it around for Eugene.

He went back to get refills on the beverages of his table.

"Have you heard of us kid?" one of the band asked.

"I don't know," Drake replied. "Who are you?"

Laughter erupted at the table, the roadies most of all.

"We're called Loverboy," Mike answered with a smile.

"What kind of music do you play?" Drake questioned.

"New Wave rock and roll," one of the roadies announced.

"Yeah, mostly," Mike added. "We've recorded a bit, and have an album coming out, and we have gotten a bit of radio airplay too. Everything helps."

"That's cool," Drake responded. "I was in a band back in Aberdeen."

"What'd you play kid?"

"Bass," Drake answered. "My band was called Fate, but we were more of a grungy metal band. It's kind of the sound in Grays Harbor."

"Well, take my advice kid," another man said, he was older than all the rest and the most conservatively dressed. "Grungy metal, whatever that is, won't ever be the next big thing like New Wave. You can write that down and take it to the bank."

"Hey kid," Mike continued. "Don't listen to him, he's our manager, and he thinks he knows everything. We appreciate any fellow musician, and all I got to tell you is stay true to your music and don't sell out. Everyone has a gift to share with the world, and I can tell yours isn't being the best busboy. Am I right?"

Drake nodded.

"Sometimes the talent a person possesses can change the world, if they choose to act with it," Mike finished.

"Hey Zen-Master Mike," one of the roadies chirped. "Maybe you should start a church and give up on singing."

"Hey, are you listening?" Mike questioned their manager. The older guy nodded. "I want that guy fired. I don't care if he's your wife's brother, or your brother's wife's cousin."

The guys around the table all laughed, including Mike and the just 'fired' roadie. Drake assumed that was an ongoing joke amongst them. The number eight light flashed up on the ceiling panel, and Drake hurriedly went to get their food out of the pass through window.

He had to make four trips to get all of their food out to them. At the end of their stay the band left a twenty dollar tip, and they thanked Drake for being so nice to them.

"Take it easy kid," Mike said, as he shook Drake's hand. "Change the world."

"Thanks, sir," Drake replied.

"Mike, my name is Mike Reno," he remarked. "And the pleasure's been all mine."

"Loverboy, huh?" Drake added. "I'll have to listen to what you've got, and I'll give New Wave a chance."

Mike smiled and headed out of the restaurant. He waved one last time to the busboy.

Sandy graciously gave Drake a five dollar tip for working her table and kept the rest of the money. Drake didn't think that was very fair, but he knew if he complained he might not have gotten what he did. The waitresses were not obligated to tip the busboys anything, and most did so just to encourage them to help.

Drake was very tired by the time seven o'clock came. It had been a very long night, and he was happy to leave. He only had a few more days before he could get his drivers license and he had already saved up nearly six hundred dollars for a car. That car wouldn't come soon enough, he thought when he got outside and started to pedal his ten-speed home. The front wheel had never truly worked well since the fight against the hellhounds, and it squeaked horribly at low speeds.

The sun had risen at twelve minutes to seven. Bright hues of reds and oranges streaked across the cyan sky, broken by thin bands of wispy clouds. The air was fresh, crisp, and smelled of late summer. Pollen tempted a sneeze from Drake as he rode the curved part of NE 6th Avenue that turned into NE 81st Street. Drake rode past the Security Pacific Bank and its rotating time and temperature sign—7:03, and 52°, declared the bank as he passed it. It was going to be a good day, Drake thought. Too bad he was going to sleep through most of it.

He braked and came to a loud squeaky stop at the light on NE Hazel Dell Avenue. This early on a Sunday morning much of the town was still slumbering. No cars were on the road, as far as he could see in either direction. He pushed off with his bike and pedaled to the right, before holding his left arm out to signal a quick turn onto NW 82nd Street. This was the second longest straight stretch of his ride home, and also the one he dreaded most since it was mostly uphill. He downshifted and began the long sloping climb. The first few times he had ridden this road it made his thighs burn, but after riding it for much of the summer he had grown to not hate it as much. Now it was more of a challenge to see how quickly he could take the hill. He rose up from the seat and pedaled hard in smooth powerful strokes. He reached the top of the hill and the athletic fields of Jason Lee Middle School were before him, across NW 9th Avenue. He looked to his watch to see how long it had taken him to crest the hill, but realized he had not looked before he started. Oh well, maybe next time, he thought.

He came to a squeaky stop of metal rubbing against metal. He turned right onto the empty road. Seagulls sat upon the glistening dew covered, green grass of the fields to his left. The sun had crested the mountains in the east and it fought with the clouds that covered the ragged top of the volcano, in an attempt to illuminate the devastated peak. Drake looked at the sun reflecting off the rows and rows of windows from the school. Dennis attended Jason Lee, but Drake had never been inside it. The school quickly fell behind him as he raced home. The cool air felt good upon his face.

He began to slow as the green road sign for NW 86th Street stood along the road to his right, because his next turn was a block away.

He always road this block slowly, not because of the turn, but because of what sat opposite of the turn. A solitary house sat upon a low hill on the southeastern corner of the intersection. It was a grand manor, with tall pillars gracing the front entry along NW 9th Avenue. The house was painted a pristine shade of white. And yet, this particular house had troubled Drake every time he passed it. Gooseflesh and raised hair on the back of his neck were the result of lingering too long by the house. So, curiously, every time he did ride past, he slowed down just enough to linger in the sensation, before hurrying on his way and casting at least one quick glance backward to see if something from that house had followed him.

He slowly approached the house, his front wheel squeaking loudly, heralding his arrival. The sensation began as it always did. A feeling of dread washed over him. Something was different, the feeling was more tangible, and the foreboding was overwhelming. His bike came to a stop before the pillared house. What was the cause of the sensation? Why did this house plague him so?

He looked at the sleepy house. There was nothing that feigned any evil, in fact it looked stately, and it possessed a simple architectural elegance. His eyes surveyed the building from the south to the north, shaking his head at the oddity of the oppressive feeling emanating from the house.

In the lawn at the corner of the property sat three large dogs that watched him upon his bike, and Drake's heart began to race, for these were no ordinary animals. Their faces were vaguely human, their eyes wicked and glowing and their mouths filled with row upon row of sharp canine teeth. Thick cords of slobber connected their mouths to the green grass beneath them. They had been sitting and waiting there for quite some time. Mangy tufts of brownish-black fur sprouted around their necks, and continued in odd clumps along their bodies. Along their backs, large boney spikes protruded. Their legs were long and sinewy, and at the end of each foot long black claws tapped the blades of grass below them, like the impatient talons of great birds of prey awaiting their supper.

"Hellhounds," Drake muttered beneath his breath. He had fought the two in the darkness of the parking lot in his rescue of Moose, but he hadn't seen them in all of their hideous glory until that moment.

Drake began to pedal again, going wide into the lane of oncoming traffic—if there would've been any. The hellhounds watched him, waiting. With a sudden turn to the left, Drake made his escape onto NW 87th Street, and he rose up off the seat and began to pedal faster, like he had up the hill. He took the chance to look back over his shoulder, just like he'd always done when he passed that house. Now the overwhelming dread made sense. It had never been the house itself. It had always been the premonition of this morning, of the hellhounds in wait for him.

Behind him, his worst fears were realized. The three hellhounds had launched themselves into pursuit. They sprinted after him. How was this possible? He had the black button in his pocket, why hadn't it shielded him from their senses? The clacking of their black claws upon the pavement echoed in the cool morning air. He thought of turning and fighting, but there was no dumpster enclosure to protect his back, so he reasoned his best bet was to try and lose them and hope to make it home. It was then that he realized he couldn't go home because that would lead the beasts right to the rest of his family, and his younger brothers. He had to fight, but he had no idea where, just yet.

Before him, the 'Y' of the road loomed, to the left was NW Westridge Street and to the right was NW 88th Street. He didn't know where Westridge would take him, since he always rode 88th Street. He figured familiarity was best at this point and turned hard to the right at nearly the last moment. One of the hellhounds sprinted down Westridge, and the other two held fast in its pursuit of Drake.

His pulse pounded in his ears as he pumped the pedals hard. The hellhounds behind him couldn't keep up, and his lead was growing. He looked to the right and saw another hellhound running through the yards of the homes along the road. To the left a fifth beast paced with him, jumping fences as it went. The hellhounds on either side glanced at him as they ran. Drake sensed a hunger inside them, and it caused a wave of nausea to fester in his stomach.

He sped through the intersection with NW 15th Avenue. He plotted and planned as he pedaled with all of his strength. Before he usually turned off 88th Street onto 21st Avenue, it split into two short one-way roads and rose up a little hill to the intersection with 21st Avenue. The street he lived on, in the house where his baby brothers slept, even now, and he knew he couldn't lead these five beasts there even if that meant he'd fall to them. Drake knew he'd make that sacrifice.

The hellhounds trailing him were keeping pace. Another had joined them. Drake was unsure if that was one of the original two, or if it was now a sixth beast.

His bike flew down the shadowed road, caused by the leafy branches of the trees that lined the southern side of the road. He quickly approached the cross street, NW 19th Avenue, and to his dismay two more hellhounds sat on either side of the street waiting for him. It had been a trap. They were leading him into their midst, into the noose, or the mouth of the beast.

He made up his mind. He'd stand and fight them. He reached for his pocket and removed the key that locked Hikari to his bike, and prayed he didn't fumble it and drop it as he pedaled furiously down the road. The lock clicked open and part of the chain swung down. Drake put the key back into his pocket and found the hilt of his sword. It was warm to his touch. He thought where he might make his stand. There were the fields next to the elementary school Albert attended, and there was the field across from their house. Wait a moment, he thought, that field was between their house and a church. The church was Holy ground. Hellhounds should be diminished on Holy ground he reasoned, and his destination was set—all he had to do now was get there.

As he passed the two sentinel hounds on 19th Avenue they ran toward him, nipping at his legs, and nearly toppling him from his bike. Before him, the shrubby median divided the road. NW 21st Avenue lay up the low hill, and he had to take that corner at a high rate of speed. He turned wide going the wrong way down the one-way road, the median tight on his right. The hellhounds to his right fell back giving him the gap he needed to take the corner. He furiously pedaled his bike to a near breaking point, crested the hill, and took to the air and leaned hard to the right. The back wheel of the bike hit the loose gravel in the middle of 21st Avenue and slid toward the far shoulder. The front wheel caught the pavement past the center line and his knee hit the road with a sharp pain that radiated up his leg. Without skipping a beat, he pedaled on. The bike rose to a more upright position and he was off to the north along the avenue.

The eight hellhounds pursued him, most came thundering out of the property around the intersection and a few on the road that had directly pursued him. Their long black claws clacked on the pavement and scrambled in the loose gravel as they fought to turn. Two fell into three others knocking all five down. Within seconds they were up and off again trailing the other three who had safely managed the turn and the rider on his bike.

One last hill rose up before Drake as he rode for his life. He passed Lakeshore Elementary on his left and drove the pedals hard with his aching legs. He caught air once again as he crested the hill. His bike hit hard on the road, nearly colliding into an oncoming car. He thought for a moment how he must have startled the driver, and actually chuckled about the fright that awaited him in his path over the hill. Behind him the car horn blared, again, and again. He looked back over his shoulder, and saw three of the beasts were closing on him. In the distance he saw the field off to his left, his home a little farther off on his right. He pedaled harder, sweat dripped from his brow into his eyes, and his breathing became labored as he pushed onward.

Next to the mowed field along the back was a path that led along the edge of the property to the church. His bike could take that narrow road, but the hellhounds would be able to run through the grass and cut him off. It was a dangerous gamble, but if he did not show his intention to head to the church right away perhaps they would just follow him down the path. If he tried to go overland through the grass with his skinny street wheels they would get him before he made the church property. There was only one real choice.

He tapped his brakes and slid the back wheel as he turned hard to the left onto the gravel lane. He pushed onward, the white spire of the church rising above the great shingled roof of the main building off to his right. The closest hellhounds fell into the chase along the path, as he had hoped. A couple of the others cut through the trees along the edge of the property and quickly caught up to their main pursuit.

The narrow lane turned to the right, bringing it straight parallel to the church property. He thought for a moment about what time it was. It was about fifteen past seven on a Sunday morning. People would be arriving for church services in an hour or so, and the volunteers and clergy perhaps even sooner. He imagined what they might think when they pulled up and found him dead amongst a pack of bloody hellhounds.

With a wry smile he steered his bike up through the grass, under a tree, and crashed over a low wall into the blacktop parking lot of the church. He tumbled onto the pavement. The pain was sharp and he was sure he had left some skin on the black surface. Without thought he went for his bike and freed Hikari from its scabbard.

Brigid's training resonated in him, and he took an offensive position, the sword raised above him and pointed back toward the oncoming hellhounds.

The monsters bounded over the low wall and out into the parking lot. First two, then three more, and then the final three—they saw their prey before them and realized he wasn't about to lie down without a fight. His sword was enchanted with some eldritch magic, burning with a faint blue fire. The hellhounds began to circle him, their breath coming out in billows of steam, and their sharp black claws clicking on the pavement as they paced.

How Drake wished Scrappy was there with him now. His barbarian blood would've boiled from the thrill of the fight... or even Freeman, or Martin. He didn't like the prospect of dying. Doing so alone was even worse, because no one would know what had happened.

One of the hellhounds tested him, and made a snapping pass at him from the side. Drake pivoted and cut the legs out from under it and part of its abdomen. It rolled into another beast that smelt its lifeblood spewing out and tore into its neck killing the wounded hellhound with a wet whimper.

Seven to one, now those odds are much better, Drake joked with himself. Little good that it did, two hellhounds came at him from different directions. Drake caught the first between its neck and shoulder spraying black blood across the parking lot. The second dug deep with its mouth into Drake's left side. He wrenched Hikari free from the dying beast before him and saw the remaining hellhounds advancing on him. He was close to falling as the beast biting him shook its head, ripping his clothes and flesh.

Brigid hadn't taught him how to get out of this. He wished he was in Gehenna where he had greater strength. The shaking and tearing pulled him to his knees, as he tried to cut into the hellhound upon him. The others drew closer, their torrents of slobber dripping onto the black pavement.

Brigid was going to be pissed she wasn't there to help him. Poor Brigid, he thought, she might never forgive herself. There was something there on the edge of his mind. What had Brigid told him about names, and invoking or summoning? It came to him as the hellhound shook him off his knees and onto the pavement. The others were so close he could smell their rancid breath.

"Brigid!" Drake shouted. "Brigid! Help!"

The advancing circle of beasts backed up. The hellhound biting his side released him and took a step backwards. Drake looked up. The sky above him had opened up and a radiant fire erupted out of the hole. Within the fire, a beautiful woman with auburn hair and richly embroidered dress stepped forward.

"I am Saint Brigid, goddess of the sacred flame, and protector of this lad!" her voice boomed, shaking the trees and sending fear through the black blood of the hellhounds. "You vile beasts stand upon Holy ground! I say you are not welcome here! Be gone, Hell spawn!"

The hellhounds cowered and began to howl at the goddess. One of them decided they should not be fearful and began to go back toward the fallen form of Drake.

"I told you to be gone!" Brigid commanded. The fire around her raged and licked the pavement near Drake, making the tar inside it boil and smell of hot asphalt.

The hellhound nearest Drake lunged at him.

Brigid advanced and the sacred fire burned over Drake. The heat was intense, like opening the oven on Thanksgiving and feeling the heat boil out from around the well-cooked turkey. But it didn't burn him. The hellhounds weren't that fortunate. The fire surged out from Brigid and consumed the hellhounds into crisp ash within seconds.

The flames died down and Brigid stood over Drake.

"You are hurt, Drake, son of Drake," Brigid said, as she looked at the blood seeping through his clothing on his torn left side. Brigid kneeled down beside him. The air had a sickly sweet aroma, like barbequed dog hair. "This wound is deep, and I must burn out the poison or the hellhounds will have won this day after all."

"Okay," Drake muttered. He looked up at the goddess. She was a vision of beauty, and she somehow made him feel warm inside. It must have been the fire, he thought.

Brigid moved his torn shirt up and placed her hands upon the deep bite. Blood seeped from the wound and over her fingers. A bright flame kindled on her hands, and it burned into Drake, searing him. Drake howled in pain and nearly passed out.

"Are you sure you can't join us, Brigid?" Drake asked

with a painful smile. "What you did just now was really kick ass."

"Unfortunately no," Brigid replied. "You were most wise to bring them here to Holy ground. As a saint, I draw power yet from these lands, and I was able to release some of my great power. Had it been somewhere else, I would have fought bravely beside you, but together we may have fallen."

"What good is all that power if you can't use it?" Drake questioned.

"There are rules that bind us all, physical laws, natural laws, and even supernatural laws," Brigid answered with a bright smile. "I must get you home now so you may rest."

Drake nodded. Brigid helped him to his feet. He tottered while she retrieved his bike. She looked at it and smiled.

"Your transportation machine has seen better days, I am afraid," Brigid stated earnestly.

"That's the truth," Drake replied. "But my birthday is coming and I'm gonna get a car."

Together, Brigid's arm under Drake's, they walked side-by-side across the field to his house.

In the church parking lot, morning parishioners found several large ash piles in the back of the church. Many assumed it was residue from an unknown eruption of Mt. St. Helens, a few thought some local kids were up to no good, and a couple believed it was a portent of God—the end of days was coming.

23

2015

SWEET SIXTEEN

THE BROTHERHOOD OF OLYMPUS
AND THE TOWER OF DREAMS

Happy Birthday
Chapter Twenty-Three
September 22, 1980
Hazel Dell, Washington

"Dad," Drake explained, "I'll be sixteen tomorrow, and I can go after school to take the driving test to get my license. All I need is a ride to go look at these cars I found in the paper."

"Is that so?" Dad asked with a chuckle. "And you think it's legal for a fifteen year-old to buy a car? Do you know what to check for to make sure it's worth buying?"

Okay, maybe Drake hadn't thought of all that, but he was absolutely sure he was done riding his beat-up and mostly broken bike. Drake was tired of being driven everywhere since the hellhound attack by one member of the Brotherhood or another. He wasn't a baby anymore.

"Let me see what you circled," Dad asked. Drake handed him the newspaper. "How much money do you have?"

"With all of my last check, eight hundred and fifty-seven dollars," Drake replied proudly.

"Then you need to look at more expensive cars," Dad stated. "Most of the ones you circled are in the five hundred dollar range, and wouldn't be much of a car, or probably has something very wrong with it. You don't need a broken car son, anymore than I need an oil-leaking jalopy in my driveway. Hey, what about this one?"

"What one?" Drake asked, as he moved over to look over his dad's shoulder. Dad pointed to an ad.

"1970 Plymouth Duster, two-door hard top, 340 racing

block, automatic, low mileage, a great car for $1000.00," Dad read the advertisement aloud, as Drake read it over his shoulder.

"Dad," Drake replied. "I told you, I have eight hundred and fifty-seven dollars, and that's a thousand dollar car. I can't grow extra money on a tree you know?"

"Drake," Dad responded with a chuckle, "you do your old man a disservice, I'm a salesman by trade, and if you want that car I can get you a better price. Call them and see if it's still available."

Drake called the number. He hated talking on the phone, and wouldn't have done it if it weren't for the very best of reasons. The car was still for sale, so Drake got an address and said they would be over in about a half an hour.

"Okay," Dad said, as he grabbed his jacket. "Let's go. Make sure bring your money, and when we get there just let me do all the talking."

Drake nodded and followed his dad out to the car.

They arrived about twenty minutes later.

"Come on," Dad said, as he got out of the car. "Let's go see if it's worth the money."

Drake quickly followed him up the driveway. Beside the garage sat a primer black car. It had a spoiler on its trunk and kind of looked like a race car. The owner, an older man with a full beard and Portland Trailblazers cap on, walked out of the house to greet them.

"Hey," the man said. "Thanks for coming out. Well, there she is, if I had more time I could have made a stock car out of her. She's got a 340 racing block, that's a prime Mopar engine. Let me start it up so you can see what I mean."

The man opened the driver's side door, climbed in and started the car with a loud VROOOOOM! The car sat and idled. Dad walked to the front and opened the hood. He studied the engine carefully, looking at the hoses, gaskets, and connections. Dad shook his head. The owner was watching him closely. Dad walked over and looked at the tires, checking the tread wear before he stood up and shook his head some more. The owner was feeling concerned, but didn't say anything. He just kept watching Dad. Finally, Dad sat in the driver's seat looking at the gauges and lights, and then he checked the odometer and shook his head again. He sat still for a moment longer and felt the car rock from side to side with the power of the engine. He shook his head one last time.

"So whattaya think?" the owner asked. "Is she a beaut, or what?"

"Well," Dad began, "you certainly aren't gonna get a thousand for it."

"Why not?" the owner asked.

"Well, it's got a nearly blown head gasket with a substantial oil leak," Dad continued. "What's it go through about a quart of oil a week?"

The owner shrugged.

"Its alternator is sparking and will need to be replaced," Dad added. "The alignment is out on the front end, and it'll need new tires, most likely. The odometer is over a hundred thousand, so its hardly low mileage. It's painted in primer paint, and the inside needs to be completely cleaned out, if not re-upholstered. Oh, and it's got a broken motor mount that's making the car rock so badly as it idles."

"Oh," the owner said dumbfounded.

"You might get four-fifty for it at best," Dad said, as he winked at Drake. Drake took the cue and pulled out five hundred dollars in twenty dollar bills from his pocket, exactly as his Dad had told him. "Son put that money away, it's not worth five hundred dollars, and he probably doesn't want your money anyway."

Drake fanned the money and began to put it away.

"Wait," the owner announced. "Five hundred is good, I'll take five hundred for the car, and I'll even throw in a case of oil I got for it in the garage."

Drake nodded to his father.

"Sir, you have a deal, five hundred dollars for the car and the oil," Dad agreed.

The owner brought out the paperwork, and it was all signed over to Dad. Drake gave the guy five hundred dollars and took the keys.

Dad climbed in and started the car. He shifted it into reverse and backed it out onto the street. The former owner waved and went back inside, happy to be five hundred dollars richer. Once Dad had the car in the street, near his car, he climbed out and talked to Drake while the engine was still running.

"You have your permit?" Dad asked. Drake nodded. "Well, you see the problem. We have two cars, and one licensed driver. So you're gonna drive your car home—right behind me—got it?"

Drake nodded with a wide smile.

He climbed in the 1970 Plymouth Duster and sat there for a moment, feeling the power of the engine as it rocked the car from side to side. He felt a joy he had no words to describe. This car was his, and he already loved it.

The next day after school, Drake got his drivers license, and they had Martin and Beth over for his birthday dinner. Mom had made fried chicken and boiled potatoes with fresh chicken gravy. The boys loved that dinner whenever Mom cooked it. Drake thought for a moment that it wasn't the same without Mark.

When they had finished dinner, Mom brought out a chocolate cake with sixteen blazing candles on it. Everyone sang *Happy Birthday* to him as the cake was set on the table in front of him. He smiled, made a wish, and blew out all of the candles.

"Who wants cake?" Mom asked, as she whisked it away to cut it.

There was a chorus of "I do, I do," in the dining room. It was a silly question since they were all going to get a piece of cake anyway. The cake came on saucers with a scoop of vanilla ice cream.

Drake got a couple presents to open, some new things

for his car and a new alarm clock from his parents, a card from his grandparents with ten dollars in it, and from Martin he got a new military issue trench-coat style raincoat like the one he had that Moose had ruined when he stole it. The family sat around afterwards talking about life, work, and school.

"So, Drake," Beth stated, "Marty told me you have some pictures up in your room. I'd like to see."

Martin nodded.

"Sure," Drake replied, as he got up from the couch and headed for the stairs. Beth followed him. Tonight Drake had noticed that Beth was dressed more girly than she normally was when they practiced at Brigid's house. She had a black knee-length skirt, white tights with a black seam up the back of her legs, black Mary Jane pumps, and a tight purple sweater that made sure everyone knew she was really a girl.

"After you," Drake stated, as a gentleman with a curt head bow. Beth smiled and began to slowly walk up the stairs. Drake noticed the almost sensual motion of her hips as she neared the top of the stairs, and of course the seam of her hosiery so reminiscent of Veronica Furfur.

Below them, Albert and Dennis were bouncing from one beanbag chair to another.

"I don't think they needed the extra sugar," Mom stated.

Once upstairs, Beth waited for Drake, who passed very close to her and opened his door, turned on the light, and stepped into his room. This was the first time that Beth had ever come into his room.

She entered and smiled.

"Wow, you have a lot of space," Beth announced. "I like how you made that area into a studio with your desk and stuff."

Drake hurried to get his tablets to share with his sister-in-law. She sat on the bed, set her purse next to her, and crossed her left leg over her right. Drake brought the tablets over and opened the first to show her. He stood in front of her. Beth patted the bed beside her with her left hand.

Drake, ever the gentleman, did her bidding and sat beside her.

"Now let's see what you got here," Beth said as she took the first tablet and started flipping the pages.

Drake noticed that her skirt had slid up revealing most of her white nylon encased thigh, which was dangerously close to touching him. It felt like Mom must have turned on the furnace downstairs.

For the next twenty minutes or so, Beth perused his artwork, asking him things like, 'what's this?' or 'what's that?' and Drake answered flatly, in great detail but without emotion or expression.

Finally Beth closed the tablets and held them on her lap.

"Drake," Beth began, "I get the feeling you don't like me. Do you like me Drake?"

Drake nodded.

"Well that's good, I guess," Beth responded. "Why don't you talk to me? You know I'm not gonna bite you… that hard, anyway."

"I guess," Drake answered. "It's 'cause you're a girl and I don't know much about girl stuff, I don't have any sisters, you know."

"Well, we can talk about things that aren't girl stuff, silly," Beth replied with a warm smile. "We can talk about Brotherhood stuff if you'd like."

"Okay," Drake responded.

"You know I watch you a lot when you practice," Beth stated. "You're different than Marty, more regal, like a knight or a prince."

Drake liked that comparison.

"Thanks," Drake stated.

"Marty talks about you a lot too, do you know that?" Beth questioned. "He thinks the world of you, and I can see why. He also told me you don't have a girlfriend."

Drake shook his head. When he thought of girls like that he still heard Uncle Wally laughing at him on the bus telling him that girls had cooties. He knew that wasn't true, but somehow he couldn't let it go.

Beth reached down to her purse, making more of her white thigh visible, and she balanced herself by placing her left hand upon Drake's thigh. He felt as though he nearly jumped off the bed in reaction to her touch. Beth brought out a small package wrapped in blue tissue paper and a birthday card in a green envelope.

"I got this for you, Drake," Beth said, as she handed him the present and the card. "Open the present first."

Drake carefully unwrapped the tissue paper. Inside the small bundle was a blue silken handkerchief. Drake didn't know what to make of it, so he just smiled to his sister-in-law.

"Thank you, Beth," Drake said sincerely.

"I know it's a silly gift," Beth explained. "But, in many old stories, brave knights would ride off to face dragons and other things for the honor of a fair lady. I know you don't have a girlfriend, and Marty's not much of a knight, so I had hoped that you would be willing to be my champion. Before you say no, it's kind of like the story in the King Arthur legend. The one where Lancelot takes the scarf of his queen, to champion her honor, and Lancelot and Arthur are like brothers. It's kind of like you, me, and Marty, except not so much because you would probably be the king and Lancelot, huh?"

Beth laughed. Drake thought she was attempting to be very thoughtful and kind, and he was stuck in his socially inept mode and struggled to return the favor to her.

"Okay," Drake muttered.

"Okay what?" Beth asked.

"I'll be your champion," Drake offered as gracefully as he could. He had such difficulty interacting with girls, and he couldn't understand it. It was almost like a curse. He'd been bold in interacting with otherworldly gods. He confronted and fought demons, hellhounds, and gods, but still was at a loss for words in the company of a girl. He'd have to research this malady later when he had more time.

"Thank you Drake," Beth said with a tight hug. Once

again Drake was caught unprepared and was sure she noticed him flinching beneath her touch. She looked up into his eyes. "Now open the card."

Drake tore the green envelope open. Inside it was a card meant to be funny, the humor was very pun centered, and to be nice, Drake smiled at his sister-in-law. He then read what she wrote:

Happy Birthday Drake,
Sweet Sixteen and never been kissed
I'll have to see about fixing that
Love,
Beth

Drake quickly processed the message, and linked it to what he had agreed to do, to champion his sister-in-law. Confusion reigned in his mind, and he thought he might pass out because his heart was beating so fast.

"Drake," Beth said, with her lips very close to his. "Are you okay?"

"It's really hot in here," Drake announced, as he bolted up off the bed and went to open his bedroom window.

Beth blushed.

"Listen Drake," Beth said, "I'm sorry if I came on too strongly. I meant no harm. I mean, you are really cute, dreamy even, and sometimes I wish I met you before I met your brother."

Except you're like four years older than me, Drake thought.

"I really do want you to still be my champion, okay?" Beth asked.

"Okay," Drake agreed from the window. A cool breeze blew in through his dark hair.

Beth looked at him standing there, the wind in his hair, and wished she hadn't been attracted to him as much as she was. She was married to his brother, after all.

Beth stood up, her eyes still upon him.

"Some day Drake," Beth began with a pouty smile,

"you're gonna make some pretty babies."

Beth turned and walked out of his room, her purse in hand. He heard her high heels on the thinly carpeted steps as she descended the stairs.

"And if we're both lucky, Drake," Beth said to herself. "We'll make them together, as husband and wife."

Drake held Beth's blue handkerchief in his hand. He thought about tossing it out the window and letting the wind take it wherever it may. But then he realized he had made a vow to champion her, and a knight, though he wasn't one yet, doesn't break a vow. Especially not one to a fair lady and after tonight, Drake would never again question the fairness of the lady who was his sister-in-law again.

24

KRTHAG, SPAWN OF KRANGATH

THE BROTHERHOOD OF OLYMPUS
AND THE TOWER OF DREAMS

The Empire Strikes Back
Chapter Twenty-Four
September 25, 1980
Vancouver, Washington

The Thursday after his birthday, Drake drove out to the new Vancouver Mall Cinemas to watch *The Empire Strikes Back* one last time. He had seen it five or six times before, but this was the first time he got to drive to the theater all by himself. The movie was held over for one final week, for at least the fifth time in a row. Drake thought that was a genius marketing ploy on their part. And he looked forward to watching the movie and its classic archetypes of good versus evil for perhaps the final time.

Drake carried his sword, slung low on his back beneath his thin blue trench coat. He paid for his ticket and entered the theater. He got a large soda at the concession stand inside and headed happily into theater four. The building of the multiplex had allowed a movie like the second Star Wars episode to play in Vancouver all summer long. In the old days when movie theaters had a single screen, that would've never happened. Drake was grateful for it because he got to watch this movie again, and again.

Once in the theater, Drake went to the back row and sat in the very center. He placed his sword across his lap, under his jacket. No one sat in the back row with him. In fact, there were only about fifteen people in the whole theater, all in front of him, and nothing but a wall at his back except the small window above him where the projected film streamed out of.

Drake watched the movie, and saw odd parallels to his

current plight. He was somewhat like Luke Skywalker, a boy uncertain of his place in the galaxy who was meant to be more than he thought possible. Aided by a motley crew of rogues, outsiders, and an odd few with extraordinary powers or knowledge, and yet Drake marveled at the simplicity of the plot. Ultimately, Luke was given the choice to stay, train with a master, or rush off to save his friends. Drake thought, 'how would I handle that same choice?' Head versus heart, and in the end Luke's heart won and it nearly cost them all. When the trap was sprung by the Sith Lord, Darth Vader in Cloud City, Drake came to a realization. How did he know that Han and Leia would go there? And on a more personal note, how had the hellhounds known to wait along the road he rode home on?

The button Aunt Carmen had given him had shielded him, he saw it work the night he fought to rescue Moose. The hellhounds went after Moose because he held Drake's jacket. They wanted nothing of Drake, except to get him out of the way so they could get Moose—who they thought was their intended prey. And that was the gist of it, he still had the button, it was in his pocket even now.

Brigid had explained that the hellhounds had only gotten to Earth through the Tower of Dreams now held by the enemy. They had yet to figure out how it worked, so they couldn't send the hosts of Hell through to seize the Earth—yet. He understood all of that. Addraemyr, Woden, and the rest were all pretty clear on the perils that lay ahead of them. What he didn't understand was how the hellhounds knew where to set their trap? He knew it was a trap, as surely as the one Darth Vader had set in *The Empire Strikes Back*. But, there weren't that many people who knew who, or what he was, and fewer still that knew he'd be riding that route. Maybe, he dared not hope he was correct, but perhaps one of his brothers had sold him out. If that was the case, who? It hurt his heart to even consider that among his Brotherhood stood a traitor. He had to trust them all—if they were to survive they had to trust each other and work together.

The action on the screen picked up and pulled the melancholy away from Drake. His pulse quickened as Luke and Vader faced each other. The music drove him higher. And the climax of the film was pure satisfaction tempered with desire to see the next movie in the series. Too bad he'd have to wait three more years to find out what happened next. Drake sat and watched the credits roll at the end of the film. The other patrons had long since left when the last of the credits cleared the screen and the house lights came up. He quickly returned his sword to its spot on his back and covered it with his jacket before any of the theater workers came in and saw him with it.

He headed down the carpeted steps, his empty soda cup in his hand, and felt the urgent need to relieve himself of excess liquid. He dropped the empty cup in the illuminated trash can near the theater door and headed out to find the restroom.

It was late, nearly eleven thirty, and most of the people had long gone home. Drake was uncertain if any movie was still playing and thought only the theater employees might be there, cleaning the now vacant theaters of spilled popcorn, candies, and soda. He was the only one on the wide carpeted hallway between the theaters, and when he turned the corner into the well lit restroom he found he was completely alone in there too.

The restroom had a counter with three sinks on it, a wall with paper towel dispensers over two large garbage cans over-filled with soiled towels and soda cups, and beyond the wall a row of three stalls enclosing toilets faced the long wall with five mounted urinals.

Drake walked to the farthest urinal. Boys learn bathroom etiquette early in life and often from their peers, you always went to one end or the other if there were more than two urinals, and if another guy was using one, you had to go to the one the farthest away. If you went next to another guy, unless all of the others were full, then, as Drake was told—you probably liked guys more than girls. Drake wasn't sure that was true, and it really didn't matter to him if someone else did like guys instead of girls, but he didn't like the way he got teased about his perceived sexuality because he was a junior in high school and had never had a girlfriend.

He unzipped his pants and took care of his business. He looked back only twice at the doorway while he urinated. In the middle stall, behind Drake, a large black foot lowered down from the toilet. It had three curled toes that flexed on the floor as it began to bear weight. The toes ended in sharp talons that cut into the tiled floor. Drake heard a scraping noise behind him to the right and looked back over his shoulder, as he began to zip his pants. A second three toed foot lowered to the floor in the middle stall.

Drake looked more intently at the two grotesque feet flexing their talon tipped toes and thought, 'that's not right at all.' He reached up to flush the urinal, but before he put his hand on the silver lever, the stall door burst open in an eruption of shattered wood, porcelain, and spraying water against him and the wall near him.

"What the hell!" Drake yelled, as he turned to face what had emerged from the stall. Drake was tall, at six foot five he looked down on much of the world, but the creature that had broken down the stall raised up to its full height and had to duck against the eight foot ceiling. It wore no clothes, and its body was more insectoid than human. It had a rough-hewn exoskeleton that had sharp spikes along the edges. Its long legs seemed to be bent backward at the knee. The segmented torso had four arms moving independently of each other, with long serrated claws where its hands should be. The neck upon the torso was thin and scaly, like that of a tortoise stretched outside its shell. Its head was reptilian, and barbed along its jaw, brows, and scalp. Shiny black eyes stared down at Drake, and cords of yellowish slobber or venom leaked from its gaping mouth full of teeth.

Drake backed up closer to the corner of the room. The exit was past the towering monster and the spraying toilet water which was now starting to pool on the floor. He reached back under his coat and slowly worked the scabbard down so he could grasp the hilt of Hikari. The creature raised its top two arms and broke the fluorescent light fixtures above it in a shower of sparks. One of the lights dangled down on its wiring, buffeted by spraying toilet water from within what was left of the stall and swinging much too close to the water on the floor.

"You are god-slayer!" the creature shouted in a deep, guttural tone. Drake shook his head at the chance the thing might let him go if it thought it had the wrong person. "I am Krthag, spawn of Krangath, Lord of Lower Gehenna, and it is custom of my people that those who we kill should know who killed them, for it gives us greater power over you in death."

"You've got the wrong guy," Drake stated. "I'm just here watchin' a movie."

"Wrong guy or not, Krthag was told god-slayer would be here," the demon replied, "though you do not look like you are capable of killing any god, skinny human. I still will have your head."

Behind the demon, a red shirted theater employee took a step into the restroom to check on what the loud noise had been moments before. Krthag turned and looked at the employee and pointed one of its serrated claws at him. The employee took two quick steps backward and ran from the restroom.

Drake took advantage of the distraction and unsheathed Hikari. He realized immediately that the narrow space of the restroom would not allow him to use his sword as it was designed. Drake quickly stabbed the torso of the demon, cracking its thick exoskeleton and drawing black demon ichor that fizzed and bubbled when it hit the pooled water on the floor. The wound was not deep enough and Krthag returned the favor by hitting Drake backward with its two lower arms before pinning him high against the tiled wall with its upper right forearm wedged under Drake's left arm and across his chest. Hikari had clanked on the tile floor from the impact of the blow.

The demon appeared to smile as it looked into the eyes of his victim, and Drake struggled against the wall kicking the armored torso of the large creature. Krthag took his upper left arm and moved the serrated claw past Drake's neck. All it would have to do was press its arm against his neck and cut downward to end the fight.

"Your head is pretty, god-slayer," Krthag stated. "Remember my name, Krthag, spawn of Krangath!"

At that very moment, three red shirted theater workers rounded the corner carrying mops and brooms. The first one threw a stiff bristled push broom at the tall creature in the corner, hitting it square in the back. Krthag turned its head and saw its new adversaries.

"More heads, good," Krthag said, as it began to turn its body away from Drake. It still had him pinned against the wall with its upper right arm, but as it turned the pressure loosened and Drake reacted by sliding his left hand in between his chest and the demon's arm enough that he slid to the ground. Water splashed as he hit the floor. He found the hilt of Hikari beneath the sparking light fixture. Krthag had advanced two steps toward the theater workers, who had begun to back up out of the restroom.

Drake jumped upward, landing upon the armored shell of the demon's back. He squeezed his legs and looped his left arm between its two left arms, like he was going to ride upon its back. Krthag turned its head back to look at its attacker. Hikari was at the back of its thin tortoise neck and with a sudden fury Drake slashed sideways severing the head from the body. Ichor spurted upward from the arteries in its neck and the head clonked along the tile floor, sloshing in the pooled water. The large body began to come down and Drake jumped free before it hit the floor with a loud splash and thud.

Drake quickly checked the two remaining stalls with his sword ready to strike. Both were empty. He decided what he needed to do in an instant. He quickly dumped most of the trash out of one of the cans to get its black plastic garbage bag. He picked up the severed head avoiding the sharp spikes along its edges and dropped it in the bag. He had kept some used paper towels in it so it wouldn't rip through the plastic. He closed the bag, sheathed his sword, and began to head out the doorway before he realized that he hadn't washed his hands. He quickly set the bag down, washed and dried his hands, wiped the sink knobs clean before tossing the damp towels into the remaining trash can, and then exited the flooded restroom.

"Wait," the broom-throwing employee said. "Is it still in there?"

"Part of it," Drake replied, as he walked toward the theater exit door, garbage bag in his hand.

"Is it still alive?" another employee questioned.

"No," Drake answered, as he walked out the door and into the parking lot. "And sorry about the mess!"

The door closed behind him. The employees peered into the restroom. The large black, multi-armed body lay in the pooled water on the floor of the broken restroom. Water still sprayed from the broken toilet. The lights at the end of the restroom flickered and sparked. Beneath the body the push broom was broken. Just inside the door, one of the trash cans was on its side and a pile of dirty paper towels and soda cups littered the floor. There were only two things missing—the garbage bag and the creature's head.

"You don't think that guy took its head, do you?" an employee asked, and most of the gathered employees shrugged.

"Don't touch anything in here," the assistant manager said, as she walked near the doorway. "I've called the police, and everything in there is part of the crime scene. We all get to stay late tonight."

"We get paid, right?"

"Nope," the assistant manager said. "You're all off work, and this is your civic duty."

A chorus of "great" and "that's not fair" erupted from

the gathered theater employees.

The Vancouver Police arrived within fifteen minutes of the attack. They cordoned off the bathroom and had the assistant manager shut off the water main to stop the flooding. The investigators heard the eyewitness reports detailing how this monster was trying to kill some guy in the restroom and three of the employees had saved him. One of the detectives had dusted for fingerprints so they could find out who the mystery guy was, the sink knobs had recently been wiped, but said there were hundreds of prints all over the bathroom, and it would be nearly impossible to distinguish who the intended victim might have been.

Two detectives stood over the body on the floor taking pictures and writing notes. They did a lot of head shaking as they worked. Finally after about two hours, the lead detective Robert York, a middle-aged man with graying hair and a thin black mustache over his equally thin lips, talked to the assistant manager again in her office with two other police officers joining them in the small room.

"I'm sorry ma'am," Detective York began. "Whatever that thing is in there, it's not human. It's like a giant headless ant or roach. This isn't a homicide. We'll send Animal Control Services to pick up the carcass. Somebody at a University or government lab is gonna want to do some research on it to find out how it got so big. The only crime here is vandalism, but even then, one of my officers said it looks like your giant cockroach came out of the toilet, so I'm thinking the guy in there was probably pretty scared when it attacked him. And frankly, you're lucky he left, he could have sued you for having such a dangerous animal in your restroom."

"What about all the damage?" the assistant manager asked. She was irritated to hear the results of the investigation after having to sit and wait so long after she should have been home. "Surely you can arrest the guy for all of that?"

"Like I said, ma'am," York answered. "He could probably sue you for the attack, and you're lucky he didn't get hurt. There's no blood in there, unless you count that black goop out of the roach. Anyway, in case he did get hurt, I've already alerted the hospitals to be on the look out for animal bites or unusual cuts."

"Miss Johnson," interrupted an employee. He was one of the few who remained for questioning—the broom thrower. They'd been sitting out in the lobby. "There's some men here from the church."

"From the church?" Miss Johnson questioned.

"To give last rights to the dead bug?" York quipped.

"Excuse me," a tall silver haired man said, as he entered the room. Another man, with blonde hair neatly combed, wearing the same black suit, white shirt, and red tie like his partner, followed behind. "I'm Brother DeCarlo, and this is Brother Hendrick. We've come from the Vatican to investigate the unusual things happening here in Vancouver."

"Right. And how would two brothers from the church know that anything unusual was going on here tonight?" York questioned.

"You shame us, officer," DeCarlo answered. "Your own police band radio has been filled with chatter this very night about dead giant bugs in a restroom."

"Not officer, detective," York replied.

"Sir," Hendrick added, "it's imperative we investigate this incident. We've been sent by order of the Pope."

"Why would the Pope be interested in giant bugs half the world away?" the detective asked. "Maybe if you were exterminators, I'd believe it."

"We are God's exterminators, officer," Hendrick replied.

"Officer, are you a Christian?" DeCarlo asked. He pulled out his passport and flashed him his identification. "We are from the Knights of Malta, the only order of Crusaders still in existence. Once our order was known as the Hospitallers, and we shared our allegiance to the Pope with the Templars and the Teutonic orders. Neither of those knightly orders exists anymore under the charter of God. We do. We are the military and the police of the church, and we have reason to believe that what is happening here is a sign of the end of days."

"Detective, my name is Detective York, brother," the detective clarified before he responded. "Now wait just a minute, Brother DeCarlo, so you and your brother here are military knights of the church, okay, I can deal with that. But now you're telling me that the giant dead roach in there is something out of the Book of Revelations? Listen, I did my time as an alter boy, I know the whole fire and brimstone spiel, seven seals, seven signs, all of that. But, I have a real difficult time believing that bug is somehow related to Biblical prophecies."

"Officer," DeCarlo replied, "we have the authority of the Pope to proceed with this investigation. You wouldn't want an international incident to start over this, or have this affect your eternal soul?"

The detective shook his head.

"My eternal soul? I can't believe you just took this there, brother. Of all the gall, you're a bigger dick than my Lieutenant, and that's saying a lot. If this was an actual crime, I'd be busting your balls all the way to the President of these here United States if I had too, brother," York responded angrily. "I'm not too keen on some Knights of Malta, the United Nations, or the Prince of England coming into my jurisdiction and taking over any of my investigations. But like I was just telling the lovely lady here, this really isn't a police matter, since the only dead thing here is a giant cockroach. So, you're more than welcome to clean up the mess."

"That's much better," DeCarlo stated. "We will, of course, need copies of all of the witness statements, and any other evidence you've collected. There was mention of fingerprints that might identify the intended victim? We would like those as well."

"You heard the man," the detective said to the two other officers in the room. "Let him have all the evidence,

Christ sakes, let the good brothers cart that piece of crap roach outta here too, while they're at it!"

The detective and his officers walked out of the managers' office past the two Knights of Malta.

"Thank you officer," Brother Hendrick stated. Detective York stopped when he heard the word 'officer' uttered one last time, and turned back to face the two Knights of Malta.

"Listen brothers, sisters, cousins, or whatever you are," York added. "You guys watch yourselves while you're here, I'd hate to see you get hurt. Oh, one more thing, we have laws here too, and it's my job to enforce them. I'll be watching you and if you so much as jay walk I'll make sure you're deported faster than you can blink an eye, international incident or not, got it?"

Detective York turned and walked away, motioning to all the police personnel still in the building to vacate the premises.

"What is this jay walking?" Hendrick asked DeCarlo. Brother DeCarlo shrugged and stepped out of the office. Miss Johnson shook her head, because her long night of civic duty had just gotten longer.

THEATER GARBAGE TROPHY

THE BROTHERHOOD OF OLYMPUS AND THE TOWER OF DREAMS

25

Dark Tidings
Chapter Twenty-Five
October 8, 1980
Hazel Dell, Washington

When Drake brought the head of the demon Krthag, spawn of Krangath in the black garbage bag to Brigid's house, quite a spirited discussion ensued.

"So, I went to watch *The Empire Strikes Back* last night," Drake announced.

"Haven't you seen that before?" Scrappy asked.

"We saw it together a few weeks ago," Freeman added. "It's pretty cool, I think it was better than the first one, which is saying a lot since most sequels aren't as good as the original."

"Anyway, guess what I found at the theater?" Drake queried.

"A girlfriend?" Scrappy responded with a laugh. Drake looked at him sourly. Beth looked at Drake with hurt in her eyes, almost like she hoped that wasn't true.

"No, I didn't find a girlfriend," Drake replied. He picked up the black plastic bag and set it on the kitchen table. "I found this."

"A bag of garbage?" Martin chuckled. "I got some of that in my apartment, right Beth?"

"Not garbage like this," Drake remarked. "Take a look inside."

Brigid had been busy tending flowers in the windows and casually listened to the discussion. Freeman reached out and pulled the bag open.

"Whoa!" Freeman yelled with a startled jump away from

the table. "What the hell is that?"

"Let me see?" Scrappy asked eagerly.

Freeman pulled the sides of the bag down to reveal the decapitated head of a demon. Its black eyes had lost their glossy shine and appeared a bit milky. Its toothy mouth was half open with a coarse black stained tongue hanging out. The sharp barbs along the jaw, brow, and scalp had poked some of the paper towels and held them there like obscene decorations.

"Is it real?" Beth asked frantically.

Drake nodded, and Beth passed out hard on the floor with a thud. Martin and Brigid quickly tended to the fallen Beth.

"That's awes!" Scrappy exclaimed. "Where did you get it?"

"This, my brothers, is the head of the demon Krthag, spawn of Krangath, and he was sent to kill the god-slayer," Drake replied.

"Were you injured, Drake?" Brigid questioned, as she held her hand on the temple of Beth.

"No," Drake responded. "Just my pride. The thing almost had my head if it wasn't for some guys working at the theater who threw brooms at it giving me the chance to kill it."

"Why were you alone, Drake, son of Drake?" Brigid asked. "After the hellhound attack I thought we agreed that you should not go out in public alone."

"Brigid," Drake answered, "I can't sit in a cage, it was a spur of the moment thing, and no one knew I was going. And that has really baffled me. I pondered it much of the night."

"What do you mean, my friend?" Freeman asked. "Perhaps we can help your pondering."

"Well," Drake began. He knew this wasn't going to be easy, no matter how he phrased it. "The hellhound attack felt like a trap, the way they sat and waited for me in greater numbers along the path I always rode. It was like they knew I was going to be there. But I also know that the charm my aunt made for me has been working, it even worked last night—this demon didn't know who I was. So how would they know when, or what road to wait on? They're not that smart, right Brigid?"

"Correct, son of Drake," Brigid replied. Beth was fluttering her eyes in response to Brigid's touch. "They be hell spawn, loyal and fierce, but not intelligent in that manner."

"So who sent them after me?" Drake queried. "Who knew my routines, my schedule?"

Martin, Freeman, and Scrappy looked at each other. The four of them and the two girls had been pretty tight for the last few months, doing most everything together. Was Drake insinuating that one of them might have betrayed him?

"Krthag here, told me who he was, it's the custom of his people to tell the ones they kill their names, so that they have more power over them in death," Drake explained.

"'Tis true," Brigid added. "Krangath is the vile daemon lord of the fourth plane of Gehenna and his minions do so believe that notion of name power over the dead."

"Anyway," Drake added, "he said he knew the 'god-slayer' was going to be there, that he was told that by someone. The question I have is, who?"

"Many lesser demons of the netherworlds have been known to work for evil lords and despots, usually for a price," Brigid explained. "Krangathian spawn have been known accomplices of hellhounds for centuries, and it is doubtless that this one came here through the Tower of Dreams like the hellhounds."

"Wait," Scrappy said with a smile. "You're saying there are more of these bad boys in the Tower for us to fight?"

"Yes, barbarian," Brigid replied. Scrappy smiled even wider at the thought.

"You know, Drake," Freeman began after much thought in a short amount of time, "hear me out before you respond. With the hellhound attack, I might have assumed that we could have a leak within this very group. Just as you have probably thought yourself."

Drake nodded. Scrappy was still smiling, and Martin and Brigid were helping Beth up into a kitchen chair.

"Such a possibility would be a grave thing, and could spell the doom of us all, when we face the might of things like that," Freeman continued, as he pointed to the demon head on the pile of paper towels in the middle of the table. "In fact, I would wager that we would not succeed at all if we had a traitor in our midst. But, my friend, you said something that undermines the demon's statement linking it to one of us. Drake, you said you went to the theater last night to watch the movie by yourself, a spur of the moment thing, and none of us knew, correct?"

"Correct," Drake replied.

"Therefore," Freeman added, "if none of us knew, how could we have told anything to any demons about where you were going to be?"

"True logic, shaman," Brigid stated.

"Drake," Martin said, stepping away from his wife, "Remember what I told you when we were first practicing CRV, that there are others out there capable of finding out things through psychic spying? What if the enemy has someone capable of doing it? They could have seen where you were going and sent their assassin out to get you."

"That is quite likely, psychic warrior," Brigid added.

"That's possible, Martin," Drake replied. "Very possible. The only weakness in it is that three people did know where I was going last night—none of you here, of course."

"Who?" Martin asked.

"Dennis, Albert," Drake stated coldly, "and Mom."

On the night of October eighth, they had gathered together, the six of them, one last time. Beth and Martin were going to be gone to visit her parents in Alaska for the next three weeks, returning on October thirtieth, the day before their assault on the Tower of Dreams. They had made plans to meet one last time when Martin and Beth returned, but fate would stop that from occurring. Little did they know at the time, that this would be the last time they all sat together—barbarian, shaman, psychic warrior, skeptic, god-slayer, and goddess.

"What're you looking at, Freeman?" Drake asked. Freeman sat at the table flipping through a thin hardcover book. He held it up and it had assorted monsters on the cover.

"This, my friend, is the *Monster Manual*," Freeman answered. "It's for the *Advanced Dungeon and Dragons* game system."

"Are we gonna play it tonight?" Drake asked.

"No," Freeman replied. "It takes a while to set it up, you have to generate characters, and someone's got to be the dungeon master, so I don't think our personal dungeon master—Brigid—has set aside any time tonight for games."

"So why are you looking at it?" Drake questioned.

"Well," Freeman answered, "the game designers did a lot of research when they created this game of mythical monsters, beasts of legends, gods, goddess, demons and devils, and races of fantasy. Their research is so good, that I find much of what they have written to be quite creditable."

"I see," Drake remarked.

"I have found many errors on this section on Celtic Mythos, shaman," Brigid stated. She entered from the living room carrying a thin purple book with two clerics doing battle adorning its cover, one clad in purple, the other in green, their deity aspects large and locked in a death struggle above them,. The title on the top of the book was *Deities and Demigods*. "First they have misspelled my name, they put a 'T' at the end, and they have called me a lesser goddess? That is untrue. It is I who the British Isles are named for, not Dagda, Lugh, or Nuada. They should have sought me out. I would have given them insight into my pantheon beyond any mere tome written long ago by humans."

"And how would they have found you, Lady Brigid?"

Drake said with a smile. "It's not like you have a telephone."

"I do so, son of Drake," Brigid stated, as she pointed to the yellow phone hanging on the kitchen wall.

"And I'm sure you're listed in the phonebook as Brigid, goddess of the sacred flame," added Drake.

"Now you are just jesting to amuse yourself," Brigid remarked. "At my expense I might add. Son of Drake, you are most lucky that I am not a vengeful goddess."

All three broke into hearty laughter.

Later, the six sat at the kitchen table and broke bread together. They talked, laughed, and enjoyed each other like friends do—like family—like brothers.

"Tonight is the new moon," Freeman stated, "the black moon, it is the first new moon since the orange full moon we had on the twenty-fourth of September. If things hold true to the pattern the next full moon will present itself as red, and that my friends is a bad omen."

"Is that true?" Scrappy asked worriedly. He looked first to Drake and then to Brigid.

"Lunar cycles have long influenced human life, though we don't like to admit it," Drake answered. "For example, the moon is on a twenty-eight day cycle, the exact same as the female menstrual cycle."

"Drake!" Beth exclaimed. "Not at the table."

"Eww," Scrappy added. "That's gross."

"I'm just saying from a science perspective that it's a curious thing when you compare humans to all other life forms. Why is it that the human female has a cycle that mirrors the moon?" Drake clarified. "Did someone plan it that way? Or did women just start to sync with the moon over generation upon generation of living beneath its gravitational pull?"

"You are quite the thinker," Brigid remarked. "Many of my kin would enjoy such discussions with you, though some would undoubtedly inform you such things exist because they made them so."

"So why is it a dark omen, Freeman?" Beth asked. "This

red moon, how can you tell if it's red? I don't think I have ever seen a red moon, or a blue moon for that matter, though I've at least heard of that."

"A blue moon," Drake explained, "is the second full moon in a given calendar month. It is a rare occurrence, but since the lunar cycle is twenty-eight days and most of our months are thirty or thirty-one days it does happen. It's not really blue in color though."

"The red moon, that follows an orange moon, and that comes after a yellow moon, is bad mojo," Freeman stated. "Beth, when you first see the full moon on the horizon, it is large and bright. And if it's tinted in color, it marks omens. Two months ago the full moon was yellow. And we saw a trap set for Drake. Last month, I watched the orange moon rise with great apprehension. And we were all witness to the demon attack upon Drake… well, at least its head. Tonight is the black moon. It's still there, only it's between us and the sun, so we can just see the dark side of it. Tomorrow we will witness the breaking of our fellowship, when you and Martin go away. I am fearful that the next full moon will be red, a blood moon, signifying a more deadly omen."

"Do they have to come in that sequence? Yellow, orange, and red?" Drake asked. He'd never heard of this moon mojo before and was very curious to know more. "What if the moon was just red, following a normal white moon? Would that be as bad?"

"A red moon any time is bad mojo," Freeman responded. "But when the progression is there, the colors of fire—yellow, orange, and red—each one builds upon the other in a geometrical sequence making the final red moon devastating. Most of the worst disasters to befall humanity have come after such progressions."

"But the tint of the moon on the horizon would be influenced by the amount of pollutants in the atmosphere," Drake added.

"Uh oh," Scrappy announced. "Geek-fest."

"That's true, my friend," Freeman answered. "Pollutants

would influence some of what we perceive. But one could argue that Mother Earth uses those pollutants to signify the coming mojo in an attempt to purify her ecosystems, perhaps by thinning mankind's increasing population."

"You two are most fascinating," Brigid interrupted. "And I do know some gods with dominion over the Earth who are not happy at the current condition of the world."

"They're also most boring for those of us who just want to fight and not talk all day," Scrappy added.

"So if the next full moon is red, that means we're in trouble?" Beth asked nervously, Martin patted her hand to comfort her.

"Don't be completely alarmed," Freeman replied. "It could affect someone on the other side of the world, be a disaster in China, a flood in Bangladesh, a tsunami in the South Pacific, or a demon attack upon one of us. But, I'm just saying the patterns we've seen with the attacks on Drake aren't promising."

"Then we just have to make sure we protect him better this time," Beth rationalized.

"Aye, maiden Beth," Brigid remarked. "If it were truly that simple, but take heart, your love of the god-slayer has not gone unnoticed."

Beth blushed. Uncertain how much Brigid might truly know of her desires, she forced the thoughts from her mind quickly because she knew that Martin would sometimes say he saw things in her mind. She used to not believe him, even though he was usually correct. Now she was not so certain. She was still somewhat skeptical of this whole adventure, but she'd seen too much to disregard it all like she once did.

"Martin, have you found anything in your searches of the three possible suspects?" Drake asked. "I have watched them all with greater suspicion, and haven't shared anything with any of them since the attack in the restroom."

"I have probed our brothers' minds covertly," Martin replied. "They both possess the awareness of someone being there, which made me have to come to them in their dreams.

Searching for anything while someone dreams is a challenge because the mind is very active with memories, fantasies, and horrors. It isn't the best place to be hanging out because you can get pulled into their dreams."

"What did you find?" Freeman asked.

"Neither seems to have the capability to be a traitor, though they feel completely responsible for the whole snake-guy incident. Oh, and I've seen the snake-guy from both of their memories, and he wasn't very pleasant, I might add," Martin explained.

"Thank you, that's how I felt about him too," Drake added.

"Quatyl was not a pleasant god, that is for certain," Brigid remarked. "And what of your mother?"

"Well," Martin responded, "that's another challenge. She has the La Madrid gift, not as much as Aunt Carmen, or Uncle Wally, but she does have it. She has many, many secrets hidden in her mind that I couldn't uncover no matter how much I dug, and near the end of my search I realized that she had been aware of me being there the whole time, and all she did was smile at me then ejected me from her mind."

"I regret to say this, but it does seem that we should be cautious of your mother," Brigid stated.

It was difficult for Drake to imagine that his own mom would've put his life in jeopardy. Why would she do it? What would she gain from such a thing? It made no sense, but the seed of suspicion was planted in Drake that evening by his brother Martin. That seed would quickly germinate inside his mind.

On October twenty-third, Freeman noted as the moon rose on the horizon that the tint was crimson red. Brigid had stood and watched it with him and they knew that it was a dark tiding.

That night, Drake dreamed the old dream that had

plagued his nights for two years. He knew all of the characters present in the dream, he knew what the tower was, and he knew he watched the dream from his view point, unable to change the outcome. It began again, on a dry, deserted plain of low rolling hills stood a massive, shiny, black tower that rose upward into the brewing storm clouds that churned through the sky—before him was the Tower of Dreams. A dull, primer-black 1970 Plymouth Duster approached the base of the tower with its exhaust spewing a thick blue smoke from the rich burning of oil. The car shook from side-to-side as it idled. Martin climbed out of the passenger side door, flipping the seat forward and letting a red-haired woman out of the back seat. It was Beth. She was beautiful, and dressed they way she had been on his birthday. Behind her the sinewy form of Scrappy emerged from the back seat of the car. He was about Beth's height because of the high heeled shoes she wore, but his proportions were beyond those of a typical man. He was built like a weight lifter, a profoundly gifted weight lifter. His rippling upper arms were bigger around than Martin's thighs. His neck was so thick it appeared to be just an extension of his shoulders. He carried two machetes, one in each hand. Scrappy was like a raw force of nature, and Drake was very glad Scrappy was there with them.

The three of them turned and looked toward Drake. They appeared to be talking to each other and to him. Where was Freeman, Drake thought? Off in the distance a wailing cackle was heard. Drake recognized the sound. Hellhounds were prowling. The howl repeated from the other side. It began to get louder. The hellhounds were getting closer. A sense of urgency came over Scrappy as he ran to the glistening exterior of the tower. Martin followed him and together they began to feel the smooth wall looking for something. The howls were getting ever so close now. Martin yelled at Scrappy and Drake for help. Scrappy found the crack Martin was pointing to and tried to get his fingers into it. He couldn't get a grip. He quickly stuck the end of one machete into the slim gap and pulled on it with a great flexing of his arms. The machete snapped in two near the tip of the black blade. He turned to Drake and stuck out his hand, demanding Hikari. Drake raised his sword and shook his head.

The howling was now nearly upon them. Martin yelled something at them and they rushed back into the dust-covered car. Beth pulled out Dad's twenty-two caliber pistol and shot at a dark form beside the tower. Drake had never seen that before, and he wondered why it was happening differently tonight. The thing stumbled and fell in front of them—to his horror, it was Freeman. Drake and Scrappy ran to the fallen Freeman. Martin and Beth barely made it in the car and closed the doors before the windows were assaulted with loud thuds by hellhounds, unsightly creatures with wild tufts of hair on the backs of their necks, a row of long bone-like spikes protruding from their spines, and overly large, human-like heads with rows of razor-sharp teeth in the slobbering maws. The hellhounds lunged at Scrappy. Ten or more of them took him to the ground. Drake slashed Hikari through the beasts in a vain attempt to save Scrap. Behind him, demons of Krangath spawn crashed into his car, shattering the windows and slicing Martin across the neck. Martin's head fell backward over the seat, attached to his body by thin strips of muscle and skin. Blood erupted from his fresh stump of a neck. What's going on, Drake thought, this wasn't the way it happened? Beth screamed, and she shot the revolver again and again into the carnage around her, until it just clicked and clicked on the empty chamber. The insectoid demons slammed the car and tore at the roof and windows. Beth somehow moved over and started the Duster with a load roar. A serrated claw of a demon slashed her fair face ripping flesh and cutting bone. Her dead foot fell hard on the accelerator and the car shot forward into the hellhounds on top of bloody remains of Scrappy, whose spine shattered from the impact of the weight of the car upon him, before careening into Drake's legs, pinning him against the Tower of Dreams. Drake looked down. His legs were broken and crushed, he couldn't feel them, and it was like they didn't exist anymore. Then he noticed three bloody holes on his chest. He'd been shot by the wayward bullets of Beth during her frenzied shooting. Light began to fade, darkness surrounded him, and he saw the smiling face of his mother and remembered no more.

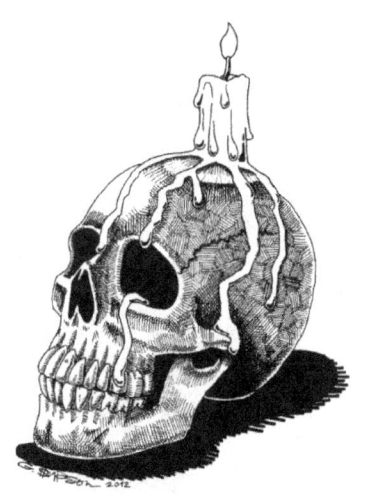

26

TIME AND TEMPERATURE

THE BROTHERHOOD OF OLYMPUS
AND THE TOWER OF DREAMS

Halloween
Chapter Twenty-Six
October 31, 1980
Hazel Dell, Washington

Martin and Beth never arrived on the day before Halloween, like they were supposed to. They had somehow missed their flight and didn't arrive at the Portland International Airport until late in the afternoon on the thirty-first. Drake had spent the night before at work freaked out about how everything was falling apart. Brigid had tried to reassure him, but even her goddess influence did little to calm him. He didn't look flustered on the outside, but inside his gut was churning like he had eaten twelve pounds of broken glass and shards of jagged metal.

"It all started with the red moon," Drake said.

"I saw the moonrise with Freeman, crimson red it was," Brigid replied.

"Yeah, Freeman couldn't even get the night off work either, so we have to come here to the restaurant. Fortunately it's Halloween, so people won't be too shocked to see us with swords and stuff. Then Martin isn't back yet. And then there's my dream. After the night of the blood-moon my dream changed," Drake added. "It'd always just been a premonition of who was there and of the tower. But the new dream had us all dying at the base of the tower, horrible deaths, so much blood and gore. We failed. And as we fall, so too does the world, all the gods told me that!"

Brigid shook her head. She had never seen Drake so upset, so vulnerable.

"My dear Drake, son of Drake," Brigid began with a soft

smile. She gently brushed his dark hair back away from his eyes. "It troubles me to see you so. I must ask you one question. Who am I?"

"Brigid, goddess of the sacred flame," Drake replied.

"And do you believe this is so?" Brigid asked.

"Yes," Drake responded. "I've seen your flame, I don't doubt you Brigid, I doubt me."

"I am glad you do not doubt me, god-slayer," Brigid said. She smiled at him again. "I need you to hear my words, to understand my passion, my belief, my love, and my faith in you Drake, son of Drake."

Drake lifted his head and looked at Brigid. She was perhaps the most beautiful woman he had ever seen. She made him warm inside by being close to him.

"I accepted this duty from my kin," Brigid began. "It was no easy task to live among humans and teach you and your brothers the art of war, and the tactics of survival that will be needed on your journey. I have always preferred art, music, or poetry to warfare. But this situation was unique. Never have my kin been in such a strait. You offer us hope. You are our only hope, Drake. In the time I've have been here, I have opened my heart to you and your brothers. If ever I were to be a patron of humans again, it would be you five. I love you, as a sister loves a brother. If not for prophecies of your offspring that Poseidon has kept close to his breast, I could love you as a woman loves a man. You are a shining light, a beacon for all who hold hope true to their hearts. If I could go with you, I would do so without question. If I had to lay down my existence for you, I would proudly do so as well."

Drake's head was swimming with all that she was saying.

"I have faith in you Drake," Brigid continued, as she stroked his hair. "You possess an ability that will change the outcome of the war that will be fought. It has been seen by many, which is why those on the dark side fear you so. In time you will learn of this gift, and you will master it. And in that time I shall come to you and ask that you remember the faith I had in you, and we shall be as brother and sister."

"I would like that, Brigid," Drake stated.

"As will I, god-slayer, as will I," Brigid responded. "But none of that shall come to pass if the fear and doubt that roots in your belly are not expelled. All warriors feel fear before a battle, but a true warrior, a leader among men, knows that fear by name and channels it into the passion of why he fights. You fight to defend your family, your friends, your world, and even my world. There is no greater passion in war than choosing to fight for your love. You, god-slayer, are a defender of love, and none have ever been truer. If you believe who I am, also believe in my faith in you, Drake."

Brigid kissed his forehead. The bile in his stomach felt different. It had settled, but it was more than that, it was like a fire inside him, churning on the passion of his love—his agápe. He knew Brigid had spoken the truth. His life had always been on this path. He was chosen for something greater, like Luke Skywalker and all the heroes of fables, myth, history, and legend before him, and he would not fail his brothers or the goddess of the sacred flame. A grim smile emerged upon the face of Drake Fraser.

It was all arranged. Scrappy would meet him at his house at eleven o'clock, and they would drive to the restaurant together where Martin and Beth would be waiting for them. They had chosen this plan because Freeman was working the graveyard shift at Danny's. They concluded that Freeman would be the most at risk in any attack because he'd be separated from the rest of them, the straggler from the herd concept. Drake had all of the gear that Martin and Beth had asked him to bring, including two of Dad's rifles and his revolver.

In the morning before school, Drake decided to warn his little brothers so that they would be safe when everything hit the fan later that night.

"So," Dennis said, squinting a bit either out of disbelief or too much belief, "these things that caught us in the big place through your secret room are coming here tonight to try and kill Frasers?"

"Well…" Drake responded. He wanted to put extreme caution in them, but not scare them senseless. "Yeah, maybe. We aren't really sure, but I don't want either of you getting hurt. You probably shouldn't go trick-or-treating tonight either. And make sure you have the buttons Aunt Carmen gave you. Remember she put some of her mojo on the house so it's the safest place for you."

"What's mojo?" Albert asked.

"Kind of like magic," Drake answered.

"Aunt Carmen is magic, too?" Albert questioned. "I thought she was like a witch?"

"Geez, Albert," Dennis remarked, "witches are magic. Sometimes you're such a dillhole."

Drake shook his head.

"I just think you two should be in the safest place you can tonight, okay?" Drake asked them.

Albert looked at Dennis and smiled. Dennis smiled back at his brother.

"Okay, Drake," Dennis said. "We'll be in the safest place we can find until you get back."

"Yeah," Albert added. "And we won't go trick or treating either. Hey, maybe we'll just keep the candy Mom got for us to give out?"

"Deal!" Dennis shouted. "And we'll still wear our costumes."

Dennis and Albert high-fived each other and Drake felt relieved that his little brothers would be safe, at least. Drake hugged them both, and that was something they thought was a little weird, but it re-enforced their idea of finding the absolute safest place to hide that night.

Drake worked until nine o'clock after he got out of school. Brigid was there, and she gave him a pressed cherry blossom to hold close to his heart.

"To remember me and my faith in you, god-slayer," she

had said.

Drake thought it was curious that he had known her for months, working with her nearly every day during that time, either at work, or training for this very day. Up until the last few days she had never addressed him as 'god-slayer,' almost like it was a title she avoided. And in truth, he didn't like it, because it seemed so big and ominous like something he really wasn't, except for a fluke of fate. But now she had used it in such a way that he began to accept it to a point that he was beginning to feel comfortable with it. Maybe it was who he was meant to be. He was Drake Fraser, god-slayer.

Brigid gave him a hug when he was leaving work. She was going to work through the witching hour, in case she could be of any help to Freeman in the restaurant. They had determined that whatever was going to happen would occur in the hour before midnight, the witching hour at the end of All Hallows Eve. That was when they had to be ready to meet their destiny—whatever that might look like.

"May love be with you, Drake god-slayer," Brigid said, as she held him tight. She rose up and kissed his cheek. "Be safe and lead well."

"Thank you Brigid, goddess of the sacred flame," Drake responded, as he hugged her back. Brigid truly was like a sister to him, and he loved her as such. "Please keep Freeman safe, if you can."

"I will do so with honor," Brigid replied.

Drake looked at her one last time and turned and left. He got in his car and started it up, heading home one last time—perhaps his final time.

When he got home he began to load gear into the inside of his car, he packed in all the stuff Martin had asked him to bring, and then filled his canteens with water, and packed the first aid kit into his duffle bag, along with a spiral notebook, two pencils, an eraser, and an ink pen. He also put some *Twinkies* in his bag, and a few packs of gum—just in case, he thought. Monique followed him faithfully. At one point she had actually climbed in his open bag, like she wanted to go with him.

"No girl," Drake said to her when he picked her up and put her outside the bag. "You can't go, I don't want you to get hurt. Your job is to keep Dennis and Albert safe, okay? Can you do that?"

Monique wiggled her little white puff of a tail and barked. She liked it when he talked to her.

"Good girl," Drake remarked. He scratched her head behind her ear. "You're such a good girl."

Drake went back into his room, grabbed Hikari and the Staff of Orkan, and carried them both down to his car. He bounded back up the stairs and went to get the Archive Room key, but it wasn't in the spot behind his *Lord of the Rings* books where it had been. Instead it was sitting on his desk near the bookshelf on a folded piece of paper. He must have already pulled it out and forgotten about it. He had been so busy trying to remember everything he needed and worried that he'd forget something. He had actually already packed *Twinkies* twice. He looked over at his duffle bag on his bed to see that Monique was sitting in it again. He shook his head and picked up the key and put it in his pants pocket. The folded piece of paper fell on his floor, unseen to him.

He packed his fathers hunting bow, his practice bow, two quivers of arrows, and extra ammunition for all three guns. He also packed their Polaroid camera, a compass in a pouch for the webbed utility belt he wore, and two hunting knives.

There was a knock at the door. Drake hadn't turned the outside light on, so it shouldn't have been trick-or-treaters. He cautiously approached the door and peered out the peephole. Outside was dark, so the peephole didn't really help. He looked at the clock across the room and it was already nearly ten-thirty. It must be Scrappy at the door, he thought, and turned the knob.

A dark form moved in front of him then moved toward him with great speed. Scrappy emerged from the darkness into the light of the living room.

"Hey brother," Scrappy said. "I would've been here sooner, except Robert wanted to come with and I had to ditch him. He don't believe in all this stuff, and he might've gotten one of us killed."

Drake clasped his right forearm against Scrappy's forearm, their hands near each other's inner elbow. They moved closer and patted each other on the back.

"I'm glad you're here Scrap," Drake stated. "I can't imagine doing this without you."

"I'm glad too," Scrap replied. "I'm finally gonna get to fight something to the death. Like you have, god-slayer."

They both chuckled.

"Come on, let's get the last of this in my car and load your stuff in there too," instructed Drake.

They accomplished their last task, getting Scrappy's gear in the Duster. They walked back into the house to make sure they hadn't forgotten anything. Monique danced on her hind feet, begging to go with them.

"I told you," Drake said, "you're not going. Your job is to guard Dennis and Albert."

"Where're your little brothers?" Scrappy asked.

"In bed, I think," Drake replied. "They didn't go trick-or-treating, and went to bed early."

"Okay," Scrappy responded.

"Come on, let's go," Drake stated. He stopped and picked up his dog, kissed her white curly head. "Love you Mo."

Drake set down the poodle and headed out the door behind the muscled form of Scrappy. He turned off the main living room light and closed the door behind them—locked. He checked it twice before he climbed into his black car.

Drake started up the duster. The radio came on, and it was already on KGON. The DJ announced the next song, *Tom Sawyer* by RUSH. It played as they drove toward the restaurant. They were both warriors, like the one in the song. As they drove, the street lights blinked out when they neared.

"What's up with the lights?" Scrappy asked.

"Maybe the electric company knows we are coming," Drake answered.

"Or maybe it's just you?" Scrappy queried. "It never does that for me, except when I'm with you, but never this much."

"Yeah," Drake said with a smile. He had begun to notice that he sometimes affected lights this way. "Maybe it's just me."

They smiled at each other as they cruised down the dark road, illuminated only by the lights of the dashboard.

They pulled into the restaurant parking lot. Drake found that one of the areas in front had no cars parked in it, over next to the gas station that fronted NE 78th Street near the off ramp from southbound I-5. Drake backed into the spot in front of the tall Danny's sign. He hoped to be able to watch Freeman through the witching hour, and this spot was perfect to see the whole pass through window and into the kitchen beyond.

Drake looked over at the rotating Security Pacific Bank sign. The first turn showed it was '11:01' and '51°.'

"Freeman should already be in there," Drake stated.

"Yeah," Scrap replied. "Unless he's late."

Drake saw the bespectacled form of Freeman walk into the kitchen. His white, tall, heavily starched chef's hat added an extra eight to ten inches to his height. Both of them were watching Freeman so intently that they were startled when someone knocked on the window of the car.

Martin and Beth stood outside the car. Drake was very happy to see that they had finally made it back from Alaska. Scrappy got out, flipped the bucket seat forward and climbed in behind Drake. Beth got into the back with Scrap, and then Martin clicked the seat back into place and sat in the front with his brother. Drake noticed it was the same seating positions they had in his dreams, both the premonition ones and the nightmare. While they sat, they attached gear to themselves, or just checked what they were carrying. Drake was keeping an eye on the kitchen to watch Freeman.

Time passed slowly. Too slowly. The time and temperature sign kept turning. '11:30' and '49°' then it was '11:40' and '48°.'

"When's it going to do something?" Beth asked. "I'm tired."

"Sometime in the next twenty minutes," Drake replied. "It has to be soon."

Drake looked back at Beth and Scrappy. They both looked as anxious as he felt. He glanced over at Martin. He was glad one of his brothers was with him, though he would've probably preferred Mark.

The moments took what seemed an eternity to pass. The sign turned '11:48' and '47°' and the level of tension inside the car had become palpable.

"This is driving me crazy," Beth declared. "I can't take it anymore, Marty, I'm tired from our flight, let's just go home."

Beth unclipped her seatbelt and began to push on the back of the seat in front of her.

"Scrappy," Martin stated calmly. "Can you help her buckle her seatbelt again?"

Scrappy nodded, reached out with one hand and moved Beth back against the seat. He deftly buckled the belt once again. She turned, her right hand raised to slap. Scrappy looked at her and wagged his right index finger before her. Beth held her hand and did not strike.

Something changed outside. A dense fog had begun to settle from above. It also seemed to be rising from the ground—something common on damp lands, but exceptionally rare on dry roads and parking lots. The sign turned, '11:50' and '45°.' The fog was becoming more and more difficult to see through. Drake worried about losing sight of Freeman inside. The sign continued to turn, '11:50' and '42°' and turn, '11:51' and '39°.'

"The temperature's dropping fast!" Drake exclaimed.

"It's coming!" Martin yelled.

"Look!" Scrappy shouted excitedly. "Out my window, what's that out in the fog?"

They all leaned to look out the drivers' side. In the distance a black shadow had partially emerged from the fog. It was an immense obelisk that reached up as far as the eye could see.

"It's the tower!" Scrappy announced. "Quick, we have to get to it before it moves again!"

Drake was uncertain, it was to the west as Addraemyr had said, but there was something he couldn't quantify about that shiny black shadow. He rolled down his window and looked into the fog. Then on a whim he looked up. Above them the thick fog churned as if they were inside a large glass tube. The stars were bright in the black sky in the circle directly above them.

"Look above us!" Drake yelled. Martin rolled down his window and looked up. Beth popped her head out next to her husband. Scrappy forced his out next to Drake.

The sign turned unseen by the four stargazers, '11:51' and '35°' because they only saw the thick tumultuous fog roiling against the invisible walls of the tube that rested above them. Far up in the night sky the stars began to swirl.

"Back inside!" Drake commanded fearful of what happening, hoping he could lead them safely, and live up to the words that Brigid had showered upon him.

"What's happening?" Beth screamed. She had begun to become frantic.

The car rocked like it was being buffeted by strong winds. Air poured in through the open windows so forcibly that it pushed them backward, but there was no wind. Drake and Martin both struggled against the oppressive air and looked at the sign as it turned, '11:52' and '34°.' The temperature had dropped fourteen degrees in twelve minutes.

Beth screamed behind them. It was a shrill scream that lingered in their ears, but seemed to fall away into nothingness.

Drake held onto the steering wheel tightly and turned to say something to Martin, and then there was only darkness.

27

THE TOWER OF DREAMS

THE BROTHERHOOD OF OLYMPUS
AND THE TOWER OF DREAMS

Wasteland
Chapter Twenty-Seven
October 31, 1980
On a desolate plain

Scrappy blinked his eyes hard. There was no difference in the depth of the darkness before him, whether his eyes were open or closed. He realized that he didn't even feel the seat of the car he had just been sitting on. Then he thought he must be dead. So this is what the afterlife was like—just darkness. He wasn't sure how he died, but as he thought about it, he became angry because he knew it wasn't fighting some horrific beast or massive barbarian to the death.

He tried to move, but found that he was kind of held in place by something unseen, a force perhaps, or maybe he was in a grave? That upset him more, when he and Drake had talked about it, if he did happen to die. He had explained that he wanted a funeral pyre. His remains would be lifted up in the fire and raised to the sky, and he absolutely didn't want to be buried.

Damn Drake, he thought, how could he bury me? Unless, Drake had died too, and at that moment Scrappy felt true sorrow for failing his brother. He was supposed to protect him in battle, to see him through to the end. And now this was the end. He felt tears flood his eyes.

The sun was so bright it was painful. Drake looked out his window. Dust swirled in the stiff winds blowing across the brown desolate plains around them. Drake turned and saw his three brothers—Martin, Beth, and Scrappy. It was still cumbersome to think of Beth as his brother, but it was more symbolic than functional. Martin was rubbing his eyes, adjusting to the bright light, Beth looked around like she was in shock, and Scrappy looked like he was about to cry.

"Scrap," Drake said. "Are you crying?"

"No!" Scrappy exclaimed defiantly.

"Well, it looks like," Drake continued.

"It looks like I'm about to punch you, too," Scrappy interrupted.

Drake shook his head and let it go.

"Where are we?" Martin asked.

"I don't know," Drake replied. "There are no visible landmarks, nothing at all to give us any clue to where we are. The only thing I'm certain of is that we were just sitting outside Danny's and it was eleven fifty-two, almost midnight."

Dry intense heat wafted in through the open windows, like that of a desert in summer time.

"And now it's well past sunrise," Scrappy added. "It's hot here too."

"It appears so," Martin agreed. "But where? This is not Vancouver anymore."

"Simple," Beth stated. "If it's midnight in Washington, where on Earth would it be daytime, and have this kind of climate?"

"Drake?" Martin asked.

"Well," Drake responded, "we could be anywhere from the Australian outback to the Asian steppes, or even the plains of east Africa. I would have to see where the sun is to try and measure the time here."

Martin looked at his watch.

"My watch says its eleven fifty-three," Martin added. "You know what, we should take some pictures. Beth, hand me my camera."

Beth found the thirty-five millimeter camera and handed it to Martin.

"Let's check where the sun is," Scrappy stated. Drake nodded and undid his seatbelt before opening the door and stepping out on the hard ground. Scrappy quickly flipped the seat forward and joined him. He appreciated stretching his legs.

The plain before them was nothing but low rolling hills, broken with scrub brush that looked like it had not seen water in decades. The Duster sat on a crude, rutted dirt road, stretching out in front of the car and behind it to the horizons. In front of the car, along the edge of the sky, a dark red storm brewed. Sporadic lightning flashed and it looked like a place to avoid. Behind them the sky was bright and free of clouds, but it also held something that Drake wasn't prepared to see. There was a sun in the sky that seemed a bit bigger than what they were used to, but that could just have been different because of the change of hemisphere. But that wasn't all. Beside the sun, halfway to the horizon, a second sun burned in the sky. It was half the size of the first and glowed with a red fire. It was like Tatooine in *Star Wars*, except that wasn't all. Farther to the right about the same height above the horizon as the first sun, a third object burned in the sky. This one was smaller than the second, and flashed a blue pulse of light about every five seconds.

"A pulsar," Drake said with an open mouth.

"Why're there more than one sun?" Scrappy asked.

"Martin, Beth," Drake began. "I don't think we're in Asia, or Africa, in fact I don't think we are even on Earth anymore. We're in a trinary star system."

Martin and Beth climbed out of the car.

"What's that mean?" Beth questioned.

"That means we're on another planet that has three suns," Drake answered.

"That's not good at all," Scrappy added. "But at least we can breathe here."

"Good point," Drake remarked. "The atmosphere does appear hospitable, but there doesn't seem to be much water."

"Except maybe in that nasty looking storm, over there," Martin stated, as he pointed to the huge red storm on the far horizon.

"So what're we gonna do?" Scrappy asked. "Do we sit here and wait in the heat, with not much water, or do we drive this road we are on and see where it takes us?"

"I think we should wait," Martin announced. "Freeman isn't with us and if we move we might lose him here forever. Assuming he came here too?"

"There's been someone here at some point, because there's a road. I say we drive and find a place to get out of the heat, but if there's water, its like Martin said its probably within that storm," Scrappy added, as he pointed toward the flashing red storm.

"I like that idea," Beth concurred. "But I say we should drive toward the suns, away from the storm, because that storm doesn't look like a place I'd want to be."

The three of them turned to Drake. Three different opinions and it was up to him to decide which was best. Drake thought about the situation. He too was concerned about where Freeman might be, but he knew sitting out in this heat with the little bit of water he had in his canteen was a recipe for disaster. He studied the dirt road that his car sat upon, looking to the suns, and then off to the storm.

"Here's what I think," Drake began. "I'm worried where Freeman might be, as much if not more than any of you. And I think waiting out here in the sun with barely any water would not end well. The road ahead of us has the storm, and it doesn't look friendly at all. Behind us may be the best choice. But there is one thing I cannot shake from my mind. When we were just in the parking lot, Freeman was in the restaurant in front of us. If we haven't changed orientation, and if he's been brought here too, he should be off somewhere in front of us."

Martin nodded in agreement. Beth shrugged, and Scrappy tipped his head slightly to the right and smiled.

"And if that storm has water, we can try to get some," Drake concluded.

"Let's go," Scrappy announced. He climbed back into

his seat behind Drake. Beth shrugged again and climbed in the back next to Scrap. Martin and Drake climbed in and Drake started up the car. It rumbled and shook as it idled. Drake shifted into drive, and off they went.

The hard dirt road was rough, and the fastest they could go was about thirty miles-per-hour. That speed didn't last long, since some of the road required them to slowly roll over the deep ruts so they didn't get stuck or break an axle of the car.

It was two o'clock in the morning on Martin's watch when Drake pulled the Duster to a stop. He shut the engine down and popped open the trunk to grab a quart of motor oil. When he bought the car, Dad had said it had an oil leak, and leak it did. Drake had to add a quart about every tank of gas he drove it. He had driven about half of the gas out of the car, and decided he should add some oil, just in case, because he didn't want the Duster to break down on some other planet.

Scrappy, Martin, and Beth got out to stretch their legs. In front of them the maelstrom of the red lightning storm raged dangerously close. Most of the energy of the storm was being spent higher in the sky, and to their dismay it didn't appear to be generating any rain. Arcs of red hued lightning flashed down to the broken hills before them while the violent clouds in the sky turned and spun in on themselves. The storm raged over a low series of hills that would've passed for mountains on this very flat land they had traveled, had they not known what true mountains looked like.

Drake punched the oil can with the pour spout and popped the hood to add the oil to the engine.

"Is there something inside the storm?" Scrappy asked. "Look up in the hills. I thought I saw something inside it."

Beth and Martin stared at the violent storm, but didn't see anything different about the storm where Scrappy had mentioned.

Drake finished adding the oil, wiped the spout clean, and returned all of the things to the trunk of the car, including the empty can of oil. He was tempted for a moment to toss the empty can along the dirt road, but remembered the whole butterfly effect from one of his science readings on the chaos theory. Should he do anything to alter the environment or change the history of this alien world, even as simple as crushing a butterfly or littering an oil can, the consequences could be catastrophic. He'd rather not be the cause of the death of this entire planet and any life that might exist there.

They started down the road again. The surface smoothed and it became easier for Drake to drive. Soon they were cruising at nearly fifty down the hard dirt road. They slowed as they crested the big hill that had loomed before them. By now the lightning had been flashing above and behind them, fortunately the major part of the storm was higher in the atmosphere. Still, the occasional lightning strike near them that blew large chunks of soil and rock into the air did nothing to ease their anxiety.

At the apex of the hill Drake slowed to a stop. Before them, in the middle of the storm, stood a wide obsidian tower that reached all the way up and was lost within the maelstrom above.

"The Tower of Dreams!" Scrappy exclaimed from the backseat.

The booming of thunder shook the ground and rocked the car.

"Did I mention that I voted for driving the other way?" Beth stated.

Drake headed down the sloping hill, toward the tower. He looked along the hillside as the lightning flashed. Black figures moved toward the tower with them. Something was in the hills following them. Drake remembered how the hellhounds had paced him into their trap.

"Look on the hilltops when the lightning flashes," Drake said as he drove. "There's something out there following us, like the hellhounds followed me."

"We're going a lot faster than you could on your bike," Martin said. "We should have time to get in once we arrive at the tower."

"So how do we get in when we get there?" Scrappy asked.

Drake and Martin looked at each other and shrugged.

"I don't know," Drake replied.

"Let's just get there first," Beth added. She'd seen the figures moving on the hillside in the lightning flashes. Two and four legged things ran toward the tower, and their destination. "I don't like the looks of those things following us."

The distance to the base of the tower wasn't as far as it seemed, and soon they were pulling up to the bottom of it. Drake stopped the Duster a car length away from the obsidian obelisk, and then the car idled for a brief moment before he shut it down as it sputtered to a stop. The engine acted like it didn't want to turn off as it sputtered and spurted. Finally the car came to rest at the base of the Tower of Dreams.

"Let's figure out how to get in there fast," Martin said. "Whatever's out there won't be out there for long, we'll have company soon."

"Make sure you grab your gear," Drake stated. "Once we get inside we probably are in there until this is done, one way or another."

Scrappy nodded. The four of them strapped or fastened their equipment and weapons to themselves quickly.

They went to the obsidian wall and began to examine it for a way in, a door, a keyhole, a locking mechanism, or anything besides the solid shiny black stone they found. They went farther and farther from the car, searching the surface of the tower in vain.

In the distance a cackling howl was heard, followed by three more around them in answer to the first.

"What was that?" Beth asked. "I've never heard anything like that before."

"I have," Drake replied somberly. "Those are hellhounds."

"Oh," Beth responded. "That's not good."

"How are we gonna get in, Drake?" Martin questioned loudly. "We're running out of time!"

"What did Addraemyr tell us?" Drake asked himself. "The Keeper had to have given us a clue, what did he say?"

"Look!" Martin screamed. "Over here, I found a door!"

Scrappy and Drake rushed over to Martin, who was almost in front of the car. Sure enough there was a small crack around a large rectangle that would pass as a door.

"How do we open it?" Scrappy asked.

Drake pulled an arrow from his quiver. About twenty yards away beyond his car, a hellhound approached. He notched it, took aim, and let loose the arrow. It went through the left shoulder of the beast and took it to the rocky ground with a cloud of dust.

"Good shooting, brother," Scrappy remarked. A second hellhound came up and began to tear at the bloodied beast. "They're eating each other."

The twenty-two revolver popped, once, then twice. Both bullets went high over the second hellhound, but the second did break off one of the spikes on its back near the spine. The hellhound jumped, forgot about its feast, and began to advance on them again.

Scrappy and Martin were desperately trying to get their fingers into the crack of the door. Scrappy took one of the machetes that hung from either side of the green webbed belt around his waist and slid the tip into the crack.

Drake pulled another hunting arrow from his quiver, notched it, took aim and let it fly. The arrow went low, missing the blood stained and slobbering jaw of the beast. With no hesitation he pulled a third arrow from the quiver and raised his aim slightly. The next arrow found its mark, piercing the eye socket of the hellhound deeply and dropping it to the dirty ground.

Lightning flashed around them, and the thunderclap that followed shook them like a massive earthquake. The car actually moved at least a foot to the right as it bounced on the heaving ground. The thick scent of ozone hung in the air, warning them of the next strike.

Scrappy pried at the door with his machete blade. It began to budge, just slightly, and then the tip of the black blade broke off in the crack with a sudden pop of metal snapping. Scrappy stepped back to survey the door.

"I need something stronger to pry it open!" Scrappy declared.

The twenty-two went pop, pop, pop, pop and Beth screamed as another hellhound fell in the near distance. Five more moved closer. At least six had begun to feed on the three fallen animals, tearing bloody chunks of flesh from their dead or dying bodies.

"They just keep coming!" Beth yelled. She reloaded the revolver in a near panic.

"Drake!" Scrappy yelled. "Give me your sword, let me use it to pry the door open!"

"No," Drake replied shaking his head. "My sword is a weapon not a crowbar."

Drake fired another arrow, dropping another hellhound into the carnage of feeding, blood, and howling that was becoming increasingly more violent. The twenty-two sounded again, pop, pop, pop, pop, pop, and then a flash so bright it blinded them as lightning struck the base of the tower a mere twenty feet above them. Their hair stood on end as they staggered and fell. The thunder that followed was so violent that Martin and Scrappy were knocked onto their backs, and both Drake and Beth slammed into the heaving car. Had it been ten feet lower they probably would've all died.

When their sight began to clear, they saw the demons milling around in the midst of the hellhounds. There were Krangathian spawn, and some that looked like tall, twisted jackals that stood on two feet, and others that resembled reptiles or combinations of beasts—lions, bears, gorillas, and great horned goats with long sharp teeth protruding from their insidious mouths.

"We have to fight!" Scrappy yelled. He raised both of his black machete blades up to the sky and bellowed.

"There's too many, little brother!" Martin shouted.

Beth had reloaded yet again. Drake loosed an arrow into the neck of one of the goat-headed demons. It howled in pain, and the horde began to advance on them. Nearly a hundred hellhounds and half as many demons closed to within thirty yards around them.

Drake realized their plight—if they stood and fought here, they would inflict heavy losses on the demonic horde, but they would ultimately fall, there were too many for the four of them to fight.

"In the car!" Drake commanded. "In the car *now*! Move it! Move it!"

Beth quickly climbed in, pulling the seat back into its place with her. Martin was in and closed the door. He had the thirty-aught-six in a shooting position out the window in a flash. The scope allowed him to aim with great precision. He fired and fractured a head of a demon, blowing skull and black ichor out of the back of its head.

Scrappy was nearly berserk with rage, building it to a level that he would release upon his enemies in battle. He held his ebon blades high above himself and shouted. Drake struggled with the barbarian to get him to move.

"Scrap!" Drake pleaded. "We gotta go, there's too many and not a defensible place to make a stand. Let's go, you will get to fight them, I promise you, you have my word as your friend and brother!"

Scrappy had heard the last part and turned with Drake back to the car. Beth fired the pistol again, with a pop, pop, pop. Scrappy climbed into the back seat and Drake pushed the front seat back with a click and climbed in. He turned the key to start the car, but the engine would not turn over. He tried again, and again. Pumping the accelerator, he tried the key again, but it wouldn't start.

Martin fired the rifle, worked the bolt to discharge the casing, and fired again. The sound of the rifle echoed inside the car like the thunder had just moments ago outside. Two demons dropped in the distance.

"Hey dumbass!" Scrappy yelled. His ears were ringing from the gunshots. "That's too loud, it hurts my head."

"It hurts their heads more!" Martin shouted back.

"Start the car Drake," Beth stated. "Start the car!"

Drake tried the car again. It didn't turn over.

"I think you flooded it," Martin said. He pulled the rifle in and frantically rolled up the window. The demonic horde advanced closer and closer.

Drake quickly rolled up his window, too. He closed his eyes and wished Brigid was with them. The demons were at the side of the car, pressing their hideous faces against the windows, pushing against the side of the vehicle, rocking it. Drake pumped the accelerator one more time and turned the key. The engine fired up with a roar.

The demons pushed harder, the car shook violently, and Beth closed her eyes to try and shield herself from their ghoulish visage. Drake shifted into reverse and revved the engine. The car shook more than before as the demons continued to rock it, and then it hit something hard behind them, blocking their escape.

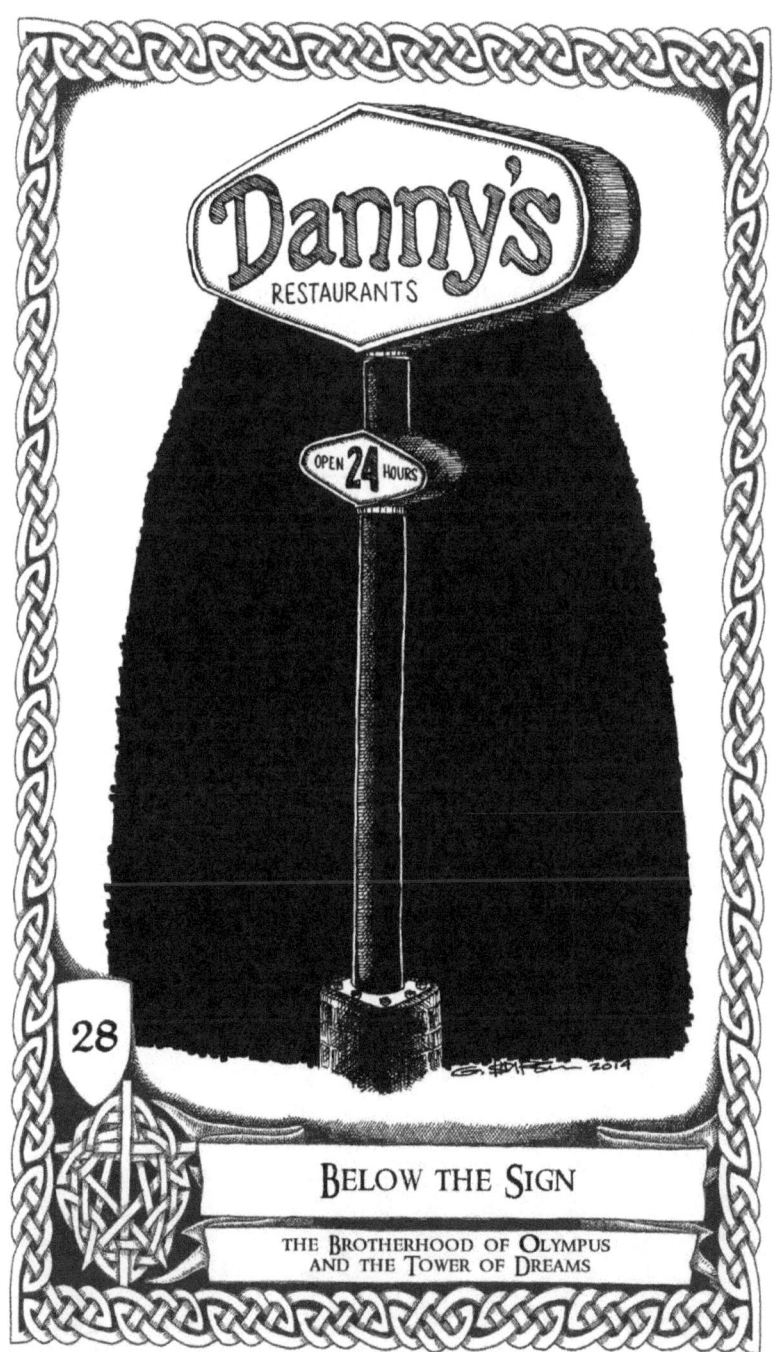

28

BELOW THE SIGN

THE BROTHERHOOD OF OLYMPUS
AND THE TOWER OF DREAMS

Danny's
Chapter Twenty-Eight
October 31, 1980
Hazel Dell, Washington

The 1970 Plymouth Duster had hit hard whatever was behind it, and it refused to yield. Drake turned to look over his right shoulder and saw the cement footing that held the steel pole that supported the large orange Danny's sign some forty feet above them. He quickly shifted the car into drive and moved the car forward and away from the cement post. The Duster idled loudly and shook with the regular rhythm of the firing pistons.

In front of them the fog was so thick they could barely see Freeman standing inside the kitchen. The clock down NE 6th Avenue continued to turn, '11:52' and '34°' and both Fraser boys stared at it in disbelief.

"What just happened?" Scrappy asked. "Something just happened, it's like we were gone somewhere, but we didn't go anywhere, we're still right here!"

"The clock's the same as it just was," Beth added after she opened her eyes to survey the surroundings. "It was all just a dream, like a daydream cause I'm awake, but more like a nightmare."

"Wait," Scrappy continued, "are you saying we've just been sitting here this whole time?"

"It's the same time it was," Beth replied. "We've only been here."

Drake and Martin sat in the front with their minds racing over the possibilities of what they had just experienced, or thought they had experienced. They both had seen the clock, and it was the same as it just was, so no time had passed. But it didn't make sense, because it all seemed so real.

"What do you remember?" Drake asked. "First thing that comes to your mind."

"A tall black tower," Scrappy replied.

"Hideous monsters," Beth added.

"A red lightning storm," Martin remarked.

"I remember all of those," Drake stated with a nod. "How could we all have the same waking nightmare? It's highly improbable."

"What's more improbable Drake, all of us having the same nightmare," Beth responded, as she leaned forward over the front seat, "or that we somehow traveled to another planet and came back to the exact moment in time?"

"Point taken, and I'm with Beth on that one," Scrappy added.

It was truly a conundrum that vexed Drake's mind. The probabilities were slim to none for either possibility, but Beth was correct, the chance that they had traveled through space and time was infinitesimally smaller. Drake looked at the dashboard of his car. The engine was still rumbling as it sat in park. He saw the fuel gauge showed he had less than a half a tank of gas.

He knew he had filled it up today, before going to work. It was still on the 'F' when he parked in front of the restaurant less than an hour ago. He looked up, the sign still turned, '11:53' and '34°,' how could he have used more than half a tank of gas in the passing of no time, if it had truly been a shared dream? There were documented cases of individuals having a shared psychosis where they all believed they had experienced the same thing, but in reality hadn't. Perhaps this was such a case. Maybe there was something in the fog that swirled around his car, like a drug or toxin that had made them hallucinate.

But what of the missing gas?

"Check to see if anything's different or missing," Drake announced. "Look for anything out of the ordinary."

They all started looking around at their assorted gear. Drake got out of the still running car to check the trunk. Inside the trunk he found an empty can of oil near the cans he normally carried there.

A rush of overwhelming thrill poured through him, like the moment the rollercoaster clears the top of a slope, hangs for a brief moment in time, then plummets downward. His heart bounded in his chest. He looked at the outside of the Duster. It was covered in brown dirt, and there were scrapes in the paint from serrated claws. Near the window beside Beth a large four-fingered handprint was pressed through the built up dirt exposing the black paint underneath.

"One of my machetes is broke!" Scrappy yelled as he held it up. The tip was broken off, and it was slightly bent like it had been used to pry something. "Look!"

"I'm missing a lot of bullets for the pistol," Beth said. She very much remembered firing the revolver, over and over in what she was sure was a dream.

"I've got three casings on the floor from the thirty-aught-six," Martin added. "Drake, how many arrows do you have?"

Drake turned his quiver and quickly counted. He had twenty razor-tipped hunting arrows when he packed his equipment earlier that very night. He counted them in twos with his fingers—two, four, six, eight, ten, twelve, fourteen, and one.

"I've got fifteen," Drake replied. And then he answered the follow up question before it could be asked. "I'm missing five arrows."

In the distance, the sign continued to turn. '11:54' and '34°.' Drake looked up and saw the thick fog above them begin to part once again. The stars became visible once more above them. He hurriedly slammed the trunk closed and walked quickly back to his seat in the car, slowing only to get all of his gear in without tearing the upholstery of the seats or breaking any of the attached equipment. When he finally slid into his seat, he saw the dirt upon his boots. He knew he had polished them the night before, and they were clean when he put them on back at the house. The conundrum hurt his head.

"Check your shoes," Drake told them.

Each of them looked down and saw thick brown dirt caked on their shoes or boots. Beth shook her head.

"It's not possible," Beth remarked. She reached down and touched her soiled shoe, leaving a streak from her fingertip through the dirt and knocking some of it onto the floorboard of the car. "It's physically not possible, unless we're still dreaming."

The sign turned, '11:55' and '32°' and Martin looked at his watch.

"Hey guys," Martin stated with audible tone of disbelief, "according to my watch it's two twenty-seven, we're missing two and a half hours."

"Marty, stop," Beth remarked. "It's not possible, it's just not."

The sign turned '11:55' and '29°' and both Martin and Drake looked at each other in horror. The fog grew thicker and churned once again in a perfect circle around the car, almost like they sat in the eye of a hurricane.

"Possible or not," Drake began, as he rolled down his window letting the frozen air spill into the warm car, "whatever happened before is about to happen again! Hold on to your gear!"

He held Hikari in one hand and the Staff of Orkan in the other, both weapons protruding out the open window.

Beth closed her eyes while the car rocked violently in her self imposed darkness.

"It's coming here!" Martin shouted in front of her.

"Roll up your window! Roll up your window!" Scrappy yelled beside her. All around her the air turned icy cold.

At four minutes to midnight, two men in black suits with red ties walked into the Danny's restaurant just off Exit Four on Interstate-Five. They shook the chill off as the inside door closed behind them.

"Someone will be right with you!" Debbie announced from the waitress station in the middle of the restaurant. One of the men waved a hand and nodded.

"Hey!" Brother DeCarlo declared. He pointed outside when the customers turned to look at him. "Anyone in here leave their car running in the parking lot? There's a black car right out there by the sign with its engine running and a window down."

29

ENTER IF YOU DARE

THE BROTHERHOOD OF OLYMPUS
AND THE TOWER OF DREAMS

Tower of Dreams
Chapter Twenty-Nine
October 31, 1980
Tower of Dreams

The icy chill left them in an instant, and they each fell from their various crouching positions, almost like they had been sitting upon invisible chairs that had been suddenly removed from beneath them, landing on the hard floor below. The clatter of metal on the warm white stone was loud.

"It's about time you guys showed up," Freeman stated in front of them. He was about thirty feet away and walking in their direction. "This is the second time I've been in here, the first time I waited like almost three hours for you. Where've you been?"

"That depends on what you believe," Scrappy responded. He sat on his butt behind Drake. Beth was on her side to his right, and Martin was in front of her—exactly as they had been sitting in the car.

Drake stood up from his knees from where he had fallen when he arrived. He quickly sheathed Hikari and moved the staff to his left hand. He reached out to help Scrappy up. Martin did likewise for Beth.

"Where's the car?" Beth asked, as she rubbed her hip and buttock. "Falling on my ass hurt."

"I don't know," Drake responded. "Nothing was different this time. We were all in the same spots, doing the same things."

"No," Scrappy remarked. "You had your window down."

"And you were holding your weapons out the window," Martin added. Drake wondered when his brother had become so observant.

"The first time I was holding the steering wheel, I think," Drake added. He looked at his equipment, the quiver, the bow, and the duffle bag. "We brought what we carried, or had attached to us."

"So you carried the car the first time?" Martin asked, shaking his head. Freeman sensed some tension and acted to diffuse it.

"Did any of you have your seatbelts on?" Freeman asked logically.

"Yeah," Beth responded. "But not just now, we had just climbed in when we were sent back to Earth, and never took time to buckle any seatbelts."

"Sent back to Earth?" Freeman inquired. "Clearly I've missed something."

"It's kind of a long story," Martin started.

"Well," Freeman replied, as he motioned around himself, "from my previous experience in here, we've got nothing but time."

Drake and Scrappy told Freeman of their adventure in the car along the road toward the tower, and of the challenges they faced once they arrived. Martin and Beth both offered some insight, clarification, or direction as the story was told.

"Fascinating," Freeman responded when the story was done. "And up until you arrived here with me, you weren't certain whether it had all been a dream, delusion, of painfully real."

"We still don't," Beth clarified. "The only difference is that you're with us now. Maybe."

"My, you're such a determined skeptic," Freeman remarked with a wide smile. He felt strangely alive in this environment. It was as if he could feel the structure of the molecules around him and almost touch the energy radiating from each and every atom. "I would be perfectly happy staying here, though I would want to see more of what's here."

Beth walked up to Freeman and poked him to see if he was real, and then nodded her head. They looked around the vast chamber. It was white polished stone on the floors and walls, with a high vaulted ceiling, frescoed to illustrate some woodland scene with animals of all sorts, including many that had never truly existed on Earth except in myths and legends. There was one doorway out of the room, and it was behind where Freeman had approached. The room appeared to be oval, with the door being at the far end of it.

"Where are we?" Scrappy asked.

"I believe we are inside it," Freeman answered.

"The Tower of Dreams," Drake added.

"Then we made it," Beth remarked. "Now we can go home, right?"

"It's not that simple," Drake corrected her. "The Keeper, Addraemyr, told me and Martin that we had to liberate the tower from the evil forces of the dark gods."

"Yes," Beth replied. "I've heard all about it when we were training with Brigid, remember?"

"Did you explore when you were in here before, Freeman?" Scrappy inquired. "Any idea where we need to go?"

"There's only one door," Freeman answered. "But I didn't go through it when I was in here by myself because I wasn't sure where you all were. And I figured if I left this room, you might have more trouble finding me."

"That was kinda my plan when we first arrived outside the tower," Martin remarked.

"Except we were like over two hours away from the tower," Drake clarified.

"Since we're all here," Freeman began, "I suggest we find out what we need to do to accomplish our task."

Among the others, he was decidedly underdressed. He had a chef's knife in a cardboard sheath tucked into his belt. He wore his white cook's shirt, starched chef's hat, brown kerchief cinched around his neck like a boy scout, except his was held with a Captain Danny's orange decoder ring. He had long flat spatula and some towels in his hands.

"It looks like we need to go that way," Martin said with a point to the doorway beyond. They all started walking that direction.

"Do you have my gear?" Freeman asked Drake, as they walked. Drake nodded and unzipped his duffle bag to remove the few things Freeman had asked him to carry. Drake pulled out his medicine bag, his spirit bag, and a few assorted books—including a couple of Dungeons and Dragons manuals. "You can hold onto my books right now, since I don't have a bag to put them in."

"Did you find a map while you were here, Freeman?" Drake asked.

"Even one like they have at the mall would be good," Beth added.

"Nope, no maps," Freeman replied. "But I sense that we are near the bottom, and we need to go to the top."

"Me too," Martin added. "And somewhere in the tower they've got Addraemyr locked up. We should probably go find him and free him. He could help us find our way through the tower."

"He's the ultimate pacifist and wouldn't help us fight," Drake stated. "But he did tell us that the tower had ways of defending itself."

"Traps," Scrappy remarked.

"Most likely," Drake replied.

"Maybe we should split up?" Martin asked. "Beth, Scrappy, and I could go and try to free Addraemyr. I can sense him, and I can find him, then he can help us."

"Wait a minute," Scrappy interrupted. "Why me? I don't wanna do any rescuing, I'm here to fight."

"Well," Martin replied, "neither of us are fighters, and Drake's already killed a god, so having you with us made the most sense. We need a fighter in each group."

Scrappy scowled. He did not like the idea of splitting up.

"You know that's what they did in *Star Wars*," Drake

stated thoughtfully. "One group went to rescue the prisoner, while the other went to complete the task to get them out. That didn't work out too well for everyone. Obi-wan died, and neither Freeman nor I want to be Obi-wan."

"I don't know," Freeman remarked. "Obi-wan kind of kicked ass… well at least until he died, of course."

"I don't think we should split up," Drake clarified. "We are all here for specific reasons, we all have specific abilities or skills, and I think we need all of them to finish this quest."

Drake waited a moment but no one protested his opinion. He began to walk toward the door, and they followed him silently the rest of the way to the door. It was close to hundred yards from where they first arrived in the chamber, but they finally arrived at the open arch of a door and they saw that it opened out into a wide concourse beyond. Martin was cautious of the doorway, sensing that it could be a trap. He pulled an arrow from Drake's quiver and stuck it through the doorway. Nothing happened and he pulled it back out.

"No trap," Martin announced with a smile. Suddenly a red light began to strobe in the middle of the doorway and with each flash it got quicker and quicker. It was like it was a countdown. White metal emerged from within the door jam, like a series of curved surfaces that when brought together would close and interlock with each other like the iris in a camera. The metal was about two inches thick and slowly moving into a closed position.

"Quick, the door is closing!" Martin shouted, as he stepped through the closing aperture. He motioned for them to follow. "We need to get through quickly before it closes."

Beth stopped in front for a moment, unsure of the door.

"Go!" Scrappy yelled.

Beth stepped through cautiously. Freeman quickly followed, but he had to climb through the moving parts, leaving Drake and Scrappy in the chamber. Both the boys realized that the door was already too small for either of them, since they were the two largest members of the party.

Scrappy made a noble attempt to hold the door open by grabbing the cool white metal. He flexed his mighty arms but still the door closed further and further.

"Be safe!" Drake yelled to the people on the other side as the door sealed closed.

"This sucks!" Scrappy yelled. He began to beat on the door.

"Looks like you and I need to find another way, my brother," Drake said with a forced grin. He had just explained that splitting the party was not a good idea, and now they were separated.

The corridor was about ten feet wide. It was made out of an illuminated white substance that glowed enough to light the structure. It was roughly circular, like a tube, and it stretched far, far to the horizon to the right of them. To the left it ended with a low door about thirty feet away, and there was another door along the other side about the middle of the distance to the end. They could see no doors down the long end of the hall.

"So that's it?" Beth asked. Her eyes opened wide and in a near state of panic. She trusted Drake, and had asked him to champion her, and now he was gone. "Now it's just us, and our two best fighters are done? This is so stupid!"

Freeman agreed with her. This was a bad way to start. But he also realized that they should have gone in a different order through the door—biggest to smallest—and the smallest shouldn't have stopped and wasted time before she went through.

"It's not my wife's fault, Freeman," Martin said after he probed the shaman's mind.

"I suggest caution with your abilities, Martin," Freeman replied. "My mind is a dangerous thing, and I wouldn't want you to get hurt inside it."

The two men faced each other.

"Marty, it's okay," Beth interjected. She wasn't sure what was happening, but she knew fighting amongst them wasn't the best thing to do. "I could have gone faster. I was scared, and now they're still in there."

"We need to move," Martin announced. "The hallway's probably not safe. It may be watched or patrolled, and I say we should find Addraemyr."

"I do agree that we need to use caution in the corridor," Freeman replied. "I don't think rescuing the Keeper's our best option. It wasn't what Drake wanted, and he leads us."

"So you think the three of us should go fight our way through the tower and liberate it from an army of demonic forces?" Martin inquired sharply.

"If we have to, yes," Freeman responded. He turned away from Martin and began to search the wall around the door that fractured the party. "But I think there's another way."

"What do you mean?" Beth asked. Martin seemed to be puffing out his chest, trying to seem bigger then he already was.

"Janua!" Freeman commanded with his right hand over the sealed door. He felt the atoms of the door react to his command, and it began to slide open, opposite of how it closed.

"It's opening, what did you say?" Beth questioned excitedly.

"Janua is Latin for door, entry, or beginning," Freeman answered. "It comes from Janus the god of beginnings and doors, and it's why the opening month of our year is called January."

The door slowly opened wider and wider. Scrappy came into view, but he stood in front of the door by himself. Beth was worried about what happened to Drake. Then as the door opened further they could see Drake's feet on Scrappy's shoulders.

"Whatever you did's workin'!" Scrappy called out to Drake above him.

"Great," Drake answered. "Now put me down."

Scrappy bent at the knee and lowered Drake enough that

he could jump the rest of the way. They quickly grabbed their gear and darted through the open door. The red light began to flash again, and the door began to close.

Martin quickly approached Drake and hugged him.

"I'm glad you're safe and that we're all back together," Martin stated. Freeman rolled his eyes.

Drake and Scrappy finished putting all their equipment back on and they surveyed the long hallway.

"Now which way?" Scrappy asked.

"Everyone seems to think we're near the bottom of the tower, so I think we need to go up," Drake explained.

"If we're in a tower," Beth asked the obvious question with a hand gesture down the long corridor, "how come the hallway goes out that way instead of up and down?"

Martin, Scrappy, and Freeman all shook their heads or shrugged. Drake alone pondered that observation.

"Maybe the space in here isn't relevant," Martin attempted to answer the question. "I mean, the tower was wide, so the circumference was pretty big. But maybe inside it everything's smaller, so it seems farther to the end of the hall, but somewhere along the way we'll find stairs or an elevator and up we go."

"Interesting idea, Martin," Drake added. "There are some corollaries of scientific theory that suggest size is mostly relative. But I think what is happening here can easily be explained by thinking inside the box, or tube in this case."

"What do you mean?" Scrappy asked. He was still concerned about being shrunken down into a smaller version of himself.

"I'm talking about gravity," Drake explained. "Inside the tower is something like a centrifuge creating its own gravity. So instead of it being up and down in here, it's left to right. It's something that scientists have discussed using in space stations or deep space ships to simulate gravity."

"Oh," Beth replied. "I guess that explains it."

"Let's check these two doors before we head down the long hall," Scrappy said. Everyone agreed and they began to walk down the corridor cautiously. Martin went first, followed by Scrappy, then Drake and Beth nearly side by side, and Freeman brought up the rear.

"Is there anything you don't know?" Beth asked Drake quietly. She flipped some hair up out of her face to see him better. Drake immediately thought of things he didn't know, and most of them centered on interactions with girls. Beth smiled at Drake and he began to blush.

Freeman, ever cautious and ever observant, took notice of how Beth acted around Drake and decided he'd have to talk to his young leader about it later.

The door halfway to the end of the hall opened into another large oval chamber. It was empty. It was bright white and made of stone, or a stone like substance. Drake decided that it seemed almost antiseptic because it was so clean and white.

They turned and walked the rest of the way down the hallway. Martin and Scrappy peered into the room without crossing the threshold of the doorway. The room was identical to the other two they had seen, except this one had occupants. In the middle of the room a detachment of demon soldiers sat on the hard floor. Scrappy immediately reached for his machetes and Martin grabbed his shoulder and tried to pull him back. He had no hope to stop the enraged barbarian, so he took matters into his own hand, and stuck the arrow through the door. The same red light began to strobe, and the door began to slide shut. In the middle of the room the demons jumped to action when they saw the red light start to flash.

Eight demon soldiers began to run for the slowly closing door.

"Don't go in there Scrappy, you'll get stuck in there," Martin advised. "The door's closing."

Scrappy backed up, contemplating his jump into the room of demons and the glorious fight he'd have inside it. But he knew he had told Drake that he'd see him through to the end and he couldn't do something that would jeopardize that promise. Martin turned to smile at Scrappy, to tell him that it was for the best not to go in the room, when two serrated claws of a Krangathian demon jutted through the closing door and sliced back across Martin's left arm. Blood splattered along the glowing white corridor as Martin fell to the floor with a thud. Beth screamed, and Drake rushed up to assist Scrappy. Freeman quickly stooped and dragged Martin away from the thrashing claws.

The demon pushed its upper torso through the closing door. All four of its deadly arms were through when the door began to crush into its thick abdominal exoskeleton.

Freeman pulled an herb from his medicine bag and began to chant over the deep gashes on Martin's arm. He pressed the green leaf into the wound and held pressure on it. Beth moved over to check on Martin.

"Oh my God Marty, you're bleeding!" Beth shouted and felt like she might pass out. The white hallway began to grow dark and she felt it spinning around her.

"Sit down, Beth!" Freeman ordered. "Before you fall."

The demon looked around with its reptilian head. Its big black eyes seemed to focus on both boys in front of it at the same time.

"Scrap!" Drake shouted. "The neck!"

"My name is Kaagerk, spawn of Krangath!" it bellowed in a guttural voice.

Drake advanced with the blue-fire of Hikari in his right hand, the staff in his left. Kaagerk turned all of its attention toward Drake. Its four clawed arms lashed out at him and Drake fought them off with both staff and sword.

Scrappy fell upon the trapped demon like an agent of death. Both machetes hit the long tortoise-like neck simultaneously about four inches apart. The result was spurting black ichor pumping out of its severed neck, and the bony head thudding on the floor next to a slice of its neck. Scrappy dipped his finger into the ichor and wiped a broad stroke of demon blood under each of his eyes like war paint.

"My first kill," Scrappy announced with a happy grin.

"There'll be more, trust me," Drake replied with a grim smile. He turned to look at Martin and saw Freeman tending to him. "How's my brother?"

"I stopped the spread of any venom or poison, but the wounds are deep," Freeman replied. "I can't stop the bleeding."

Drake turned and looked at his burning blade. He knew how to stop the bleeding, but it was going to hurt a lot.

"Martin!" Drake exclaimed. "Martin, I need you to focus on Beth, look at her, don't take your eyes off Beth."

"Ooh..kkk..ay," Martin stammered.

Drake laid the burning blade of Hikari in the blood and torn flesh of Martin's arm. Martin screamed as the fire burned and seared his flesh. Just as quickly it was done. The bleeding had stopped and the wounds were cauterized.

"Get them up," Drake said to Freeman and Scrappy. "We need to move and I don't know how long that door is going to stay blocked like that."

Freeman and Scrappy helped the other two up and began to aide them in walking the other way down the corridor. Along the way they passed the door on the left and then the closed door to the chamber they started in. Behind them the dead body of the demon in the door was beginning to move. Drake was not sure if that was because the door was still crushing the body, or if the other demons inside the room were trying to dislodge it.

"Quickly, quickly," Drake said as he moved in front of the others. "I don't know how long that's gonna keep them out, and I don't wanna wait around and find out."

Seconds turned into minutes, and minutes turned into what seemed like hours as they moved briskly down the hallway. Finally they came to more doors along both walls, and the corridor itself opened up into a larger chamber. Drake slowed them down cautiously as they approached any possible new dangers.

Beth and Martin had both been walking without assistance for a while by then, so Freeman and Scrappy moved up and helped Drake as they approached the first door along the right side of the corridor. Inside the room, they saw a green field full of wildflowers under a blue cloudless sky. The aroma of the pollen and the fragrance of the flowers poured out of the room.

"Is that home?" Scrappy asked.

They looked at the scene before them. Suddenly a herd of small greenish-blue lizards ran through the grass. The lizards were running on two and four legs. They were capable of both and it just depended on how high up each wanted its head, or so it seemed. Their heads were large for the size of their bodies, roughly the size of a medium dog, but their heads kept drawing the attention of the spectators. The lizards had what appeared to be beaks, a thick bony plate behind their small eyes, and a series of colorful frills around their necks. They ran like they were afraid.

"Those are archaeoceratops, from the Early Cretaceous period, they're herbivores," Drake announced, "but I don't think we want to see what's chasing them."

Drake stuck the end of an arrow into the door and it began to flash before starting to slowly close.

"Those were dinosaurs," Scrappy said. "Those were real dinosaurs! How's that possible?"

"Clearly, the Tower of Dreams does open up to lots of different realities like you said, Drake," Freeman remarked.

"We need to be even more cautious than I thought," Drake contemplated. "If these are doorways into the past, present, and future, then we don't want to do anything that will alter the past and change the future, or present. Like if we accidently killed one of those little dinosaurs it might have changed history to the point that humans never appeared and we would just cease to exist."

"Do you think we would cease to exist, or do you think we would still be here, since we are outside the time continuity?" Freeman asked.

"Good point," Drake replied.

"Hey geeky boys," Scrappy interrupted. "How about we

438

keep on moving and talk about that brainiac stuff later when we're not being hunted by demons and dinosaurs."

They passed by many doors after that, doors that were open and unopened, and they found that most of them had a touch sensitive pad on the left hand side that would open the door. It made them wonder if the original door they struggled with had one and they just failed to notice it, but none of them had any desire to go back and check. The worlds they saw were snippets of history, the future, what could only be described as fantasy or fantastical. Villages and cities—from primitive to futuristic, unicorns and great winged beasts, and whole worlds with coloration that was so different from their own, and they all were accessible from within the tower.

"We could explore lots of places from here," Drake mentioned as they walked. "Provided we could make it back out of each room."

Freeman and Martin nodded in agreement. Martin had slowly regained some of his strength as the herbs and magic from Freeman's medicine bag had begun to work on his wounded arm.

They made their way to the beginning of another wide chamber. Freeman held them up at the threshold of the door.

"There's something at the far end of this chamber, guarding that door," Freeman whispered. Scrappy squinted and couldn't see anything. Drake and Martin nodded, and Beth stepped out and looked, before quickly moving back against the wall.

"Demons," Beth announced quietly. "Four of them, two of the bug ones, and two of the jackals. And the door is different, it's like swirling lights."

Drake and Freeman looked at each other. Scrappy shrugged. Martin took the thirty-aught-six and leveled the scope toward the far end of the room. He nodded.

"You could see all of that, Beth?" Freeman asked.

"Yeah, you guys can't?" Beth replied. They all shook

their heads.

"She's right," Martin added, as he lowered the rifle.

"So here's our problem," Freeman explained, "we have demons ahead of us, across a large open space with no cover. Any ideas, gentlemen, or lady?"

"Fight 'em," Scrappy replied.

Beth and Martin shook their heads.

"Well," Drake responded, "the challenge isn't the distance. It's the lack of cover. They're also guarding the way we have to go. So I think the greatest concern of an attack on them is that once they see us coming, one or more of them would slip through the doorway and go to warn the others still ahead of us. We're a formidable force, but we're only five, and five against an army isn't good odds, no matter how formidable we are."

"That's what we'd do in the military," Martin remarked. "Someone's gotta spread the word, and let the rest of them know."

"Can you hit them with the rifle if they head for the door?" Drake asked Martin.

"Yeah," Martin replied. "Even with a bum arm. I just need to get a bit closer to be a hundred percent sure."

"Okay, this is the plan," Drake stated, as he looked at each of them in turn, "Scrappy and I will run forward to engage them, and hopefully draw them to us. Freeman, any of your mojo support would be appreciated, but stay close to Beth. Beth, use the twenty-two to protect Freeman and Martin, but be careful where you shoot since we'll be out in front too. And Martin, as soon as you think you're in range, scope them out and drop any of them heading for the door."

"Let's do it," Scrappy remarked eagerly. Everyone nodded in agreement. They all understood the plan and their individual parts inside it.

They began to slowly make their way into the long chamber, right down the middle of the white floor. The ceiling was high and arched. Drake had been observing it since they arrived and he finally concluded that the architecture a weird mash-up of Gothic with its vaulted ceilings, arches, and stone work, and futuristic modern with all the illuminated white walls and touchpad doors. They saw no signs of anyone else in the great room as they advanced.

About halfway across the stone floor, Martin dropped to one knee and raised the rifle up, using the scope to sight his target. He raised his right hand to signal that he was ready. Beth and Freeman moved a little closer and stayed wide to the right of Martin's line of sight. Drake looked at Scrappy and nodded, and then he raised Hikari in a salute to his brother.

The two boys smiled at each other, raised their blades, and began to run forward to battle. Scrappy cried out a bestial call of war, and the demons jumped up at his challenge.

The Krangathian demons immediately began to run to engage their attackers. The jackal demons waited, like they were talking, before one rose and moved away from the door they guarded toward the oncoming attackers but then stopped to wait. The fourth demon turned to go into the doorway. The thirty-aught-six sounded with a loud bam. The bullet entered the left side of the jackal head and the right side splattered out brain and ichor. The demon fell to the floor.

The remaining jackal turned and saw its comrade on the ground, dead. It knew its orders, to guard the door, but also to send word of any attack.

While the jackal demon debated its course of action, Drake and Scrappy clashed with the Krangathians. The demon standing before Scrappy slashed and then pulled back its four long arms, waiting to finish the human when he lunged into its range. Scrappy smiled and held the broken-tipped machete in his left hand low in front of him, his other machete he held back above his right shoulder. He paced to the right, making the bug turn and widen its stance. He continued to slowly pace, and the demon pivoted on its right three-toed foot, widening its stance. The demon flashed its four clawed arms in a sudden half-hearted lunge to try and draw its attacker inside the four claws that could become a cutting machine if it could get Scrappy inside its grasp. But the barbarian kept pacing around the demon and it finally had to lift its right foot to turn, and when it did, the fury of the barbarian was unleashed upon it. Scrappy hacked at every joint between the exoskeleton plates he could reach. Its two left arms fell to the floor at the elbow, but its right arms swung wildly for the head of Scrappy. The serrated claw of the upper arm hit the machete in his right hand. Beth saw the lower claw moving for Scrappy's waist and prepared to shoot the revolver. With a burst of speed, the machete in his left hand parried the claw aimed for his torso. He smiled and then yelled. This was what he was made for. This was his calling in life. The demon pulled back both arms to attack one more time, its body leaking vast amounts of ichor from its wounded joints and severed arms. Scrappy looked up at the monstrosity before him and with a grin he pulled the blades of his machetes upward and outward, crossing at the thin neck of the demon. Its head flew backward and its broken body collapsed.

On the other side, Drake engaged the remaining Krangathian. He held Hikari high, and the Staff of Orkan low in his left hand. Both weapons burned with a low blue flame.

"This is for the bathroom, demon!" Drake shouted as he attacked. The demon pulled back its upper arms while its lower ones fended him off. Without the constraints of the small size of the bathroom, Drake was able to use Hikari to his advantage. The two arms that fended him off flew away with a trail of black ichor following their arc as Drake slashed through his adversary. Electricity surged in the staff and the demon's upper arms spasmed from the lightning that shot out when it attempted to cut down Drake from above. Drake spun to his left and sliced Hikari through the chitinous exoskeleton in one smooth stroke. The upper body of the demon slid down upon the lower body, and ichor pumped from its severed core. Drake realized that his strength was augmented here, like it had been in Gehenna, just not to the same degree.

The remaining demon turned to run, to warn the others of the attack, and Martin pulled the trigger. The skull of the demon fractured open as ichor and brain splattered out. It fell where it stood.

Drake wiped Hikari on his pants and sheathed the blade. He approached Scrappy and clasped his right forearm to Scrappy's in the handshake they had made their own.

"Today," Drake said, "we are truly brothers of battle."

Scrappy tipped his head back and roared. He was home.

They pulled the dead jackal demon away from the door so they could better examine the entryway. It was an odd yet fascinating thing. Inside the doorway a spiral of pulsating energy spun. It cycled through the colors of the rainbow. Around the doorway, an archaic or alien language was written. Both Freeman and Drake looked long and hard at the glyphs but neither could recognize them.

"I don't think I wanna go through that," Beth stated.

"The demons have gone through it," Scrappy added. "If they can do it, I can."

When the pulsating color changed from violet to red, beginning the color spectrum again, the lettering around the door shifted and changed.

"That's cuneiform!" Drake exclaimed. He touched the inscription that was carved into the hardware around the door. He wasn't sure how he could feel a carved inscription that just a moment before was an alien language. It was like it was generated with a three-dimensional emulator.

"Can you read it?" Martin asked. Drake began to study it. As he slowly worked his way up the left side of the door, the color inside the doorway cycled again, from violet to red. The language shifted again. This time it was a series of pictoglyphs.

"Hieroglyphics," Drake announced, as he felt their textured relief in the door frame. It fascinated him that each new language was carved into the doorway.

"Can you read that one?" Martin asked. Drake began to decipher the words to the best of his knowledge.

"It says something about each must enter alone and find what you most need, or seek," Drake explained. "Or that could also be find your doom."

"I didn't need to hear that," Scrappy remarked.

The color changed from violet to red, and the language shifted again, to a language Drake couldn't identify.

"It looks Arabic," Drake stated. "But I don't think it is, because the characters are too squared off."

They sat and watched the language shift through three more scripts that none of them recognized. Then finally, as it shifted from violet to red one more time, it was carved in English, although the syntax was off. Drake pulled out his notebook and quickly wrote it down. Above the door it stated: *Challenge of the Spirit*. Along the right side of the door it stated: *The Individual Must Enter and Through Their Needs They Must Pass*. And down the left side of the door it stated: *Desires Are Not Sought and May Lead to Their Doom*.

"What does that mean?" Beth asked.

"I think it means we walk through thinking of what we need," Martin answered.

"And not what you desire," Scrappy added. "Cause that would be bad."

"That does seem to be what it says," Freeman agreed. The color in the doorway shifted from violet to red and the language changed to another alien script. Drake was excited and wrote hurriedly in his spiral notebook. "Why are you grinning?"

"Well," Drake said. "It's like the Rosetta Stone. If I'm here long enough, I can write down each of these languages and I already have the English translation so I would have a key to decipher more of the languages, if we encounter them again."

"Okay," Martin said. "Since we are supposed to enter individually, while we wait for Professor Drake, who wants to go first?"

"I'll go," Scrappy announced. "I'm not afraid and I know what I need too. I need a sweet weapon like Drake's got instead of just these machetes."

"I'll go after Scrap," Drake said, as he wrote down the next set of characters.

"What do you need?" Scrappy asked.

"Don't know," Drake answered. "Maybe some answers, or a map."

"I'll follow Drake," Freeman volunteered. "And I need to know more about my magic here, what I can or cannot do. This place is very alive with magic, I can feel it, I just don't know what I can do with it."

"I think you should go after Freeman," Martin said to Beth. "And I'll go after you to make sure you're safe."

"And what do you need?" Freeman asked.

"I think I need to know about Wally," Martin answered.

"Isn't that more of a desire?" Drake questioned.

"No," Martin replied. "It's more of a burning need I've had since he died, I need to know why. And I'm not gonna let an opportunity like this pass me by without trying."

"What about you, Beth?" Freeman inquired.

"I don't know what I need," Beth answered. "Except maybe I need to know if we're gonna make it home safe."

They waited about twenty more minutes until the languages cycled back to English and Drake had recorded each of the inscriptions. Martin looked at his watch. It was four twenty-one in the morning, and he thought they should all be sleeping. Scrappy stood in front of the doorway. He decided he'd enter when the color was indigo, the closest it got to black.

"Wish me luck," Scrappy said. And then he stepped into the swirling energy like he was walking into a wall of water. It formed around him and he stepped completely through. "It tickles."

Scrappy was gone. Drake waited for his turn. He decided to enter when the color was blue. Drake looked back and smiled a worried look at them. Then he stepped in as the color shifted to blue, and then he was gone. Freeman waited until the color shifted back to red and quickly stepped through and was gone.

Beth and Martin remained.

"I'm scared Martin," Beth stated. "I don't want to go in there alone. Hold my hand."

Martin tipped his head sideways and thought, that shouldn't be against the rules, as long as she went in front of him, one at a time.

"Okay," Martin replied. He grabbed her left hand in his right. And Beth stepped into the door, the color was green, Martin would've preferred to wait until it was yellow again— Wally's favorite color. But he had no choice and stepped in to the color as it began to shift to blue. Holding hands they disappeared.

Glossary of names, locations, phrases, and items

Abyss. (ăh·bĭs) Legends exist of a netherworld made of 666 interlocked layers that get progressively darker and more sinister as you descend into what appears to be a bottomless pit of festering evil. There may actually be more or less than 666 layers, since the number was attached by religious philosophers using the Biblical number of the beast as their reference. Few have ever travelled into the Abyss and returned to tell the tale. This netherworld is a huge place inhabited by many insidious creatures, daemons, dark or disgraced gods, demons, devils, and a multitude of damned souls. Great demon armies reside here waiting for their call to battle. In classic mythology, the Abyss was referenced as the primal chaos before creation, or a bottomless infernal region.

Acheron. (æk·əh·rən) A wasteland of a netherworld, it has many realms within it, but little is accomplished because of the nature of those that reside there. The prime belief in Acheron is 'Law above Evil,' which is a conundrum for most of its residents. The upper lands are ragged iron plains, buffeted by silica sands, and very inhospitable for human life.

Denizens of the wastes are primarily of goblinoid, draconian, orcish, or demonic races, and damned spirits from other planes. The Pit of Despair exists within Acheron. In classic Greek mythology, Acheron was a river in Hades, but over time became more synonymous with infernal regions, the underworld, or Hell.

Addraemyr. (ăd·rā·mir) Keeper of the Tower of Dreams, and Lord of Dreams, he was of the guizor caste of the huisum race that was created by the Elder gods to serve as guardians of the mythic Towers of Ominous Power. Addraemyr possessed a precognitive ability that allowed him to see the future. The huisum were made to be neutral observers, scientists, chroniclers, and collectors of life in all its forms. Many gods, daemons, and other greater powers have sought to control them over the eons, but the huisum have managed to remain neutral.

Adramelech. (ăd·rā·mĕl·ək) He was an Assyrian sun god, cast into the netherworlds with the arrival of the Judeo-Christian monotheism. This was an easy transition for the barbarous god who favored wealth and trinkets of power. In art many different depictions exist of him, he has been described as humanoid with the hind of an ass and the tail of a peacock, or as a well defined man with an inferno raging around his skeletal head.

Aesma. (æ·smă) He was a daevas in the service of Countess Furfur. He was a demon with a terrifying reputation, the demon of wrath and fury, of the bloody mace, and of slaughter during war. He was incorporated into the Zoroastrian pantheon from the earlier prehistoric Indo-Iranian period of human development. His true form was documented in ancient texts from the early 5th-6th century, but was lost during the later Islamic expansion into Persia. *See Daevas.*

Aeon. (æ·än) He was the god who was the personification of time, from the Greek pantheon of mythology. He was also known as Khronos, not to be confused with the Titan Cronus. He was elusive in his allegiance during start of the

Covenant War, often operating in his own best interest. In art he was depicted as an old wise man with a long, gray beard bearing a long handled scythe. Images of him form the root of the "Father Time" myth.

Agápe. (ăh·găp·ā) One of four independent words used to define variations of love used by the ancient Greeks. It is a selfless love, a love that was passionately committed to the well-being of others. The term predates the old gods, and is part of the language used by the huisum, who measure the value of a person by the agápe in their heart.

Amun. (ăh·mən) He was the god of creation, the wind, and knowledge, from the Egyptian pantheon of mythology. He created himself, represented the essential and hidden knowledge, and was the champion of the poor. Later he became known as Amun-Ra and assumed the titles of sun god, and the Lord of the Sky. He took a strong liking to Drake Fraser because of his pursuit of knowledge. In art he was depicted as a tall, slightly blue-skinned man who wore an intricate turban adorned with two massive Nile Goose feathers.

Brigid. (bri·jəd) She was the Celtic goddess of the sacred flame and all things perceived to be of relatively high dimensions such as high-rising flames, highlands, hill-forts and upland areas; and of activities and states conceived as psychologically lofty and elevated, such as wisdom, excellence, perfection, high intelligence, poetic eloquence, craftsmanship—especially blacksmithing, healing ability, druidic knowledge and skill in warfare. Today, whether seen as goddess or saint, she is still largely associated with the home and hearth and continues to be a favorite of both polytheists and Catholics. She was the daughter of Dagda and one of the Tuatha Dé Danann, her feast day was Imbolc, on February first, which became St. Brigid's Day in the Catholic Church, during which they celebrate St. Brigid of Kildare. Known by a variety of derivative names, including Brigantia in what would become Britain. In art she is depicted as a statuesque woman with auburn to red hair, and possessing an eternal flame either in her hands or hovering above her head.

Carpe Diem. (kär·pĕ dē·ĕm) [Latin] English translation—seize the day.

Chalat'. (chă·lăwt) They were the indigenous people of the western Olympic Peninsula who lived in the shadow of Mt. Olympus. They resided in the river valleys carved from the glacial runoff from the mountain. This is the ancient name of the people of the Hoh Rainforest, also known as the Hoh Indians.

Chehalis. (shə·hā·lĭs) They were the indigenous people to the south of the Olympic peninsula who lived in the Chehalis river valley. The river empties into Grays Harbor and the Pacific Ocean. The Chehalis were the trading partners with the Olympic Peninsula people and the Cowlitz and Chinook to the south.

Code. (kōd) The virtues and rules required of knights to remain in the order in which they serve. Each order of knights had a unique code, though many borrowed the grander concepts of chivalry into their scripture.

Council of Olympus. (koun·səl ŏv ō·lĭm·pŭs) The gathered council of the gods, daemons, spirits, and other entities who did not all support the Covenant of Reason, but did still want humanity to survive. They were a party to the signing of the Covenant, and are thereby bound to its tenets. They were instrumental in the initial formation of the Brotherhood of Olympus in the Middle Ages, and now see the Brotherhood as their champions on Earth.

Council of Retribution. (koun·səl ŏv rĕt·rə·byū·shən) The gathered council of the gods, daemons, devils, and other entities who sought to end the Covenant of Reason and gain dominion over the Earth and all of humanity. They were a party to the signing of the Covenant, and have begun to strike against those who would hold them in check. They orchestrated the accident that killed Walter Reuss and listed the Brotherhood of Olympus as their enemy.

Covenant of Reason. (kŭv·ə·nənt ŏv rē·zən) This

agreement was signed by the greater powers that once influenced the day-to-day lives of mankind that banned them from contact or further intrusion into the lives of men. It was agreed to by the benevolent powers as being necessary to keep the benign powers from running havoc over the mortal world, the benign powers viewed it as banishment but did agree to the terms, even though it cost all of them their ability to be directly involved in the development of humanity. Many banished individuals have plotted for centuries how to circumvent the agreement and once again enter the mortal world. Some of the benevolent had prophesized that a war over the Covenant loomed somewhere close by on the horizon of time.

Daemon. (dæ·mən) These were evil beings of greater power and influence over the lesser demons and devils of various netherworlds. Often seen as being akin to gods or demigods within netherworld pantheons, many were the offspring of gods or goddesses and lesser demons or devils. They often ruled over dominions or keeps within these netherworlds.

Daevas. (dæ·vəs) Prehistoric Persian name for seven demonic entities of vileness and destruction, even among gods the daevas were thought to be dangerous and wicked. They have been known to kill minor gods in the past, and have historically been tied to the struggles of humanity. It was speculated that a god owning their allegiance would have powerful pieces to move on the board game of the Covenant War.

Dagda. (dăg·də) Was the Celtic high king of the Tuatha Dé Danann whose name has been translated roughly to mean the 'good god.' His reign over the lands ended after the invasion of the British Isles by the Gaels (the Irish). Legends exist that Dagda died of wounds during the third battle of Magh Tuiredh, afterwards the Tuatha Dé Danann left the lands to the Gaels and departed for the Otherworld through the sídhe, the earthen mounds that dot the Irish landscape. He was the father of Brigid. In art he has been depicted as a handsome figure of immense power, armed with a magic club and associated with a cauldron. The club was supposed to be able to kill nine men with one blow; but with the handle he could return the slain to life. The cauldron was known as the Undry and was said to be bottomless, from which no man left unsatisfied.

Demon. (dē·mən) Powerful creatures often referred to as entities, who originate from many of the netherworlds of the outer planes. They form vast armies and legions in the service of daemons, greater devils, and dark gods. Singly they have been documented to torment or even possess humans throughout much of recorded history. Demons have great contempt for humanity and its life force and ability to love. Their physical appearance ranges from beautiful to the grotesque, usually an odd combination of animal parts that maximize the horrific concept or the sheer destructive brutality of the creature.

Deshnak. (dəsh·năk) Was a monstrous daemon of barbaric proportions that was known as the Despoiler because of his history of slaughtering entire villages, cities, and some complete counties of humans. He had no regard for the lives of humans, killed other daemons, and legends depict him single-handedly destroying an entire demonic legion to get to a daemon lord who had wronged him. He was a member of the group that destroyed the Brotherhood of Olympus in 1469, and laid siege and conquered the Tower of Dreams in 1980.

Doquebatl. (dōk·ă·băt'l) He was the greater spirit of change to the Klallam people. This was another name of K'wati. *See K'wati.*

Einsichtmeister. (īnz·ĭçht·mīs·tĕr) [German] English translation—knowledge master. One of the masters of the Brotherhood of Olympus who served as a deputy to the High Master of the order, typically either the knowledge or strategy master served as the leader of the Brotherhood and reported directly to the High Master. However, during the 1460s, the High Master of the Teutonic knights was also a member of the Brotherhood himself. The knowledge master was responsible for knowing as much as possible about as many things as possible, to be a resource for the Brotherhood in making timely decisions. The last recorded Einsichtmeister was Berchtold von Wensing, who died in 1469, at the Battle of Mohrungren Fields.

Elder god. (ĕl·dər găwd) Deities of primal forces, who had dominion over Earth and many other realms before the pantheons of gods that rose to prominence during the early days of human civilization, but they have since been nearly wiped from all history and memory. They constructed many wondrous things, including the Tower of Dreams, before they disappeared.

Eldritch magic. (ĕl·drĭch măj·ĭk) Magic from an archaic source, often synonymous with wizardry, that could also be described as being eerie, or weird in nature. One plausible origin of the root word being from the Middle English word, *elfriche*, which meant elf kingdom or fairyland; usually a magic or magical item of greater power.

Éros. (ĕr· ōs) One of four independent words used to define variations of love used by the ancient Greeks. It is romantic, physical, or sexual love.

Ethereal Plane. (ē·thər·ē·əl plān) A realm or plane of existence that connects many other realms together, it borders many of the known planes and some of the undocumented planes. It is a dark, windswept land of blackish green vapor. Some mystics have claimed that humans could travel trough the ether to visit these other realms. It is the home of the Mordgeists, and a place where many spirits gather with unfinished business before moving on to another plane of existence.

Ganesha. (gə·nā·shə) He was the god of wisdom, prophecy, and prudence, remover of obstacles, from the Hindu pantheon of mythology. He was also known as the Lord of Beginnings and would be invoked before a task began. He was a vocal proponent of the Brotherhood of Olympus. In art he was depicted as a short, pot-bellied,

yellow-skinned man with an elephant head that had a broken
right tusk. He had four arms, one holding a shell, another
holding a chakra, another holding a mace, and the final one
holding a water lily.

Gehenna. (gĭ·hen·uh) It is a fiery and ice-filled series of
realms beyond the ethereal plane, that is also a netherworld.
In some mythology, this is a place of torment for lost souls
after death. It lies beyond the ethereal plane of existence and
is home to many dark citadels of daemonic powers. One
such place is the Grand Library of Gehenna, located on the
side of an ever-erupting volcano, said to hold infinite
knowledge that may rival the Tower of Knowledge, because
of the aggressive acquisitions of the Librarian throughout
history.

Guizor. (gī·zôr) The ruling caste of the huisum race, few
of them still exist, and all of them are revered for their
wisdom. *See Ranthalion or Addraemyr.*

Hecate. (hĕk·ā'tē) She was the goddess of fertility, later
associated with Persephone as queen of Hades, from the
Greek pantheon of mythology. She was also known as a
goddess of the underworld, magic, witchcraft, necromancy,
crossroads, gates, and doorways. In art she was depicted as
three women—a young maid, a statuesque matron, and an
old crone.

Hellhound. (hĕl·hound) A monstrous canine-like
creature indigenous to many netherworlds, it was widely
believed that they originated within Hell itself before
spreading out into the Abyss and other planes. They were
ferocious hunters, were more intelligent than most animals,
and were devoutly loyal to their master. They were often
used in armies as shock troops, or to attack the flanks of
slower adversary. They tended to be cunning, crave blood
and fresh meat, and have even been known to turn on each
other if one of them was wounded.

Hephaestus. (hĭ·fĕs·təs) He was the god of fire,
metalworking, stone masonry, forges, the art of sculpture, and
blacksmiths from the Greek pantheon of mythology. He

crafted nearly all of the magic weapons within Greek myth and legend, employed cyclopean titans within his forges, and was regarded as a friend of humanity. In art he was often depicted as having a hunched back, twisted feet and legs, or other deformities. He was almost always shown with a hammer, anvil, or near fire.

Hikari. (hǐ·kär·ē) [Japanese] English translation—light. The name given to the sword crafted by Masao Norishige for Henry Reuss, who in turn was going to gift it to his son Walter, before finally giving it to his grandson Drake Fraser. The sword was of a rare tsurugi ōdachi design, with a matsukawa-hada blade. [The name is pressed into the steel of the blade: 光]

Hochmeister. (hôk·mīs·tĕr) [German] English translation—high master. The title of High Master was unique to the Teutonic Order, unlike the other two orders of Jerusalem founded crusader orders that simply used the Grand Master title. The High Master was like elected royalty, having complete authority over the operation of the order, and served a term for life. The High Master swore fealty to the order, and to the Pope—the one person who had power over the position. The High Master had many deputies, and he also took reports from the Master of the Livonian Brothers of the Sword, and the Master of the Brotherhood of Olympus. Heinrich Reuss von Plauen was the only High Master to own the title while still belonging to the smaller, covert Brotherhood. The High Master lost oversight of the Brotherhood of Olympus in 1469, by order of the Pope, when it was decreed to cease to exist.

Hoh Rainforest. (hō rein·fôr·ĭst) It is one of the largest temperate rainforests in the United States, located on the western side of the Olympic Peninsula. The trees of the forest are nearly all covered in long blankets of mosses and lichens. Some of the old growth trees, Sitka Spruce and Western Hemlock, grow as high as 312 feet, and 23 feet in diameter. It is also home of the Duncan Tree, the largest western red cedar in the world.

Hospitaller knights. (hŏs·pĭ·tăl·lər nīts) Also known as the Order of the Knights of Saint John, formed in Jerusalem in 1099. Originally a hospital organization, they became a military order escorting pilgrims to the Holy lands in their distinctive black mantles with a white cross emblazoned upon it. They rose to prominence over their peer Orders after the forced disbanding of the more successful Templar knights in 1312, and the Teutonic knight's focus on the Northern Crusades, the Hospitallers also stayed within the favor of the Pope. They are the only one of the three orders of crusaders that still exists today on their original charter. They are still involved in the affairs of the Vatican, and are rumored to operate as the secret military of the Pope. (*also known as the Knights of Malta*)

Huisum. (hu·ēs·əm) The gray skinned race of neutral observers created by the Elder gods who still serve their long lost creators through the technology of the Towers of Ominous Power. In art and legend they are often depicted as gray alien creatures with enlarged heads and almond shaped eyes.

Hurricane Ridge. (hûr·ĭ·kān rĭj) It is a mountainous area in the northern part of the Olympic National Park, accessible from Port Angeles. At an elevation of 5,200 feet, it was named for its intense gales and winds. From this location many of the mountains of the Olympic range are viewable, including Mount Olympus to the south.

Ichor. (ĭ·kôr) The blood of demons, or demonic creatures that is most often black in color and reeking of sulfur. Some ichor contains poisons or acids that will burn through whatever it is spilled upon. It has been used in some eldritch magic as a component in powerful spells. It does not tend to wash out of clothing.

Imbolc. (ĭm·bōlg) The midwinter feast of the ancient Celts held on what is now February first, and currently celebrated as St. Brigid's Day. It was a day of weather prognostication, and is a forerunner of the American Groundhog Day. It was also a day upon which families would seek the blessing of the goddess, and later the saint. One of four Celtic seasonal holidays, which also included Samhain, the predecessor of what would become modern day Halloween

Janus. (jā·nəs) He was the god of doorways, passages, gates, bridges, and all beginnings from the Roman pantheon of mythology. He was also known as a god of the past, present, and future. In art he was depicted with two faces, facing the opposite directions.

Joe E. Brown. (jō ē broun) American comedic film actor who made nearly sixty movies from 1928 to 1963, he was a gifted athlete who gave up a professional baseball career to be an entertainer. He was known for his large mouth and overly expressive face as a sight gag during his movies. He was an ardent supporter of Allied troops during World War II, and was one of two civilians to earn a Bronze Star for his service to the USO.

Kanzler. (kŏnz·lər) [German] English translation— chancellor. Chief officer or assistant of the High Master for the Teutonic knights. The chancellor took care of the keys and seals and was recording clerk of the chapter. Gregor von Rautenberg was the chancellor who pulled off the secretive Hochmeister Hoax of 1469-70, and acted as the Hochmeister following the decree of Heinrich Reuss von Plauen.

Krangath. (krăn·găth) He was a Daemon Lord of Lower Gehenna, and a great progenitor of demon warriors who served in the legions of many netherworld garrisons. His demon offspring, or spawnlings, stood over eight feet tall, were roughly insectoid in appearance, bipedal, with six appendages—the four arms ending in sharpened serrated claws, the body is covered by a thick exoskeleton, and their heads and necks were rather long reptilian looking. His spawn were created for one purpose, to be soldiers—to fight and kill for their masters.

Kildare. (kĭl·dâr) A small town in Eastern Ireland, some thirty miles from Dublin, that was the site tied to the transition of goddess Brigid to Saint Brigid. Saint Brigid's

Cathedral still stands near the site of the Holy well that had been tended by nuns for centuries after Brigid had become a saint. Also one of the surnames, Brigid would sometimes use when she visited Earth.

K'wati. (k·wăt·ē) He was the god-like spirit of change and enlightenment for many of the indigenous people of the Pacific Northwest mythologies. Known as the 'Changer,' he was the greater spirit who created mountains, rivers, and gifted the peoples of the region with the abilities they needed to survive. The Olympic Peninsula was under his domain, and he granted the establishment of the Council of Olympus to exist in its new location in the Pacific Northwest of North America. In art he was depicted as a wise man wearing cedar bark clothing lined with white fur, often seen with either a broad woven cedar hat, or eagle/thunderbird feathers woven into his hair. He was also known as Doquebatl by the Klallam.

Leprechaun. (lĕp·rĭ·kŏn) One of a race of elf-like creatures often referred to in Irish folklore and mythology. According to most sources, they were often slightly mischievous, protecting a hidden treasure, somehow connected to rainbows, and rumors persist that their use of magic often leaves lingering rainbows.

Lilac. (lī·lŏk) [Syringa vulgaris] It is a flowering plant common to much of the United States and in herbology it has been used for its powers of exorcism and protection. Lilac has been used to drive away evil where it has been planted or strewn. In New England, lilacs were originally planted to keep evil from the property.

Livonia. (lĭ·vō·nē·ə) During the Northern Crusades led by the Teutonic knights against the heathens of northern and eastern Europe, ancient Livonia was colonized by the Livonian Brothers of the Sword, later called the Livonian Order, and the name Livonia came to designate a much broader territory known as Terra Mariana on the eastern coasts of the Baltic Sea, in what is the present-day northern part of Latvia and southern part of Estonia. Its frontiers were the Gulf of Riga and the Gulf of Finland in the north-west, Lake Peipus and Russia to the east, and Lithuania to the south. The original Brotherhood of Olympus was created from a group of knights and laymen who belonged to what would become the Livonian Order, during their service in Transylvania in the 13th century.

Lucifer. (lū·sə·fər) An ancient name of Indo-European root, meaning 'morning star,' that has long been associated to the fallen angel who according to myth and legend presided over Hell. There was a feudal system in place amongst the netherworlds, with daemons, greater devils, dark gods and goddesses assuming titles of nobility—Baron, Countess, Duke, Prince, et al. There was never a king or queen of Hell, rather the highest ranking title was Crown Prince, and that was associated with Lucifer. He predated the Judeo-Christian monotheism, and was once a god of the morning light prior to written human history. Lucifer always possessed a darker side, and it was easy for him to assume the 'Satan' role in the early years of the religion. This title, gave him enormous credibility within the netherworlds and through his power-broking he was awarded the Crown Prince title and has possessed it ever since. In art he is often depicted as having goat features, being strikingly handsome, having large feathered wings sprouting from his back, and being capable of radiating a bright illuminating aura.

Masamune. (mă·să·mū·nə) Was widely recognized as Japan's greatest swordsmith, he created swords and daggers, known in Japanese as tachi and tantō respectively, in the *Soshu* tradition. No exact dates are known for his life and he has reached a legendary status amongst swordsmiths and collectors. It is generally agreed that he made most of his swords in the late 13th and early 14th centuries, 1288–1328. Some stories list his family name as Okazaki. He was believed to have worked in Sagami Province during the last part of the Kamakura Period (1288–1328), and it is thought that he was trained by swordsmiths from Bizen and Yamashiro provinces, such as Saburo Kunimune, and

Awataguchi Kunitsuna. His students were many, the ten greatest are known as the *Juttetsu* or "Ten Great Disciples of Masamune," among them was the legendary Saeki Norishige.

Matsukawa-hada. (măt·sū·kä·wə – hă·də) [Japanese] Pine tree bark pattern steel in the blade of sword, a technique mastered by the legendary Saeki Norishige.

Mojo. (mō·jō) A term used to reference magic, or mana, or the perception of good fortune. It originated from African shamanism, through what became Caribbean vodooism, before becoming part of American popular culture.

Mohrungen. (môh·rŏng·ən) Was an ancient Prussian town that changed hands during the Middle Ages, Germany, Prussia, Poland, and the Teutonic knights all ruled it at some point. It was the location that Heinrich Reuss von Plauen made his encampment, and was said to be where he died in 1470. It was known as the location where the original Brotherhood of Olympus made their last stand in 1469. It is now a Polish town known as Morąg.

Mordgeist. (môrd·gīst) They were inhabitants of many netherworlds; their origin was lost in antiquity, and their name literally means 'death spirit.' They have often been seen in locations where humans have recently died, or will soon die. They are harbingers of death. They have often worked for daemons, gods, or spirits with greater power or force, making them quite mercenary in their activities. In art they have been depicted as skeletal creatures, shrouded in gray or black robes and mists, with unnaturally long teeth and glowing red eyes.

Netherworld. (nə·thĕr·wûrld) A world lying beneath or below by definition, often thought of as planes of existence inhabited by the dead, demons, and devils. These worlds were typically ruled by deities who aspired to be more than they were, that were unhappy in their roles, or who took great pleasure in their roles as tormentors of dead humans.

Nu Kua. (nü kwă) She was the goddess of creation, from the ancient Chinese pantheon of mythology. She created mankind from the mud of the Earth. She was an ardent supporter of the Brotherhood of Olympus. In art she was depicted as remarkably beautiful woman with jet black hair, with a large, coiling body of a serpent below her waistline.

Ōdachi. (ō·dă·chē) [Japanese] A term used to describe a Great Sword. Any sword with a blade over three *shaku* was considered to be an Ōdachi. (A *shaku* was a unit of measurement approximately one foot in length)

Philia. (fĭl·ē·ă) One of four independent words used to define variations of love used by the ancient Greeks. It is the love between friends as close as siblings in strength and duration. Such as the love of brothers for each other, or a friendship where there is a strong bond existing between people who share common values, interests or activities.

Pictoglyphs. (pĭk·tō·glĭf) Writing using characters or images instead of letters to construct a message, such as Egyptian Hieroglyphics.

Pirates of Penzance. (pī·rĭts ŏv pĕn·zăns) Is a comic opera in two acts, with music by Arthur Sullivan and libretto by W. S. Gilbert. The opera's official premiere was in New York City on December 31, 1879, it is widely used in community theater and high school drama productions.

Poseidon. (pō·sīd·ən) He was the god of the sea, earthquakes, and horses from the Greek pantheon of mythology. He was the brother of Zeus and Hades, and was considered one of the most influential of gods during the era of Greek civilization, prior to the arrival of the Judeo-Christian monotheist movement. He, unlike many of his pantheon, always tried to stay connected to humanity and his list of demigod offspring was quite extensive.

Prussia. (prŭsh·ə) Was the territory that was situated at the southern end of the Baltic Sea, comprising lands that are now part of Russia, Lithuania, Poland, Germany, and Austria. Much of the Prussian Frontier was settled during the expansion of the Teutonic knights during the Northern Crusades. The House of Reuss originated in Prussia.

Plane. (plān) A level of existence or reality with finite, or near infinite borders, where laws of physics, energy, and time are mostly consistent, our contemporary Earth exists within one such plane. It has been speculated by many that alternate realities or divergent timelines may exist within the plethora of planes. Travelling between planes requires powerful magic, talismans, or established gates or portals. Some of these planes of note include, but are not limited to, the Ethereal, the Astral, Gehenna, Asgard, the Abyss, Gladsheim, and the Prime Material—where Earth as we know it exists.

Quatyl. (kwŏt·ĭl) He was the god of the night sky, and reaper of souls, a death god of an ancient Meso-American pantheon that pre-dated the Mayans. Because of his lesser god status, he had long sought to expand his death god position by being assimilated into the feudal hierarchy of the netherworlds. He was more daring or aggressive in his actions because he was always trying to make a name for himself among the other gods. He did not like daemons or devils who occupied titled positions within the hierarchy because he felt he was above them, and not below them. He fought Drake Fraser in single combat in the Grand Library of Gehenna. He appeared as a serpentine creature, with four arms, two large bat-like wings, with a distinctive reptilian head, and as a sky god he was capable of radiating a glowing aura.

Queets. (kwēts) They were the indigenous people of the western Olympic Peninsula who lived to the south of the Chalat', and the north of the Quinault. They were absorbed by the larger Quinault tribe after the 1855 Treaty of Olympia, and have since disappeared as a recognized tribe.

Quileute. (kwĭl·ē·yūt) They were the indigenous people of the western Olympic Peninsula who lived to the north of the Chalat', and the south of the Makah. Their language was not of the Salish family; instead it was of the same origin as the Chimakum. According to their tradition, K'wati transformed wolves to make the first of the Quileute.

Quinault. (kwĭn·ălt) They were the indigenous people of the western Olympic Peninsula who lived to the south of the Queets, and the north of the Chehalis. They were given one of the larger reservations in Washington as a result of 1856 Quinault Treaty, though they have not thrived economically. George and Freeman Kalama were from the Quinault Tribe.

Ranthalion. (răn·thăl·yən)   Keeper of the Tower of Infinity, and Lord of the Garrison of Infinity, he was of the guizor caste of the huisum race that was created by the Elder gods to serve as guardians of the mythic Towers of Ominous Power. The huisum were made to be neutral observers, scientists, chroniclers, and collectors of life in all its forms. Many gods, daemons, and other greater powers have sought to control them over the eons, but the huisum have managed to remain neutral.

Raven. (rā·vən) He was the god-like spirit of creation and trickery for many of the indigenous people of the Pacific Northwest mythologies.   Known as the 'Trickster,' he was the greater spirit who dropped the stone as he flew that formed the land humans later inhabited. He was always seen as playing an angle or attempting to outsmart mankind for his own benefit. In art he was depicted as a black bird, or as a spry man with black hair and mismatched clothing, often containing baubles or colorful feathers.

Rose. (rōz) [Rosa 'Mister Lincoln'] It is a flowering plant common to much of the United States and in herbology it has been used for its powers of luck, protection, healing, love, love divination, and psychic powers.   Roses and the wood of the plant itself have been used to as protection when they are carried.

Saeki Norishige. (sā·kē   nôr·ĭsh·ĕg·ē)   He was a swordmaster who hailed from Etchu province of Japan, and was a student of the legendary Masamune.   He was the master of the art of Matsukawa-hada, his skills were passed down through his family. Masao Norishige, who worked as a blacksmith in the Aberdeen, Washington area during the first half of the 20th century was his descendent, and through Masao's skill the sword Hikari was created.

Saurva. (sôr·və) He was a daevas in the service of Countess Furfur.   He was a demon with a terrifying reputation, the demon of pestilence, rape, genocide, and deformity. He was incorporated into the Zoroastrian pantheon from the earlier prehistoric Indo-Iranian period of human development. His true form was documented in ancient texts from the early 5th-6th century, but was lost during the later Islamic expansion into Persia. *See Daevas.*

Salish. (sā·lĭsh) Family of indigenous languages that were interwoven along the coastal regions of what is now British Columbia and Washington, primary amongst these was the Skagit-Nisqually or Lushootseed. Many Salish terms were incorporated into the Chinook Jargon, which consists of terms and words from the languages of all the trading partners, used amongst indigenous people, the French, the British, and the Americans. A number of these words are still in use in the region as place names, rivers, mountains, and other things.

Sésquac. (sés·kwŏch) This is the Salish name of a 'wild man' who lived in the forest. The Sésquac, or Sasquatch, lived in the mountainous regions of the forests and was equally feared and revered by the indigenous people of the region. They were described as large ape-like proto-humans, covered in long hair, and standing between seven and twelve feet tall in some legends.

Shou Lao. (shō lă·ō) He was the god of longevity and knowledge, from the ancient Chinese pantheon of mythology. He also ruled over the date of death for every living thing. In art he was depicted as a small man with a very prominent bald head, bushy white eyebrows and random white whiskers, he often was shown carrying a staff and a golden peach.

Staff of Orkan. (stăf ŏv ôr·kăn) This was an ancient wooden staff, said to have been crafted from a branch of Yggdrasil, the World Tree. It was imbued with powerful magic, the primary one being control over weather, hence its name 'Orkan' which is Norwegian for hurricane. It had long been in the possession of Woden within his armory. It was an item crafted of Eldritch magic.

Star-Cross. (stär-krôs) This is the combination of two

powerful symbols, the pentacle and the cross. The pentacle has long been used to represent the divine, or spirit over the four elements. It is a symbol of great power over the spiritual world, but has often been mistaken for the corruption of the symbol when it was inverted with a single point facing down, and two points facing up in a goat horn analogy. The cross, from Christian theology symbolizes divine forgiveness, divine power, and sacrifice. The combined symbol was first used by the Brotherhood of Olympus sect within the Livonian Brothers of the Sword, that later became an autonomous sub-division of the larger Order of Teutonic knights.

Storgé. (stôrg·ā) One of four independent words used to define variations of love used by the ancient Greeks. It is love through the fondness of familiarity, family members or people who relate in familiar ways that have otherwise found themselves bonded by chance. An example is the natural love and affection of a parent for their child. It is described as the most natural, emotive, and widely diffused of loves: natural in that it is present without coercion; emotive because it is the result of fondness due to familiarity; and most widely diffused because it pays the least attention to those characteristics deemed 'valuable' or worthy of love and, as a result, is able to transcend most discriminating factors.

Succorbenoth. (sū·khôr·bən·ŏth) He was a daemon who served many of the rulers in the netherworld known as the Abyss. He had dominion over gates, and has often linked to any daemonic incursions unto Earth because of his ability to make gates from the netherworlds to Earth through the manipulation of human hosts on the Earth side of the gate. He has also been linked to the death of Walter Reuss, and was firmly in the Tiamat camp within the Council of Retribution. In art he has been depicted as being a massively tall humanoid surrounded by a purplish-black aura, with a lion's mane of fiery red hair, and an overlarge smile filled with many interlocking fangs.

Taktikmeister. (tăk·tĭk·mīs·tĕr) [German] English translation—strategy master. One of the masters of the

Brotherhood of Olympus who served as a deputy to the High Master of the order, typically either the knowledge or strategy master served as the leader of the Brotherhood and reported directly to the High Master. However, during the 1460s, the High Master of the Teutonic knights was also a member of the Brotherhood himself. The strategy master was responsible for knowing as much as possible about strategies, tactics, probabilities, and odds of success, to be a resource for the Brotherhood in making timely decisions. The last recorded Taktikmeister was Leopold von Schmidt, who died in 1469, at the Battle of Mohrungren Fields.

Telekinesis. (tĕl·ĭ·kə·nē·sĭs) Is a type of psychokinesis— the psychic ability allowing a person to influence a physical system without a physical interaction, using just the mind or a thought to make something happen in the physical world. Specifically it is the movement and/or levitation of physical objects by purely mental force.

Templar knights. (tĕm·plər nīts) Also known as the Poor Fellow-Soldiers of Christ and of the Temple of Solomon, they were the most wealthy and powerful of the European Crusader orders. The organization existed for nearly two centuries during the Middle Ages. Officially endorsed by the Roman Catholic Church around 1129, the order became a favored charity throughout Europe and grew rapidly in membership and power. Templar knights, in their distinctive white mantles with a red cross, were among the most skilled fighting units of the Crusades. The Templar's existence was tied closely to the Crusades; when the Holy land was lost, support for the Order faded. Rumors about the Templar's secret initiation ceremony created mistrust and King Philip IV of France, who was also deeply in debt to the Order, and he took advantage of the situation. On Friday, October 13, 1307, many of the Order's members in France were arrested, tortured into giving false confessions, and then burned at the stake. Under pressure from King Philip, Pope Clement V disbanded the Order in 1312.

Teutonic knights. (tū·tŏn·ĭk nīts) Also known as the Order of Brothers of the German House of Saint Mary in Jerusalem, they were a religious military order of Germanic knights formed in 1190 for the Crusades. In their white mantles with a black Teutonic cross, they served honorably with the brethren of the larger Templar and Hospitaller orders during the occupation of the Holy lands. After the Crusader forces were defeated in the Middle East, the Order moved to Transylvania in 1211 to help defend the South-Eastern borders of the Kingdom of Hungary before being expelled by force of arms by King Andrew II in 1225, finally they accepted the offer to settle near the Baltic Sea. From their new base of operations they began the Northern Crusades, an invasion of Prussia, Lithuania, Livonia, and the other Baltic territories intended to Christianize the region. The Order created the independent Monastic State of the Teutonic Knights, expanding through military prowess they conquered Prussian, Polish, and Lithuanian territory, before conquering Livonia, and adding the Livonian Brothers of the Sword to their brethren. It is from their ranks that the first Brotherhood of Olympus was formed.

Thuringian. (thû·rĭn·jē·ən) A person or object from, or having to do with the region of Thuringia in what is now central Germany. Now known for its forested lands and winter sports heroism, this historic land was the home of Heinrich Reuss von Plauen.

Tiamat. (tē·ə·mät) Was the goddess of the sea, a primordial goddess of chaos, who took the form of sea serpents and dragons and created all the monstrosities of Mesopotamian myth and legend. She was the mother of all evil dragons. She was slain by her own children, and then took up residence in the Abyss as a more sinister goddess. She became one of the most powerful deities in the netherworlds through her pacts and alliances with others, and coveted the crown possessed by Lucifer. Succorbenoth was one of her lieutenants. In art she has been depicted as a beautiful woman with draconic or reptilian features. She has also been described as a mutli-headed dragon, with each head representing a different type of dragon she created. This concept was further advanced by the description of her as the chromatic dragon in the *Dungeons and Dragons* game system.

Tower of Dreams. (tow·ər ŏv drēms) One of a series of mythical towers built by the Elder gods that predate the rise of the Old gods, the Tower of Dreams served multiple functions for the other towers, it was the hub through which communication and travel occurred between towers, and it was the source of the linkage between the others through the control panel that contained the Dream Stones—one for each of the towers. It also existed within all possible realities, since its power resided within the dreamscape. The Tower of Dreams freely traveled through the planes of existence. Although myths exist that the tower travelled in some mathematical pattern, few were ever been able to plot or even guess at its course through the planes.

Tower of Infinity. (tow·ər ŏv in·fĭn·ə·tē) One of a series of mythical towers built by the Elder gods that predate the rise of the Old gods, the Tower of Infinity granted visitors the ability to see into the infinite streams of time and space, among other things. The Tower of Infinity was rumored to exist in a remote mountainous region of the Ethereal Plane.

Tower of Might. (tow·ər ŏv mīt) One of a series of mythical towers built by the Elder gods that predate the rise of the Old gods, the Tower of Might developed, acquired, and deployed weapons and warriors to protect the other towers. They never violated their protect and serve mandate, even though there were some of the huisum who talked of being an offensive force to enhance their role in protecting and serving. The legends surrounding the Tower of Might suggest it was able to physically move by some unknown force or magic to respond to an emergency.

Towers of Ominous Power. (tow·ərs ŏv ŏm·ə·nəs pou·ər) A series of mythical towers built by the Elder gods that predate the rise of the Old gods, such as Woden, Amun, and Nu Kua, each tower was given dominion over an aspect of reality. Within legends and myth there were seven towers known to exist usually depicted in a hexagonal pattern with the last tower situated in the middle—the Tower of Infinity, the Tower of Life, the Tower of Science, the Tower of Might, the Tower of Knowledge, the Tower of Magic, and the Tower of Dreams. The central tower was the hub around which the others operated, and it was through this tower that all the huisum who controlled the towers traveled to and from each other, and to a large part communicated with each other. The towers were created to be neutral observers to the development of reality, life and death, and the struggles of species both sentient and non sentient.

Tsuka. (sû·kə) [Japanese] The hilt or handle of a sword usually wrapped or decorated in a way to personalize the weapon for its owner.

Tsurugi. (sû·rû·gē) [Japanese] A double edged broadsword, these were common in the early years of Japanese sword making prior to the creation of the single edged, curved bladed katana, or what is commonly known as a Samurai sword. The art of the straight blade double edged sword, using the same metal folding technique and construction was lost to antiquity, except for within the Norishige family line.

Tuatha Dé Danann. (tû·ăthə dē dā·năn) Celtic pantheon of gods, usually translated as tribe of the goddess Danu, also known by the earlier name Tuath Dé—tribe of the gods. Led by their king, Nuada, they fought three Battles of Magh Tuireadh during their time of dominion over the British Isles. In the first they defeated and displaced the native Fir Bolg, hundreds of years later they fought and won the Second Battle of Magh Tuireadh against the Fomorians. Finally in the third battle they fought the Gaels—the modern human inhabitants of Ireland—it ended in what was considered a stalemate, the Gaels sought to divide the land between the Tuatha Dé Danann and themselves, they cleverly allotted the portion above ground to the Gaels and the portion underground (the Otherworld) to the Tuatha Dé Danann. The Tuatha Dé Danann were led underground into the Sidhe mounds by Manannán mac Lir, and it is said they still reside there today. Brigid was from the Tuatha Dé Danann pantheon.

Übersinnlichmeister. (über·sĭn·lĭch·mīs·tĕr) [German] English translation—supernatural master. One of the masters of the Brotherhood of Olympus who served as a deputy to the High Master of the order, the supernatural master was responsible for knowing as much as possible about the paranormal, paranormal phenomenon, psychic abilities, and preferably had a practical use of them all allowing him to be a resource for the Brotherhood in dealing with the foes they encountered. The last recorded Übersinnlichmeister was Wilhelm von Essen, who died in 1469, at the Battle of Mohrungren Fields.

Vatican City. (văt·ĭ·kən sĭt·ē) The sovereign city state that houses the organizational and governing structure of the Catholic Church located within Rome, Italy. It was built upon the ruins of the Circus of Nero and has been the seat of Papal authority for most of the last fifteen hundred years. It also houses multiple museums, archives, libraries, and much of the recorded history of the Judeo-Christian monotheistic religion.

Veni, Vidi, Vici. [Latin] English translation—I came, I saw, I conquered.

Waffenmeister. (vă·fən·mīs·tĕr) [German] English translation—weapons master. One of the masters of the Brotherhood of Olympus who served as a deputy to the High Master of the order, the weapons master was responsible for knowing as much as possible about weapons, how to use them, possible weaknesses and strengths, and to a large part was the best fighter among the Brotherhood. The last recorded Waffenmeister was Steffan von Dienheim, who died in 1469, at the Battle of Mohrungren Fields.

Woden. (wō·dĕn) He was the All-Father, greatest of the Aesir, and leader of Asgard, from the Norse pantheon of mythology. He was also known as Wodanaz or Odin. He has been known as a god of war, battle, victory, death, wisdom, magic, poetry, prophecy, and the hunt. Wednesday was named after him, 'Woden's day.' He was the god who was instrumental in the creation of the Brotherhood of Olympus in its modern form. In art he was depicted as a large man with a long white beard, bearing an eye patch, often seen with a large golden spear (Gungnir), two ravens (Huginn and Muninn), and an eight legged horse (Sleipnir).

Zaubermeister. (zou·běr·mīs·těr) [German] English translation—magic master. One of the masters of the Brotherhood of Olympus who served as a deputy to the High Master of the order, the magic master was responsible for knowing as much as possible about the magic, magical beings, defense against magic, and preferably a practical use of magic allowing him to be a resource for the Brotherhood in dealing with the foes they encountered. The last recorded Zaubermeister was Valten von Holdau, who died in 1469, at the Battle of Mohrungren Fields.

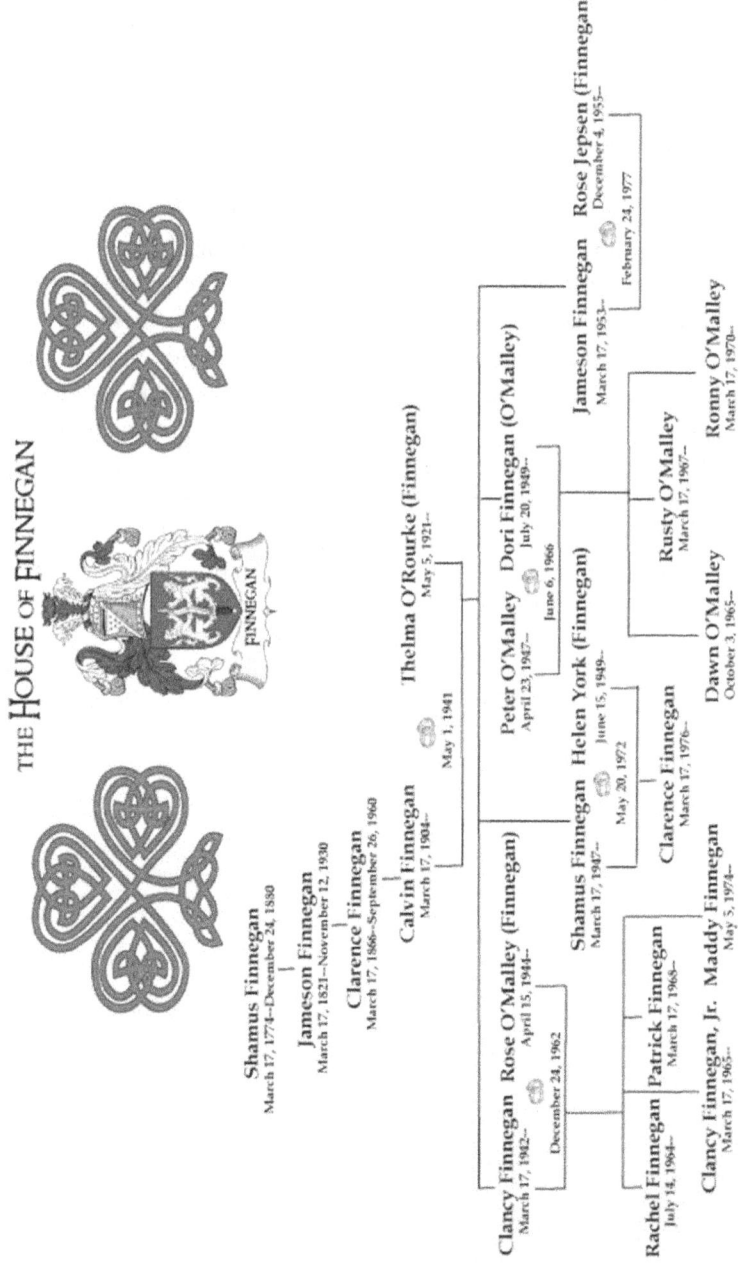

THE HOUSE OF FINNEGAN

Shamus Finnegan
March 17, 1774–December 24, 1850

Jameson Finnegan
March 17, 1821–November 12, 1930

Clarence Finnegan
March 17, 1866–September 26, 1960

Calvin Finnegan
March 17, 1904–

Thelma O'Rourke (Finnegan)
May 5, 1921–

May 1, 1941

Clancy Finnegan   Rose O'Malley (Finnegan)
March 17, 1942–   April 15, 1944–

December 24, 1962

Shamus Finnegan   Helen York (Finnegan)
March 17, 1947–   June 15, 1949–

May 20, 1972

Peter O'Malley   Dori Finnegan (O'Malley)
April 23, 1947–   July 20, 1949–

June 6, 1966

Jameson Finnegan   Rose Jepsen (Finnegan)
March 17, 1953–   December 4, 1955–

February 24, 1977

Rachel Finnegan   Patrick Finnegan
July 14, 1964–   March 17, 1965–

Clancy Finnegan, Jr.   Maddy Finnegan
March 17, 1965–   May 3, 1974–

Clarence Finnegan
March 17, 1976–

Dawn O'Malley
October 3, 1965–

Rusty O'Malley
March 17, 1967–

Ronny O'Malley
March 17, 1970–

THE HOUSE OF FRASER

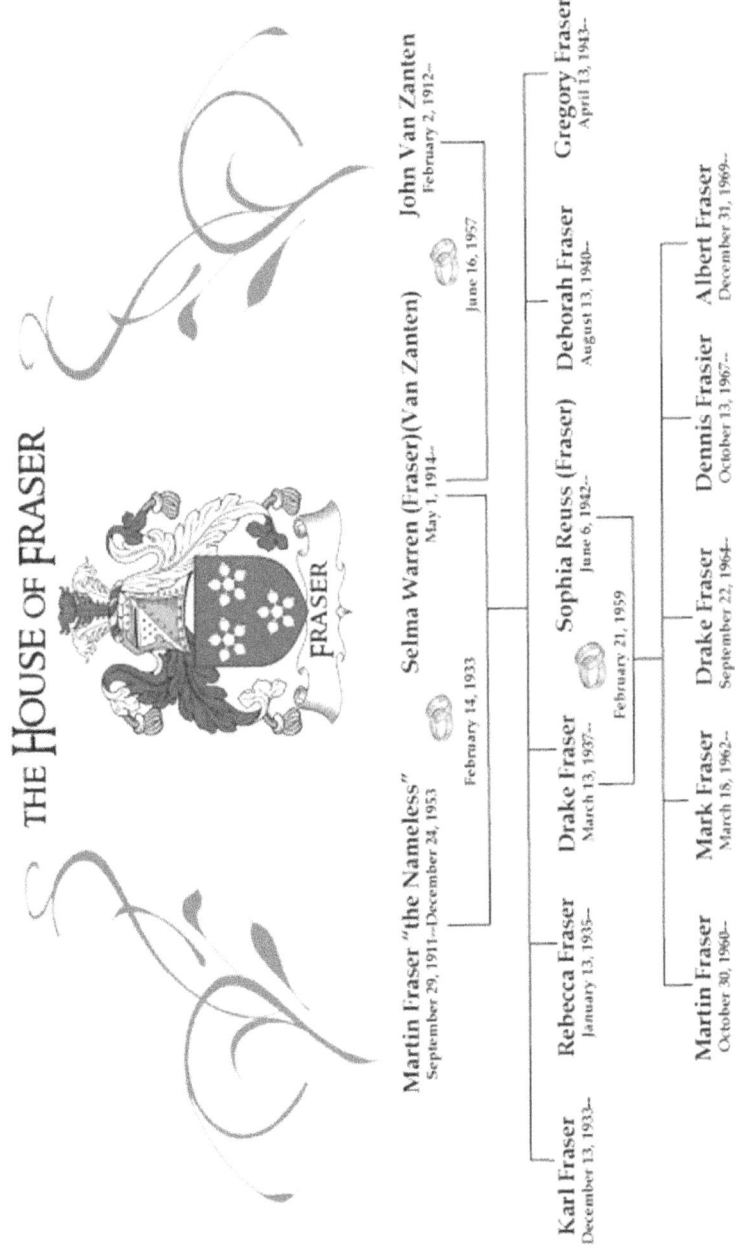

FRASER

Martin Fraser "the Nameless"
September 29, 1911–December 24, 1953

February 14, 1933

Selma Warren (Fraser)(Van Zanten)
May 1, 1914–

June 16, 1957

John Van Zanten
February 2, 1912–

Karl Fraser
December 13, 1933–

Rebecca Fraser
January 13, 1935–

Drake Fraser
March 13, 1937–

February 21, 1959

Sophia Reuss (Fraser)
June 6, 1942–

Deborah Fraser
August 13, 1940–

Gregory Fraser
April 13, 1943–

Martin Fraser
October 30, 1960–

Mark Fraser
March 18, 1962–

Drake Fraser
September 22, 1964–

Dennis Frasier
October 13, 1967–

Albert Fraser
December 31, 1969–

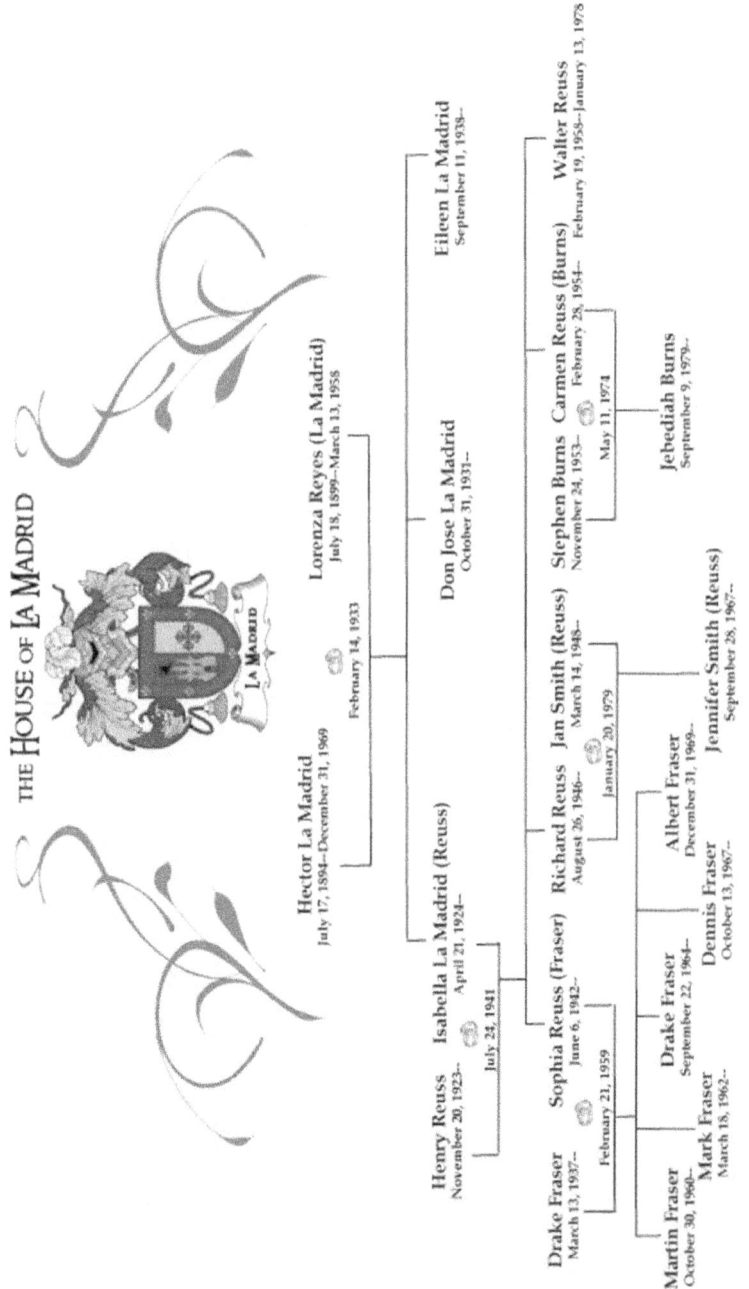

THE HOUSE OF LA MADRID

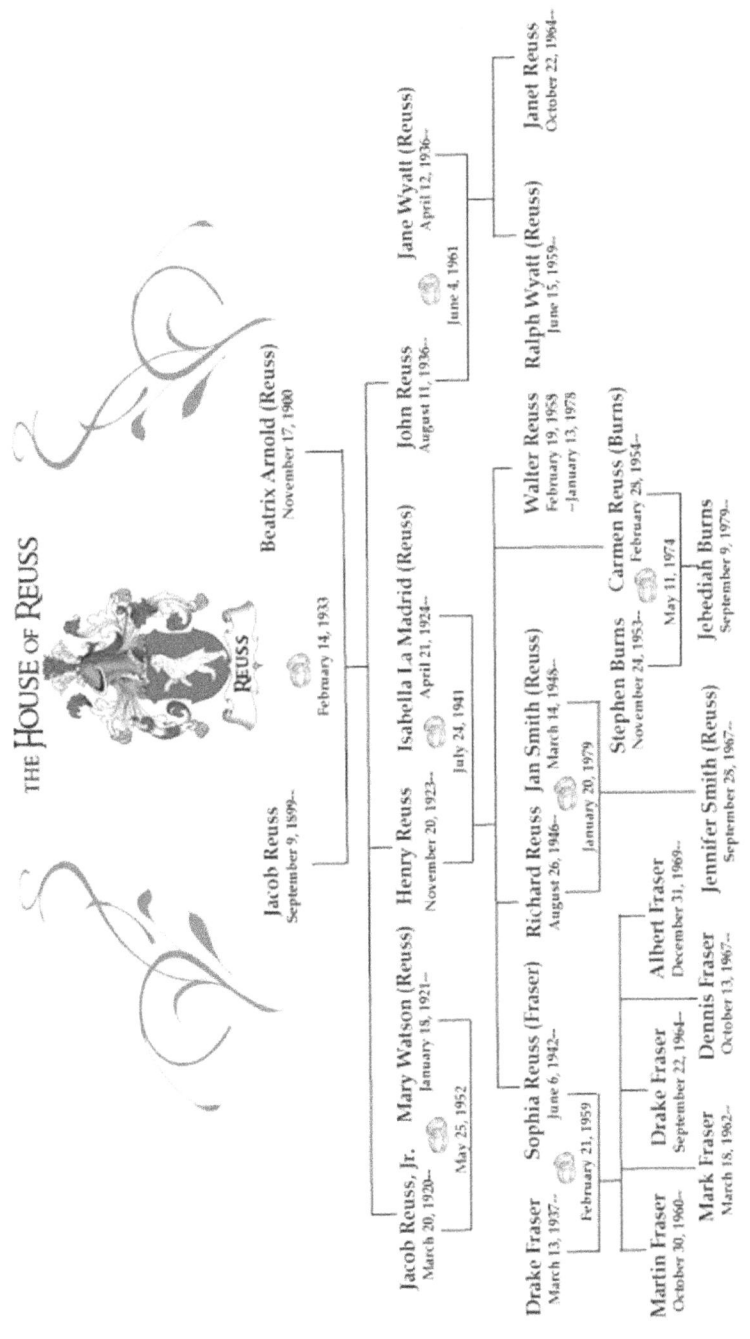

DISCUSSION GUIDE

After the publication of the Brotherhood of Olympus and the Deadliest Game the author was invited to book clubs and classrooms to discuss his literary work. It became apparent through his discussions with book club members and middle and high school English teachers that providing a resource of guided questions could be extremely valuable for anyone looking to add a book to their club, or classroom literary circles. The author enlisted the aid of four English teachers with over 40 years of experience between them to craft a set of literary questions for his books, aligned to CCSS. Questions, comments, feedback, and of course photos of examples of student work can be directed to the author's website:

https://guysimpson.net

Last Stand of the Brotherhood of Olympus
Tower of Dreams Prelude

- Predict why the prelude, set 500 years in the past is important to set the scene for the story?

- Predict where might the Hochmeister have gone when he was leaning against the Tower?

Page 22 – "The Brotherhood of Olympus ceased to exist on that grim Friday the thirteenth, in the year 1469."
- Identify superstitions surrounding Friday the thirteenth?

Page 22 – "So, too, was the succession of knighthood ended, and the Code lost for Antiquity."
- Describe what the author meant by the above quotation?

Author note:
The first book in the series, *The Deadliest Game,* is referenced early on through behaviors, items, or events. How do the following link directly to the previous novel?
Page 14 – "In turn each of the masters of the Brotherhood knelt and kissed the forehead of the Hochmeister." "The five of them turned, each placing his right hand in the center of their impromptu circle and one by one they held their hands on top of each others." Page 15 – the Staff of Orkan.

Chapter One: To Everything There is a Season

The author uses song lyrics numerous times in his stories.
- What is the effect of using lyrics to convey meaning?

- What insight might this give about the author?

Chapter Two: Project North Star

Page 36 – Martin tells Drake he needs to lead the brotherhood.
- Why would Martin defer his elder brother status and not assert himself as the natural leader of the group?

- The author uses the term 'brotherhood' throughout the story and in his title; what significance does the term 'brotherhood' play in the story, considering the multiple definitions?

Pages 38-40 – Martin falls out his window. He hung in the air, as if he was suspended by an invisible cushion that slowly jostled him as it deflated under him. Captain Spenser

witnesses the fall from the window. 'That series of events changed many things for Martin Fraser.'
- Identify the 'series of events' and how might it change things for him?

Page 44 – Project North Star is a top secret project including military use of psychic spies, through the use of trained psychics, mastering telekinesis, and Coordinate Remote Viewing (CRV).
Many people believe that humans only use a small portion of their brain and that things such as telepathy, psychics and telekinesis are possible.
- Generate a list of terms associated with people having psychic abilities. Then, label them as having either negative or positive connotations?

Page 47 – According to Captain Spenser, the Tower of Dreams travels through time and space and appears randomly. Addraemyr, the only known inhabitant and the Keeper of the Tower of Dreams, appears to be a grey alien.
- What prior knowledge or background do you have of aliens?

- How are they portrayed in the media, literature, and movies?

Chapter Three: It All Came Crashing Down

Page 62 – The boys find their dad crying and quickly learn of their mom's infidelity. The boys remove all the guns from their parent's room, and Drake sits with their distraught father. He went to get water and on his return, "heard the sound of the chamber of the revolver spinning, the metallic click of the trigger pulling back. Dad had the gun to the right

side of his head and he pulled the trigger."
- What emotional effects would could this have on a child?

- How might you expect Drake to respond to his father's suicide attempt?

Page 67 – Reference to the chapter title: "Drake saw the bloom that was their family, blossoming as recently as the prior weekend at Martin and Beth's wedding, shriveling, turning brown, and withering on the vine. Personally he had lost Rachel, his mother betrayed his father, he nearly lost his father, and now he was going to lose all the benefits he had worked for at school. His friends, his class presidency, his band, his place on the basketball team, and everything else he had slowly struggled to achieve. In his viewpoint, everything in his life had just come crashing down around him."
- Discuss other instances in literature where a character has experienced a loss of nearly everything they value, or have achieved?

- Compare and contrast how Drake responded to the characters in other stories facing similar situations?

Author note:
More family back story is shared by Drake's great uncles outside Martin and Beth's wedding. Drake recalls the photo of the boys from 1965 that triggered his memories in the summer of 1979.

Chapter Four: Hikari

Pages 69-71 – Drake dreams of the black tower on the barren wasteland again, many people remember their dreams and

some believe the dreams are trying to tell people something.
- What do you think Drake's nightmare trying to tell him?

- What could it be foreshadowing?

Chapter Five: The Journey South

- Identify elements of foreshadowing in this chapter and what they might be alluding to?

- What subtle hints does the author give the reader?

Pages 91-92 – Drake argues with his mother; she doesn't understand him or his life. She states that he needs to grow up and stop being such a baby. He replies, "Do you even know anything about me? Do you know how much effort it took me to run for class president? I could only do that because lots of people knew me, and because of Rachel. Do you even know anything about basketball? You have only come to one of my games, one game. During my freshman year, and that's it." Drake's relationship with his mother is growing strained.
- What are the underlying reasons?

- Predict the direction their relationship will go in the future?

Chapter Six: A Plot Revealed

Introduction of the fantastical setting of the underworld Gehenna, home of Countess Furfur. The use of mythology to build the fabric of the world inhabited by Drake and his brothers was first introduced as a dream sequence in *The Deadliest Game.*

- Describe why the author would move the mythological characters and settings from a dream world to the real world?

- The author uses varied mythological characters, what background knowledge is needed to appreciate the mythological references?

Chapter Seven: One Step Forward, Infinite Steps Backward

Page 116 – Drake went for what was safe at lunch time; he saw a social outcast table and sat there.

- People often perceive their own social value, describe how that can be both beneficial and an obstacle to achieving personal goals?

Pages 118-126 – Drake was determined to make basketball his sanctuary away from the awkwardness of the new school, but Moose Caine had other ideas about the new kid joining 'his team.'

"Hey Fraser, Stop crying, and learn to play basketball. You're a freaking joke, you pansy." Later when revealing how his first day went to Mark, he said, "It just sucks! I hate it all!"

- How do nicknames/terms strengthen familial bonds?

- How can they also be destructive?

Chapter Eight: Chronicler

Drake is pessimistic about Martin's claim he is a psychic spy. Martin tells him of his training, of going to New York and working with Ingo Swann, of becoming a skilled practitioner of Controlled Remote Viewing, during which the CRV psychic draws things on a tablet. Just like Drake has always done.

Pages 132-133 – In Drake's sketchbooks were rough sketches of a massive black tower. Martin described it, 'This black monolith is the Tower of Dreams. It's a tower of legendary origin created by a very ancient race that came before the gods of myth and legends. The Keeper of the tower, Addraemyr, told me about the Brotherhood of Olympus, and some things about a medieval order of knights. The Keeper said I had to keep you safe, that you possessed the key to what's to come."

- Describe what is the draw or the appeal of the Tower of Dreams to the characters?

- Predict what would affect the likeliness of Drake to believe Martin?

Page 133 – There's a dimensional war on the horizon. The Keeper warned that it will be difficult to tell allies from enemies.

- Give examples why is it sometimes difficult to tell your allies from enemies?

Chapter Nine: River Rising, Fraser Falling

Page 141 – What is the purpose of having the teacher describe a Pedigree Chart?

- Predict why discussion of demigods is important to the story?

Page 147 – Drake knew he could play basketball at a higher level, he just had not shown it yet. Finally, after being pushed hard by Moose, Drake steps up on the basketball court and at the end of practice Coach Arthaud states, "The River's rising gentlemen!" Many authors using phrasing that have multiple meanings.
- What possible meanings might the author have been implying by using "the river's rising?"

Pages 149-151 – Moose Fights Drake after practice, some of the boys try and intervene, most chant, "Fight! Fight! Fight!" Drake doesn't fight back. 'Drake pulled his shirt free from Moose, his fight or flight instinct was welling up inside of him.'
- What does 'fight or flight' mean?

- Describe a time that you may have had a similar feeling?

Page 153 – 'With quick reasoning, Drake surmised that such a punch to a knocked out opponent like Moose might result in death. He acted, not to save Moose, but to save James.'
- Why did James Kirk rescue Drake?

- Describe how Drake saved James?

Chapter Ten: To Seek Out New Life

Page 163 – George Kalama states, "Drake and I are basketball brothers, we are on the same team, we face the same foes, and that makes us brothers." The author is laying the groundwork for the use of the word brotherhood in his work.
- List ways that the term brothers or brotherhood is used by the author?

- Compare and contrast other uses of similar words?

The author uses lots of cultural references to *Star Wars*, J. R. R. Tolkien, Robert E. Howard, *Conan*, etc. in the dialogue of the boys at the lunch table.
- Explain why the author included those references?

Page 168 – Ryan Healy brings up love and brotherhood. "Mrs. Mulkey said that the Greeks were smart to split love up into four different words, *Agápe*, *Éros*, *Philia*, and the other one."
Page 169 – George further clarifies it. "I think *Agápe* love—unconditional love—can be even more powerful when combined with *Philia* love."
The author introduces the reader to origins of words in this chapter.
- Explain why this is important to the reader?

- Describe how it is important to the story?

Author note:
Many things are happening in the dialogue of this chapter, the

Fibonacci sequence is introduced. George explains his motivation—to be better, "My uncle Freeman took me to a sweat lodge and I asked the great spirits what I could do to fix it, and I was told to be better. That's what I'm going to do. I'm going to be a better person, a better friend, and a better brother." First literary reference of Freeman Kalama occurs, a future member of the Brotherhood. The concept of being better is introduced. "Now you're Scrappy the Barbarian," Drake stated with a smile, this is the first appearance of the name and title linked together.

Chapter Eleven: Go River

Page 173—After the tough loss to Fort Vancouver with a chance to go to the state basketball tournament, the author adds this philosophical phrase, "Some things in life are just not meant to be, but some could argue at times that the ride along the way is more important than the destination."
- Explain what the author is trying to convey?

- Describe how the increased amount of people keep coming to the table at lunch seems to parallel the philosophical phrase used?

Chapter Twelve: Raven and the Key

Page 184 – Raven delivers the key for Furfur, and then flies back into Drake's room to bring him a message: "Aw Caaaa! Aw Caa!" Raven exclaimed. "Be cautious young Fraser! If I can find you, they can find you! You're not safe anymore doing nothing! Prepare! Prepare! War comes!"
- Predict what Raven might be warning Drake about?

The Archive Room was first seen in *The Deadliest Game*, now Drake has been given the key.
- List ways the Archive Room could be used by Drake and his brothers to advance the story?

- Predict how Albert knowing about the key and the room might be important to the rest of the story?

Chapter Thirteen: The Adventures of Dennis and Albert

Dennis and Albert get themselves separated from the key and inside the Archive Room, and they wind up in the Grand Library of Gehenna. Dennis and Albert seem destined to get into trouble.
- List other examples in literature of characters with similar traits or behaviors as them?

Pages 208-209 – Drake listens to the two demons guards talking about eating his brothers. 'In his mind he saw Moose. He felt the shame of being pummeled by him in the locker room. Drake had experienced too much bullying, and could not move past these two talking about his brothers that way. It was one thing to pick on him, but don't ever pick on his brothers.'
Page 210 – "No one's gonna eat my brothers," Drake said, as he walked away from the carnage he never knew he was capable of inflicting. Hikari blazed as the black demon blood burned off the blade.
- Describe how the two passages above link back to events in earlier chapters?

Drake defeats Quatyl.
- Predict how that might change the perception of the brothers among their allies and their enemies?

Chapter Fourteen: To See Addraemyr

Page 219 – 'Going back to school after killing demons and a god was an odd juxtaposition of realities for Drake. '
- What does juxtaposition mean?

- What other words could the author have used to describe what Drake was feeling?

Page 219 – The Power of words: 'He thought of the old English adage, 'Sticks and stones may break my bones, but words will never hurt me,' and knew it wasn't true. Those cheap words, sissy, pussy, faggot, and the like laid an oppressive weight upon his soul. The cut in his arm was healing—sure it was still sore and the stitches had started to itch—but it was getting better; however, the wounds caused by those words would never go completely away.'
- Describe how this demonstrates the power of words?

- Identify a statement you have heard that has stuck with you.

Page 229 – "God-slayer, it is not up to us to determine the worth of a person, or of a people," "All humans are capable of being greater than they suspect, the brothers Fraser are just further along or more open to the possibilities of their genetics. We do not measure the value of a person by their outward appearance, rank, or species, rather by the sum of the agápe in their heart. Your value in the cosmos is greater

than precious metals or the rarest of jewels. Humans have the potential to take us all into a period of great enlightenment, or to our ruin. The choice will ultimately be yours."
- Explain what agápe means?

- Predict what choice humans will make and describe what that might look like?

Chapter Fifteen: Devotion to a Dream

Page 235 – 'Life for Rachel took an ominous turn in mid December. She began to experience a series of unfortunate events.'
- Describe the author's purpose for using the word ominous?

Trials and tribulations of Rachel, she is thrown from a moving car, stung by a scorpion, locked in an old refrigerator, nearly drowned in the public pool, and molested by her step-grandfather. Each time she nearly dies she is sent back by Aeon.
- Explain why the god declared his allegiance in the coming war on the side of Rachel Finnegan?

Rachel is nearly drowned by unseen attackers, but is saved by her friends and the giant hand of water that slams the creatures into the bottom of the pool and back into the ether.
- From your understanding of classical mythology predict who might be able to manipulate water in such a way?

Page 251 – Rachel hears who has orchestrated her attacks when the daevas, Aesma and Saurva are talking to her step-

grandfather, whom they are possessing. In the darkness of her own personal hell she resolves to fight.
- Describe how her family dynamics and decisions made by Rachel affect her character?

Chapter Sixteen: Council of Olympus

Page 265 – Woden states, "The conviction of a man is measured through his heart and the love that resides within it. You will know your brothers when you meet them, and they will, of course, rise to the challenge of your bidding. Do not fret over such things, my boy. Those you seek will be great and noble warriors for our cause. And one might say that they have been searching for you and what you offer for their entire lives." This is another reference to brothers and the brotherhood.
- Describe how Woden's comments reinforce the author's meaning of the terms?

Chapter Seventeen: Aunt Carmen

Drake's dad is insistent that he should get a job for the summer.
- Predict what implications might this have on Drake and his future?

- What is Drake dad's motivation for insisting he work?

The author once again makes a pop cultural reference to the 'Force' from *Star Wars*.
- Describe whether it advances the plot by letting readers make inferences, or simply to further develop Martin's character as a science fiction aficionado?

Page 285 – Drake gets hired at the restaurant, despite planning on intentionally blowing his interview. 'Drake thought to himself that the benefits of the job included hanging out with Mark, possibly working with Scrappy, making some real money,' among other things. 'The drawback, and it was a big one, was Moose Caine. Drake was done running and hiding from Moose and all his other fears. He would have to face him to overcome this weight that hung on his soul like an albatross."
- Describe the image created by the author's simile?

- What other literary device might describe Drake's present state?

Chapter Eighteen: Magic Man

Page 294 – Drake fixes Freeman's glasses.
- Describe what this action informs the reader about Drake's character?

Page 294 – Freeman's quote: "I'm a shaman and magic man. Just like you're a barbarian, we each have our own calling, and if we are brothers, we complement each other's strengths and protect each other's weaknesses." This is another concept of brotherhood—to complement strengths and protect weaknesses.
- Explain how this concept would help a group be successful?

Page 296 – Freeman asks to join the Brotherhood, the line-up at this time included Drake, Martin, Scrappy, and possibly Mark. Though Drake is certain Beth will join because of his dreams.

- The new Brotherhood may seem a congregation of misfits at first; is this group stronger or weaker than the Fraser brothers (from *The Deadliest Game*)?

- Which factors contribute to your opinion?

Page 299 – Brigid, goddess of the sacred flame. "I volunteered my service to train and tutor your brothers for the coming war, my name is Brigid, goddess of the sacred flame, and I'm here to help."
- Describe how Brigid's character challenges traditional gender roles within literature?

Chapter Nineteen: Risk

Page 308 – Drake asks Brigid, "I know your name, Brigid, so I can summon you?"
- Predict how this information might be important for Drake as the story moves forward?

Page 312 – The dilemma between Martin and Beth. Brigid offers a solution.
"The simplest choice always lies the closest to you," Brigid stated. "She wants to be included in your life. This is part of your life. Include her. Show her why you must do this, bring her into the Brotherhood."
- What message is being reinforced by this statement?

- What implications does this have on Drake and his future?

Page 312 – "Wait a minute," Scrappy interrupted. "You're saying bring a girl into the Brotherhood? Wouldn't that make it more of a sisterhood?"
"My dear Scrappy," Brigid said, "the Brotherhood is not about gender. It is about the love between you. A female could easily join the Brotherhood and fight along side you for everything that was right and just in the world."
The author has been building to the concept that 'brotherhood' is based upon agápe—the unconditional love of your fellow man, or woman.
- Explain how this aligns with the use of the term in other sources of literature?

Chapter Twenty: Moose Caine

Page 327 – Why did Drake save Moose? Drake answered, "The difference between you and me, is that I honor my commitments, to my friends, my team, my brothers, and even my co-workers. Yeah, you've been a dick to me, but it's like Ryan said, what makes us better is our ability to love each other, to rise above the pettiness and become something stronger because of that love in our hearts. You've been my teammate and my co-worker, and those hellhounds were going to kill you. I couldn't just turn away and let a defenseless guy get eaten, not if I could prevent it. I had to help you, I had no options." Drake seems to be developing a 'Code' of chivalry as the events in the story progress.
- How does this add to your understanding of Drake and his motivation?

- Do you operate by similar principles? For whom or what would you make such a sacrifice?

Pages 329-330 – Events happening in Vatican City.
- Describe how this passage of the book further links to the events of the previous chapter and the prologue?

Chapter Twenty-One: Of Mark and Drake

Brigid is upset by the hellhound attack and thinks its time to bring Mark back into the Brotherhood. Mark has other plans and has avoided telling Drake because he didn't want to hurt him.

Page 336 – The brothers talk. Mark states he cannot allow himself to believe in the paranormal, or the world he knows would make no sense at all. "I know," Drake added. "Trust me, I've been there, done that. The foundation of my reality has been reshaped a million times since Wally died. But, damn it Mark, you were there with me. Only you and I could go back in and face Succorbenoth and the mordgeists. Only us. It was real."

"I don't know what was real anymore," Mark replied. "That day was like a bad dream to me, little brother. I can't live my life that way, I just can't. That's not my path, not my destiny.
- How can one event affect two people in such different ways?

The author uses the lyrics of a song to convey a secondary feeling to the flashback sequences as Mark is leaving, looking back at Drake standing in the parking lot.
- Describe the effects of using song lyrics in a story, in terms of the reader's connection to the text?

- Are song lyrics more powerful than a simple quote? How?

Chapter Twenty-Two: Flight to Home

Page 345 – Freeman states "Numbers are symbolic and possess power."
- How have numbers been used symbolically or superstitiously in history?

- How are they used now (do we still attach symbolism and superstition to them)?

- Do you attach symbolism or superstition to any particular numbers?

Page 346 – Drake isn't sure he wants to be the leader, with all the responsibilities, and he isn't so sure he possesses free will. 'Sometimes, usually when he was tired, he dreaded the whole thing and wondered what he had gotten involved with. Mordgeists, hellhounds, demons, daemons, gods, and goddesses, it was almost oppressive to think about. It seemed that they all spoke of him having choices, and that the future before them was unwritten, and yet it was like he had no real choice at all. He was simply cast to play this part, and he wasn't really sure he wanted to audition for it in the first place.' Drake is at a crossroads in terms of choosing to take the responsibility of leading the Brotherhood.
- Based on your understanding of his personality so far, predict the path he will choose?

- Explain how a person could uphold responsibility while still exercising free will?

Page 349 – Drake encounters individuals along his path who give him clues and encouragement, "Sometimes the talent a person possesses can change the world, if they choose to act with it."
- Identify a time in your life where you were so caught up in the day-to-day grind of work and responsibilities, you failed to notice bigger signs the world was trying to show you. Which clues did you miss? Did you realize it before it was too late?

Page 352 – Drake pushed off with his bike and pedaled to the right. A solitary house sat upon a low hill... Gooseflesh and raised hair on the back of his neck... The sensation began as it always did. A feeling of dread washed over him.
- Describe a time when you had a similar experience with 'gooseflesh and raised hair on the back of your neck?'

- What do experts call that feeling?

- What do they say about listening to it?

Chapter Twenty-Three: Happy Birthday

- How did Drake's dad get the price of the car reduced by $500?

- Which adjectives would best describe Drake's relationship with his father up to this point?

Page 366 – Beth gives Drake a birthday present that comes with a price, "You're different, more regal, like a knight or a prince... Brave knights would ride off to face dragons and other things for the honor of a fair lady." Drake initially accepts the vow, but then ponders it further.

'Drake held Beth's blue handkerchief in his hand. He thought about tossing it out the window and letting the wind take it wherever it may. But then he realized he had made a vow to champion her, and a knight, though he wasn't one yet, doesn't break a vow. Especially not one to a fair lady.'

- What message is being reinforced by Beth's statement?

- How is Drake's 'Code' of chivalry further developed and reinforced in this chapter?

- What implications will this have on Drake and his future, once he embraces it?

Chapter Twenty-Four: *The Empire Strikes Back*

Drake watched the movie, and saw odd parallels to his current plight and started to see how it appeared as though someone might be betraying him.

- How is the pop culture of the *Star Wars* references used in this chapter?

- Explain why Drake takes the severed demon head with him?

Pages 379-380 – The men in black state, "We are God's exterminators... We are from the Knights of Malta, the only order of Crusaders still in existence. Once our order was known as the Hospitallers, and we shared our allegiance to the Pope with the Templars and the Teutonic orders. Neither of those knightly orders exists anymore under the

charter of God. We do."
- Predict how the introduction of the Hospitallers impacts the story?

Chapter Twenty-Five: Dark Tidings

Pages 386-387 – 'On the night of October eighth, they had gathered together, this would be the last time they all sat together—barbarian, shaman, psychic warrior, skeptic, god-slayer, and goddess.' The foreshadowing of this statement is rather ominous.
- Predict the chain of events that could occur to make this true?

- What is the likelihood that the Brotherhood will remain intact? Why?

Page 391 – 'It was difficult for Drake to imagine that his own mom would have put his life in jeopardy. Why would she do it? What would she gain from such a thing? It made no sense, but the seed of suspicion was planted in Drake that evening by his brother Martin. That seed would quickly germinate inside his mind.'
- If Drake's mom was innocent, explain who would benefit most from him suspecting her as a traitor, and why?

Pages 391-394 – That night, Drake dreamed the old dream. Except this time, everything turned out horribly wrong and they all died. At the end of his dream one image remained, 'he saw the smiling face of his mother and remembered no more.'
- Explain how this dream helps or hurts Martin's claim that their mother may be the traitor?

- What is it about the bond between a mother and child that makes these events even more troublesome?

- How would the situation be different if the possible traitor were someone besides her?

Chapter Twenty-Six: Halloween

Pages 398-399 – Drake was feeling upset and vulnerable, the plans they made were not working, and Brigid feels the need to give him a last pep talk. "Never have my kin been in such a strait. You offer us hope. You are our only hope, Drake. In the time I've have been here, I have opened my heart to you and your brothers. If ever I were to be a patron of humans again, it would be you five. I love you, as a sister loves a brother... You are a shining light, a beacon for all who hold hope true to their hearts. If I could go with you, I would do so without question. If I had to lay down my existence for you, I would proudly do so. I have faith in you Drake. You possess an ability that will change the outcome of the war that will be fought. It has been seen by many, which is why those on the dark side fear you so. In time you will learn of this gift, and you will master it. And in that time I shall come to you and ask that you remember the faith I had in you, and we shall be as brother and sister... All warriors feel fear before a battle, but a true warrior, a leader among men, knows that fear by name and channels it into the passion of why he fights. You fight to defend your family, your friends, your world, and even my world. There is no greater passion in war than choosing to fight for your love. You, god-slayer, are a defender of love, and none have ever been truer. " Brigid has the highest level of faith in Drake.
- Based on your understanding of Drake's character, how will

having the unconditional support, confidence, and faith of someone like Brigid affect his actions and choices?

Page 399 – 'Brigid kissed his forehead.' The author uses this as a form of saying good-bye, for the Fraser family, and then it is demonstrated by Brigid.
- Explain whether you believe this endearment was appropriated by the goddess after watching the Frasers, or if you think it is a broader culturally appropriate action that she possessed before meeting them?

Page 402 -- What is written on the folded piece of paper with the key?

- Predict what you think might have been written on that paper?

Page 404 – 'Time passed slowly. Too slowly.'
- Describe situations where time seems to expand or slow. What causes that feeling?

Chapter Twenty-Seven: Wasteland

Page 411 – It was like Tatooine in *Star Wars*.
- If you have prior knowledge of Tatooine, how does this reference aid your understanding of the text?

Page 414 – 'He was tempted for a moment to toss the empty can along the dirt road, but remembered the whole Butterfly Effect from one of his science readings on the chaos theory.'
- Explain what is the Butterfly Effect, as used in this context?

Page 414 – 'At the apex of the hill Drake slowed to a stop. Before them, in the middle of the storm, stood a wide obsidian tower that reached all the way up and was lost within the maelstrom above.
"The Tower of Dreams!" Scrappy exclaimed from the backseat.'
- Describe the references or literary premonitions the author has provided to prepare you for this moment in the story?

- Explain which version of Drake's dream/nightmare was closest to what happened outside the Tower of Dreams?

Chapter Twenty-Eight: Danny's

Page 421 – They arrive back in the car in front of the restaurant, was it real or just a dream? Beth stated, "It was all just a dream, like a daydream cause I'm awake, but more like a nightmare."
- Describe evidence provided to support either position; was it real or a dream?

Page 422 – 'It was truly a conundrum that vexed Drake's mind. The probabilities were slim to none for either possibility, but Beth was correct, the chance that they had traveled through space and time was infinitesimally smaller. Drake looked at the dashboard of his car. The engine was still rumbling as it sat in park. He saw the fuel gauge showed he had less than a half a tank of gas.'
- In the passage above, what does the author mean by a 'conundrum'?

- What other words could have been used to describe what

was happening to Drake?

- The author also uses the word 'infinitesimally,' what does it mean, and how does its usage make the passage more meaningful?

Chapter Twenty-Nine: Tower of Dreams

Pages 428-429 – Freeman feels differently inside the Tower, 'He felt strangely alive in this environment. It was as if he could feel the structure of the molecules around him and almost touch the energy radiating from each and every atom. "I would be perfectly happy staying here, though I would want to see more of what's here."
- How might Freeman's use of magic be different in this setting?

The Brotherhood has finally made it inside the Tower of Dreams, Martin suggests that they split up to accomplish two tasks, and Drake disagrees.
- Choose one side or the other and explain your position using examples from history and literature along with this book to support your position?

Page 446 – The rainbow doorway stands before them. The inscriptions around the doorway cycles through various languages and says something about each must enter alone and find what you most need, or seek. Each entered in turn, but Beth convinced Martin to hold her hand while she entered and disappeared.
- Predict what implication not entering alone might have for Beth and Martin?

- Why did the author end his story here?

ADRAMELECH & THE PIT OF DESPAIR

THE BROTHERHOOD OF OLYMPUS
AND THE DREAM STONES

This tale is based upon actual events...

Scrappy the Barbarian
Chapter One
October 31, 1980
Tower of Dreams

The indigo color tickled his skin like the buzz of a nine-volt battery upon his tongue. He actually giggled as he stepped through the veil of radiance. It took him three steps to clear the energy doorway and he stepped out into a dark and smoky alleyway. The buildings around him were lit with torchlight and the smoke from the flames hung low in the air. Scrappy turned to look behind him, and all that was there was a black stone wall.

"Guess I'm not going back the way I came," Scrappy said. The question though was, where was he? And he didn't have an answer. He stepped aside because he knew Drake was following him. He waited for Drake for what seemed like hours, but he never walked through the wall to join him.

Finally Scrappy realized he was on his own and that maybe he wasn't even out of the doorway yet, since he hadn't encountered any of his needs. The rotating inscription around the doorway had said, *The Individual Must Enter and Through Their Needs They Must Pass.* It was also supposed to be a Challenge of the Spirit. If this was a challenge, he knew he was courageous enough to face it, just like Scrappy Doo, the plucky little Great Dane on *Scooby Doo,* and his namesake. He had lived his whole live waiting for an adventure, and now he had one. He smiled, rose up, and began to explore this dark new world.

Carefully he crept down the cobbled roadway. No one appeared to be out. The world was dark, except the flickering of fire light from what appeared to be torches arranged as street lights, there wasn't any other movement, just the heavy, humid darkness. Maybe he was entirely alone? No, someone had to start the torches that burned in front of him, so he knew that couldn't be right.

He cautiously started to walk toward the crude street lights. From what he could see, he appeared to be in a medieval town or village. He passed what appeared to be a blacksmith shop with a sign hanging above it containing an anvil. He thought about going in a looking for a weapon, but decided to keep exploring first. Most of the buildings looked like houses and he tried to stay away from the ones with light inside. After what seemed like an hour or more of creeping in the shadows of the cobblestone roadway, he realized things looked oddly familiar. He realized the road he was on had circled all the way back around to where he started. He debated making his way back to the blacksmith shop and rummaging for an axe or sword, but decided he needed to move about a bit more while he still had the cover of darkness and the village seemed to be asleep.

He decided to venture toward the middle of the town. In the black of night he couldn't tell what existed in the center. He walked cautiously along the first straight road he came to, into the heart of the village.

There were more signs now. He couldn't read the writing, but some of the pictures helped him. An inn, a tavern, a general store, perhaps, and then a sign with an arrow pointing straight ahead, 'damn it,' he thought, why couldn't Drake be there with him? Drake would be able to understand or read the writing.

Dogs began to bark in the distance behind him. He went a little farther and saw a massive black stone castle with three tall crenellated towers looming out of the darkness before him. There were guards placed at the portcullis amid the high stone wall. Each of them held a long pole-arm that ended in a nasty point. Scrappy had to come up with a plan. He needed a weapon, one better than his machetes, and he was pretty sure that's what he was thinking about when he first stepped into the doorway. But then it tickled and he thought about a stupid nine-volt battery. What if all of this was just to give him a battery?

He decided to go 'look' at the weapons in the blacksmith shop. He walked back along the quiet cobblestone road and found the circular road again. He turned and followed it until he came to the sign above the blacksmith.

Scrappy looked around the building for signs of people. There was an upstairs, so he thought the smith himself might be asleep up there, and maybe his family, and an apprentice or two. He checked the barn-like door at the front of the building, and it gave off a loud creak as he touched it. Dang it, he thought.

He crept around to the side of the building, and saw a single wooden door was left partially open. Perhaps they had cats? It made no difference to him now, as he slowly slid past the door and into the building.

Scrappy looked around in the near darkness of the room. A low fire burned back toward the wide barn doors. It appeared to be the forge itself, with hot embers providing a faint red glow and warmth. Scrappy hadn't even realized he was cold until he approached the forge and basked in the heat. His eyes quickly adjusted to the different level of light and he saw the hilts of swords in a basket against the far wall. He stepped over and began to look at the weapons in the basket. They appeared to be iron, or low grade steel at best. He drew one out of the basket, it was heavy and crude, but he thought it would do better against the exoskeletons of demons than a machete. He walked over to the forge to look at it better. It was a broadsword, thick and ungainly. It would take someone with a lot of strength to wield it in battle, but fortunately he was such a person. Scrappy smiled, and turned to leave. He heard a loud creaking noise behind him. It sounded like the noise of the door, but louder.

"Halt!" shouted a voice from the now open barn door. Scrappy turned. Four figures stood there, with sharp pole-arms lowered at him. He looked at the broadsword in his hands. He smiled.

"I didn't come here with any friends," Scrappy said. He rushed into the four guardsmen, breaking the line and two of the wooden shafts of their weapons. "And I doubt I'm leaving with any!"

In the street a unit of guards had pulled up. They were led by an angry man on horseback who was barking orders to his men. Scrappy looked at them in the dim torchlight. The men had small horns along the eyebrows and their skin seemed to be a mottled yellow. They wore plate armor over black mail, tall black boots, and most of them sported oval shield emblazoned with a crude yellow dragon on a black field.

Great, they have armor, he thought, and they must have been passing by just as he snuck into the building, or else they have a pretty good alarm system.

"Halt!" the commander barked from astride his horse. "Drop the blade, thief!"

"I'm not a thief!" Scrappy yelled. "I'm a barbarian! And I needed a sword!"

"You need to drop the blade, thief!" the commander shouted back. "Archers!"

Some of the soldiers in the back of the unit moved forward. Sure enough, they were archers. They had short bows and quickly notched their arrows and pulled them back read to fire. There were twelve of them. Scrappy thought he might be able to knock down two or three arrows with the sword, more if he had the machetes out since they were lighter and he had trained with them. But twelve arrows weren't going to be an option. What had Drake told him, that some times its better to not fight now and live to fight another day, or something like that? He was sure Drake made it sound cooler. Scrappy realized his predicament and dropped the sword on the cobbled road. Soldiers moved up quickly with ropes and they tied his arms behind his back. They tied a short length of rope between his ankles so he could walk but not run, and finished it off with a noose around his neck that they used to lead him down the road toward the black castle in the center of the village.

That walk was one of the worst experiences of his young life. The shame and inhumanity of being bound and led like an animal through the streets caused tears to form in his eyes. He kept thinking to himself, what would Drake do? What about Scrappy Doo? Or what about Conan, what would he do to get out of this? Conan be damned, he'd have fought, and lived, because he's a fictional character like Robert used to argue at the lunch table.

Scrappy was taken to a cell in a dank dungeon under the castle. A small window let in the light of the day, because the sun had finally risen when the iron door was slammed shut and locked sealing him in.

Two more sunrises followed before he was finally brought out to face the crown and answer for his crimes. He had overheard the jailers talking about the prisoners they were taking before the Duke today. Once again, his arms were bound, but this time in iron manacles, and his legs were shackled with a short length of chain between them. They didn't put a noose around his neck, relying on the sharp point of spears to prod him along the halls and stairs to his date with justice.

He entered the throne room of the Duke. Tapestries hung along the walls that depicted battles between knights, dragons, and various other monsters. Very few were scenes of knights against knights. At one end of the big room sat a high black stone throne atop a large dais of what looked to be obsidian. On the throne sat a fat, old version of the commander who had arrested him three days prior. Except the Duke, he assumed, had a long white beard and he wore an iron crown with a yellow dragon rampant upon the top. About a hundred other prisoners were in chains and waiting along the wall with Scrappy and his jailer escorts. Few others were in the throne room—a handful soldiers, and perhaps the other lords of the city lined the far wall. Bright yellow dragons were on the two large tapestries that hung behind the Duke. They were like massive curtains.

"All rise for the honorable lord of night, Duke of the Iron Plains of Acheron, Khaeron son of Khaeros!" shouted a bannerman of the Duke.

"Your Grace," the chief jailer stated from the middle of the throne room floor. He had bent to one knee. "We bring before you this morn the criminals of the south cell block for you to pass judgment upon them."

The Duke rolled his hand urging the chief jailer to get on with it. The chief jailer turned back and motioned for some of the chained criminals to be brought forth.

"Your Grace," the chief jailer began again. Seven individuals, an older balding man, a younger man, a woman, and four children of different ages down to what appeared to be a toddler, were presented to the Duke in irons like Scrappy bore. "This is the family Karessi, whose child Stephos walked on the wrong side of the roadway on the Duke's Day."

The gathered lords all began to chatter.

"Silence before the throne!" the Duke yelled. The clamor came to a sudden end, like someone had sucked all the sound from the room. "Which one is Stephos, lord jailer?"

The second to the smallest was pushed forward.

"Stephos," the Duke stated, "do you deny the crime you are charged with?"

The child looked to his mother with confusion on his yellow horned face. She nudged him out farther.

"No," Stephos finally said in a low voice that was barely heard.

"Very well," the Duke stated. "I thank you, good Stephos for your loyalty to the crown and the law of Acheron. Law above Evil."

"Law above Evil!" a chorus of voices echoed back.

"The punishment for breaking a Duke's Day law is to be fed to the Dragons," the Duke decreed. "And as family to a law breaker, you share his blood, you share his sentence!"

"Thank you my Grace!" the old man in chains said as he fell to the ground. "Law above Evil!"

The jailers took the family of seven up the dais, past the high stone throne, and toward the big dragon curtains. Ropes pulled back the curtains on either side. Scrappy could see deep in the chamber behind the throne were yellow dragons, long necked beasts with great leathery wings and spikes upon their heads. The dragons awaited the family of seven who walked willingly into the dragon den. The dragons had done this before and knew the people in chains were food. They fought over the people, ripping and tearing them in half or eating some whole. All the while the lords and jailers cheered, as did most of the criminals.

'What kind of place did I walk into?' Scrappy thought about what the punishment for his crime might be, and decided that taking his chance with the arrows was better than his chance with the dragons.

Two more cases were quickly decided with chants of 'Law above Evil' and ended with the prisoners being led to the dragons to be eaten. The next case was similar, but the criminal demanded a challenge of spirit. Scrappy had heard that not too long ago, somewhere, if he could only remember.

"A Challenge of Spirit has been asked, your Grace," the chief jailer stated.

"I accept your plea, Barhtien," the Duke decreed. "You shall be flayed on the stone of retribution and left for the vultures until your spirit heals or you die."

"Thank you, your Grace, thank you," Barhtien said as he humbled himself on the floor before the Duke. Scrappy was pretty sure being flayed meant being skinned, and that didn't sound much better than being dragon chow.

Then the jailers with Scrappy pushed him forward.

"Next we have an outlander, your Grace," the chief jailer announced. "Look at his dark skin, he may be from the Abyss or one of the Hells. He hasn't confessed his crime, but he was caught stealing an iron sword three days past."

"What is your name, outlander?" the Duke asked.

"My name is Scrappy!" he shouted.

"Why are you in my lands outlander, Scrappy?" the Duke inquired.

"I'm a barbarian and I needed a sword!" Scrappy yelled.

"Thievery is evil, is it not outlander?" the Duke continued to question. "Even in your lands, is not thievery evil?"

"Yes," Scrappy responded.

"I cannot hear you outlander," the Duke said.

"Yes!" Scrappy yelled.

"Law above Evil!" the Duke bellowed. "The punishment for thievery is to be fed to the Dragons after having your hand removed and hung from the plaza for all would-be thieves to admire."

"That's not fair," Scrappy uttered as he fell to his knees. "I walked into the door, to the challenge of spirit, and wind up getting fed to dragons?"

"Your Grace!" the chief jailer shouted. "The outlander has stated he wants a Challenge of Spirit."

The Duke looked down upon the form of Scrappy, bound in chains and on his knees before him.

"Law above Evil!" the Duke shouted. The chorus answered him. "I accept your plea, outlander. You shall be dropped into the Pit of Despair where you shall have the chance to heal your spirit or die."

The jailers came forward and roughly picked up Scrappy and carried him out a side door. They threw him into the back of a wagon and locked his chains to a hook on the floor.

"Waggoner," the jailer said, "take this outlander to the Pit of Despair for his Challenge of Spirit."

The waggoner gave a hand motion and then snapped his reins, making the horses move pulling his creosote soaked wagon along the cobblestone road. The wagon lurched and rocked as they made the trip out of town. Scrappy realized as they left that the little town or village he thought he was in was actually a sprawling metropolis separated by thick walls and massive gates.

It was nearing sunset when they finally left the outer gate of the city.

"How far to the Pit of Despair?" Scrappy asked.

"Four or five nights," the waggoner replied. "Depending on the winds."

Scrappy examined who else was with them on the journey. Two soldiers rode on horses behind them, a smaller, hunched back horn-face sat up on the bench of the wagon near the waggoner. Both the driver and his companion were covered by a thick canvas canopy. Scrappy sat alone in the back of the wagon, uncovered and exposed to the world— whatever this world was.

That night they stopped to rest. Scrappy found that sleeping in iron chains on hard creosote coated wood wasn't comfortable at all, and when the winds blew it became miserable. He only had a t-shirt on for warmth and shook and shivered all night long. He slept at times during the day when the sun was warm upon his skin, before it got blistering hot. By the second day, Scrappy had learned that the little hunched back horn-face was named Scurros. The waggoner and the soldiers had no concern or care for their cargo. They were abiding by the law, and Scrappy had learned that the law in Acheron superseded evil.

Scrappy hadn't figured out whether Acheron was the name of the city the Duke presided over, or the name of the world he found himself in, but information among other things wasn't very forthcoming during his journey to the Pit of Despair.

"Scurros," Scrappy said, "what is this Pit of Despair?"

"Are you stupid, outlander?" Scurros replied. "Everyone knows of the Pit."

"Then I must be stupid," Scrappy stated. "So what is it?"

"It's where the damned are left to stew in their own evil," Scurros answered.

"But the Duke said I had a chance to heal my spirit," Scrappy continued. "Has anyone ever come out of the Pit?"

"I don't know, has anyone, waggoner?" Scurros asked and the waggoner shook his head. "No, outlander, none have ever healed their spirit."

"So it's just a big hole?" Scrappy asked.

"No outlander," Scurros replied with a demonic chuckle. "In it you will find the challenge of spirit you seek. Each is different."

"I seek a sword," Scrappy stated.

"And by this sword you will probably die," Scurros responded. "Law above Evil."

"Law above Evil," the waggoner added.

"Why do you keep sayin' that?" Scrappy asked.

"All Acheron is banner pledged to the great houses of daemons, the High Lords of the Abyss and the Hells," Scurros answered. "But where their evil is ripe with chaos, we follow Law above Evil."

"So I'm in a... what did Drake call it? A notter, no, that's not it. I'm in a netherworld?" Scrappy inquired, Scurros and the waggoner nodded. "That explains a lot, actually."

Two more days passed before the winds finally hit hard. The hurricane force wind ripped shards from the hard iron plains and drove them like darts into Scrappy's skin. He turned and hid his face as best he could, but his skin seeped blood from the hundreds of puncture wounds he endured. The waggoner, Scurros, and the two soldiers put their horses behind the wagon and shielded themselves from the iron shards as best they could. Scrappy was sure they were safer than he was in the back of the wagon.

On the fifth day, he was not given the ration of jerky and cup of water-like liquid that had been sustaining him. He soon found out why when the wagon came to a stop on a ledge above a huge sloping hole, maybe a mile across, or more. It was what he imaged the Grand Canyon would be like, except the Pit sloped always to the middle, down into the black nothingness.

"May you be tested well, outlander," Scurros said, as he jumped into the back of the wagon to unlock Scrappy from the hook. The soldiers approached with their pole-arms lowered, the sharp nasty points at his heart. Scrappy was stiff and sore, but he had his pride. He walked to the end of the wagon and jumped down, falling to his knees on the hard iron ground.

"On your feet, outlander," a soldier ordered. "Your Test of Spirit is at hand."

Scrappy rose and moved ahead of the points that jabbed his wounded flesh. Toward the edge of the cliff they prodded him. He looked down and saw the hole at the bottom of the Pit was thousands of feet down. A feeling of vertigo overwhelmed him.

"Jump outlander!" Scurros encouraged him. "Law above Evil!"

Scrappy shook his head. The soldiers stabbed his back with the wicked points of their pole-arms and prodded him over the edge. He fell nearly a hundred feet before he landed in the coarse sand that seemed to constantly be moving down into the mouth of the Pit. He tumbled and rolled, the sand rubbing against the iron shards stuck in his skin, causing more bleeding as he moved closer and closer to the hole. The two wounds from the spears in his back were deep. He hoped they missed vital organs, but he wasn't sure he'd live anyway, so it didn't really matter.

He finally neared the mouth of the Pit, and a sense of dread flooded over him. But he could do nothing but slide toward the hole. High above on the cliff, he was sure he heard his four companions yell, 'Law above Evil!' And then he fell into the nothingness.

It seemed like hours that he fell through the darkness, and finally he hit the bottom. It broke his body, and he felt his blood seeping out of him everywhere. He closed his eyes and thought of home. He thought of the silence he used to love, silence was his friend. And that made him think of

Drake. He began to cry.

"I've failed you my brother."

He awoke in a hole filled with straw. He looked at his body and saw that he was intact. He wasn't dead or disfigured, and he was no longer bound in chains. He stood up and tried to look out of the hole. His head barely rose out of the earthen hole. Around him were thousands of holes, he assumed each had another person inside them. The feeling of dread came over him again, and he saw something approaching him from above. It was a machine of some sort. It hovered above the holes, and on top of it rested a chair, or maybe the chair was part of it. It was hard to tell from his position in the hole. On the chair upholstered in human flesh and dragon scales, sat a dark god. His red skin was thick and pitted, his muscles were big and sinewy, and he wore oversized, blackened metal shoulder pads over a black leather tunic, and high black boots adorned with skulls and articulated metal plates. His head was encircled with fire, and his facial features were skeletal. He had no visible eyes or flesh upon his head, only flames.

The god stared at him, or would have stared if he had eyes, for a few moments as if he was analyzing him.

"You are a human? I do not get many humans here, outlander," the god stated. "None the less, you have been condemned to a Challenge of Spirit."

"Is it truly a challenge," Scrappy asked, "or just a punishment?"

"Why it is truly both, human, and that makes it so deliciously wicked, does it not?" the god answered. "What did you seek?"

"A sword," Scrappy said. "All I needed was a sword."

The god bent down and stared an empty eye-socket stare into his soul. Then sat back up and laughed.

"I know you, James Kirk," the god cackled. "And I have the ultimate Challenge of Spirit for you. You fancy yourself a barbarian, so every day you shall meet one of my condemned in battle, and should you win, you shall receive your sword. But should you fail, I will repair you each night and in the morn you shall battle again. That shall be your Challenge of Spirit."

"Let me see the sword," Scrappy demanded.

"My, such a feisty human. I have not had the pleasure of a living human to work with in hundreds of years, are all humans this feisty now?" the god responded. Scrappy shrugged his massive shoulders. "Very well, if it helps you understand the price you shall pay."

From within a shimmery cloud of black dust, that formed by his left boot, the god produced the sword. It was a wicked looking blade, curved slightly like a scimitar but with two barbs upon the top of the sword. The blade itself seemed to possess an aura of red energy. The end of the blade curved down below the start of the hilt, along the length of the sword, above the blood groove archaic characters spelled something he couldn't read and the letters were outlined and highlighted by stylized flames. The hilt was two handed and wrapped in supple leather strips folded along the side in the style of the samurai. It had a silver divider placed two thirds of the way up on the hilt near the blade, and the pommel was a wicked spike upon a curved silver claw.

"That appears to be a fine sword," Scrappy remarked.

"Yes it is," the god replied. "I have had it for over two thousand years. Hephaestus forged it for me. And I will have it for over two thousand more."

"It's mine, if I pass this test?" Scrappy asked.

"Truly," the god answered. "I shall keep my word, and my word in the Pit of Despair is law."

"And Law above Evil, right?" Scrappy questioned.

"Absolutely human, you flatter me," the god replied. "Shall I introduce you to your opponent? I have chosen him especially for you."

"Please do," Scrappy said. If all he had to do was beat someone in combat to claim the sword, and he had multiple times to do so, it would take him a week, or a couple weeks at the most, he figured. Then he could go back and help Drake, if he could find him.

"Here you go, James Kirk, meet your eternal opponent," the god announced. Scrappy was now standing on a dirt field and strewn on the ground around him were assorted weapons. It reminded him of movies he had seen about gladiators in ancient Rome. A large man walked toward him. He was taller than Scrappy by about three feet, and wider by about the same amount. He was a mountain of a man. His skin was dark black, his hair a thick matted afro. He had a full, thick beard and an iron collar around his neck with long sharp spikes.

"Do you recognize him?" the god inquired with glee. "Of course not, I have made him bigger, of course. But you haven't seen him since you were what, three years old? Meet your adversary barbarian, your father Jamal."

A flood of recognition washed though Scrappy, it looked like his memories of his dad. Could it be?

"Come here you little mulatto freak!" Jamal yelled. "Let me give you a hug, you little bastard!"

The god cackled and rose up on his hover disk. Jamal picked up a spear and threw it at the shocked boy, his son. The spear sunk deep into his abdomen and Scrappy slumped to the ground. Jamal laughed above him.

"Mulatto bastard!" Jamal yelled, as he brought his wide fist down upon the back of Scrappy's head. The pain was overwhelming.

Scrappy woke up, back in his hole. He took a piece of the hard straw and scraped a mark into the wall. One day down. He'd do better today.

Day after day passed, each ended with the same result— Scrappy laying dead on the ground. Scrappy had over five hundred marks scraped into the wall of his hole. He ritually counted them again each morning, and he realized he was running out of room. He had changed over the time he was in the Pit. He had begun to grow a mustache and had a prickly bunch of hair upon his chin. He also had gotten stronger and often spent much of the day grappling with his demonically enhanced father.

"Dad," Scrappy pleaded. "Join with me! I don't want to kill you! Together we can escape. Let me save you!"

Jamal would ignore his son and brutally attack him, ending the battle for the day. And the next day would unfold much the same way. Scrappy couldn't understand. He was demonstrating love. He was showing that he was capable of loving his father, the man who abused him verbally and physically when he was a child and then walked out of his life leaving him fatherless. How was that not overcoming this challenge? Once he even just got down on his knees and said, "I love you, Dad," and Jamal had stabbed him with a rusty sword, again and again.

On the seven hundred and forty-fourth day he prepared to once again face Jamal in a fight to the death. And that's when it hit him. He was Scrappy the Barbarian, and he wasn't the son of Jamal Kirk anymore. He was hoping to save his father, to love his father, and in that fallacy he forgot to love himself, to honor who he was, and who he had become. He was Scrappy, he was small and insignificant, but he mattered, and he had courage. He possessed the courage to fight his father, to beat his father, to become who he was meant to be.

That day on the gladiator field Scrappy found an axe, and he stood firm against Jamal's attacks.

"I do love you, Dad," Scrappy said, "but I'm not the little kid you left. I'm not your mulatto bastard anymore!"

Jamal attacked with a sword, furious and fast came the hacks and slashes, each expertly blocked by the barbarian who had fought his opponent seven hundred and forty-three times to the death before. He knew his movements, could see the strategy Jamal used before it happened, and this day he finally utilized it.

"I'm not your bastard any more, Dad!" Scrappy yelled. He turned on the larger Jamal, springing the axe down on the flat side across his back, knocking him to the ground. "I'm Scrappy the Barbarian! Scrappy, damn it!"

He swung the axe over Jamal's head, who parried it with his sword. Before Jamal could get up, Scrappy backhanded the axe upward, catching Jamal under the chin. The blade of the axe cut skin, muscle, and bone. Jamal's lifeless head lopped onto the dirty ground behind him. Red blood gushed from the stump of his neck. Scrappy picked up the sword Jamal had dropped and stabbed it viciously into his chest, before pulling it out and raising both the axe and the sword above his head in triumph. He bowed to his fallen father.

The god reappeared in an instant on his hover disk.

"What is this?" the god questioned. "How can this be? You lacked everything you needed to defeat my champion, you foolishly believed you could love and save him, like a pathetic human would, but somehow you have triumphed. This cannot be—it cannot be."

"You owe me a sword, god," Scrappy stated.

"I owe you nothing, human," the god snapped back.

Scrappy threw the axe cleaving much of the disk, bringing it crashing to the ground. He'd realized during his time in the gladiator field with Jamal that he had augmented strength like Drake described when he fought the snake-god in a netherworld. He had just chosen not to reveal it until he was ready.

The god looked at him, and if he had eyes Scrappy was sure they would be opened wide and in shock. Scrappy shifted the sword of his father into his right hand, and with a mighty leap he jumped high in the air and came down sword first on the god. The blade rested just above his heart.

"Shall we see if you can repair yourself as easily as you repaired me?" Scrappy asked.

"Barbarian," the god responded with his hands raised. "Barbarian please, I am certain we can work something out."

"Law above Evil!" Scrappy growled, as he pushed the tip of the blade through the black leather tunic and drew black blood from the god's chest. The god hadn't expected

Scrappy to attack him at all, and now the human had drawn his blood. Death isn't a concept most gods ponder, but at that moment he did, and he decided he didn't want to die.

"The sword is yours, barbarian!" the god squealed frightfully.

"Tell me your name!" Scrappy demanded. He remembered what Brigid had said about knowing the name of an entity, the power of name-magic. He pushed the tip of the blade farther into the flesh of the god.

"My name is Adramelech, god of fire," the deity whimpered. "Please do not kill me barbarian. You have my sword, and I shall return you to your path."

"Let my father go, release him from this place, and send him to heaven," Scrappy commanded.

"As you wish, barbarian, I will release him. Jamal Kirk has lost his value to me, after all, and I will see him delivered as close as I can get him to your heaven," Adramelech answered.

"See that you do, and don't just drop him off somewhere random, either," Scrappy barked. "Now, I'll be taking that sword you promised. Oh, and I will be back to finish this Adramelech, mark my words. So start counting your days until I come back, skull-head, you've made an enemy that you'll regret having!"

Scrappy had the wicked blade that oozed faint red plasma in his hand, its leather and metal scabbard hung on a crude belt around his waist, and he finally stood on the other side of the door he had stepped through almost two years ago. He smiled and turned and looked for Drake, as the spectrum of colors cycled one after the other.

ABOUT THE AUTHOR

Guy T. Simpson, Jr. is the author of the Brotherhood of Olympus Saga. He is an award winning artist and illustrator, possessing a graduate degree in education from The Evergreen State College. He has worked as a middle school science and leadership teacher in rural Washington State, as well as a plethora of other jobs throughout his career. He still resides in the Pacific Northwest with his wife, three college student children, and a number of dogs and cats. He is currently at work on the third installment of the Brotherhood of Olympus Saga.

For more information see the author's website:
www.guysimpson.net

Coming Soon:
THE BROTHERHOOD OF OLYMPUS
AND THE
DREAM STONES

Also Coming Soon:
THE BROTHERHOOD OF OLYMPUS
AND THE
LABYRINTH OF ANANSI

www.ingramcontent.com/pod-product-compliance
Lightning Source LLC
Chambersburg PA
CBHW061022030726
47504CB00002B/224

* 9 7 8 0 9 9 6 1 8 1 4 1 9 *